The Red Rock Ranch Collection: Books 1-3

Brittney Joy

Brittney Joy/Horse Girl LLC

www.brittneyjoybooks.com

The Red Rock Ranch Series Collection, books 1-3 / Brittney Joy; Horse Girl LLC --1st ed.

Ebook ISBN: 979-8-9852294-9-3

Paperback ISBN: 978-1-958178-00-3

Contents

Dedication

"All horses deserve, at least once in their lives, to be loved by a little girl." -Unknown Author

Newsletter Invitation

Never miss a new release ~ Sign-up for Brittney Joy's newsletter:

http://www.brittneyjoybooks.com/newsletter

LUCY'S CHANCE
THE RED ROCK RANCH SERIES
- BOOK 1 -
BRITTNEY JOY

Lucy's Chance: Book 1

Sixteen year old Lucy Rose is spending her first summer away from home and she has two things on her mind: an abandoned, violent horse and a blue-eyed cowboy. Only neither is hers.

Lucy has never attracted much attention from boys, but she can't seem to ignore her blue-eyed co-worker, Casey Parker. A true cowboy, Lucy is fascinated by his gentle way with the horses at Red Rock Ranch. However, she is very aware that Taylor Johnson, rodeo queen extraordinaire, already has her spurs in him. And there's no crossing Taylor.

… Not until a mysterious horse appears on the ranch and pushes Lucy and Casey together. The two are willing to do anything to save the black gelding that doesn't want a thing to do with them or the human race. But every step forward with the broken animal makes Lucy fall harder - for him and for Casey.

Turn the page to start reading...

One

It was four minutes past noon and I was chasing a two hundred pound steer down the barn aisle. At three minutes past the hour I had my butt planted on the long wooden bench in the tack room and was halfway through my turkey-mayo sandwich. My first swig of Dr. Pepper fizzled down my throat and I closed my eyes, reveling in the cold, wet gulp. The cool air in the tack room reeked of worn leather and dirt.

Amidst my gulping, I'm not sure which came first: the frustrated hollers from Marilynn or a chocolate-brown blaze of fur and hooves flying past the open door. Either way, I dropped my pop can and scrambled out into the barn aisle, looking from one end to the other. Marilynn stood with her hands on her hips in the barn doorway. Her five foot, petite frame didn't make much of a silhouette against the sun, but her voice made up for it. She pointed at the steer trotting down the aisle. "Get that little bugger," she yelled, and I turned, racing straight for him.

I ran like I knew what I was doing, but I didn't. I pumped my arms and tried to lengthen my stride, but cowboy boots do not make great running shoes. Their slick leather soles slid against the concrete floor instead of gripping it. Trying not to twist an ankle, I steadied my long legs into a safer speed, but the steer didn't slow a bit. In fact, he picked up his pace. With his tail flagged high over his back, his hooves clipped against the floor as he darted out the opposite end of the barn.

Marilynn had spent the morning showing me the ropes. Mucking stalls, grooming horses, packing hay bales around—those were all going to be part of my job. I didn't recall her saying anything about tackling cattle, but I didn't want to let her down. Not on my first day. So I ran.

I burst out into the sunshine and gained speed on the gravel road leading to the pastures. The weathered fencing ahead stretched out for miles, dotted with horses and cattle, and the steer had already stopped, grazing on the lush grass like he was supposed to be there. A few of the ranch horses poked their heads over the fence, extending their necks out to sniff the visitor, and I slowed to a jog as I approached him. He picked up his head and stopped chewing, looking straight through me. "Easy, buddy," I said through heavy breaths. I raised my arms as I stepped closer, showing him that he needed to stay put.

In all the years I had worked with horses, I had never been around cattle. I assumed they were similar to horses. They were about the same size and they had the same gentle brown eyes. I would have called the animal in front of me a cow, but I was informed earlier that day that he was actually "a steer." And, *the steer* in front of me had long black eyelashes and a baby pink nose. His brown coat looked slick as silk and I felt the need to touch his big floppy ears. He reminded me of our neighbor's golden retriever, Bart, who wandered over to our house whenever I was outside, wiggling his whole body in happiness. Seeing no immediate threat, I dropped my arms to my sides and headed straight for the steer's shoulders. I didn't have a halter, but I could put my hand under his throat latch and lead him back, just like I would with a horse.

Wrong. Very wrong.

He was standing there, so sweet and quiet, like a little puppy waiting to have his head scratched. I didn't expect him to lurch forward like a shot cannon. And, upon this rash reaction, in instinct I jumped in front of him, trying to stop him from running past me. This brilliant idea only gave him nowhere to go but up. I watched it happen in slow motion and couldn't do a thing about it. In a split second, two hundred solid pounds lifted off the ground in an attempt to jump over my head. I don't know where that cow wanted to go, but he made it very clear that I was not going to be giving him any directions.

A month ago, I squealed like a cut pig when I got the job. I hung up the phone after talking to Mr. Owens, the ranch's owner, and jumped around the kitchen for fifteen minutes. I would be spending my freshman summer as a stable hand at the Red Rock Ranch. What could be better? Now, I heard a different type of squeal and I was certain it was also coming out of my mouth. I threw my arms in front of my face and just had time to brace myself for the hit. The steer didn't quite make it over my head. Instead, his chest slammed into my shoulder, spun me around, and put me face first into the grass.

Lucky for me, all four of his hooves missed my body as they found the ground. I picked my head up, thankful I didn't get stomped, and watched the steer run off along the fence line, holding his head high in the air flaunting his escape. Mental note: Cows are not like horses. Do not let the big brown eyes fool you.

Then, I watched the brown steer trot straight towards a boy with a bucket in his hand. The boy shook the bucket as he opened the pasture gate and that dang steer trotted in right after him, following the sound of grain rattling against metal. He didn't give that kid any lip or try to knock off his head. The boy overturned the bucket and grain piled onto the ground. The steer dug his nose right into the trap, licking up the goodness, and the boy walked away, untouched, shutting the gate behind him. I rested my cheek on the grass, trying to make my head stop spinning. Maybe cows *were* more like horses than I thought.

Marilynn's boots crunched through the lawn as she jogged over and then stood, looking down at me. "I didn't mean you had to wrestle with the steer." She shook her head and tried, unsuccessfully, to hold back a grin. "They don't usually take kindly to that."

I rolled over onto my back. "I'll remember that for next time."

To further emphasize my over-dramatic attempt at catching a cow, a second body came into my vision. "A little grain in a bucket is usually enough to get their attention," the ball-capped cow-whisperer noted with a wink. "You must be the new girl."

Marilynn assisted with the introduction when she realized I wasn't going to respond. "Lucy Rose, this is Casey. He's the other stable hand."

I stared at their faces, assessing the situation. It was my first day at work and I had been football-tackled by a mere baby cow. I was now lying on the ground, surrounded by my two co-workers. I probably had dirt on my face and grass stains on my shirt. I reached out my hand. "Hi, I'm Lucy. Nice to meet you."

With ten minutes before I had to be out the door, I scrambled for something to wear to the ranch sorting. Rummaging through every piece of clothing in my suitcase, I tried on five different shirts. I found something wrong with each of them.

Ignoring the mess of clothing scattered across my bed, I pulled a long sleeve t-shirt over my head and stared at the purple cotton top in the full-length mirror hung from the wall. A leggy, skinny girl stared back. I turned sixteen three weeks ago, but my body seemed resistant to catch up to my age.

And what was my hair doing? The stick-straight, mousy brown strands hung on my head, brushing the middle of my back. I poked at them with a comb trying to muster up some volume. Sigh. *I guess a ponytail will work.* At least I had all the dirt smudges washed off my face and blades of grass plucked from my hair.

Looping an elastic around my hair, I looked away from the mirror and examined my home for the summer. The one-room bunkhouse had a twin bed tucked in the corner, a small oak nightstand, and a matching three-drawer dresser with brass knobs. A single light hung from the center of the A-frame ceiling. It was simple and perfect.

The employee bunkhouses were a quick walk from the ranch's outdoor arena, but the clock on my nightstand was blinking at six-fifty-four. I only had six minutes to get there. Yanking on my trusty tan cowboy boots, I hopped out the screen door, hustling down the three stairs to the dirt path. Pointed towards the arena, I examined the neat row of bunkhouses as I passed by. There were at least ten and they reminded me of a village of miniature log cabins. I wondered which one was Marilynn's. Which one was Casey's? Right now, they appeared dark, deserted.

Farther ahead, the big fluorescent arena lights buzzed as they warmed up and, beneath them, swarms of people gathered on and around the bleachers. It became obvious *everyone* was at the ranch sorting. Crossing my arms, I approached the mob of people and scanned the bleachers for Marilynn. There was quite a variety of people in the audience, but the ranch guests were easy to pick out. Scattered throughout the crowd were families and couples outfitted in GAP jeans and shiny new cowboy boots. Cameras hung from their necks and visors sat perched on their heads. Their kids danced around in plastic cowboy hats and yelled things like "yehaw" and "giddy-up."

The regulars also stuck out, sporting worn-in wranglers and real cowboy hats. Belt buckles shined from their waists. They chatted and joked together, hanging in a tight circle by the edge of the arena. A few of the girls were balanced up on the fence, eyeing the cowboys warming up their horses. They looked like they put a little more effort into getting dressed for the occasion.

I slowed to a stop on the outskirts of the crowd, feeling like an intruder. Marilynn did say to meet at seven o'clock, didn't she?

As though she heard my internal screams for help, Marilynn came into view. Clean, crisp jeans and a hint of lip gloss. "Hey!" Marilynn waved from inside the arena. "Over here!"

I rushed to her side with a few curious looks from the crowd of regulars.

"You ready for your first ranch sorting?" Marilynn asked as she pushed her mahogany hair behind her ear. The blunt ends brushed the top of her starched collar. I nodded. "You're going to be my assistant at the gate, okay?"

I grew up around horses but had never participated in a ranch sorting. I wasn't quite sure what it was. I assumed it had something to do with the ranch...and sorting?

"Sure, what would you like me to do?"

Clipboard in hand, Marilynn instructed, "I'm going to round up the competitors in the arena and send them over to the cattle pen as the announcer calls out their names. You stand by the cattle pen gate and let them in and out. You are the official gate girl."

The official gate girl. *Okay, not the most impressive title, but I'll take it. That will put me close to the action and away from the crowd.* "I think I can do that."

Just then the Star Spangled Banner crackled over the loud speakers and a single horse and rider loped through the gate at the far end of the arena. The crowd grew quiet and stood at attention, hats off and hands placed over their hearts.

American flag in hand, the rider's perfectly curled blonde hair bounced with each stride as she rode around the edge of the arena. Her horse's chestnut coat gleamed like a new penny and its flaxen mane and tail almost matched the color of the rider's own golden curls. Her blouse glittered with crystals and her tan leather chaps were the same color as her cowboy hat. She looked like a Barbie doll.

"Who is that?" I whispered to Marilynn without taking my eyes off the rider.

"Taylor," Marilynn paused. "Taylor Johnson. Rodeo queen extraordinaire."

I digested Marilynn's statement. I couldn't tell if she was being sarcastic or matter-of-fact.

"She's really pretty," I said, also admiring her stunning horse.

"That she is," Marilynn noted. "Taylor and her mom are regulars here at the ranch. They've spent the last few summers here as guests."

Taylor didn't look like the rest of the guests in the audience. She looked like she grew up on the back of a horse...or came from the pages of Seventeen Magazine. One or the other.

"Her family has money. They rent out one of the guest houses for the summer and Taylor always brings her horse, Star."

"Oh." I scanned Marilynn's face noting her unimpressed facial expression.

Taylor guided her horse to the middle of the arena for the end of the Star Spangled Banner. The crowd clapped and the announcer thanked her as she trotted Star towards the back gate, waving and flashing her smile to all the cowboys on the way out.

"Okay, now we can get this show started," Marilynn said as she left to locate the first team of riders.

I moved to my position at the cattle pen gate, wondering how long Taylor had been working with Star. They made such a pretty picture together.

Lost in thought, I jumped when the announcer's voice boomed over the loud speaker. "Welcome to Red Rock Ranch's first ranch sorting of the summer!" His voice thundered and the crowd cheered. "Our first team is ready to enter the pen. Let's make some noise and see how fast they can round up those steers!"

That's my cue. I opened the gate plenty wide for two riders and looked up just as they trotted through.

"Watch out for those steers, Ms. Lucy." The sarcasm laced in the rider's voice was too familiar. "They can be a bit tricky."

Casey. He shot a smirk my direction as he rode through the gate. *Funny guy. Funny guy.*

"Cowboys and cowgirls, let's welcome a few local cowboys, Casey Parker and Austin Jones! Representing the town of Three Rivers!"

Locking the gate in place, I peered through the metal bars at the two riders, recognizing Casey's dapple gray horse. The big gray gelding dominated the field this morning while Marilynn and I fed the ranch horses. I scooped oats into buckets hanging along the fence line and the gray gelding was the first to dig in. He pinned his ears flat against his neck as he ate, showing the other horses who was boss. Not one horse dared to mess with him. But now, his ears were forward and pricked. He stood still and glared at the herd of cattle on the other side of the circular pen.

Then Casey leaned forward and the gray horse sauntered towards the herd. The pair stepped into the herd of ten, creating a barrier between the herd and a single black steer, marked on his rump with a spray-painted number one. The steer spun and tried to run back towards the others, but Casey and the gray shot forward to cut him off. Then, loping close behind the steer, they followed him along the edge of the pen and through the opening to a second circular pen.

Casey and his partner were a blur, taking turns to separate each steer from the herd and move them into the second pen. The horses hopped and weaved, chasing the steers in numerical order according to the spray-painted numbers on their rumps. While one rider was chasing a steer, the other rider blocked the rest of the herd from a premature entrance into the second pen. The object of the event soon became clear to me. That's why they call it "sorting."

The gray gelding seemed to listen to every quiet movement of Casey's body. They communicated with a language that no one else could hear, but I was certain it wasn't sarcastic. Casey and the gray worked together as a seamless team.

Before I knew it, the two riders had worked their way through the numbered herd and the crowd jumped to their feet as Casey chased the last steer into the second pen. The clock stopped at thirty-one seconds.

"What a way to start off the summer!" the announcer shouted and the crowd roared. Casey headed back towards me and I opened the gate. He tipped his hat at me as the big gray trotted by, barely winded, and I watched as they maneuvered out into the arena, greeted with high-fives and hoots from the other riders. That was obviously not his first ranch sorting.

As the night went on, I opened and closed the gate for another thirty pairs of riders. I watched each sorting with intensity. Although, it seemed like no one could match up to Casey and his partner's time. The closest were two sisters on matching palominos who managed to hit forty-two seconds.

The metal latch rattled as I closed the gate after the last pair of riders trotted out into the arena.

"Nice job, gate girl," Marilynn said as she came up behind me.

"Thanks," I grinned. "That was fun to watch."

"It's even better when you're in the saddle. You should give it a try. You could always use one of the ranch horses."

My body shuddered when I thought about riding in front of a crowd like that. I took a breath to respond but got distracted as I glanced over Marilynn's shoulder. Next to the arena bleachers, Casey was talking and smiling with Taylor, the blonde rodeo queen. She reached out and touched his arm, laughing at something he said that must have been hilarious and brilliant.

Marilynn caught my line of sight and turned to see what I was staring at. She wrinkled up her nose. "Wow, that didn't take her long to hunt down Casey."

Hunt down? It didn't look like he was in distress.

"Figures. Taylor tends to like the spotlight." Marilynn shrugged. "And she also seems to be attracted to guys in the spotlight. Last summer it was Justin, but only after he won the bull-riding title at the St. Paul Rodeo. Appears she's got her eye on Casey this year."

It did look that way.

"Anyhow, I'll see you in the morning," Marilynn said as she turned to leave, clipboard still in hand. "After chores, I'll need your help with a ride into Mount Hood."

My eyes snapped back to Marilynn and I forgot all about Casey and the rodeo princess. My first trail ride into the mountain? "I'll be there bright and early!

Two

I actually beat Marilynn to the barn the next morning. The air was crisp before the sun came up and I zipped up my canvas Carhartt vest. My leather work gloves were stuffed in my pockets along with a pocket knife and a granola bar. I was ready for whatever Marilynn needed me to do today.

A few horses gave a soft nicker as I flicked on the barn lights, illuminating the aisle. My boots clicked along the floor and, one right after the other, the horses poked their heads over their stall doors. Their sleepy eyes blinked at the bright lights.

About halfway down the aisle, I recognized the chestnut with the flaxen mane and tail, Taylor's horse Star. The wide blaze on her delicate head was chalk-white and her forelock lay in a neat braid. Her ears pointed forward and she watched me as I came towards her. I reached out to rub her pretty face when, without notice, her ears pinned flat against her neck and a flash of teeth grabbed for my arm.

Jumping back, I yanked my arm away and stood, stunned, a safe distance from the stall door. I couldn't believe how the pretty mare looked so ugly with her ears still flattened, moving her body from side to side over the half door.

"She's a cranky one, isn't she?" Marilynn had just entered through the barn door with a thermos of something hot in her hands. "Very punctual, I see. That's good."

"Yeah," I said, keeping my eyes on Star. "I was up around five this morning. Had a little trouble sleeping."

"She was like that when she came here last summer too," Marilynn noted, pointing her thermos in Star's direction. "Taylor spends a lot of time trailering to rodeos and rodeo queen competitions. Star spends a lot of time in trailers and stalls and, when she's not doing that, Taylor has her in full time professional training. I'm not really sure she remembers how to be a horse."

At once I felt bad for the little mare that almost took a chunk out of my arm.

"She got better over the summer last year. She gets pasture time with us and Taylor tags along on some trail rides every now and then. Star gets a break here."

"Seems she needs it."

"She does," Marilynn agreed. "Ready to feed all these hungry ponies?"

"Sure am," I answered, grabbing a grain bucket in each hand.

The ponies were fed, their stalls cleaned, and the barn aisle swept. It felt good to push a wheelbarrow and throw bales of hay, but it would feel even better to swing up into a saddle and head out into the mountain.

I shed my vest when the morning warmed up and it looked like the sun was around to stay. *Blue skies and sunshine. What a gorgeous day for a ride. How could it get any better?*

Outside the barn, Marilynn brushed hay bits off her jeans. "Change of plans. It looks like I'm not going on that trail ride after all."

The smile dropped from my face.

"Mr. Owens has some friends staying at the ranch and he asked me to give their little boy a roping lesson this morning." She shrugged.

I tried not to let my disappointment show. "That's okay. Is there anything you need me to do in the barn while you are giving the lesson?"

"Yeah, you can help Casey tack up the horses. You're still going on the ride. Casey will lead it," Marilynn stated. "He's rounding up the horses now."

Following Marilynn's new instructions, I hurried to the horse pasture to find Casey, eager to show him I knew my way around a horse much better than a cow.

Casey already had five horses tied up along the pasture fence and was cinching up the big gray gelding he rode last night. The horses looked content basking in the morning sun and swishing at a fly here and there.

Casey had his back to me, but the gravel crunching under my boots gave me away. "You sure you don't want to tackle a steer or two before we head out?" he said, turning his head to face me. His mouth curled up in a grin.

"No, I got that out of my system yesterday," I said, narrowing my eyes at him. *I wish he'd forget about that already.*

Casey just chuckled and picked up a second saddle from the ground. "Who would you like to ride today? You point to the horse and I'll throw a saddle up for you. Every one of these steeds will treat you well."

The horses seemed to know they were being scrutinized as they turned their heads to see what we were blabbing about.

"The little palomino on the end looks sweet."

"She is," Casey replied as he went over and threw the pad and saddle on the palomino's back. "This is Sunny."

I watched Casey pull the cinch under her belly and wrap the saddle's leather latigo through the metal loop. The sleeves of his black-and-red flannel were rolled up to his elbows and he brushed his sandy hair from his eyes with his forearm. "I think I'm supposed to be helping you tack them up," I said and immediately realized I sounded ungrateful for his kindness. "Marilynn said," I added.

"If you insist." Casey nodded to the stack of saddles and bridles. "Everything is labeled with the horses' names. Next to Sunny are Jack, Freckles, and the sorrel pony is Sharkie."

I studied the tiny sorrel pony with the hay belly and raised an eyebrow. His back wasn't much higher than my waist and his frizzy, thick mane stuck out in every direction. He resembled a cartoon character.

"Sharkie?" I asked.

"Don't let his cute face fool you. He's a spitfire out in the pasture. He takes on horses twice his size. Marches around out there like he's king," Casey said, shaking his head. "But he's a teddy bear for kids."

"He looks more like a 'Sweetie' to me," I said, walking to the pile of tack. I threw a baby blue saddle pad on Sharkie's short back and scooped up a tiny brown leather saddle.

"Who's that?" I asked, nodding my head towards the big gray gelding.

"This is my horse, Rocky." Casey ran a slow hand over the gray's muscled rump. "His mom, Babe, was a ranch horse, but she colicked when Rocky was only a month old. I bottle-fed him and Mr. Owens said he was mine after that. That was five years ago."

"You two made quite the team in the ranch sorting last night."

"Thanks. He's a good boy. Takes care of me."

Casey patted Rocky, quiet and lost in a thought. It was obvious how much he cared for the big gelding.

"You headed out for a ride?" The new voice came out of nowhere and her question broke my stare. Taylor strutted right by Sharkie's tail, focused on Casey. She didn't seem to notice I was standing there, a few feet away.

"Taylor," Casey said, standing at attention. "Yes, taking some guests on a ride in about fifteen minutes. Care to join us?"

Taylor's jean shorts just covered her butt and I wondered if she cut them that short or if she in fact bought them like that. Not proper riding attire. But she did have her cowboy boots on.

"I would, but I'm supposed to have brunch with my mom and Mr. Owens. Can I take a rain check?" Taylor cocked her head and played with the end of her perfectly messy side braid, twisting the ends through her fingers.

"Sure," Casey said, clearing his throat. "Lucy and I have rides scheduled all week. Pick your day."

Her nose wrinkled at my name and Casey's eyes shifted from Taylor to me.

"Taylor, have you met Lucy?"

A sense of panic shot through me, as though I wasn't supposed to be there. Taylor turned and I became aware that I probably had hay pieces stuck in my hair and manure on my hands. I wished I was saddling up one of the regular-sized horses so I could just duck and hide behind them.

"Hi, I'm Lucy." I wiggled my fingertips at her.

"You must be the new help," Taylor said flashing a forced Hollywood smile.

Interesting way to put it.

"I'm the new stablehand," I corrected her. "Here for the summer."

Taylor turned her attention back to Casey. "Casey, here, doesn't need much help," she cooed. "He's quite the cowboy."

Now I knew I definitely wasn't supposed to be there.

"Maybe I'll run into you later, Casey. Going to the bonfire?"

"I think so," Casey said, his cheeks a shade of pink.

"You should." Taylor winked.

As Taylor sashayed away, I caught Casey's gaze lingering on her departure. Her hourglass figure was accented further by the turquoise beaded belt wrapped around the waist of a tight t-shirt.

An impatient Sharkie started pawing at the ground and the sound broke Casey's trance. He looked back at me and then diverted his eyes to the ground. "You want to saddle Freckles and I'll get Jack? The guests should be here any minute," he said, walking towards the saddles.

"No problem." I wondered if Taylor had that effect on every guy she came into contact with.

Three

There was nothing better than the back of a horse. The rhythmic swaying in the saddle never failed to sooth me. I rubbed Sunny's neck with my free hand and ran my fingers through her cream-colored mane. She was a sweet, quiet mare. Reminded me of my horse, Stella, at home.

Casey was leading the trail ride, followed by Freckles and Jack carrying Lisa and Steve, a California couple on vacation with their son, Simon. Simon was ten years old and couldn't wait to gallop. I'm not sure he knew what a gallop was, but that's what he told me in the first thirty seconds of meeting him.

"I feel like a real cowboy!" Simon exclaimed to me over his shoulder and then proceeded to drop his reins and circle his hand in the air, twirling an imaginary rope. Sharkie just kept moving along. The squirmy little boy didn't bother him in the least.

"Real cowboys have to hold onto their reins," I reminded him.

"Oh, yeah. I forgot." Simon grabbed the reins resting on Sharkie's neck.

The air tasted cleaner in the mountain. We had only been riding for twenty minutes or so, but we were in the thick of Mount Hood. Trees rose a few hundred feet above our heads and created a green canopy, letting only a few rays of sunlight though. The ground was covered by ferns; moss worked its way over roots and up the base of trees. And we rode single file following a well-worn path through it all. I could do this all day long.

"How old were you when you started riding?" Simon asked, pulling his straw cowboy hat off his head to examine it, but still keeping one hand on the reins.

"I was about your age," I said, thinking about all the days I spent on Stella's back. I would run out to the barn at the first sign of daylight and ride and brush and love on Stella until Dad made me come in for dinner. And then I'd spend the evening telling Dad all of my horsie adventures.

"I want a pony." Simon interrupted my thoughts. "But Mom said they don't allow ponies in the city so I got a cat instead. His name is Bob and he's orange and really hairy."

I chuckled. "Cats are nice too."

"Yeah, Bob is a nice cat. He sleeps with me every night. He likes to sleep on my head sometimes," Simon said as he pushed his cowboy hat back on. "Whoa! I think I see a cow!"

Looking past Simon, I could see Casey and Rocky walking through a bright opening and out of the dense trees.

"Let's catch up. You want to trot, Simon?"

A squeal came out of the little boy's mouth and he nodded his head as fast as he could. I gave Sunny a gentle squeeze with my calves and we jogged up next to Sharkie. Sharkie followed and broke into a choppy, quick trot to keep up. Side by side, Simon and I trotted out of the forest. The rest of our group was waiting for us on the edge of a huge emerald field dotted with hundreds of cow and calf pairs. The snowcapped tip of Mount Hood hovered above us.

I slowed Sunny to a stop next to Casey and Simon trotted Sharkie over to his parents to tell them how much he loved the little brown pony.

I couldn't take my eyes off the scene sprawled out in front of me. "This looks like a postcard."

Brown and white cows and calves grazed on the abundance of grass. Many were laying in the sunshine chewing their cud. Their fat bellies spilled over on the ground and they paid no attention to the new visitors.

"Do all of these cattle belong to the Red Rock Ranch?" I asked.

"Yeah, there's about three hundred head total. We push them up to these higher pastures during the summer to graze. I ride up here a few times a week just to check on the herd," Casey said, relaxed in the saddle and scanning the field. "I always bring my rope just in case there's a sick or injured animal."

Movie scenes from John Wayne's westerns flashed through my head. "You rope and treat them by yourself?"

"Not by myself," Casey noted. "Rocky is always with me."

And there wasn't a drop of sarcasm in his voice. In fact, he said it like it was no big deal. Speechless, I gawked at Casey, realizing I could probably learn a thing or two from this cowboy.

Unaware of my stares, Casey watched Simon laugh and trot circles around his parents. "We better get going. Let's take these guys for a trot through the field and then head back down the mountain," Casey said, nudging Rocky forward.

I waited for Lisa, Steve, and Simon to follow and then Sunny and I fell into step. I wished Casey and I had more time to talk. I had a thousand questions for him about the ranch, the horses, the mountain. Instead, we walked in a line along the edge of the field, next to the giant fir trees. The tall grass brushed Sharkie's chest and he bit off the tips of the wispy blades as he walked.

"Silly pony." Simon giggled and patted Sharkie on the rump.

As Casey turned to ride out through the field, something jostled in the trees. In a split second, twigs snapped, branches cracked and I realized something big was bulldozing its way through the brush, straight for us.

Sunny jumped sideways and trampled through the field backwards, moving away from whatever monster was lurking in the woods. "Whoa, girl. Easy..." I grabbed the saddle horn and tried to sound calm. Bringing her to an unwilling stop, I glanced up. All five horses were now facing the rattling brush.

Sunny's ears were so far forward that the tips were almost touching. Was the bull out in this pasture too? Would a bear attack a group of horses in the middle of the day? Scenarios traced through my head.

But, before anyone could react further, a big black figure burst through the bushes, screaming at the top of its lungs. The wild-eyed beast stopped abruptly in front of us and it took me a second to realize...it was a horse.

The second scream came from Simon and I turned to see pure fear rush over the little boy's face. He dropped his reins and wrapped his body around the saddle horn. In the same instance, Sharkie pinned his tiny ears flat against his curled neck and reared up, striking out at the foreign animal.

This display prompted the black horse to lurch forward, teeth first, at the tiny pony and screaming boy.

My instincts kicked in. Leaning forward, I kicked Sunny into a lope. Two swift strides and I had Sharkie's reins in my hand. Without pausing, I spun Sunny away from the black horse and we pulled the reluctant pony with us, ending up behind a stunned Jack & Freckles.

Not sure what to do next, I looked back towards Casey for help and caught the tail end of a rope soaring through the air. The loop slid around the black horse's neck and Casey wrapped the opposite end of the rope around his saddle horn. He braced his feet in the stirrups, ready for a wild reaction.

Rocky backed until the rope slammed tight around the wild horse's neck, causing a series of violent bucks and rears. I watched, frozen in disbelief, as the horse flailed his body through the air. His front legs lashed out at the rope as though he was trying to pick a fight with it.

Pulling back against the uproar, Rocky dug his hooves into the ground, using all of his body weight.

Realizing he was trapped, the black horse stood still, glaring at us. His nostrils flared, taking in our scent. His sides heaved from the fight, but he was not giving up. He was ready to fight again at any prompting.

Simon was crying by this time. His mom was off her horse and holding the boy.

"What the heck?" I gasped. It was the only thing I could think to say.

Casey caught my eye and then assessed the guests. His shoulders relaxed a bit when he realized no one was hurt and he nudged Rocky forward one step, giving the black horse a little slack in the rope.

"You just roped a mustang," I said, staring at Casey. In pictures, mustangs exuded freedom and beauty, but I had never been close to one. We were on his territory and he obviously didn't like it.

Casey shook his head. "He's not wild."

Did he just miss the part where that horse charged through the trees and then proceeded to attack us? "What are you talking about?" I shrieked.

But, in the midst of second-guessing Casey's eye sight, I noticed a thin strap of leather hanging loosely around the black horse's neck. It looked like a worn dog collar and a number plastic tag hung from the buckle. Number thirteen. Everything about this horse screamed bad luck.

"Everybody okay over there?" Casey asked as Simon's crying turned into a quiet whimper. My heart ached for the little boy who was so excited for his first horse ride just a few minutes ago. Now he probably just wanted to go back to the city and snuggle with his fat cat, Bob.

"We're fine," Lisa responded, rubbing the boy's back and then setting him on the ground. "A little shook up, but fine."

Unsettled by the crying, Sharkie turned his head and nudged Simon, rubbing his whiskered nose on the boy's arm.

"Do you know what Sharkie just did?" I asked and Simon looked up at me, confused and blinking away tears. "Sharkie was just trying to protect you. He didn't mean to scare you."

Simon was quiet, thinking about my words. He craned his neck to check on the black horse who was now securely detained by Casey's rope. Then he looked the pony in the eye. "Good boy," he whispered and patted him on the forehead.

Lisa took a breath and mouthed the words, "Thank you."

I turned back to Casey. "What do we do now?"

"Well, we can't leave him out here. I can't take a chance at having that happen again. And I have no idea where he came from." The black horse whipped its head back and forth and pawed at the ground. "Lucy, can you lead these guys back? I'll follow and hopefully we can get this horse back down to the ranch. Then we'll figure it out from there."

"Yes...yes, I can do that." I gathered my thoughts and my reins. "Simon, can you and Sharkie help me lead this trail? I really need your help."

Simon stared at me and then slowly nodded his head. He wiped his runny nose on his sleeve, took hold of Sharkie's reins and put a boot in the stirrup.

Four

Back at the barn, I rushed to tie the horses to the fence. I yanked their saddles off and threw the tack in a pile on the grass. "Come on, girl," I said, clucking at Sunny and pulling her towards the pasture. Sunny didn't seem to be as rattled as I was, but she trotted anyhow.

"What's the rush, Lucy?" Marilynn asked, walking out of the barn.

I didn't turn around. I closed the gate behind Sunny and hurried back to the other horses. "Hello!" Marilynn yelled, waving her hands in the air. "Did you hear what I just said?"

"Casey roped a horse...a crazy black horse." I started untying Freckle's lead from the fence.

"What are you talking about? We don't even have a black horse on the ranch." Marilynn's face scrunched up, ready to scream profanities at me, when a high-pitched whinny shrieked from behind the barn. We both stopped in our tracks and whipped around.

"That...*that* is what I am talking about."

The black horse was dripping sweat, but still fighting. Head raised, he whinnied again, prancing and pulling his weight against the rope. Poor Rocky was getting jerked and pulled on, but he just kept walking.

"What are we supposed to do with that?" Marilynn asked, staring at the mess of a horse as it approached the barn.

"Open one of the barn paddocks," Casey directed, still wrestling with the rope. The horse seemed to be fighting with the same grueling intensity. Casey had to be exhausted by now.

"You're going to put that thing in the barn?" Marilynn questioned him. "Are you crazy?"

"I don't know what else to do with him. He's just going to cause problems if we let him go."

Marilynn shook her head. "Fine. Put him in the last paddock. He shouldn't bother any of the other horses over there, but I swear I'm going to freak if he kicks through the barn walls."

I sprinted towards the barn, leaving Freckles tied, and swung the paddock gate open. There were ten individual paddocks, each connected by a Dutch door to a barn stall, but they were reserved for the guests' horses. On the opposite end of the barn, Star barreled out of her stall. Assessing the situation, she pranced around her paddock, tail held high, adding unneeded chaos.

Casey tried coaxing the black horse into the paddock, but he balked at the sight of the open gate. Every muscle in his body stiffened and his hooves dug into the gravel, refusing to move forward. From a safe distance behind, Marilynn and I waved our hands in the air. *Just take a few steps forward. Get in there. Get in there.*

And then he did, by grand scale. The black horse leapt straight to the sky, soaring over an invisible jump, and landed square in the middle of the paddock, frozen.

In the few seconds he was still, distracted by his surroundings, Casey grabbed the loop of his rope. At his touch, the horse reversed at light speed, ramming his hind end into the fence, but Casey held tight and the rope popped off the horse's head. Turning Rocky, Casey hustled him out the gate and I slammed it shut.

And there the black horse stood. His feet planted firm on the ground, afraid to move. His coat dripped in sweat and a stark white rim lined his eyes. All three of us gawked at his sudden silence. The rattling metal gate was now the only sound.

"Well, we got him in there. Now what do you suggest we do?" Marilynn crossed her arms, looking back and forth between Casey and me. "Mr. Owens is not going to want a crazy, wild horse running around in his barn."

"I think he would like it even less if that crazy horse chased down his guests *again*," Casey shot back, tired of her lip.

"He chased you down?" Marilynn glared at the black horse, tapping the toe of her boot. "Well, you guys figure it out. And, please figure it out quickly... before Mr. Owens gets involved."

At that, Marilynn marched back to the barn without another word.

Casey sighed, dismounting from Rocky. "Well, she's not very happy with me," he said, wiping his forehead with a handkerchief.

"We did the right thing. We couldn't just leave him up there. Who knows what would happen the next time we rode through." I paused, looking at the black horse. "And he's lost. Somebody has got to be looking for him. Even if he is crazy."

"Yeah, you're probably right," Casey agreed, stuffing his handkerchief back in his pocket. "By the way, you did a great job out there."

The random compliment broke my thoughts and I turned to face him. "You roped a wild horse and pulled it down a mountain. What did I do?"

"You pulled that little boy out of the way before I could even get my rope in the air. It could have been a total disaster if you hadn't been there with me." His blue eyes actually looked sincere.

"Thanks," I said, squirming under the unneeded compliments.

The black horse whinnied again, but this time he sounded shaky and unsure. "He's going to need a bucket of water and some hay after he cools down."

"I'll get it," I offered. "Go take care of Rocky. He looks like he needs a hose down."

"Thanks, kid." Casey smiled and held my gaze just long enough to make me uncomfortable.

Four-thirty-six Sunday morning and I was staring at the blinking numbers on my alarm clock. Rolling over, I slid the quilt over my head, trying to force my body to sleep. Just one more hour. Squeezing my eyes shut for a few more minutes, I decided it was useless. There were too many images racing through my head. I pictured that black horse, drenched in sweat, standing alone in his paddock, scared out of his mind...and I hoped he was okay. Throwing my covers back, I sat straight-up in bed. I needed to check on him.

Outside, a pink haze outlined the mountain and rain pattered on the grass. The quiet was eerie yet comforting as I headed along the path. The barn door squeaked as I rolled it open and Star nickered a soft welcome. She looked cozy in her pink plaid sheet, but I didn't let her sweet face fool me this time. I threw a few flakes of hay over her stall door before she could flashed her teeth at me.

I tiptoed down the dim aisle, not wanting to scare the black horse, but I didn't hear a single noise as I approached the last stall. The horse hadn't kicked the wall, pawed at the floor, or even given his shrill whinny. Peering over the door, I scanned his stall. It was empty. The bucket of water and his hay were untouched. My gut sank. Marilynn is going to freak if he broke through the fence and ran off.

I quickly opened the door to assess the damage, but, at my entrance, something banged hard against the paddock fence. I focused my eyes past the stall and into the attached paddock...and there the black horse stood, pressed against the fence and soaking wet in the drizzling rain.

I crept further into the stall. There was not one hoof print in the shavings. He had been out there all night. Why wouldn't he come out of the rain and into the barn?

Putting both flakes of hay under my arm, I picked up the water bucket and walked towards the paddock. I didn't take my eyes off the black horse as I remembered what he was like yesterday. One quick movement from him and I would be jumping for the door.

But, he didn't move. He watched me as I set the bucket and the hay just outside the stall and then we stared at each other.

His drenched coat emphasized his ribby sides. "You should really eat something," I whispered and backed away, locking the stall door behind me. I couldn't believe he stood out in the cold rain all night when he could've slept in a warm, dry stall with a belly full of hay.

Out of his sight in the barn aisle, I munched on my strawberry pop tart and looked around for something to do while I waited for Marilynn. *The tack could use a good cleaning, I guess.* Grabbing a bridle, rag, and leather cleaner from the tack room, I took a seat on the long wooden bench. I was about to turn on the radio when I heard the slightest bit of rustling from the end of the barn.

Setting the bridle down, I tiptoed along the stall fronts and peeked over the black horse's stall door. The sun was coming up and I could now easily see into the paddock. The black horse was just outside the stall with his head to the ground, carefully wrapping his lips around a few strands of hay. He stretched his neck out, keeping his body a safe distance from the foreign building. But, when he finished chewing, he stepped one foot closer and ripped a big mouthful, shaking his head and spreading the flake at his feet.

I held my breath, making sure not to giggle at his overzealous bite. I didn't want to alert him of my hiding spot and I watched in silence as the black horse filled his hungry belly. Standing there, chewing on his hay, he didn't look scary or mean. He just looked frightened...unsure.

The black horse ate a portion of the hay and then dipped his nose in the water bucket and gulped. Ripples of skin ran up the bottom of his neck as he drank. When there was nothing left, he raised his head and licked his wet lips, water dripping from his whiskered muzzle. He finally seemed content.

Just then, the barn door to my left swung open and chaos took over. In one swift movement, the horse spun on his hind legs, sent his bucket flying, and lunged himself to the farthest point of the paddock. In the commotion, I tried to step backwards, but, instead, tripped over my own feet and landed on my butt facing Marilynn.

Marilynn stepped through the door and pulled back the hood of her yellow raincoat.

"What are you doing?" Marilynn looked at me with one eyebrow cocked and then turned to peer into the stall. "And what is that crazy horse doing?"

I stood up and brushed the dirt from my jeans, feeling a bit silly. "He was eating. I moved his hay out in the paddock because he won't come into the stall. I think he's scared of the barn."

Marilynn's eyebrow rose further. Then she turned to survey the stall and what she could see of the paddock. "He didn't destroy anything overnight?"

"Doesn't look like it." I shrugged my shoulders.

"Well, that's a plus. Maybe it's better if he stays out of the barn."

I looked at the black horse, pushed up against the end of the puddled paddock. The white around his eyes had returned and he was on full alert again, staring at us. I felt like I needed to stick up for him, but I didn't know what to say.

I carried on with morning chores without a mention of the black horse but managed a glance in his stall each time I passed by. Throughout the morning, his mound of hay slowly disappeared and I didn't witness any more commotion. Hopefully, that meant he was settling in.

Sunday was a quiet day on the ranch. Marilynn and I finished chores and there weren't any trail rides scheduled for the afternoon. Instead, I spent the extra time pampering the ranch horses. A bucket of brushes in hand, I moved from one horse to the next, making my way through the pasture. Each horse got their share of rubbing as I combed their manes and curried their bodies while they napped in the afternoon sun.

After the evening feeding, I walked the trail back to my bunk. The rain and fog had burned off by noon and the sun was glowing in the open sky. It was only six o'clock and I had no idea what I was going to do for the rest of the evening. Contemplating the task of organizing my bunk, I remembered Marilynn mentioned a bonfire at the main lodge. She said everyone was welcome. *It wouldn't hurt to check it out.*

A quick wardrobe change and a baseball hat later, my bunk's screen door slapped shut behind me. There was no way I could sit inside and ignore the summer weather.

Past the outdoor arena, I made my way up the hill towards the main lodge. The long log cabin sat squarely against the mountain backdrop. A covered porch wrapped the front of the cabin and a handful of guests swayed and chatted on wooden rocking chairs. A trail of smoke rose from the massive stone fireplace, protruding from the middle of the roof, and country music hummed through the air. I took a deep breath and could taste the campfire.

The music started to blare as I walked around the back corner of the lodge, setting my eyes on an orange blaze. A massive bonfire roared in the cozy circle of land between the back of the lodge and the multiple guest cabins. And, a dancing mass of people bounced to the music of three guitars, a violin, and a sassy female singer.

The band was perched on the lodge's back deck and their catchy tunes forced my head to bob in rhythm. The upbeat country music reminded me of home and I started my way through the dancing crowd, scanning the back deck for a place to sit. But, instead of a seat, I got a sharp elbow to the ribs from a little spinning flash of blonde curls.

"Watch where you are going," Taylor snapped, her face just inches from mine, but she barely made eye contact before spinning back into the arms of a waiting cowboy.

Slightly stunned by her lack of manners, I stood there watching as the dancing couple rocked back into seamless rhythm. His hand found the small of her back and Taylor threw her slender arm around his broad shoulders. Reaching up, she snatched the black cowboy hat from his head and placed it on her own. Hatless, her dancing partner brushed his sandy brown hair out of his eyes as Taylor swayed her hips to her own beat.

The sandy haired cowboy was Casey.

I couldn't get out of there fast enough. I turned to retreat, but there were dancing couples in every direction.

In the midst of my shuffling, Casey caught my eye. "Lucy?" he asked, peering through the mob.

Trapped, I stood in the crowd feeling like a stalker. *I should have stayed in my bunk.*

I waved my hand and forced a smile, still looking for somewhere to retreat, but Casey made his way towards me. Taylor was close behind.

"Hey, glad you decided to come to the bonfire. Pretty fun, huh?" Casey's smile was welcoming, but it didn't make me feel any more comfortable.

"Pretty fun," I responded, avoiding Taylor's glare as she stood at Casey's side. Even without eye contact, I felt her looking me up and down, accusing me of something hideous.

"How's the black horse doing?" Casey asked, oblivious to Taylor's stares.

"Pretty freaked out," I said. "But he's eating and drinking now. And, he hasn't broken anything in the barn so far."

"That's good," Casey nodded. "Wanted to let you know I stopped by the sheriff's office earlier today. Asked if anyone reported a lost horse, but no one has. I left a description of the black horse and told the sheriff he was at the ranch if anyone came looking for him."

My mind raced back to images of the frightened horse. "I'm not really sure how someone loses their horse, but hopefully they can find him now."

Casey shrugged. "I'm not sure either, but he's got a place to stay while we figure it out."

"Sarah?" Taylor burst out the question as though she hadn't listened to a word of our conversation.

Casey and I both stopped and looked at her.

"Excuse me?" I asked when she didn't say anything else.

"Sarah. You're the new girl working at the barn." She said, like she was proud to remember who I was.

"Lucy," I responded.

"Lucy, Sarah. Close enough," Taylor said, rolling her eyes.

As the band started a new song, Taylor fully lost interest in our conversation.

"Let's dance!" she squeaked and tugged at Casey's arm.

Casey opened his mouth, but no words came out before Taylor pulled him back into the crowd. I was left standing by myself, again. *Sarah...that is not even remotely close to my name.*

I maneuvered a path to the deck and half-listened to another song. I watched everyone dance and laugh around the bonfire. And, the more I watched, the more I felt like I didn't belong. Feeling homesick for the first time, I snuck out and headed back in the direction of my bunk.

With the country music fading in the background, the ranch felt cold and quiet. The sun had set and there wasn't another soul within ear shot. My empty bunk didn't sound too appealing either.

Maybe I should check on the black horse? Being in the barn would be much better than sitting in my bunk by myself.

I shuffled down the barn aisle to the black horse's stall and peeked inside, trying not to scare him again. In the paddock, he nibbled on the last strands of his hay, but, when he noticed my presence, he whipped his head up and backed a few quick steps.

"It's okay, boy. I just came to check on you." I said, resting my arms on his stall door. I let him assess me in silence and, after a few minutes, crept inside the stall to sit down in the unused cedar bedding.

"You know, this bedding is pretty comfortable. You should give it a try," I said, resting my head against the stall boards and wrapping by arms around my knees.

The black horse didn't move. He stared at me, his ears pricked forward and head cocked. "I know how you feel," I whispered, watching him in the paddock. "It's kind of scary being away from home, but it will be okay. You don't have to be scared." I took a deep breath, half-reassuring myself of the same thing. "We'll find your owner. Don't you worry."

The black horse blinked his eyes and stepped closer to his hay. He never took his eyes off me, but seemed to accept that I wasn't a threat...at the moment.

In the quiet, I pictured Taylor's blank face as I reminded her of my name. She really didn't care what my name was. I'm not sure why that irritated me, but it did.

The black horse chewed his hay.

"Black horse...you deserve a name. You deserve to be called something other than black horse." I twiddled my thumbs, trying to think of a fitting name. "You deserve a name no one will forget."

He needed something strong. Something to give him confidence. *Thunder? No, too intimidating. Ebony? No, that's not quite right.*

"You just need a chance to prove yourself."

The black horse cocked his head again at my whispered statement.

"Chance? Do you like that?"

The black horse picked his head up from his hay, nodding up and down. He was probably just shoeing a fly from his nose, but I took it as a sign that he liked the name. That he would choose that name for himself. And I thought it fit.

"Chance it is," I smiled. "Thanks for keeping me company, Chance."

Five

Monday flew by. I finished feeding the horses and cleaning stalls just in time to saddle up with Marilynn for the scheduled afternoon trail ride. Again, I tailed the end of the ride on Sunny, but today's adventure was less eventful than yesterday's...there was no charging wild horse and no one cried.

As the sun set, I helped Marilynn load the saddles back in the tack room.

"I can't believe how late it is already," Marilynn said as she heaved the last saddle on the wooden rack. "I'm starving."

"Me too," I said as my stomach growled. I hadn't noticed any hunger pains until Marilynn mentioned food.

Scanning the tack room, Marilynn nodded. "Okay. We're done for the day. Let's go ransack the kitchen."

I followed her lead.

With a belly full of homemade chili and a stack of chocolate chip cookies in my hand, I walked through my bunk door and slumped down on my bed. My body felt like jelly but, even as tired as I was, the silence in my bunk was overwhelming. With the excitement of the day slipping away, the homesick pangs returned.

Trying to ignore them, I grabbed *Summer Dust*, the book sitting on my night stand, and picked up where I left off last night. It was the third book in my favorite series and I was sentences away from the start of the Kentucky Derby. I read on as Summer, the longshot filly with the big heart, entered the starting gate, but placed the open book on my chest when I realized even the suspense of the race couldn't keep my attention.

The silence surrounding me was deafening. It gave me too much room to think. I closed my eyes, hoping for a food-coma to kick in. *You're fine. Just tough it out. You'll get used to being here. You'll make friends. Just think about the time you get to spend in the barn, with the horses, in the saddle. Keep thinking about that.*

So I did. And, as I laid there thinking about the horses, I realized there was someone else at the ranch fighting my same battle...Chance. He was away from home and he didn't know anyone either. *Maybe we could wallow in our newness together?*

The next evening, when Marilynn said good night, I grabbed my dinner to-go and made my way to the barn.

"Hey there," I whispered, sliding open Chance's stall door. My entrance wasn't loud enough to startle a mouse, but Chance stumbled backwards and then stared at me from the paddock, neck arched and eyes wide. I stepped inside the stall, trying to ignore his not-so-welcoming demeanor.

"You mind if I have dinner with you?" I asked, half-looking for an approval. When Chance didn't move, I found a comfy spot in his clean bedding and sat down cross-legged to unwrap my tuna salad sandwich. Most horses would be curious as to why I decided to sit on their stall floor. They would mosey close and sniff me all over. Probably try to nibble on my dinner or nuzzle my hair. But, Chance wasn't like most horses. He stood in his paddock like a coal black statue. He didn't even blink.

I took a bite out of my sandwich anyhow.

I chewed and let my eyes slide shut. The quiet here was different. It wasn't foreign like my bunk. The barn was filled with sounds of rustling hay and soft snorts. The scent of sweet grass and cedar bedding filled my lungs. And, being near Chance felt familiar, even if he wasn't as warm & cozy as my Stella at home. Even if he didn't want to come near me.

Lost in the comfort of the barn, my eyes jerked open when a crunching noise snuck up on me. I yanked my legs out from underneath myself, scrambling to jump for safety. Images of flailing black hooves flashed through my mind. But, turning my head towards the paddock, I froze with my feet out in front of me, realizing Chance had only taken a few steps closer. His neck lowered, he watched my every move, eyes wide with a mouth full of hay.

"Geez," I exhaled and rested my arms against my knees. "You scared the crap out of me." Touching my hand to my thumping chest, I was amazed I avoided a heart attack. "For a second there, I thought I was going to see the bottom of your feet."

Chance continued staring at me, hay pieces sticking out of both sides of his mouth. Certain I wasn't going to get up, he started chewing.

I shook my head and chuckled. "You almost made me choke on my tuna salad sandwich."

The next few evenings I spent in Chance's stall, eating my dinner and telling him stories. I told him anything that came to mind and he listened, from a distance, as he chewed his hay. I told him about Stella, my mare at home, and the home cooked dinners my grandma makes every Sunday. I told him about Taylor and her mare's sour attitude. And I told him how Casey ended up with Rocky. Chance kept his eyes on me through every story, hanging on each word. He still wouldn't come within ten feet of me, but I did notice a few hoof prints in his stall bedding. Maybe our evening talks were starting to make him feel comfortable too.

Back at work, I unclasped Star's halter and shut the gate to one of the smaller pastures. She pranced away from me, shaking her head and hopping around in the afternoon sun. Her flaxen mane rolled in the breeze as her hooves sprung from the ground. I smiled as she put her nose to the grass and began nibbling.

Throwing the halter over my shoulder, I turned back towards the barn, but stopped in my tracks as I witnessed the chaos. In a blur of black, Chance ran back and forth at end of his paddock, frantic and screaming. A man in a cowboy hat and jean jacket walked towards him with a halter and lead dangling from his hand. Chance reared up and I held my breath until his feet reluctantly hit the ground. He was either going to jump over the fence or go through it. I took off in a dead sprint for the barn.

Marilynn stood at the front of Chance's stall and watched me as I raced down the aisle.

"What's going on?" I yelled, hoping that man hadn't gotten any closer to Chance. Marilynn opened her mouth to respond, but I didn't wait for her words. I pushed open the stall door and scrambled inside.

The man was still walking towards Chance, now with his hands held high in the air, giving Chance nowhere to go. Chance crashed his shoulder against the metal gate, making it ring, and when the man didn't retreat, he reared towards the cowboy, feet flailing and ears pinned flat. I was too late. Somebody was going to get hurt.

"You can't do that!" I screamed from the stall just as the man shielded his face with his arms and ran backwards.

Unharmed, he turned and stomped past me into the barn aisle. "Apparently not," he said, tossing the halter and lead on the ground and staring back at Chance. "I was just trying to catch him," the man stated, wiping his wrinkled brow with a handkerchief. "What is *wrong* with that horse?"

Marilynn shot me a glare as I stepped into the aisle and shut the stall door. Chance ran back and forth at the end of the paddock as though the man was still in there with him. A cloud of dust circled his legs and clung to his sweaty body. My heart pounded in my ears.

The startled man was in his sixties, tall and trim. Silver sideburns poked out from underneath his black cowboy hat. His hands were rough, but clean as though he had worked hard in his life, but not in some time. "We can't have something like that here at the ranch." He directed his statement at Marilynn. "He's a law suit waiting to happen."

"I know, Mr. Owens," Marilynn responded. "He's only been here a few days. Casey has been checking with the sheriff's office to see if anyone has reported a lost horse, but no one has. I'm not sure what to do with him."

"Let's try to get him loaded in the stock trailer and I'll haul him over to the livestock auction in Three Rivers."

An auction? I looked back at Chance, pacing and pawing at the fence, practically frothing at the mouth. No one would buy him. No one would take the time to see the good in him. He'd end up getting shipped off to slaughter.

"Please...please let him stay," I blurted out as my gut flipped.

Mr. Owens stared at me for a few hard seconds. "And you are?"

"This is Lucy Rose," Marilynn jumped in and flashed me a look like I had better shut my mouth. "She was hired to help me with the horses for the summer. Lucy, *this* is Mr. Owen's. This is his ranch."

I swallowed what little spit was left in my mouth, wishing I had made a better first impression.

Mr. Owens brushed the dust from his weathered jean jacket. "Every horse here earns their keep and I can't have one just standing around eating hay and taking up space. Not to mention, he could hurt someone."

"He's just scared." I said, wondering if Mr. Owens and Marilynn could hear my voice waver. "He needs some work."

"That's an understatement," Mr. Owens replied, wide-eyed and searching my face for a better answer.

"I'll work with him," I offered. "I'll do it. He just needs time. I'm sure he could make a great ranch horse." Both of their mouths dropped open.

I wasn't sure my statement even made sense. I didn't know if Chance could be broke...or even touched for that matter, but I did know Chance didn't deserve to be shipped off to an auction. Mr. Owens owned the ranch, the horses, the cattle. He must have a soft spot for the animals or he wouldn't have them. My eyes shifted between Marilynn and Mr. Owens, waiting for a response.

Mr. Owens sighed, shaking his head. "Fine. The auction isn't for two weeks. If I took him to the stockyards now, I'd have to pay to keep him stalled until the auction." He looked me straight in the eye. "You have two weeks to work with him. If you can't get him broke in that time we will have no choice but to take him to auction."

"I understand. Thank you, Mr. Owens," I said, as he turned his back to me and walked out of the barn.

Marilynn stood in the same spot with her hands pressed firmly on her hips. She closed her mouth, only to start snapping her gum. "You might be crazier than that horse. What exactly do you think you are going to do with him?"

We turned to stare at Chance who had worked himself into a dripping, frothy sweat.

"I don't really know what I am going to do with him," I whispered as he continued pacing in his paddock.

Marilynn and Casey rode off with a group of guests on an afternoon trail ride and I was in charge of cleaning up the barn. I picked the stalls, swept the aisle, and organized the tack room. Satisfied with my work, I made my way to Chance's stall, hoping he had calmed down after this morning's episode with Mr. Owens.

Chance's head hung low and heavy as he stood in his paddock. The once-frothy sweat had dried and chalk white lines were left in its place. That poor boy needed to be brushed. He needed a good bath. He needed some love. But, how could I do any of that if I couldn't even get close to him?

Maybe I couldn't tame him, but I knew I had to buy Chance time until I could find out where he came from. Somehow, he was far away from home, lost and scared.

I tossed a few flakes of hay into his paddock and sat cross-legged in his stall. Chance stared at me, his eyes glazed over with exhaustion. "I'm not going to chase you, Chance. Don't worry. Eat your hay."

Chance watched me for a few silent minutes, and when I didn't move, he moved to the hay. He nibbled but kept his dark eyes on me. His ears flicked towards each noise in the background but pointed in my directions as my stomach gurgled.

"Did you hear that?" I asked him, realizing I forgot to eat lunch. "I guess it was pretty loud."

Good thing I carried a reserve. Reaching in my pocket, I pulled out a peanut butter granola bar and ripped open the crinkly silver wrapper. Enjoying my first chewy bite, I noticed Chance extending his neck, just a few inches. His nostrils flared with small puffs of air as he tried to identify the new smell.

"Does that smell good?" I mumbled as I tore off a chunk and offered it in my flat hand. "It's peanut butter."

I reached my hand out as far as possible without leaving my seat on the stall floor. Chance balked at my gesture.

"I'm not going to hurt you, Chance," I whispered, holding my hand still. *I wonder how long I can keep this position.*

And, as I contemplated, Chance began to inch closer. His hooves were planted firmly on the ground, but he reached his nose out, farther and farther, until he was inches from my hand. I held my breath as he sniffed and nuzzled the unknown item with his whiskered top lip...and then he snatched it from my hand. His lower jaw moved in tiny circles, grinding the granola bar. His head bobbed up and down as he finished the treat and then he stood there, staring at me, ignoring the pile of hay at his feet.

I ripped off another piece of the granola bar, but froze when I heard voices outside the barn. Chance's ears pricked forward and he stepped back. *Dang. They must be back from the trail ride already.*

Sighing, I stood up and brushed the bedding from my backside. *I wish I had just a little more time alone with Chance.*

"Hey, Lucy," Casey said, breaking my thought as he walked down the barn aisle, bridles hanging from his shoulder. "How's the black horse doing?"

I glanced at the gelding that was just inches from my fingers. "Better. He's better."

"Good to hear," Casey said, pulling open the stall door to get a better look.

"Have you heard anything from the sheriff's office?"

Casey shook his head. "Still nothing. I just can't believe no one around here is looking for a lost horse. If Rocky went missing, I would be calling every neighbor and police station within a hundred miles. I don't get it." Casey shrugged his shoulders and his eyes drifted towards the paddock.

"I don't get it either," I agreed, watching Chance chew a few yellow strands of hay.

Casey leaned his shoulder against the stall door, looping his thumbs in his jean pockets. "So, Marilynn told me about your introduction to Mr. Owens this morning."

I stopped breathing. *Great. Casey thinks I'm crazy too.*

"That was pretty bold," Casey noted.

I met his eyes. Bold? Was that a nice way of calling me stupid? I searched for a way to explain myself, to explain Chance, to tell Casey that I really didn't know what I was doing...but I stopped as a warm smile graced Casey's face.

"I'm excited to see a change in that black horse. Glad you're up for the challenge."

I mulled over Casey's use of the word challenge but was thankful someone was taking my side. "Thanks," I whispered.

"And let me know if you need any help," Casey offered as he turned towards the tack room, pulling the dusty brim of his baseball hat over his eyes.

"Hey, Casey?" I called after him and poked my head out the stall door. "I don't want to call him the black horse anymore. He deserves a name...and I thought we could call him Chance."

Casey nodded. "I think that sounds perfect."

Six

Chance's black nose wrinkled as his wet tongue rolled across the palm of my hand. A smile grew on my face, but I kept from giggling. My secret weapon, the peanut butter granola bar, had cast a surprising spell on Chance.

This was the third evening attempting this trick-- breaking a bar into several small pieces and waiting patiently as each treat lured Chance closer and closer. Kneeling on the stall floor, Chance's breath warmed my open palm. He was as close as he had ever been and I couldn't help but to touch him. I brushed his muzzle with my fingertips and Chance jerked his head sideways, shooting an accusatory glare my way.

I lowered my hand. "You've got to trust me, Chance. You have to trust me so I can help you." Sighing, I repeated the words again in a soft rhythm as I raised my opposite arm, offering another piece of granola bar, this time with a halter and lead dangling from my forearm.

Chance arched his neck at the foreign object but was fully aware of the treat before him. "Trust me, Buddy. Trust me," I whispered, and his ears flicked forward again. Unable to resist the bar, Chance lowered his muzzle to my hand and, as he relished in the treat, I slipped my hand past his nose to hold it against his cheek.

Chance stopped chewing and we stared at each other. Touching and eye-to-eye, I became terribly aware how close this thousand-pound animal was to me. My head told me to back off, but my heart wouldn't let me. I didn't pull away...and neither did Chance. Frozen in silence. Each of us waited for the other to make a move.

And then Chance did. He started chewing again. He didn't run away. He didn't throw his head. He just watched me and chewed and my hand moved with the circular motion of his jaw.

I grabbed another treat from my pocket and Chance lapped it up without hesitation. Happy with our progress, I began humming along with the country music playing on the barn radio and I slowly stood, rolling my hand up to his neck.

I pushed back his tangled mane and stroked his smooth, black coat. I'm not sure if it was the humming or the rubbing, but Chance licked his lips, a sign of relaxation. I blew a tense breath from my lungs.

I hummed every song from the radio's top-ten countdown and rubbed on Chance until my shoulders ached and the sun set behind Mount Hood. With his head lowered and eyes droopy, Chance didn't seem to notice as I slipped the halter over his nose and quietly clasped it behind his ears.

"Now, let's take that ratty leather collar off of you." I said wiggling the rusty buckle and pushing until the leather broke free of the metal. The attached plastic tag, marked with a number thirteen, broke in half as the collar hit the ground. Good riddance.

I studied Chance, sporting the new nylon halter. "You look good in royal blue," I smiled.

Chance cocked his head towards me, blinking those big brown eyes. "Okay, I'll hum you one more song and then I have got to get some sleep."

That night I pulled my covers up to my chin and fell right to sleep. And, I dreamed of being on Chance's back, galloping through the open mountain field where the cattle grazed. The cool air rushed into my lungs and whipped through my hair. Chance's black neck stretched out in front of me and his body moved under mine splitting the tall grass. Each powerful stride felt like an achievement. Nothing could have felt better.

Then my alarm clock screamed and ripped me from my fantasy. I slammed the snooze button and pulled a pillow over my head, aching to go back to sleep. I needed to fall back into my dream...even for five more minutes. Why did 5:30 have to come so fast?

I laid there in protest, refusing to get up, thinking about Chance. Coming out of my sleepy haze, I remembered our evening together and couldn't believe I got a halter on him. It was a far cry from galloping through the fields, but at least we were moving in the right direction.

And, this afternoon I have a few open hours while Marilynn takes out a trail ride. In fact, she told me to get working on *that black horse* while she is gone. Apparently, Mr. Owens was asking for updates and Marilynn couldn't bring herself to tell him I didn't even have him out of the paddock yet.

But I did get a halter on him yesterday and I wanted to try a saddle today.

The afternoon sun beat hard on my shoulders as we made our trek from Chance's paddock to the arena. Chance cautiously followed my lead and second-guessed every distraction along the way. He jumped sideways when the wind rustled the bushes, baulked at a funny looking rock, and just about lost it when a squirrel crossed our path. I kept coaxing him, hoping he wouldn't bolt back towards the barn, taking me with him.

By the time we walked through the arena gate, my arms were sore from getting yanked around and my grand idea of galloping through the mountain seemed decades away. Needless to say, I was *not excited* to find Taylor in our destination. I didn't need an audience for this. Especially an audience made up of Taylor Johnson.

Taylor loped past us without even a glance in our direction. Star was tacked up in an English saddle with a zebra print saddle pad and matching leg wraps. Taylor donned tan breeches and a black velvet helmet. She steered Star towards a two-foot jump and they breezed over it like it was nothing.

Rounding the arena, Taylor took notice of Chance and trotted over, posting in the saddle.

"Are you going to stand there?" she asked, stopping Star in front of us.

"Excuse me?" I responded. Did this girl know how to say hello?

"Are you going to stand right *there*?" Taylor repeated, slower. "You're kind of in the way of my jump."

I tried to process her rude attitude but decided it would be best not to start a fight with one of the ranch's guests. "I'll stay out of your way," I stated, wondering if she ever learned how to share. "I didn't know you jumped Star."

Taylor fiddled with the chin strap on her helmet. "We just started training before we headed here for the summer. Kind of bored with the rodeo queen thing at the moment," she shrugged.

Taylor didn't look like she was just learning how to jump. She looked like she could walk into a show ring and win the class.

"Is that the wild horse that Casey roped?" Taylor asked as she eyed up Chance. "Looks a little rough around the edges."

"His name is Chance," I informed her.

"Chance...like half-a-chance?" Her overly white teeth gleamed in the sun as she laughed at her own joke, shaking her head.

My mouth gapped open. Who did this little brat think she was? I turned on my heels and clucked to Chance before my mouth spewed out what I really wanted to say.

"Oh, come on. It was just a joke," Taylor whined as I walked past.

I just kept walking. How could Casey possibly be interested in that girl? Her pretty face masked a nasty attitude. The more I got to know her, the more I disliked her. She was not nice. In fact, she was downright mean. But, maybe Casey was too entranced by her blonde hair and perfect body to care?

I watched Taylor jump Star again, in flawless form, as I lead Chance towards the saddle and brushes I dropped off earlier. Stopping him at the fence, I grabbed a rubber curry and started rubbing circles on his neck. He stiffened, for a second, and then gave in to the massaging action of the curry.

Chance sniffed the saddle hanging on the fence, blowing short breathes over the leather.

"Are you going to let me put that on you today?" I asked, pushing Taylor's comments out of my head.

Now that I was gaining his trust, this could be easy. In fact, he could be trained under-saddle for all I know. But, it was also possible he had never seen a saddle. Today might turn into a rodeo bronc show. My heartbeat picked up at the thought.

I grabbed the saddle pad and rubbed it all over Chance's body, getting him use to the feel of the coarse wool. He didn't flinch. I kept rubbing until I noticed Taylor riding out of the arena. She was on her cell phone and giggling about something. At least we wouldn't have an audience.

"Okay, let's give this a shot."

I positioned the pad on Chance's back and pulled the saddle off the fence. I held my breath as I gently placed the heavy leather saddle on his back. I let go, allowing the saddle's full weight to rest on Chance and, to my surprise, he didn't move. He didn't do anything except watch me with his left eye.

I looked for any sign of body language as I tightened the girth, waiting for Chance to explode. Still nothing. I took a step back and looked him over. He was quiet. Almost frozen. Not the reaction I was expecting.

Maybe I was making a bigger deal out of this than I needed to be.

"Good boy, Chance," I whispered, taking a breath and placing one foot in the stirrup. I paused as I pressed my body weight on the saddle. If he exploded, I could still jump back. But, he had no reaction. It was almost spooky, how quiet he was.

I grabbed hold of the saddle horn and swung my body into the seat, quickly putting my other foot in the stirrup. I had the lead in one hand and both hands wrapped around the saddle horn, expecting the worst.

Chance was like a solid statue. Not moving. He didn't even seem curious as to why I was on top of him.

I lightly squeezed my legs together and clucked my tongue.

"Let's try walking, boy." I clucked again, trying to give him some motivation.

Nothing. It was like sitting on a rock.

I went to squeeze him again, but I must have hit a different button...because I got the reaction I was initially expecting. Plus a little more.

Chance didn't explode. He shattered.

He reverted back to the first day I met him. Putting his head to the ground, Chance launched himself forward so hard that my chest slammed against the saddle horn as his feet returned to the ground. I didn't have time to react as his throat made a primitive guttural noise and all four hooves cut through the air, kicking out with such force that I simply couldn't hang on.

My body unwillingly flipped through the air and all I saw was the arena dirt. I landed hard, face down, the wind pushed from my lungs.

Then, moving only on instinct, I rolled as fast as my body would let me, avoiding flailing hooves.

At a safe distance from the explosion, I pushed myself to my hands and knees and spit the earthy dirt from my mouth.

"Oh my God! Are you okay?" Taylor shrieked as she trotted Star over and closed her cell phone.

I didn't respond right away, partially because I had no air left in my lungs. "I'm okay," I forced out, but I wasn't sure if I was. Adrenaline pumped through my veins, but it didn't numb the throbbing pain in my shoulder or the sharp imprint the saddle horn left in my chest.

"What is wrong with that horse?" Taylor asked, scrunching her face up in disgust instead of concern.

I crawled to a kneeling position and tried to brush the dirt from the front of my tank top, but it was useless. I must have skidded across the ground when I hit. Dirt ground against my skin, under my clothes, as I moved.

I patted my body, checking for signs of broken bones or blood. And, when I was sure I was in one piece, Chance's rodeo show came to a halt. He stood facing us from a distance, his sides heaving and white blaring in his eyes.

"It's not his fault," I sighed, shaking my head. *Stupid, stupid, stupid.* "I pushed him too fast."

"Umm, he just put your face in the ground," Taylor said, accenting the word *face*. I didn't need a reminder. "I'd be pissed if I were you."

I couldn't concern myself with Taylor right now. Limping myself into a standing position, I wiped my grimy face and moved towards Chance. I crept across the arena and Chance leaned his body weight backwards, ready to run again. When I snatched up the end of the lead rope, dangling on the ground, Chance propelled backwards.

"Easy, Easy, boy," I pleaded and followed, holding tight to the end of the lead rope. "It's okay, Chance. It's okay. I promise." And, thankfully, Chance slowed his feet as he realized I wasn't mad...at him.

"Have fun with that mess," Taylor said, turning to walk Star out of the arena.

How stupid of me. I should have taken more time to get him used to the saddle. He was scared frozen. I pushed him too hard. It was my fault.

I loosened the girth and slid the saddle from Chance's back, dropping it to the ground and fighting back every feeling of defeat.

Back in the barn, I closed Chance's stall door and leaned against it, processing what just happened. I'd never been on a horse that bucked like that. I could have gotten hurt. I could have gotten Chance hurt. My head spun with the frightening possibilities that hadn't happened.

"What the heck happened to you?" Marilynn asked, walking out of the tack room and stopping abruptly, her eyes as big as saucers. I was sure I looked like a complete mess, dirt smeared across my face and ground into my clothes. I tilted my head to the ceiling, fighting the tears building in my eyes.

"I hit the dirt," I squeaked out, wiping the tears from my cheeks. The back of my hand slid across the grit on my face.

"Well, that's obvious," Marilynn stated, approaching the stall. Then she pointed an accusing finger at Chance. "Did he do that to you?"

I shook my head, letting out a long, shaking breath. "I did it to myself."

Marilynn raised an eyebrow, and I braced myself for a harsh lecture. But instead, she patted me on the back like a small child. "Listen. It's okay. I know you want to help him, but maybe you just can't."

My eyes shot to Marilynn's face, stunned by her statement.

"Don't take it the wrong way, Lucy. I just meant that maybe he needs a more experienced rider, more time. I've *never* seen a horse react to people the way he does. Makes me wonder how he was treated before he ended up here...and that might take a very long time to undo."

Marilynn's words ripped at my heart, making my tears come in waves. But, maybe she was right. Chance probably needed more experience and more time than I had. *I can't give him what he needs.*

"But what if he goes to that auction and no one wants him? Or worse, what if he ends up with someone who doesn't understand him? Someone who would hurt him?" I closed my eyes, trying to rid the violent visions from my brain.

"Lucy, you're just going to have to trust that he will find a good home...or that his old owner will speak up and come get him."

I shuttered. I thought I wanted Chance's old owner to find him, but the more time I spent with Chance, the more I was certain he didn't come from a good place. I couldn't let him go back. I couldn't let him go to the auction and I couldn't let him go home. I looked over at Chance, standing in his stall. His ears flicked back and forth, listening to our conversation, searching our faces with his eyes.

"I know you're just trying to keep me from getting hurt, Marilynn, but I can't stop trying until his time is up at the ranch."

Marilynn sighed. "Well, you do what you've got to do. Just don't break any bones. You're not much help to me then," Marilynn warned as she patted my arm again and walked off.

I cringed, her touch reminding me of my throbbing shoulder. I better put some ice on that tonight.

Seven

I discovered, if needed, I could survive with only one arm...at least for a few days. Chores around the ranch were awkward, but I devised new techniques to complete them. My Olympic-discus-thrower method frightened the ranch horses a bit, but they stood still as I wrapped my good arm over the top of each saddle and used gravity to spin my body and launch the heavy piece of leather onto their backs. Thank God for obedient, trusting horses.

I also realized I could clean stalls by gripping the middle of the manure pick handle and using my armpit as a leverage point for the end of the long, wooden pole. I only placed my other hand on the handle, for appearances, when Marilynn was in sight. I don't think she noticed my newly devised stall cleaning technique. Either that or she was determined to ignore it.

Casey was more observant. He stopped in his tracks when I pulled a hay bale from the feed room and dragged it down the barn aisle by one strand of twine, leaving a trail of hay bits in my tracks.

"Need some help there?" he asked, forming his words slowly. "I can carry that for you...if you want."

"No, thank you," I replied, still dragging the bale and avoiding eye contact. "My left arm needs to get worked too. Been using my right arm too much lately."

I continued on in silence as if that was a normal response. Stopping at the end of the aisle, I cut open the bale, feeling Casey's eyes on my every move and awaiting his next question.

"Grab an extra bridle, Casey," Marilynn yelled from just outside the barn. "We're one short."

"Sure. Be there in a minute," Casey replied and turned to enter the tack room, keeping any sarcastic comments to himself.

I began feeding the horses, hoping Casey and Marilynn would head out on their trail ride soon. My next task was to dump a wheelbarrow full of manure. I hadn't quite figured out how I was going to accomplish that one yet.

I made it through the workday with no major mishaps or further injuries and my one-armed techniques seemed to give my shoulder some time to heal, to loosen up. Although, I knew I had to avoid the same situation tonight. My body wouldn't take kindly to another rodeo-bronc disaster. After a day of work, I realized how important each one of my limbs is and I didn't need to injure another one.

The arena was quiet this time. There was no one lingering around to judge Chance...or my dreaded cartwheels through the air. I took my time brushing his black coat and we relaxed together with each new stroke. Chance eventually cocked his back foot, resting the tip of his hoof on the ground, and took a slow breath, his lower lip hanging loose.

"Not so bad, is it?" I smiled at him.

Convinced we were both ready to give it another shot, I grabbed the saddle and winced as I used both arms to lightly set it on his back. I knew Chance wouldn't stand for my Olympic-discus-thrower move.

Tightening the girth under his belly, I watched, horrified, as Chance transformed out of relaxation. Every muscle hardened as he planted all four feet on the ground. His black neck arched and his nostrils flared, showing the pink skin inside. The image was a replica of yesterday.

I jumped backwards, hoping to distance myself from the explosion, but Chance's stance didn't change. He just stood there, on the verge of destruction, and I racked my brain for my next move. *Maybe I should just let him buck...without me in the saddle.*

Moving with caution, I unclipped the lead rope from his halter and switched to a lunge line, a long cotton rope that would allow Chance to move in a large circle around me.

I stepped back again and clucked my tongue. "Just walk forward, Chance. That's all you need to do," I said, raising my free hand in the air. I should have flinched at my aching shoulder, but the adrenaline racing through my body seemed to mask the pain. And, just like yesterday, his frozen body broke into a blur. Only this time I watched the rodeo show from the ground.

Chance lurched forward into a series of rears, kicks, and snorts. He was stuck in his own world, blinded by fear, as he circled around me. And then, my gut flipped when Chance whipped his body towards the fence and I realized he didn't understand he was connected to anything...or anyone.

I should have let go, but I didn't and my whole body jerked forward with him. I found myself yanked into a run, my feet grazing the dirt every ten feet or so. I was nearly flying before the lunge line ripped from my hand and I tripped over my own feet, rolling and then skidding to a stop on my butt. Reunited with the arena dirt, I sat and watched as Chance gallop around the arena with the lunge line dragging behind him.

I rested my head in my hands. *I don't think I'm doing anything good for him.*

"Chance giving you a hard time?"

I stopped breathing at the question and peeked through my fingers to find Casey, sitting on top of Rocky. How long had he been on the other side of the fence watching me? I wanted to dissolve into the ground, melt away, run back to my bunk. Having Casey watch me fail was a thousand times worse than having Taylor watch me fail.

Swallowing what was left of my pride, I stood up and brushed the dirt from my jeans. At least I didn't have to spit it out of my mouth this time. "I'm not sure what I'm doing wrong," I confessed.

Casey scrunched his eyebrows together, slouching to rest his forearms on the saddle horn. He was quiet, processing the situation. "I think you're on the right track," he noted. "It looks like Chance is too anxious to accept the saddle right now."

"Maybe a horse-sized Prozac would help," I said, rubbing my shoulder as Chance blazed another lap around the arena.

"Probably," Casey chuckled. "But I think you just need to get his mind in the right place."

"I was trying to do that," I sighed. "I took an hour to brush him and rub on him and I thought he was ready. Apparently, he wasn't." I shook my head.

"I think he needs a longer warm-up. He needs to work out his fears first. Then he'll be more accepting of the saddle...and a rider."

"Think about it this way," Casey continued. "A horse is a prey animal. His instinct is to protect himself from a predator...through fight or flight. Right now Chance is in flight mode. He's trying to run away from the scary saddle strapped to his back. You have to give him some time to realize that the saddle isn't going to hurt him." Casey nodded towards Chance. "Can I help?"

Casey was making sense, but I didn't want his charity. I wanted to do this on my own.

"Come on," Casey urged. "Before you hurt the other arm and you have to pull hay bales around with your feet." Casey's lips turned up at the corners and I rolled my eyes.

My two week trial period with Chance was getting shorter by the minute. I didn't have time to spare. "I guess," I said, giving in. "I'm not very handy with my feet."

Casey sat up in the saddle. "Okay then, let's see if we can round up Chance together."

Casey guided Rocky through the gate and I closed it behind him. The two rode out into the middle of the arena and Chance's running came to an abrupt stop. He whinnied at the top of his lungs and trotted across the arena in sharp strides. The lunge line had been snapped off and shortened during his outburst. It was now dangling from his halter, barely brushing the ground.

Chance approached the gray gelding and stiffed at his nose and neck. Rocky stood still, ignoring Chance and listening to Casey. And, while Chance was distracted, Casey grabbed what was left of the lunge line and wrapped it around Rocky's saddle horn. Chance didn't seem to notice until Casey asked Rocky to walk forward.

Chance baulked when the rope tightened and pulled at his halter, but Rocky continued walking and Chance was forced to follow. Casey moved both horses into a trot and quickly to a lope. And, loping, Chance wrenched his head down and jumped hard, making that awful guttural noise. I clenched my eyes shut, listening to the horses thunder around me. A few laps and the guttural noise stopped. I opened my eyes, searching the arena, and found Chance loping shoulder to shoulder with Rocky, following his speed.

Realizing my stubby nails were digging into the palms of my hands, I released my fingers and wiped the sweat on my jeans.

"You got him to stop bucking," I said, my mouth gapping open as Casey slowed the two horses to a walk in front of me.

"That was a start," Casey replied. "He needs more time before you can get on him, but I think he's accepted that the saddle isn't going anywhere. And that it isn't hurting him."

"Thank you . . .," I started, trying to find the appropriate words and wondering if Casey should be the one helping Chance.

"We're not done," Casey responded, cutting me off. "I think we should take him for a real ride. I was going to head into the mountain to check on the cattle yet tonight. Let's take Chance with. That will give him some more time to get used to the saddle."

"Okay." That sounded like a good plan. "I'll go get Sunny out of the pasture and saddle her up."

Casey stretched out his hand. "Hop on with me."

I almost fell backwards onto my butt again.

"Come on," Casey urged. "The sun will be down soon and it will take too long to saddle up Sunny."

Realizing my face was probably broadcasting my shock, I cleared my throat. Casey did have a point. We didn't have much time before daylight was gone. I managed a slow step towards Rocky and placed my foot in Casey's stirrup. I grabbed hold of Casey's hand and he pulled me up.

I landed behind his saddle and sat in silence for a few moments, not sure where to put my hands. Feeling rushed to make a decision, I gripped the cantle, the back of the saddle seat.

"You ready back there?" Casey turned his head and pushed his sandy brown hair from his eyes.

"Ready," I squeaked out, thinking I might feel more comfortable on Chance's back.

Casey gathered his reins, clucked to Rocky, and the four of us walked out of the arena toward the mountain.

Eight

My heart rate hovered near a normal rate by the time we were deep in the woods, but I couldn't keep my fingers from fidgeting. I moved them in circles, rubbing the smooth leather of the saddle. I focused on Chance, his body next to my dangling leg, his head bobbing with each stride, and I searched for something to say. Silence felt strange being this close to another person.

"So, how'd you end up working at Red Rock?" I asked, hoping his story would fill the quiet, calm my nerves.

Casey paused and, for a second, I thought he didn't hear me.

"I can't stay away from horses," he responded.

I waited for Casey to continue, but he patted Rocky's thick gray neck instead. "Okay...Did you grow up here? In Three Rivers?" I prodded, not quite understanding his statement.

"Nope. Grew up on my grandpa's cattle ranch in eastern Oregon." Casey's body swayed in the saddle, moving side to side with Rocky's easy rhythm. "My Grandpa bought me a pony when I was four. Crazy Alice. She hauled me all over that ranch. Kept up with the big horses."

Casey's words felt warm and genuine. Not a hint of his usual sarcasm. "Sounds like a perfect place to grow up," I noted.

"Yeah, my grandpa and that pony taught me everything I know about horses."

"How'd you end up in Three Rivers then?" I asked, trying the next logical question.

Casey paused again and then cleared his throat. "My Grandpa passed when I was eleven."

The silence became ten-times more uncomfortable. "I'm sorry," I said in one quick breath, wishing I had chosen a safer question. "That's horrible." Now, I felt horrible. I opened my mouth and managed to remind Casey of a painful childhood memory. I should have asked him about the ranch horses, his favorite food, anything but that.

"I guess that didn't really answer your question though," Casey continued. "About how I ended up in Three Rivers."

"You don't have to tell me. I mean…I didn't mean to be so nosey." My apology came out a little bossy.

"It's okay. Might as well finish my story," he said, and I kept quiet while he continued.

"My parents couldn't afford to keep the ranch after Grandpa passed. We moved to Three Rivers when my dad got a job at a friend's auto shop. I have to admit I was pretty angry with the world for a while. Thought I didn't want to see another horse for the rest of my life."

"I couldn't imagine my life without horses," I whispered and glanced at Chance. *Even crazy ones that make me eat dirt.*

"Well, turns out I can't either," Casey responded, leaning forward to smooth Rocky's mane. "My Mom took me to one of Red Rock's ranch sortings a month or so after we moved. Watching the horses brought back so many great memories and I knew my grandpa wouldn't want me to give up on horses…on ranch life. After that, I started helping out at Red Rock after school and I was hooked again. The horses are what really saved me." Casey tipped his head to the side, peeking at me with the corner of his eye. "I guess that sounds kind of sappy."

"No, no," I said right away, shaking my head back and forth. "Not sappy at all." I understood. Horses could heal any ailment, any problem. It made total sense to me.

"So...are you ready to exercise these ponies?" Casey asked, shying away from the current subject.

"I'm ready," I replied, not sure what he had in mind, but I wasn't asking any more questions at this point.

"You might have to hold on a little tighter then." And, Casey slanted his body forward in the saddle. At his cue, Rocky jumped into a lope. Chance raised his head, startled by the quick change in pace, but didn't hesitate to follow Rocky's lead.

Almost sliding off Rocky's rump, I grabbed for Casey, in instinct, and wrapped my arms around his chest. Before I could process what was happening, my body was pressed against his back and the wind whipped through my hair. Trees flew by our sides in a deep green blur as we headed up the mountain trail, suddenly intertwined.

I clasped tighter as we burst out into the open field and blazed a path through the middle of the cattle herd. With my arms wrapped around Casey's soft cotton t-shirt, it was impossible to ignore his solid frame. My face flushed hot, even in the cool wind.

The cows only watched as we thundered by, interrupting their evening peace.

As we approached flat ground, Casey sat back in the saddle, pushing against me. "Whoa, Rocky. Whoa, Chance." His words rolled out in an even tone.

The two horses slowed to a stop and halted on a cliff that seemed to overlook the world. The brown and white cattle dotted the field beneath us and, over the swaying tops of the fir trees, the ranch and the town looked miniature. The view went on and on until the ground blended into the peach and pink tones of the sky. I sighed from the bottom of my lungs.

"Beautiful, isn't it?" Casey said, taking in the scene as though he had never seen it before. I let every image soak in, not wanting to forget one detail. And, we sat there in silence. Only this time it didn't feel uncomfortable.

At least not until I realized I was still wrapped around Casey, my cheek resting against his shoulder. My stomach jumped and, not sure what to do, I sat straight up and yanked my arms back. Once again, I didn't know where to put my hands.

"You okay?" Casey turned towards me, his ice blue eyes meeting mine, his smooth skin bronzed from the afternoon sun.

"Just-taking-it-all-in," I said, my sentence blurring into one word. I felt like I should look away from his gaze, but I just couldn't.

Then Casey broke our eye contact, nodding towards Chance. "I think his mind is in the right place now."

I swallowed the knot in my throat and turned my attention to Chance. He stood with his head lowered next to Rocky's shoulder, relaxed. "He looks a lot different than he did in the arena."

"You should get on him."

I instantly pictured my face skidding across the hard ground. "Here?"

"Why not? Come on...I won't let you get hurt."

I stared at Casey again, blinking this time. And for some odd reason, I believed him. I nodded.

Casey directed the horses back down the embankment to the grassy field. He moved Rocky within inches of Chance's saddle and then Casey turned towards me.

"Swing around so both of your legs hang between Rocky and Chance," Casey instructed, and I contorted my body to sit sideways on Rocky's rump, trying not to kick Casey or the horses in the process.

"And relax," Casey said, but I only stiffened as he slid an arm under mine, wrapping it around my back and clasping his fingers against my side. "Chance will only stay relaxed if you do...you have to stay calm for him."

And then I remembered what we were doing. And, I remembered I needed to concentrate on Chance.

"Put one foot in Chance's stirrup and I will help you get in the saddle. Even if he bucks, he's not going far. Rocky won't let that happen. I won't let that happen."

I took a deep breath, preparing myself for the unknown as I put the tip of my boot in the stirrup. And, before I could second-guess myself, Casey picked me up by my torso and set me in the saddle. As soon as my jeans touched the leather, I wrapped both hands around the saddle horn, waiting for Chance to explode underneath me, hoping Casey could hold on to him.

But Chance only lifted his head and took two quick steps to the side, balancing himself under the new weight. He didn't buck. He didn't run. Instead, Chance curled his neck around to assess me. He sniffed my boot with short, inquisitive breaths and, after an intense few minutes, licked his lips in acceptance.

I couldn't believe it. I was sitting on Chance's back. Sitting...not hanging on for my life.

Casey was grinning when I finally looked over at him. "Alright cowgirl. Let's see what you can do," he said and clucked his tongue. Both horses responded to the cue and moved forward, beginning to trot. My body followed Chance's uneven strides as he zigzagged beside Rocky, unsure of my legs bouncing next to his ribs. I followed his every move until the zigzagging stopped and Chance moved forward with ease.

The cattle herd parted for us, creating a wide path through the grassy field and the horses took advantage of the space, surging into a lope. My hips rotated with Chance's rhythmic motion and my white knuckles began to regain their peach color as I loosened my grip on the saddle horn, my confidence increasing with each steady stride.

Then, I released one hand from the saddle horn, dropping my fingers by my thigh. Loping along on Chance, I felt free, suddenly safe. And, without thinking, I threw both arms out to my sides, like temporary wings. I tilted my head to the sky, letting the mountain air wrap around my whole body and fill my lungs.

I glanced over at Casey, still riding by my side, but now shaking his head and laughing. Without taking his eyes off me, he leaned forward and we broke into a gallop.

The horses made their way down the mountain in the dark, but even the night couldn't hide my smile. My first real ride on Chance was beyond perfect and the scene played over and over in my head. And, I couldn't deny that Casey helped to make it happen.

"Thanks for helping us take flight," I grinned, as we approached the barn.

"Any time," Casey laughed as he put a hand on my shoulder.

I leaned into his touch, closing my eyes for a second, but my thoughts were broken by an irritated question.

"Going to check on the cattle, huh?" Taylor stood with her arms crossed and her shoulder resting against the barn. I didn't know how long she had been there.

"Hey Taylor," Casey said as he stopped both horses a few feet in front of her. "Yeah, Lucy was my helper tonight."

I slid down from Chance's saddle. "I bet you were," she mouthed the words to me with one eyebrow cocked. I didn't know how to respond. *What exactly did she think I was doing with Casey on the mountain?*

"Casey was also helping me with Chance," I noted, feeling like I needed to explain our evening.

But, before Taylor could go on, Casey stepped down from Rocky's saddle and Taylor's face morphed to pure sweetness, placing her delicate hand on top of Casey's forearm.

"I was just stopping by the barn to see if you wanted to go get pizza with me in town. I figured you'd be pretty hungry by the time you got off the mountain." She batted her long, black eyelashes waiting for his answer.

"Sure, just let me take care of Rocky and I'll join you. Lu, you want to come too?"

Taylor's head snapped towards me. Obviously, Casey didn't notice her disgust.

"Thanks, but I don't like pizza," I blurted out and shifted my eyes away from Taylor's. I loved pizza, but it was the first excuse that came to my head. I certainly didn't want to be a third wheel. Especially when I felt like Taylor might push me out of a moving vehicle to get to Casey.

"Who doesn't like pizza?" Casey laughed. "You're a funny girl, Miss Lucy."

"Yeah, *super* funny," Taylor chimed in, cocking her head. "Maybe next time you can come with and we'll all hit up the burger joint."

It was clear Taylor's invite was not genuine.

"Yeah, we'll definitely have to do that," Casey said gathering Rocky's reins. "I'll see you tomorrow then, Lu. Have a good night."

"You too, Casey," I said, trying to ignore the possessive stares from the petite blonde standing next to him as she grabbed Casey's hand and directed him towards the barn.

"Sweet dreams, *Lu*," Taylor said looking over her shoulder.

I watched the couple walk down the barn aisle, hand in hand, and an unwanted twinge of jealousy physically gathered in my gut. I closed my eyes to erase the image and Chance bumped my back with his nose, knocking me back into reality.

"Sorry, boy." I turned. "I didn't mean to ignore you. You were amazing tonight." I rubbed the tiny white star on his forehead. "Now I know we can impress Mr. Owens if we just keep working at it. Hopefully he'll let the ranch be your new home." Chance sighed, lowering his head. "Let's get your saddle off and give you a well-deserved grooming. I think I even have a granola bar for you."

Nine

"Looking good, Lu," Casey said, climbing the boards to sit on top of the arena fence.

"Thanks," I said as Chance and I trotted past. "I've been spending every spare minute working with him."

"I can tell."

A smile crept across my face at the praise, but I kept long trotting Chance around the arena, focusing my attention back to him. This week I crawled out of bed an hour earlier, spending that extra time with Chance, in his stall, brushing and rubbing on him, gaining his trust. Then, after evening chores, I led Chance to the arena to ride, lunging him first to work out any anxieties. But, after a few days, Chance gave up on the bucking. In fact, I think he was starting to enjoy our time in the arena.

Leaning my body forward in the saddle, I made a kissing noise with my mouth, asking Chance to lope. Knowing he was supposed to speed up, he extended his trot, clipping along faster and faster. I balanced myself through the quick, choppy strides and kept encouraging him until he broke into a smooth lope, and together we moved steadily around the end of the arena. My heart swelled seeing his improvements.

As we started loping through the middle of the arena, I was so immersed in Chance that I didn't notice Taylor until Star was a few strides in front of Chance's nose. Realizing we were headed for a collision, I tightened the reins, pulling Chance into a small circle. Chance came to a jerky stop, shaking his head in objection to my sudden pull on the reins.

"Might want to spend some time working on his stopping skills," Taylor sneered as she posted in the saddle, not missing a beat and trotting back to the rail.

I growled under my breath. The only negative thing that came out of my evening on the mountain was that Taylor decided to put a target on my forehead. Instead of ignoring me, she was on a mission to keep tabs on me, to put me in my place. And, I wasn't a big fan of this new game.

Collecting my reins in my hands, I rubbed Chance's neck. "Sorry, boy. Didn't mean to yank on the bit. Let's try this one more time."

Accepting my apology, Chance trotted off. I kissed and squeezed my leg, asking for a lope again. Chance extended his trot to the point that I had to concentrate on keeping my butt in the saddle seat, but I kept on him and he broke into a lope, following the reins as I guided him in a big circle.

"Nice job!" Casey shouted from the fence, clapping his hands together. Taylor wrinkled her face in disgust as she halted Star. I wasn't sure if the revulsion came from her opinion of my riding skills or from Casey's excitement.

Casey jumped off the fence as Chance and I slowed down to a walk. "You're doing a great job with him," he smiled.

"Thanks," I beamed, patting Chance on the rump, but my joy was short-lived as I caught a glimpse of Marilynn running down the path from the barn.

She waved her hands over her head to catch everyone's attention. "We have a problem," she shouted. Marilynn was out of breath as she crawled through the fence boards and jogged over. "I must not have latched the gate this afternoon when I left the quarantine paddock," she said, her panicked expression contrasting her usual confidence. "The heifers that Mr. Owens just bought from the cattle auction got out. I don't know where they are. They must have wandered out into the mountain."

"The heifers that the vet was just out to take a look at?" Casey asked, his eyes widening.

"Yes," Marilyn shouted and then slapped her thigh. "Ugh, I can't believe I did that!"

"What's wrong?" I asked. I didn't like the way Marilynn and Casey were responding to this.

"Other than the fact that we have ten heifers roaming the wilderness?" Marilynn put her hands on her hips, still breathing hard. "The vet is concerned they were exposed to IBR at the auction. A heifer purchased the same day is showing symptoms and the auction house called Mr. Owens last night to warn him." Marilynn shook her head.

"What is IBR?" I asked, my concern growing.

"Infectious Bovine Rhinotracheitis...IBR," Marilynn responded without taking a breath. I stared at her. That didn't help me at all.

Casey chimed in with an answer. "It's a viral respiratory disease and highly contagious in cattle. The vet didn't find any symptoms this morning, but it usually takes a week for symptoms to show up after they have been exposed. And, to make it worse, IBR generally causes miscarriages." Casey started towards the fence. "It would *not* be good if those heifers found the rest of the herd...the pregnant cows. We need to find them before that happens."

I pulled my foot out of the stirrup, throwing it over the saddle to dismount. "How can I help? Can I go get Rocky and Sunny for you guys?"

"No, the horses are at the far end of the pasture. It would take too much time to get them and saddled up. We need to be looking for those heifers now." Casey stopped, locking his eyes with mine. "We need you to help us with Chance."

I froze, one foot still in the stirrup. I had only been riding Chance for a week and I had yet to ride him out of the arena on my own. I had a feeling we would be more of a problem than a help.

Casey put a hand on the top board of the fence and launched himself over in one clean swoop. Marilynn slid her petite body through the bottom boards and they both looked back at me.

"Come on, we need you!" Marilynn yelled. "Casey and I will get the ATVs, but we need a horse to search the areas we can't get to."

They needed my help. There was no other choice, no time. What was I waiting for? I had to make this work. I tightened my grip on the reins and slid back into the saddle. "Get the ATVs and I'll start heading towards the mountain," I said, clucking to Chance.

Taylor loped Star past me before I could finish my sentence. "I can help too," she offered.

I didn't like the idea of having to spend more time with Taylor than necessary, but at least we'd have the help of another horse and rider.

"That'd be great, Taylor. We need all the help we can get," Casey said before he turned and sprinted with Marilynn.

I cued Chance into a trot and followed Taylor out of the arena. The ATVs buzzed in the distance as we made our way along the pasture's fencing, headed towards the thick timber. Taylor, in her English attire, had Star collected and loping along like we were on our way to the show ring. Did she hear Casey when he said we needed to search the *wilderness* for cattle? Did she think she was going to win a blue ribbon for this?

Chance's body was ridged. His head held high, unsure of the chaos. I tried to balance myself with his uneven, cautious strides, but I accidentally bumped his belly with my heel. He pranced sideways, shaking his head in disapproval.

"Sorry, Chance," I whispered, gathering my reins and pushing him forward with a gentle squeeze of my legs. Responding, he extended his stride and, as we inched closer to Star, he began to settle, lowering his neck. Maybe it was a good thing Taylor was with us. The presence of another horse would keep Chance's mind at ease.

The ATV motors whined in spurts as their gears shifted, and soon they were on our tails. One right after the other, Casey and Marilynn whizzed by our sides and took over the path ahead. Star didn't seem bothered by the commotion, but Chance instantly felt like a grenade on the verge of bursting.

Resisting this new adventure, Chance lurched his head down and started hopping. I knew we were approaching bucking-bronco status so I braced my arms, keeping his head from getting too low. I would lose all control then. Leaning forward, I gave him a swift kick with my heels and it vaulted him out of his hopping episode. Chance loped a few quick, panicked strides and I clenched my fists as I tried, without success, to keep him from bouncing off of Star's hindquarters.

Jostled by our hit, Taylor whipped around and shot me a glare. "Think you can keep your beast under control back there?"

I really wasn't sure if I could, but Taylor's reference to "a beast" made me want to gallop up beside her and push her princess butt right out of the saddle.

"I'm going to do my best," I replied through gritted teeth.

"You think your best is good enough?" Taylor asked over her shoulder. Her words seemed to ricochet off the mountain as she extended Star's lope to catch up to the ATVs.

Chance chomped at the bit as Star pulled ahead and I tightened the reins to keep him from launching forward. "Come on, boy. Easy. Don't let her get to you," I whispered to Chance, but I was really talking to myself.

By the time we got to the edge of the woods, Marilynn was off her ATV and had discovered fresh, muddy tracks lining the old logging road that zigzagged up the mountain. "Casey and I are going to follow the logging road all the way up and see what we find. Hopefully, the heifers didn't veer far off the road," Marilynn said.

"And, hopefully, they didn't make it to the top of the road," Casey added. "This road ends at the clearing on the far side of the field where the cows and calves are grazing."

"What can I do to help?" Taylor asked, directing her question at Casey as she tucked her blonde waves behind her ears.

"We need you and Lucy to stay together," Casey responded, and I almost screamed. The thought of being alone with Taylor made my head hurt. "Slowly walk this road and see if you can spot the heifers in the trees. Marilynn and I will let you know if we find them further up."

"Here." Marilynn handed me a walkie talkie. "If you see anything, let me know."

"Of course," I said as Marilynn jumped back on her ATV and they sped off, leaving me alone with Taylor. Not exactly the person I wanted to go on my first cattle round-up with.

"Seriously?" Taylor asked, but she wasn't talking to anyone in particular. Star's reins were lying across her mane and Taylor had both hands on her cell phone. "My Facebook Ap doesn't work here."

My mouth dropped open. *Unbelievable.* Not really the time to be worried about updating your Facebook status.

Taylor rolled her eyes and stuffed her phone back in her vest pocket. "Okay, let's get this over with. It'll be dark soon and I am *not* looking for those stupid cows in the dark. I've got better things to do."

Taylor's only concern was herself, but she was partially right in her statement. There was no way we were going to find the heifers after the sun went down. We didn't bring flashlights or ropes or anything. We had about a half hour to find the small herd.

"Let's get going then," I said, guiding Chance to the left side of the logging road. Taylor and Star began to walk the right side and we both scanned the dense forest for signs of cattle. The horses kept a steady pace on the inclining road, their hooves marching in time. They didn't seem bothered by the tense silence. They made a better team than their riders did.

"You can't have Casey," Taylor said, out of nowhere. The words rolled sharp off her tongue, like little daggers.

"What are you talking about?" I asked as her eyes narrowed on me.

"Please," she said, pushing out one hard laugh. "I see the way you've been looking at him. Big puppy eyes, goofy smile. It's hilarious actually."

I diverted my eyes to the road ahead as my face flushed hot. I didn't know what to say. Maybe I did have a little crush on Casey, but I didn't know I was being so obvious about it.

"You know he's just helping you with that horse, right? Nothing else," Taylor said, digging her claws in deeper, making sure she left a mark. "Why would he be interested in you...when he has me?"

Each word slapped me across the face. I couldn't believe how much they stung. I felt stupid. I wanted to turn Chance around and run back to the ranch. I wanted to sit in Chance's stall and wrap my arms around my knees and bury my face. I blinked my eyes to keep the tears from forming. "Well, you're wrong," I said without looking at Taylor. "I don't like Casey...not like that."

"Could have fooled me," she said, but then she shrugged and examined her french-tipped fingernails, bored by our conversation. "I hope they find those dang cows soon."

I wanted to find those cows just so I could get away from Taylor, but before I could grind over her words again, a deep, drawn-out bellow boomed from the valley to my left. I walked Chance to the edge of the worn gravel road, following the sound.

"There they are," I said, looking down the hillside to a small band of heifers, mostly hidden by thick brush and trees. One chocolate colored heifer was staring at us. She must have been the one calling out.

"Holy crap," Taylor exclaimed. "We can't ride down that hill. It's too steep and there is too much brush. No way we can get to those cows."

I didn't care if Taylor followed me. *I hope she stays on the road and lets me do it myself.* Chance and I were going down there.

I pushed the talk button on my walkie talkie. "Marilynn? We found them. We are at the second switchback on the logging road."

The walkie talkie made a static noise and then Marilynn's voice came through. "Try to get behind them and start pushing them down the mountain towards the ranch. Casey and I will head back down and keep them from crossing the road. We are quite a way from you, but we'll hurry."

I clucked to Chance and leaned back in my saddle as he stepped off the road and started down the steep embankment. Chance didn't hesitate at my request.

"Are you nuts?" Taylor asked, squeaking at the end of her question.

"No, but have fun hanging out on the road by yourself," I responded.

Chance took baby steps down the steep footing. Branches snapped under his hooves and tiny rocks dislodged and bounced their way down the hill. I leaned so far back that the saddle rested against the middle of my spine. I could hear Taylor grumbling in the background and I was thankful for every step Chance was taking away from her.

"Good job, boy. Easy does it," I said as Chance worked his way down the hill, thoughtful about every hoof placement. Even though we were moving down a near vertical slope, I felt safe in the saddle. Chance was taking care of me. I put slack in my reins and let Chance choose the safest path.

As we neared the bottom of the embankment, I watched the cows. The herd was still a few hundred feet away, but they were aware of our presence. They were starting to move, sticks snapping at their feet and calling to each other in warning of an intruder. My palms started sweating. The last thing I wanted to do was to scare the herd further up the valley.

But that is where they wanted to go. The herd started moving as one unit with their noses pointed uphill. They pushed through the brush and picked up speed. We needed to get in front of them. We needed to stop them.

Chance picked up his head, his ears pointed at the running herd. I tilted my body forward and Chance read my mind. He picked up a high-stepping trot and wasn't deterred by the thick brush. The herd was running alongside the creek and we trotted parallel to them, but the herd was picking up steam. We needed to get in front of them, to cut them off.

There was a clearing ahead, a short cut towards the creek and I gave Chance the reins, urging him to speed up, to cover more ground. He charged forward, but the trees had blocked my view of a major obstacle. I gasped when the fallen tree came into view. Its massive trunk covered the forest ground, stretching nearly to the creek. For a second, I thought about trying to jump it, but I knew it was too risky.

I tightened the reins to slow Chance, but he resisted, pushing forward against my grip. *This is where some stopping skills would come in handy.* There was only a stride between his chest and the fallen tree and I had no choice...but to go with him.

I leaned my body forward just as Chance launched himself into the air with a determined force. His knees tucked tight to his chest and my face hovered inches from his mane as we sailed over the tree trunk and landed on the other side. Chance didn't miss one beat as we glided back into stride.

Trees whizzed by as I crouched close to Chance's body, my head dodging hanging branches. We were now nose and nose with the lead cow and Chance dug in harder to push us ahead of the herd. As we neared the creek I sat back in the saddle, gripping the horn for balance. Chance skidded through the mud, coming to a sliding stop in front of the startled herd. I was shocked that I didn't end up in the water.

Chance stared at the chocolate lead cow, his sides heaving, and I caught a crazed look as it flashed through her eyes. I remembered how that young steer tackled me on my first day at the ranch. Only this time it was an entire herd of cows that wanted to get by me. My fingers gripped the saddle horn tighter, but Chance didn't move a muscle. And, after fully accessing the big black horse standing in her path, the chocolate cow turned and started to trot downhill. The herd followed her lead.

Adrenaline pumped through my veins as Chance picked up a trot to follow the herd along the creek. I couldn't believe it. We stopped them. We turned the whole herd around by ourselves.

In the distance, I heard voices and glanced to the logging road to where both ATVs were parked. Marilynn and Casey were jumping up and down, hooting with their fists in the air. Taylor and Star were about twenty feet down the embankment. They had turned back towards the road.

My walkie talkie buzzed on my hip. "Nice moves, Lucy! You and that black horse just saved the day!" Marilynn said, her voice brimming with relief. "Keep them moving along the creek and we will be there to help you as soon as you push them out of the trees."

My heart pounded as my smile returned. "Did you hear that, Chance? We saved the day!"

Ten

"You should've seen us, Dad," I said, pressing my cell phone to my ear as I skipped along the dirt path. "Chance was amazing! It's like we really clicked out there on the mountain. He understood exactly what I needed him to do."

"That's fantastic, Lu. It sounds like Chance is really coming around."

"He is, Dad. He really is. We pushed the whole herd out of the woods on our own and then helped Marilynn and Casey guide them right back into the quarantine pasture. Chance did such a good job." My heart warmed remembering how Chance took care of me.

"It sounds like you're the one doing a good job with him, Lucy. Has Mr. Owens made his decision on the auction yet?"

"Not yet," I sighed. "But, Mr. Owens has got to let him stay on the ranch. I can't even imagine having to load Chance on a trailer and say goodbye to him now."

"Well, taking care of a horse is expensive. You know that, Lucy. I just don't want you to get your hopes up too high."

"I know, Dad." I understood what he was saying, but I couldn't accept it. Chance was improving every day and I just knew that Mr. Owens would notice his progress and see his potential as a ranch horse. "I'll try not to get my hopes up," I said, lying.

"Where are you off to now? It sounds like you're outside."

"Headed to the main lodge. Mr. Owens invited Marilyn, Casey, and I for a prime rib dinner as a thank you."

"Quite the thank you," Dad noted and then paused. "So, what is this Casey boy like? Do I have to worry about any hanky-panky going on while you are there?"

Hanky-panky? Who says that anymore? "No, Dad. Don't worry. We are just friends." I kicked the dirt as the words left my mouth and a few rocks bounced down the path. *I wish there was something he had to worry about.*

"I figured that, but I just wanted to make sure. Have a good dinner, honey, and call me tomorrow. Love you."

"Love you too," I said, stepping on the front deck of the main lodge. Guests swayed in a line of wooden rocking chairs and I smiled in greeting as I grabbed the handle of the double screen door.

Dinner was in full swing, and the dining room bustled. The thick smell of comfort food filled my lungs and my stomach growled in response. Long rustic wood tables adorned with white candles and fresh wildflowers were fully occupied by guests. A gray stone fireplace separated the dining room from a cozy sitting area and everyone chatted as dinner was served, country music radio playing in the background.

I'd been in the lodge before, but never during dinner time. The ranch employees had their own kitchen next to the bunk houses and it was always well stocked. I had no reason to venture elsewhere, but I was excited for this congratulatory meal.

Scanning the dining room, I picked Marilynn and Casey from the crowd. They were sitting at the table closest to the fireplace, talking with Mr. Owens. And, as I started towards the table, I noticed another familiar face.

Across the room Taylor was poking her fork at her prime rib dinner, a look of complete boredom plastered on her face. The woman sitting across from her was, without a doubt, her mom.

The wavy blonde hair, tiny frame, and matching golden tans made the two look like sisters. Taylor's mom held a full glass of red wine in the air and tilted her head back in laughter. The men sitting next to them looked smitten and Taylor's mom was soaking up the attention.

Taylor sighed as she rolled her eyes and glanced around the room. Neither her mom nor the men seemed to notice her misery and I hurried along before she laid her eyes on me. And, decided to let out her frustrations.

"Good evening, young lady," Mr. Owens greeted as I took my seat next to Marilynn.

"Good evening," I replied. "Sorry I'm a few minutes late. My dad called."

"Did you tell him about your adventure last night?" Mr. Owens asked, shaking a few packets of sugar into his iced tea.

"Yes, sir," I responded.

Casey smiled from across the table and my heart fluttered for a beat. *I wish I could control that.* But, he did look handsome decked out in a baby blue starched button-down, the color matching his eyes.

"We were just telling Mr. Owens who found the cows and pushed them down the valley," Casey said.

"I didn't really do *that* much," I said, but realized they thought different as I looked at the faces around the table.

"Well, I appreciate having three reliable, knowledgeable ranch hands and I also appreciate hard work," Mr. Owens chimed in. "Marilyn and Casey were telling me how much time you have been spending with that black horse. Seems to me it's paying off."

I bit my lower lip, hoping he would say Chance could stay. "He's a really good horse, Mr. Owens. He's smart and athletic and he's a quick learner. It just took him awhile to figure out I wasn't there to hurt him. I know he will make a heck of a ranch horse." I could hear the pleading in my voice.

Mr. Owens turned to Casey. "You haven't heard anything from the sheriff's office?"

"No. No one has reported a lost horse."

"And, it's been almost two weeks," Marilyn added. "If someone wanted him, we would have heard it by now."

"I want him," I said. I meant for my statement to stay in my head, but it just blurted out.

Mr. Owens cracked a grin. "Okay then. The black horse has earned his place on the ranch."

I grabbed the edge of the bench to stop from falling out of my seat.

"He'll be your mount for the summer, Lucy," Mr. Owens instructed. "Ride him as much as possible and I'm convinced he'll be ranch-broke by the end of the summer."

"Oh, thank you, Mr. Owens." And, I meant it from the bottom of my heart. "You won't be disappointed."

"Good, now let's bring on this prime rib dinner," Mr. Owens said and motioned to the kitchen staff.

Nothing ever tasted so good.

I flicked on the barn lights and Chance nickered from his stall. His ebony neck stretched out over the door and his head bobbed in anticipation.

"Good morning. Are you ready for your breakfast?" I asked, walking down the aisle to the feed room.

Chance nickered with more enthusiasm as I dug into the grain bin for a scoopful of oats. I opened his stall door and Chance stepped back to let me in. His ears perked forward and he watched me dump the grain into his feed bucket.

I rolled my hand down Chance's neck, brushing his thick black mane aside as he nibbled on his grain.

"You get to stay here, Chance. Mr. Owens said you earned a place on the ranch." Happiness flooded my body as the words left my mouth. "You're safe here with me."

Chance's ears flicked back and forth as he lapped up the last few kernels of grain sticking to the bottom of the bucket. Finished, he sniffed the stall floor and then bumped my arm with his nose.

"No hay in your stall this morning, Chance," I said and rubbed my fingers across the star on his forehead. "Mr. Owens said you can go out in the pasture with the rest of the ranch horses." I slid the halter over his nose and clasped the buckle. "You ready for this?"

Chance stared at me, wondering why there was a change in his morning routine, but he followed as I stepped out the stall door. His hooves clip-clopped on the barn floor and the other horses popped their heads over their stall doors as we passed through the barn aisle. They nickered and paced in their stalls, not approving of the change. In the last stall, Star flattened her ears against her neck, squealed, and pawed against her door with her front leg.

"Easy, ponies. I'll be right back to feed you."

Outside, Chance and I walked to the horses' pasture. The ranch horses gathered at the front fence, grazing and awaiting their morning grain. At the sight of Chance, Sharkie whipped up his head and whinnied a shrill greeting. Chance began to prance at the end of his lead and nickered a soft, unsure response. The rest of the horses turned to see what all the fuss was about as I opened the gate and led Chance in.

"You're part of the herd now," I said as I unclipped the lead from Chance's halter. He looked at me, frozen for a moment, and then turned on his haunches and galloped out into the field, bucking and prancing through the hazy morning fog.

Curious about the new-comer, Sharkie trotted in sharp strides to Chance. The two met nose to nose and sniffed until the pony pinned his ears and struck out with his front leg, shaking his head to show his dominance. Chance squealed and pranced away with his tail held high in the air and the little pony followed him around the pasture as Chance checked out his new surroundings.

After a few more introductions, the herd lost interest in the drama and went back to nibbling on the grass. However, Sharkie stood at the edge of the herd and kept a close eye on Chance as he romped around the field, sniffing and snorting.

I shut the gate and leaned on the fence, crossing my arms on the top board. He looked so free...so happy. Dancing around the field and weaving through the fog, he looked like he was meant to be there.

I sighed with relief.

Eleven

Despite the happiness I found in my growing bond with Chance, my new joy couldn't take away the words Taylor threw at me on the mountain. Her harsh statements worked their way into my head and made me doubt myself...her words bothered me. *I wish I could say they didn't, but they did.* So I did the only thing I could think of to keep Taylor from attacking me again -- I started avoiding Casey. I figured Taylor would leave me alone if I left Casey alone. And, I wanted her to leave me alone.

Avoiding Casey wasn't an easy task as his bunk was next-door to mine and we worked together, but I gave it an honest effort. I had to avoid him. Lately, when Casey was near, my heart rate jumped and my mind flashed back to our ride in the mountain. I remembered my arms wrapped around his chest and my cheek pressed against his back. I thought about his soft cotton t-shirt and how he smelled like a combination of pine and vanilla. I couldn't push the thoughts out of my head. It was too much to deal with...so I just tried to *not* deal with it.

Instead, I poured my energy and time into Chance. Like before, I spent my evenings riding Chance, but I avoided the arena and the possibility of running into Casey or Taylor. I volunteered when Marilynn needed someone to check the fences for broken boards and hanging wire. Chance and I rode the fence lines, surrounded only by animals and nature and peace. My saddle bags filled with nails, pliers, and a hammer.

I wasn't a very good shot with the hammer so I was happy I didn't break any fingers, but the riding cleared my mind and strengthened Chance's body. In his short three weeks at the ranch, he was filling out, putting on weight and muscle. His black coat was starting to shine and there was a fresh gleam in his eyes.

"Good job today," I said as Chance trotted off to meet his new buddies in the pasture. Chance and I led our first trail ride today and I was so proud of him. He marched forward, leading the ride with confidence. The guests had a great time and even tipped me ten dollars. *I might have to go buy some more granola bars.*

I reopened the pasture gate for Marilyn and she led both Sunny and Sharkie through. She unclasped their halters and Sharkie loped across the field, straight to Chance. Chance nickered a soft welcome and nuzzled the pony's outstretched nose. Sharkie was miniature next to Chance's tall, lanky body. The chestnut pony looked like he could have been Chance's baby.

"He fits in well," Marilyn noted as we walked out of the pasture and shut the gate.

"He certainly does," I smiled. Marilyn's attitude towards Chance had flipped ever since our cattle-chasing adventure. I guess Chance proved his worth to Marilyn. I already knew his worth.

"Okay, so grab some lunch and then meet me in the arena at two o'clock. We are putting on a junior wrangler event this afternoon and we have twenty kids signed up."

"Junior wrangler event?" I asked, throwing Chance's halter over my shoulder. "Sounds fun. Do you need me to set anything up?"

"No, Casey and I have been setting up the arena all morning while you were leading the trail ride."

The mention of Casey's name altered my feelings toward the event. "Is Casey going to help too?"

Marilyn squinted one eye at me, trying to decipher my question. "Um...yes," she responded. "Did I mention we have twenty kids signed up? We are definitely going to need his help."

I guess I couldn't avoid Casey forever.

"There's a tray of cookies in the bunkhouse kitchen," Marilyn instructed. "Can you grab that on your way to the arena?"

"Sure. I'll see you in a few hours," I said, thinking how I could dodge Casey at the junior wrangler event. I'm sure I could lose him in a mass of twenty kids.

Carrying a plastic tray stacked with chocolate chip cookies, I walked through the arena gate and scanned the mayhem. From the looks of it, I wasn't sure this group needed more sugar in their diet. A mob of small boys and girls, wearing plastic cowboy hats, bounced and weaved around their parents. Their high-pitched voices echoed off the mountain as they shrieked with excitement.

Small pens were setup on one side of the arena and the makeshift petting zoo seemed to be a popular spot. A group of children fed handfuls of pellets to the five spotted ranch goats. The goats' actual purpose was to eat the overpopulating blackberry bushes in the pastures, but today they were basking in treats, hugs, and kisses from the kids.

In the next pen, a chocolate momma cow chewed her cud, unimpressed by the audience of screaming children, and her cream-colored calf hopped and skipped around her in circles. A little girl with pigtails pulled at her mother's shirt, pointing at the calf's show.

A line of antsy kids stood next to the petting zoo, holding their parents' hands, and waiting for a pony ride. Tank, the big bay gelding, and Freckles, the leopard appaloosa, were the chosen veteran horses for this event.

Marilyn led Tank as he carried two red headed twin sisters through the crowd. He plodded along, not at all disturbed by the commotion.

"Put the cookies on a table," Marilynn said, pointing to the picnic tables in the middle of the arena. "And grab Freckles. She's tied to the fence, saddled and ready for the kids."

I nodded and headed towards the picnic tables. Mr. Owens was making rounds through the crowd, patting heads, handing out plastic cowboy hats, and chuckling like a jolly old man. The sight made me smile.

I stroked Freckles neck as I led her to the line of waiting kids.

"Looks like you're the next lucky girl," I said to the first kid in line.

The little girl's pink plastic cowboy hat jiggled on her head. She couldn't have been much over four years old, but she wasn't the least bit scared as her dad picked her up and set her in Freckle's saddle.

"Ok, now I want you to hold onto the saddle horn and your Dad is going to walk beside you. Are you ready to ride Freckles?" The little girl bobbed her head and beamed as we started our walk.

Making our way to the opposite side of the arena, I couldn't help but to scan the crowd for Casey. And, it didn't take me long to spot him, surrounded by a group of attentive kids. He was showing the group how to toss a rope lasso in the air. A row of hay bales lined up behind him, each pinned with a plastic cow head. He was occupied with the roping lesson and I was thankful to be on pony-ride-duty. Maybe I *could* make it through the afternoon without running into Casey.

After multiple laps around the arena, all of the kids got their time in the saddle. Marilyn and I unsaddled Tank and Freckles and put them in the empty pen next to the momma cow and calf.

"Time for the stick horse races." Marilyn's voice boomed over the crowd as she handed me an armful of wooden broomsticks attached to stuffed horse heads. The yarn manes and miniature leather bridles sent the kids into a tizzy, jumping around me in circles, grabbing the stick horses from my hands. I was surprised to make it out of the kid-tornado unharmed.

"All junior wranglers must report to the obstacle course," Marilyn shouted and pointed to Mr. Owens who waved his hands in the air. The kids jumped on their stick horses and skipped, galloped, and whinnied to his side.

Casey was still giving his roping lesson and, with the rest of the kids occupied, I peeked over the shoulders of his audience. Parents snapped pictures as their determined, miniature wranglers flung ropes in the air. Giving a demonstration, Casey swung a wide lasso loop over his head and tossed it over a plastic cow head, effortlessly. The kids cheered and then tried to mimic his motions.

My heart melted watching his kind, patient actions with the kids, his big smile. And, in that instant, I remembered why I was trying to avoid him. I needed to focus on something else. Something that wouldn't turn me into a blubbering idiot.

As I turned towards the stick horse races, I heard one of the parents challenge Casey. "Let's see you rope something that moves. I think you've got that plastic cow head mastered," he chuckled.

The kids squealed in unison and pleaded with Casey. They wanted to see the real cowboy in action. As I walked away, I felt bad for the goats. It sounded like they were going to become part of the roping lesson today.

I walked on but was baffled by the abrupt silence behind me. Peeking over my shoulder, I wondered what hushed the crowd and gasped as a flash of rope circle over my head and tighten around my chest. In a matter of seconds, I was roped, turned around, and facing Casey as he began pulling me towards him.

I had no choice but to walk back to him. All the attention was now on me and it would look bad if I yanked the rope off my chest, threw it to the ground, and ran away. So I played along instead.

He reeled me in and the crowd clapped. Casey bowed and the kids jumped up and down, screaming for more. We locked eyes and I tried to contort my face into a state of annoyance, but I couldn't help it...I laughed instead.

"Now, you guys try it on each other," Casey said, still holding a gentle tension on the rope. And, the kids ran in circles trying to rope one another and giggling at their newfound game.

Casey stepped in closer to loosen the rope. He slid it over my head, the lasso rolling up my back, his blue eyes watching me. The combination made me shiver.

"Thanks for being such a good sport," he smiled, winding the rope back into his hands.

I grinned and brushed the dirt from my t-shirt. "That's me. Always a good sport." My response came out laced with sarcasm.

"I figured that was the best way to get your full attention," he said, pausing. I diverted my eyes to the running kids. "Have you been avoiding me lately?"

"No. What do you mean?" My words felt cold and full of lies. I knew exactly what he meant.

"You're being weird," Casey said, stepping in my line of vision, forcing eye contact. "Did I do something wrong?"

His forehead wrinkled and worry flashed through his eyes, making me feel guilty. Casey really didn't do anything wrong. *It's not his fault that Taylor attacked me. It's not his fault that I have some silly crush on him and he just sees me as his buddy.*

I sighed, grinding the toe of my boot into the arena dirt. "No, sorry. I've just been spending a lot of time with Chance. I'm not trying to avoid you or anything." I hoped the lie fooled him.

"Okay, well, we need to go for a ride again. I could use some company to go check on the cattle tonight. This time maybe you can give Rocky a break and ride your own horse up the mountain?" He smirked and tapped my arm with his fist.

How could I be mad at him? "Yeah, I can do that."

"Meet you at the barn around six?"

"I'll be there."

I was still torn about Casey, but I needed to deal with reality. He was my co-worker and he was dating Taylor. My crush would have to stay just that...a crush. At least I knew he enjoyed my company as a friend. And, I was excited to ride with him again. I couldn't wait to saddle-up Chance and race Rocky through the open mountain field. *I should bring a rope and see if Casey can show me a trick or two.*

"You're excited too. Aren't you?" I patted Chance's neck and he danced a little jig next to me as we walked. Looking ahead, I saw Casey swing open the barn door and jog in my direction. But his jog turned into a run and, as he got closer, I noticed the frantic look on his face. I had never seen him look anything but calm and collected. This new look scared me.

"Turn around," he said, waving his hands. "Hurry, take Chance back to the pasture and . . ."

"What's wrong? What's going on?" I asked, not knowing what could be so bad that Casey would tell me to turn around and get out of here.

Casey didn't wait for me to process his statement. He grabbed Chance's lead from my hand and pulled his head away from me, trying to turn Chance around. He raised his free arm and clucked to Chance.

"Come on, Chance. Come on!" Casey begged, nearly yelling. But before Chance could react, Mr. Owens, a police officer, and a tall, scruffy man walked out of the open barn door.

The man paused and seemed to assess Chance before he pointed and shouted, "That's it. That's the horse that was stolen from my property."

I felt like the air had been knocked out of my lungs. I turned back to Casey and Chance. Casey stood motionless, still holding Chance's lead, and Chance morphed back into the scared horse we found roaming the mountain. He backed with frantic steps, pulling Casey with him. He reared, tossing his head back and forth, and jumped sideways in an effort to run. If I had been holding him, he would have ripped the lead from my hands, but Casey held tight. I wished he would let go.

"Easy, boy, easy," I pleaded. The white rim around Chance's eyes popped against his black skin.

"Yeah, that's definitely him. Crazy lunatic of a horse," the man grumbled and spat on the grass. A wad of chew jutted from his bottom lip and he wiped the brown splatter from his chin with the back of his hand. His skin was leathery and his shoulders broad, but he couldn't have been much over thirty.

"And you're obviously the rat who stole him," he said, pointing at Casey with his dirty fingernails.

Casey's jaw clenched tight. His eyes narrowed. His strong hands gripped Chance's lead until his knuckles flashed white. I thought he might charge at the man, but instead, he stood there, brewing.

"Now, now," Mr. Owens stepped in-between the two. "I won't have anyone making those kinds of accusations here. For one, your horse showed up here and we took him in. We contacted the police with the horse's information."

"And he showed up here skin and bones and scared to death," I shouted at the man and all heads snapped in my direction. "No one stole your horse. He obviously ran away from you. Could you blame him?" My heart was ready to beat out of my chest. I couldn't believe those words rolled off my tongue. I didn't know this man, but I saw how Chance was reacting to his presence and my gut told me to keep this person away. Far away.

Mr. Owen paused, staring at me, and I was afraid he was going to tell me to shut my mouth. Instead, he turned back to the man.

"Listen, no one here stole your horse. That I can guarantee. And how do I even know this horse is yours?"

"His registration papers are filed somewhere in my Dad's house along with all the other *horse crap* he accumulated over the years."

I cringed at his obvious distaste when he said the word "horse."

"Provide the papers and you can have him back," Mr. Owens said.

I couldn't believe it. Didn't Mr. Owens see how frightened Chance was? Chance didn't want to go with this man.

The man growled a few curse words and stomped off, headed to his rusty brown pickup truck. Slamming the door, he peeled out and gravel ricocheted off the barn.

A lump of tears balled up in my throat. Why was this man claiming Chance now? He didn't care about him. Someone who cared about him would have been searching for Chance right away.

I stepped towards Chance, his nostrils flared and head held high. Casey handed the lead rope back to me and gripped my hand. "I'm sorry. I was trying to warn you," he whispered. He looked about as stunned as I felt.

"It's not your fault," I said and rubbed my hand over Chance's forehead.

Gathering my thoughts, I turned my attention to the sheriff. "Who was that?"

The sheriff made a few notes and shoved his small yellow notepad in his front shirt pocket. "Billy Jackson," he stated without emotion. "His Dad passed away earlier this year and left his estate to Billy. He lived a few miles outside of Three Rivers and apparently had a collection of horses, dogs, cats, sheep and chickens. Now the animals are Billy's. He came to the police station this morning claiming a stolen horse."

"But it took him three weeks to figure that out? Did he even know he was missing?" I asked, annoyed at the sheriff's calm demeanor.

"I'm not sure why it took him so long, but, if he can prove that is his horse, you'll have to give him back."

Turning to Mr. Owens, the sheriff continued. "I have your phone number and I will notify you of further details. Have a good evening."

"Wait, what about the other animals at his place? What if they are in danger?" I asked. I had a gut feeling that the other animals on his property wanted to run away too.

"I will send an officer out tomorrow to assess their living situation." And with that, the sheriff turned and started back towards his squad car.

I didn't know what to say. The sheriff left Casey, Mr. Owens, and I circled around Chance and staring at each other, without answers.

"He can't take him. He can't have him back." I said, breaking the silence.

Mr. Owens shook his head. "I wish he could stay, but there's nothing we can do if Billy proves that Chance is his horse. We'll just have to wait and see what happens."

Wait and see? I couldn't just wait around hoping that angry man didn't come back and claim his *possession*. Chance deserved better than that. He deserved a happy home and a person who loves him.

"There isn't anything we can do?" My heart pounded hard in my chest. I thought about pulling Chance's halter off and letting him run back to the mountain.

Chance's brown eyes blinked at me. He must have been wondering what made me so upset. He trusted me now. I couldn't break that trust and send him back to a place he hated. What could I do to make sure that didn't happen? What did Billy want?

"Money," I shouted out as quickly as the thought entered my mind. "It's obvious that Billy doesn't really care about Chance. Maybe he'll care about money? I'll scrape together every penny I've got."

The look of concern didn't leave Mr. Owens' face. Didn't he hear me?

"Listen, don't get your hopes up, but I will bring that option up if Billy follows through with registration papers and still wants him back." Mr. Owens sighed. "But there's nothing we can do until we hear back from him."

Twelve

I couldn't force myself to sleep. I squeezed my eye lids shut, but that only produced visions of losing Chance. I laid in my bed, wide awake, and thought of ways to pull together the cash to buy Chance from that man. I had five hundred dollars in my savings account and I could talk to my Dad about selling my saddle. I think I could come up with fifteen hundred dollars. *I hope that is enough to make Billy Jackson go away.*

Chance was happy at Red Rock Ranch. His whole attitude had changed in the few weeks since Casey and I stumbled upon him. He went from a snorting, striking, fearful creature to a trusting, playful, eager partner. I knew all of those wonderful traits would be lost if Billy took him back.

I asked Marilyn and Casey to lead the trail rides that next day. I wanted to stay close to the barn in hopes of an update from Mr. Owens, but, so far, there was no news. After my evening ride on Chance, I kissed him square on his whiskered muzzle before he pranced through the pasture to join his herd. The sun was setting behind the mountain and my body was feeling the effects of a few hours of sleep. I needed a hot shower and my pajamas.

As I grasped my fingers around my bunk door's metal handle, I saw Mr. Owens walking down the dirt path. I strained to read his body language as he walked towards me, but dusk made it hard to tell if he had good news or bad news or no news.

"Hey, Lucy. I was hoping I'd catch you before you got tucked in for the night."

"Were you able to talk to the sheriff today?" I asked, but the deep creases in his forehead became clear. I clasped the handle of the door, bracing myself for his news.

"Yes, the sheriff called about an hour ago. They sent an officer by Billy's house to check on the other animals. Apparently, the house and the barn are empty. Billy said he sold all the horses and various critters and Chance is the only one left, simply because he couldn't get near him without getting trampled." Mr. Owens grimaced. "And he wants him back."

I couldn't breathe. The sky was caving in on my shoulders, crushing me to the ground.

Mr. Owens continued. "He gave the officer his registration papers and the pictures on the papers match Chance's star and left front sock. Chance is his horse."

I gripped the metal door handle until the inside of my palm throbbed. "Did you tell the sheriff that I wanted to buy Chance from Billy? If he sold the other horses, he must be willing to sell Chance too." The words spilled out of my mouth.

"I did, kid," Mr. Owens said, but the long pause between his words unsettled my stomach. "He wants five thousand dollars. Claims his bloodlines are worth it."

"He wants how much?" I felt like puking. "He wants five thousand dollars for a horse he hates and he couldn't even get near without getting trampled?" I couldn't believe what I was hearing. I didn't have five thousand dollars and there was no way I could come up with that kind of money.

"I'm sorry, Lucy. I wish I had better news. I even offered three thousand, but he's not willing to negotiate and I can't be spending that kind of money when I have twenty other horses to feed and a business to run. He's coming to pick up Chance tomorrow morning."

My mouth hung open. I was processing Mr. Owen's words, but I couldn't understand them. All I heard was that I was going to lose Chance and that I couldn't stop it from happening. I couldn't keep him safe with me.

"I'm sorry, kid," Mr. Owens said, scratching his head as he turned and walked away.

The air felt like a thick fog as I stumbled through the door and into my bunk. I crawled onto my bed and curled into a tiny ball, pulling my pillow to my chest, trying to get some comfort. Silent tears rolled over my cheeks. I was helpless. I couldn't stop Chance from going back to Billy. I couldn't keep him here on the ranch with me. I was going to have to say goodbye.

Why would this wonderful horse come into my life just so he could be ripped away? What a cruel game for God to play...for me and for Chance. I pictured Chance being pulled into a trailer tomorrow morning, frantic and scared, and having to watch. I could already see the fear in his eyes. He would wonder why I wasn't helping him, why I wasn't there for him. The images pierced through my head and I slammed my eyes shut, grasping my pillow tight to my chest.

I couldn't let that happen. I had to run away with him. No one was going to help me save Chance and I had no choice. I didn't know where I would take him, but we had to get out of here...before tomorrow morning.

My revelation jolted me out of bed and I skidded across the floor. Pulling on my hooded sweatshirt, I loaded the front pocket with granola bars and stuffed my cell phone in my jeans. My bunk door squealed as I threw it open and it rattled shut as I rushed into the cold dark. The last thing I expected was to run into a solid, warm body.

Casey. He was standing on my front stairs and I slammed into his chest, catching myself on the wooden railing.

"Are you okay?" Casey asked, grabbing me by my shoulders. I stared at him, his warm eyes swimming with worry. "I didn't mean to scare you."

"It's okay," I mumbled, but I knew that nothing was okay. I stood frozen in his grip.

"I was with Mr. Owens when he got the call from the sheriff. I heard the news," he said, his grip holding me in place.

My lower lip quivered. I looked to the sky, trying to stop the tears, but Casey's compassion made it impossible. The tears stung as they rolled out of my eyes and across my lips. I could taste the salt as Casey pulled me in and wrapped his arms tight around my shoulders. I buried my face in his chest and my body shook.

Casey pressed me hard to his chest and, any other time, I would have felt safe there. But, I knew he couldn't fix this for me. I swallowed hard and raised my head from his chest. Casey loosened his grasp on me but didn't let go. Instead, he tipped his head down to meet my eyes. His lips placed only inches from mine. For a few quiet moments, all I focused on was his ice blue eyes and his warm breath on my face. I could feel both our hearts beating.

"I have an idea," he whispered.

I stood there leaning on his support, waiting to hear his idea.

"I want you to be my partner in The Three Rivers Cowboy Race."

I blinked the tears from my eyes, wondering what he was talking about.

"The what?" I asked.

I was standing on my front stairs, pressed against Casey's body, inches from his lips, and about to lose my horse. I wasn't making the connection. What did a race have to do with any of this?

"The Three Rivers Cowboy Race," Casey repeated as he loosened his arms and let his hands slide back to my shoulders. The cool air blew between us and I shivered, standing on my own two feet again. "It's a race, by horseback, through Mount Hood." His eyes read my face with each word. "Teams of two have to complete a ten-mile course filled with obstacles. And the first team to cross the finish line wins...and I don't have a partner."

I wiped my cheeks with the sleeves of my sweatshirt. I was shocked that Casey wanted me to be his partner for this race, but, honestly, I had a bigger issue to worry about at the moment.

Casey continued. "Did I mention the winning team gets five thousand dollars?"

"What?" My response came out as a squeak as I tried to swallow the lump in my throat.

"You could keep Chance if we won."

I repeated his words in my head. My bottom lip shook again and I didn't know if I was delirious from the crying or dazed from being so close to Casey, but I started nodding my head.

"Yes...yes." I nodded over and over. "Yes. Chance and I will be your partners."

The ends of Casey's lips curled up in a smile. "Okay, then. Why don't you try to get some sleep now. I'll meet you at the barn at sunrise and we'll wait for Billy. We're going to have to convince him to wait the two weeks until the race and then he can have his money." Casey rubbed my arms and leaned in like he had a secret for me. "Oh yeah, and we're going to have to *win* that race."

Gravel crunched and the breaks on the brown pickup truck squealed as it came to a sharp stop next to the barn. Attached to the pickup's bumper was a one-horse trailer covered in rust and green mildew. My skin crawled as the door slammed shut and Billy shuffled out.

His baseball hat was pulled down to his eyebrows and dark curls covered the back of his neck. Sweat and dirt had deepened the brim of his hat's red fabric to a coffee color. A rope hung loosely on his shoulder and his leather work boots kicked up dust as he marched towards me. I stood in the barn doorway, wondering what made him so mad at the world.

Chance was in his stall, finishing a few flakes of hay. At sunrise, I brought him in, brushed his shiny black coat, and told him I wouldn't let him go. His ears flicked back and forth, listening to my whispers. Chance didn't have a clue what this morning would bring, but he was content to absorb my attention, my love.

"Where's my horse?" Billy said, walking past me into the barn.

I glanced down at the pasture but didn't see a sign of Casey or Marilynn. They were feeding the horses but should be back any minute. *I wish they would hurry.*

"I want to talk to you about something, Mr. Jackson," I blurted out and jogged to his side.

"Unless you have five thousand dollars in your pocket, all I want is for you to point me to that horse."

"But I do...have the money."

Billy stopped mid-stride and rotated towards me. Square on, his intimidation increased. He reeked of gasoline and earth. "*You-...have five thousand dollars?*"

My shoulders stiffened as Billy's dark eyes waited for an answer. I wanted to look away, but I didn't. "I mean, I'll have the money for you in two weeks. I'm going to enter Chance in the Three Rivers Cowboy Race and the prize money will be yours."

Hearing my voice, Chance poked his head over his stall door. Billy muttered a few choice words, waved me off like he was shooing a fly, and started walking towards Chance's stall. "I'm not waiting two weeks on some crazy scheme you have. You either have the cash or you don't. And, from the sounds of it, you don't," he growled.

Billy Jackson didn't give me a second look. He grabbed the rope off his shoulder and Chance's hooves scraped against the stall floor as he bolted into his paddock. My heart jumped into my throat as Billy threw the stall door open. *How could I stop him now? What could I do?*

I followed Billy inside the stall to witness Chance pacing against the paddock gate, trying to find an escape. I wanted to calm him, to comfort him, to save him from this man.

"You don't have to rope him," I shouted as Billy started to loop the lasso over his head, putting Chance in his sights. "I can catch him. I'll get him for you."

I needed to distract Billy so I could get to Chance and open the gate. At this point, my best option was to let Chance run.

But Billy didn't seem to hear a word I said. The lasso whizzed in circles over his head, picking up speed and threatening Chance with every loop. As Billy released the lasso, I reacted in instinct hurling my body in front of Billy to block the rope with my arms. I turned my face away as the stiff rope slapped my wrists, burning them. Frozen with my hands in the air, I opened my eyes to watch the rope hit the ground.

Billy cocked his head at me and his face flashed red. "*Get*...Out of my way," he growled and pushed me to the side.

His force threw me to the ground and I bounced across the dirt, stopping only as my back cracked against the fence. The board's sharp edge jabbed me in the ribs, but I was too stunned to feel it. No one had ever pushed me like that. No one had ever touched me in anger. My eyes searched past Billy. I needed to find Casey or Mr. Owens or Marilynn. I scrambled to get my feet underneath me.

Dust still circling my body, I caught a blaze of black from the corner of my eye and I looked up to watch Chance flatten his ears, rear up, and strike out at Billy. His front hooves flashed just inches from Billy's face, knocking the coffee-colored baseball hat from his head, sending it spinning through the air.

Greasy, dark curls exposed, Billy covered his head with his arms and tried, without success, to run backwards. Instead, his boot heel caught in his own rope and he toppled to the ground. His back thudded against the earth and air burst out of his lungs in a solid whooshing sound. For a split second, Billy laid still. Then his eyes caught mine just as Chance slapped his front feet to the ground, creating a solid barrier between Billy and I.

I didn't move a muscle, perched on my hands and knees, but Billy shot to his feet and scrambled over the fence. Chance snorted, spilling a heavy haze of snot through the air. In that same moment, Casey and Marilynn ran up from the pasture.

Billy screamed obscenities, but he didn't look back. "Two weeks! You have two weeks with that lunatic!" Billy hollered. "I'll be here the night of the race. I don't expect that thing to win so you'd better find a way to come up with the cash!" He stomped off, waving his arms and shouting more insults.

Casey left Marilynn in the dust as he ran towards me. "Are you okay? What happened?" he yelled as he threw the paddock gate open. I looked at him, from the ground, and the confusion on his face turned to rage. With his hand still on the gate, Casey slammed it shut and turned in Billy's direction. He took five huge strides before I could stand up.

"NO...no, no!" I shouted after him and Casey slowed his pace, coming to a stop at the edge of the barn. "It's okay. I'm okay." *I think I'm okay.* Everything happened in a blur.

I pushed my hair from my face and stepped towards Chance. He was standing motionless with his head craned to the side, keeping his eyes on Billy. I laid my hand on his curled neck and we watched the truck and trailer pull out of sight, leaving only a cloud of dust in its tracks.

Thirteen

The canvas covered wagon rolled out at the crack of dawn. The wooden wheels pointed towards the mountain as the ranch's two blonde Belgian draft mares, Ying and Yang, pulled it along at a steady pace. Casey and I packed the wagon to its brim with tents, sleeping bags, loaded coolers, and firewood before Ernie, the head cook, and Dusty, the ranch handy man, stepped on board. Ernie and Dusty occupied the wagon's front bench and waved as they started their trek up the old logging road.

The help of all twenty ranch horses was needed for the overnight trail ride. Mr. Owens and Casey led the ride and Marilynn and I followed behind, making sure the guests rode safely in-between. The day was spent navigating tight trails and shallow creeks, breathing in fresh air. Rocking back and forth in the saddle, the drama of yesterday melted from my head.

Strolling through a grassy clearing, the guests snapped picture after picture. Lilac and yellow wildflowers peppered the wispy grass field and tall, dark fir trees marked the edge of the forest. The rocky, snowcapped tip of Mount Hood stood proud overlooking it all.

My thoughts lost in the scenery, I didn't notice Marilynn until she moved Sunny within a few feet of Chance. "This is great endurance training for the race," she noted, her cheeks rosy in the warm Oregon sun.

Marilynn was quick to voice her doubts when Casey and I told her our plan for the race. And her doubts were valid. To be honest, I was skeptical of our plan, but I couldn't come up with a better way to make five thousand dollars in two weeks. We just had to make it work.

Marilynn rested her forearm on the saddle horn. "You and Casey have a lot of work to do in two short weeks," she said, pausing to raise an eyebrow. "You'll have to be ready for anything. The ride is tough...on you and on the horses. And they throw some crazy obstacles in the mix. Herding, jumping, whatever."

"I know," I said rolling my hand over Chance's black neck. "We have a lot of work to do. I'm just glad Casey is my partner. I couldn't ask for a better shot at winning."

"Yeah," Marilyn agreed. "Did you know Casey's Grandpa won the first Three Rivers Cowboy Race twenty years ago?"

My mouth dropped open.

"Casey's been training Rocky for this race since he started riding him. He didn't tell you that, did he?" Marilynn asked when I didn't respond.

"No." I shook my head. "He left that information out," I half-whispered. He was relying on me to win something so important to him? Surely, he could find a more experienced horse and rider to compete with. I didn't want to be the reason he lost.

"There's Diamond Lake." Marilynn pointed ahead, realizing I needed a distraction. "You're going to love it up here. Come on," she said as she clucked Sunny into a trot. I focused my eyes on the scene ahead and tried to forget the uncertain thoughts pulsing through my brain.

Ernie and Dusty had the camp ready for the crew. Five canvas tents sat in a half circle around a smoky campfire. The covered wagon was parked next to a weathered corral where Ying and Yang happily grazed. Their black leather harnesses hung from the fence posts. And, behind the tents, a crystal-clear lake reflected the white and silver tip of Mount Hood.

Trotting closer, the hearty smell of beef stew wafted through the air. A Dutch oven hung over smoky coals and Marilynn's voice echoed over the crowd.

"Everyone, unsaddle your horse and lead them into the corral. It's dinner time!"

"You ready to relax, boy?" I asked, patting Chance's neck as we came to a stop. Dismounting, I couldn't help but notice Taylor and Star. I managed to avoid her sight for most of the afternoon as she was attached to Casey's hip at the front of the ride. It was easier on me if I didn't see them together.

Taylor swung her leg over Star's neck and sat side-saddle, watching while Casey untacked Rocky. Her skin-tight jeans were tucked into her tall, black leather boots, intricately stamped with red and silver flowers. A matching bandana was tied neatly around her neck and her golden curls were wrapped in a loose bun. I wondered how many suitcases she packed for her summer here on the ranch.

I should have turned away, but I watched, in self-torture, as Casey helped Taylor to the ground. She put her hands on his broad shoulders and pressed her body to his as she slid out of the saddle. As her toes hit the ground, Taylor locked eyes with me. Realizing I was watching, she smirked.

My stomach flipped and I turned away, leading Chance to the corral. I tried to erase the image of them together but it was burned into my mind. I understood Casey was hers. And not mine. She made that perfectly clear. There was no need to flaunt it in my face.

The cool evening air rolled over my bare arms as I pulled my grey sweatshirt from my saddle bags. After a hearty beef stew dinner, everyone gathered around the blazing campfire, sharing stories, laughing, and roasting marshmallows. I slid the cozy sweatshirt over my head and inhaled the sweet, earthy mountain air. *I could live up here.*

Heading back towards the campfire, I noticed a silent silhouette by the lake shore. Casey. He was sitting, legs dangling in the water, perched atop a fallen tree. I started towards him, and then stopped, looking over my shoulder for any sign of Taylor. Hearing Taylor's distinctive cackle echo from the campfire circle, I knew it was safe to approach Casey.

"No s'mores for you?" Casey jumped at my question, but he smiled when he turned to see me.

"Actually, I already ate three," he answered and scooted over on the log.

Grinning, I kicked off my boots and rolled up my jeans. I took a seat next to him and dipped my achy feet in the cool water, listening to the crackling fire and story-telling voices in the background. The yellow moon bounced its reflection off the black lake and lit Casey's perfect face.

I took a breath, knowing there was something I needed to ask. Something I needed to know. "So, Marilynn told me that your grandpa won the very first Cowboy Race. And, that you've been practicing for the race since you started training Rocky." I tapped my toes on the glassy surface of the lake, making ripples. "Is that true?"

Casey nodded his head, watching the water run off my feet. "Yes," he responded.

"Listen, I don't want to be the one to keep you from winning this race...a race that means so much to you," I said, half-irritated at his casual response. "I can find another way to get the money for Chance."

Casey snapped his eyes up, his forehead wrinkled. Now he looked irritated. "What are you talking about, Lucy?"

"I'm sure you know of a more competitive rider." I paused, thinking about the words I was about to say. They hurt before they even came out. "Taylor could help you win."

Casey's face didn't move, but a spark flashed through his eyes. He sat there frozen and took his time coming up with an answer, but when he finally spoke his words rolled out low and even. "I don't want to win with Taylor," he said. "I want to win with you. I *want* to help you get the money for Chance. Is there something wrong with that?"

I tried to follow his logic, but I just couldn't. "I don't understand. Why wouldn't you want to ride with your girlfriend?"

This time Casey's mouth dropped open. He looked like he wanted to respond, but his words were stuck at the back of his throat. "You think Taylor is my girlfriend?" he blurted out.

I about fell out of my seat and into the shallow water. "Well, isn't she?"

Casey straightened his shoulders and stared out over the lake. "I didn't know you thought that. A lot of things make sense now."

Did I really make an incorrect assumption here? I guess I never did *ask* Casey if Taylor was his girlfriend.

"I mean...you guys were at the dance together...she's always flirting with you...you're always flirting with her." The words toppled out of my mouth. I was babbling. Maybe those things weren't concrete evidence. I started to feel like I should shrink up into a tiny ball and roll away. Far away.

"We did go on a few dates . . ." Casey admitted, his voice trailing off.

"I'm sorry," I said, trying to make sense of our conversation. "I didn't mean to bring up an uncomfortable subject."

"No," he continued. "Please...let me finish. I was going to say...we went on a few dates, but that was before I got to know you."

What? Did Casey just say what I think he said? Does he mean what I think he means? Turning his body towards me, his blue eyes radiated in the moonlight making my body numb, from the toes up.

And then Casey leaned towards me.

In slow motion, Casey wrapped his hand around the back of my neck and laced his fingers through my hair. He pulled me in with a soft touch but stopped just short of placing his lips on mine. I couldn't hear anything in the distance anymore. Casey's breathing and my heart pounding were the only sounds.

My eyes closed as he pressed his warm lips to mine. Time stopped and I placed my shaking hands on his chest. For a moment, wrapped in Casey's grip, I was lost in a world I didn't know existed.

And then it came. A shriek so shrill it broke our perfect kiss. Both of our heads whipped in the direction of the screech.

My eyes had a hard time focusing in the dark, but when they did, I gasped. Although I couldn't see her face, I recognized the tall black boots. Taylor's body was rigid, her hands balled up in tight fists against her sides. And I didn't have time to move before more bodies came spilling out of the tent circle.

"What's going on?" Mr. Owens shouted as he ran through the grass, frantically shining a flashlight towards Taylor. Instead, the light discovered Casey and me, still wrapped up in each other.

No one moved. Not Casey. Not me. Not anyone watching us. The silence was awful.

"Lucy. Casey. I'd like to have a talk with you," Mr. Owens said, clicking the flashlight off and turning back towards the tents. I was thankful for the darkness. "Now, please."

My eyes shifted to the ground. The silence was deafening as Mr. Owens stood in the tent's open doorway, arms crossed. His body made a tall, dark silhouette against the backdrop of the dying fire.

"Do I need to have a talk with you about boys?" Mr. Owens asked. I could tell he was uncomfortable without looking at his face.

Oh my God. How embarrassing. "No, Mr. Owens."

"I realize you are sixteen," he continued. "And both you and Casey are good kids, but I don't want anything inappropriate going on while you are under my care for the summer."

Until tonight, I didn't even know Casey thought of me…inappropriately. I still couldn't comprehend that he kissed me.

"And I don't want to have to give your dad a call."

Mr. Owens' comment shot me back to our discussion.

"You don't have to worry, sir. I promise I won't do anything inappropriate."

He paused. "I will take your word this time, but I'm keeping an eye on you two."

"Understood," I said as I sat down on my cot and watched Mr. Owens walk to the tent on the opposite side of the campfire. He was probably going to give Casey the same talk.

Crawling onto my cot, I pulled the flannel lined sleeping bag up to my chin and zipped the side. I should have felt bad for getting in trouble, but my blood was still pumping from Casey's kiss. The recent memory took over every thought in my head.

What the heck just happened? Casey likes me? More than a friend? My heart fluttered at these new thoughts. I stared at the canvas tent ceiling, eyes wide open, wondering how I was going to fall asleep tonight.

Mr. Owens popped into the barn more than usual for the next few days, but he didn't mention anything further about the awkward scene on the mountain. I was thankful he avoided the subject.

"What are you practicing tonight?" Marilynn asked as she took a seat on the wooden tack box.

I had Chance cross-tied in the barn aisle and finished wrapping a tiny rubber band around the end of his braided forelock.

I patted him on the forehead. "Casey wants to work on roping with Chance and then we are going to long trot around the pastures. Build up more stamina for the race," I said as I ran my hand down Chance's slick, ebony neck.

"I watched you working those steers with Casey last night in the arena. Chance is a natural. You guys work well together."

"Thank you," I said, beaming with pride at Marilynn's support. Every day Chance was making progress and my heart swelled at how much effort he put into our riding. Chance was quite the partner.

"Well, good luck with the roping," Marilynn said as she hopped off the tack box and patted Chance on the rump. "I just walked by the arena. Taylor is down there riding."

I swallowed hard.

"Try not to make her scream again," Marilynn smirked. "Although, it was pretty funny."

My body stiffened in the saddle as Chance stepped onto the arena dirt. Taylor hadn't muttered a word to me since she stumbled upon *the kiss*. On the ride off the mountain, I caught her staring at me, over and over, and I was afraid darts would shoot out of her eyes.

The arena footing was freshly tilled and Star's hoof prints seemed to be the only tracks. Taylor was riding in her western saddle and it looked like she had a whole obstacle course set up.

Orange cones, poles, barrels, and jumps were scattered across the arena.

Taylor trotted Star over a series of red and white striped poles and then moved her into a canter as they headed towards a line of hay bales, stacked two high.

"Eyes up," a woman barked from the middle of the arena. "Look at the jump ahead of you, not at the ground."

The woman pointed sharply at the hay bales and adjusted the white visor on her head as Star sailed over the jump.

"Again!" she yelled. Her long, blonde braid swayed back and forth as she crossed her arms and shook her head in disapproval.

It looked like a perfect jump to me. I kept Chance walking along the opposite side of the arena, hoping she wouldn't yell at me next. *That must be Taylor's trainer.*

Out of the corner of my eye, I saw Casey trotting Rocky into the arena. Even with Taylor's uncomfortable stares, I couldn't help but to smile at his arrival.

"Hey," Casey said without a glance towards the lesson on the other side of the arena.

"Hey," I blushed.

Casey and I hadn't really talked about our kiss on the mountain. We were more focused on the race right now...and not getting in trouble with Mr. Owens. But, I couldn't stop thinking about it.

"Are you ready to try roping with Chance?" He patted a coiled rope hung over his saddle horn. "You've got your swing down. Now we just need to teach Chance a thing or two about roping."

I nodded. "Chance and I are as ready as ever."

Chance and Rocky walked side by side towards the roping dummy – a plastic cow head attached to a hay bale. Lost in my own thoughts about Casey, I forgot about the loud lady in the middle of the arena.

"Are you guys going to rope right there?" she asked as though the arena wasn't big enough for the four of us.

Not waiting for a response, she sighed and turned to Taylor. "Let's take a break while they ride. Otherwise, they will be in your way after the hay bale jump. I have to return some client calls anyhow since I had to cancel a week's worth of riding lessons for this race."

Taylor nodded as she trotted to the middle of the arena and dismounted. The lady stomped out of the arena without another word or glance back, fumbling in her pocket for her cell phone.

I looked at Casey. *Did I hear her right? Did Taylor's trainer just mention something about the Cowboy Race?*

Star lowered her head and licked her lips in relaxation as Taylor loosened her saddle's cinch.

"That's Linda Green. Ten-time World Champion," Taylor stated while grabbing ahold of Star's reins. Standing in front of us, her perfectly plucked eyebrows scrunched up into a deep "V" and her eyes were cold and accusing. She stared directly at me without blinking.

Linda Green. I didn't even recognize her without a trophy in her hand. Images of her wins were plastered all over the pages of the horse magazines stacked on my bedroom floor. She was one of the few trainers that excelled in rodeo competitions and the jumping world. Although, I had also read that she didn't exactly play fair. She did anything to win.

"Linda Green is training you for the cowboy race? The Three Rivers Cowboy Race?"

Taylor's lips curled up in a dark smirk, and the sparkle returned to her eyes. "Yeah, I heard you two were partners in the race," she said, pausing for dramatics. "And I couldn't resist. Thought it would be fun."

"Fun?" The word blurted out of my mouth just as fast as it entered my head and my worried tone only fueled Taylor's delight. I didn't understand why it would make her happy to mess with my only way to save Chance.

"And one more thing," Taylor added. "Linda *is* training me for the race...but she is also my partner. See you guys at the starting line on Sunday."

Taylor turned on her polished heels and whistled a happy tune as she walked Star out of the arena.

The gate clattered shut and I stepped into the damp, cool pasture. The moon was just bright enough to create silhouettes of the sleepy horses. Gathered together, their heads hung low and relaxed, but one black shadow perked up at my entrance. Chance nickered and stepped out of the sleepy circle.

"Hi there, big boy," I said as Chance walked over. He nickered again and placed his whiskered lips in the palm of my outstretched hand. "Sorry, Chance. I didn't bring any treats tonight. My mind's been on other things."

I couldn't sleep. My stomach turned. There were three days before the race and that was not enough time. In three short days there was no way I could gain the experience that Taylor's team had. And, I couldn't think of anything worse than letting down both Chance and Casey.

"We've got a big day ahead of us on Sunday."

Chance's ears flicked forward and his big brown eyes blinked at me.I wrapped my arms around his neck, tears welling in my eyes as I thought of losing him. Chance stood perfectly still, listening to me sniffle, letting me hang from his body.

Pressing my face into his coarse mane, my heart ached to be even closer to him. Through the tears I wrapped a hand in Chance's mane, jumped once, and pulled myself onto his back. On top of him, I felt safe until I realized what I had done. I didn't have a halter on his head. No lead to hold on to. There was nothing to stop Chance from running.

But, instead of reacting in fear, Chance curled his neck to the side and nuzzled the tip of my boot. Then, without a second thought, he put his head to the ground and nibbled on the cool grass.

Letting out an overdue sigh, I scooted back and laid my chest across his warm body, my legs dangling at his sides. Closing my eyes, I listened to Chance chew and breathe steadily. My tears stopped and my body melted into his.

The past month played through my head.

"Do you remember the first time I got on your back?" I asked, twirling a piece of his mane in my fingers. "You made me eat dirt."

It wasn't funny then, but the thought now made me grin. I kissed his withers and placed my cheek against his slick coat.

"You really trust me now. Don't you, Chance?"

I couldn't believe the leaps and bounds we had made together. And, we needed to make one more very big leap.

Fourteen

Our entrance reminded me of a parade. The Three Rivers High School band split the crowds of onlookers as they marched down Main Street. Batons spun, trumpets blared, drums crashed and I was glad we were further back in the line-up.

Twenty teams signed up for the Three Rivers Cowboy Race and each team rode in twos behind the band. As team thirteen, Rocky and Chance walked shoulder to shoulder. Their hooves clip clopped along the pavement. Rocky was solid and calm, walking through the cheering crowd like it was an everyday occurrence, but Chance was unsure of the loud, congested scenery.

I tightened my reins as Chance pranced, every muscle showing in his upright neck. "It's okay, Chance."

"We just have to make it a few more blocks and we will be out of this mess and close to the starting line," Casey tried to reassure me.

My knuckles turned white as my grip tightened further. I attempted to smile, but my face was stiff, just like the rest of my body. I couldn't force myself to relax and I knew Chance had picked up on my nerves. He needed me to be brave for the both of us.

Rubbing Chance's neck I moved him closer to Rocky, hoping Rocky's quiet composure would rub off on him, but I over-steered. Chance got a little too close and I bumped Casey's knee with my leg. At the jostle, Casey's ice blue eyes caught mine and he grabbed my shaking hand. The background noise muffled at his touch.

"We got this, Lucy. We got this," he said.

The certainty in his eyes was so strong. Maybe what I really needed was Casey's confidence to rub off on me.

Casey continued to hold my hand as we rode through the last few blocks of burgundy brick buildings and through the blinking lights of the carnival. Past the bustling crowd and carnival rides, the teams of two were lining up in the open field. Chance and Rocky trotted to the starting line, a long yellow ribbon strung between two wooden posts, and I was glad to be out of the claustrophobic side show.

Each horse held their nose just inches from the yellow ribbon, and the last team, Taylor and Linda, trotted into place. Taylor was still waving at the crowd behind her as though she just won a beauty pageant. I was surprised she didn't wear a tiara for the occasion.

A little boy skipped along the yellow ribbon handing out sealed white envelopes to each team as a gray-haired man, dressed like an actor in an old western movie, gave directions over a bullhorn.

"Ladies and gentleman, cowboys and cowgirls, the twentieth annual Three Rivers Cowboy Race will begin in five minutes."

The crowd filtered in and gathered behind the announcer, standing proud at the wooden post.

He directed the bullhorn at the teams. "You may now open your envelopes to find the race map as well as a description of the first obstacle."

Paper ripped violently as each team pulled out an intricate map of Mount Hood.

"There are four numbered obstacles marked on this map. You may make your own path to each obstacle, but must complete them in numerical order. There will be a race official located at each obstacle. When your team has successfully completed that obstacle, the official will hand you an envelope containing instructions for the following obstacle."

"Two of the obstacles are team obstacles and two are individual obstacles," the announcer continued. "The individual obstacles cannot be completed by the same team member. And the first team to come back and race across this same yellow line, will be the winners of the twentieth annual Three Rivers Cowboy Race and the five thousand dollar prize!"

The crowded roared and cackled with excitement.

"There is exactly one minute left on the clock and the race will begin at the sound of my gunshot. Good luck to all twenty teams!"

Casey and I examined the race map in our last minute, deciding on our path to the first obstacle.

"Obstacle number one is at the base of Fallen Creek," Casey said, pointing at the red "X" on the map. "That's not far past the edge of the woods. Follow me after the gunshot. What does the obstacle description say?" Casey asked as I pulled the obstacle card from the white envelope.

#1 - TEAM Obstacle
On the hidden side of Fallen Falls, numbered rocks await you. Each team member must find your team's numbered rock and present both rocks to the race official.

"The hidden side of Fallen Falls?" I asked and looked to Casey for an answer.

"Ten, Nine, Eight . . ." The crowd chanted the countdown and the whole line of horses began dancing, reacting to the tension in the air. I tightened my grip on the reins just as the gunshot sounded.

The horses exploded forward in one unit, breaking the yellow ribbon and launching into the open field, but the gunshot was too much for Chance.

Chance reared straight up, balancing on his hind legs. I threw my body against the saddle and stayed curled in that position, waiting for his front feet to hit the ground. It felt like an eternity, but when Chance came down, he planted his feet and stood there, stunned. For a few long seconds we watched the horses galloping out in front of us, including Rocky.

"Go, Chance, Go!" I screamed as I snapped back into the game. I leaned forward and Chance pushed off into a full gallop. He ran, his legs flying in every direction, towards Rocky.

I held my reins halfway up Chance's neck and gripped the saddle horn with my other hand, holding my body in a forward position. Casey peeked over his shoulder and slowed Rocky when he realized we weren't by his side.

"Sorry," I exclaimed, out of breath, when we caught up to Casey. I steadied Chance with my hands. "I don't think Chance has ever heard a gunshot before."

"We can make up the distance. Let's just get to the first obstacle," Casey said and both horses picked up their speed heading towards the forest.

The herd of riders entered the trees in different spots and Casey pointed to an opening further down. "That should put us closer to the base of the creek."

I followed his directions and, reaching the opening, we slowed the horses to a trot and filed into the dense brush. Chance stayed close to Rocky, trailing only a few feet behind on the narrow path. His ears flicked back and forth, scanning the new surroundings. His feet were light, ready to jump in any direction away from danger.

"Trust me, Chance. I wouldn't ask you to do anything that would put you at risk," I whispered, lacing my fingers through his mane as we followed Rocky up a steep embankment.

On top of the hill, the base of Fallen Creek lay out before us. The horses stopped and we accessed our first obstacle. The creek poured off gray slate stone into a cascading waterfall and crashed into a small lake. Riders lined up along the brushy edge of the water, coaxing their steeds to jump in.

We trotted over and, reaching the edge of the lake, I gave Chance an encouraging squeeze with my legs.

"Look, it's not that deep. You can see to the bottom," I said.

Chance pawed at the line between the sandy shore and the water and then took two tentative steps in. Casey walked Rocky in beside us. That was easier than I thought.

"Now we just need to get those rocks," Casey said. He nodded towards the waterfall and I understood what the card meant by "the hidden side of Fallen Falls." We had to ride *through* the cascading water.

Rocky and Chance waded through the knee-high lake and the waterfall sprayed as we got close, mist rolling through the air. Droplets collected on the horses' manes.

"Just go for it. Don't let it intimidate you," Casey yelled over the sound of the crashing water. He motioned Rocky forward and, before I had time to protest, the waterfall engulfed both Casey and Rocky's bodies. They disappeared.

When Chance could no longer see Rocky, he screamed at the top of his lungs, questioning the monster in front of us. He stood frozen, muscles tight, staring at the waterfall that just ate his friend. And I questioned it too. I didn't know how we were going to do this, but we couldn't waste any more time. There were already more teams riding into the lake's edge.

I clucked to Chance and, to my complete surprise, he launched forward into the waterfall without a moment's hesitation.

Following the jolt, I threw my head forward and the heavy water crashed on my shoulders, pulled down the leather brim of my hat, and ricocheted off of Chance. We soared through in one swift jump, landing on the other side of the falls where Casey was waiting for us. He smiled from ear to ear at our arrival. I was just happy we made it through alive.

Inside the cave, Rocky stood in a shallow pool of teal water protected by a room of slate stone. Sunshine streamed through the waterfall at our back and illuminated the stone. The only sound was the crashing water.

"I guess that's one way to do it," I said before Chance shook like a wet dog, sending my body into the same convulsions and shaking away some of my nerves.

I adjusting myself back into the saddle and Chance picked up a high-stepping gait, splashing through the teal pool with Rocky. We headed towards the back of the cave where numbered rocks were scattered on dry ground. Stopping Chance, I threw my leg over the saddle and jumped to the floor, searching for a rock marked with a thirteen.

Casey was on foot too. We fumbled through the rocks until we both shouted, in unison. "Got it!"

We held up our rocks, both marked with a thirteen, and jumped back in the saddle just as another team burst through the waterfall.

Fifteen

A renewed energy surged through my body as we rode out of Fallen Falls and into the warm sun. I brushed the water from my bare arms and followed Casey onto shore. If we could do that, we could do anything. Thrilled with our triumph, I patted Chance on the rump as we approached the first race official.

"Congratulations," she said, exchanging our rocks for another envelope. "You are team number ten to complete this obstacle."

Team ten? My joy melted away with her words. We were in tenth place? We had some serious ground to make up. I turned Chance on his heels and loped off after Casey, ripping open the new envelope with my free hand.

"Obstacle number two looks like it's about half way between here and Diamond Lake," Casey shouted over his shoulder, holding the map in front of him. "Let's connect up with the old logging road. That's the easiest path up to the lake."

"Okay, I'm right behind you. I'll read the obstacle description while we ride." I pulled the card from the envelope and focused on the words through the bouncing.

#2 – INDIVIDUAL Obstacle
Rope, Pull & Race.
Pick one member from your team to rope a log, marked with a red
X, and drag it past race official #2.

"It's an individual obstacle and it's roping," I said, stuffing the card in my jean pocket and extending Chance's trot to catch up to Rocky. "This one is all yours Casey."

"Are you sure you want me to do it?"

"Of course," I responded without hesitation. "I watched you rope and pull a wild horse out of the mountain. A log will be a piece of cake."

Casey grinned and nodded at Chance. "He's not so wild anymore, is he?"

The horses' hooves crunched against the gravel as they stepped onto the old logging road. We covered about a mile of rugged ground, but Rocky and Chance weren't even breathing hard. All of those evening rides were paying off.

I pushed the damp hat off my head and let it hang from my neck by the leather string. Beams of sunlight shot through the tree tops and warmed my cheeks.

"We've got to make it to the top of the logging road for the next obstacle," Casey noted.

I looked up the steep incline and my eyes followed the zigzagging road back and forth up the mountain. The road had to be a couple of miles long.

"We've got to make up some distance," I said, noticing a pack of riders on the highest part of the logging road.

"I know," Casey agreed. "But we have to be careful not to push the horses too hard. They're going to need energy for the other obstacles. We can't just gallop up this road."

"Well, let's go straight up then," I said. My idea made perfect sense to me. "What's the shortest distance between two points? A straight line."

Casey gave me a blank expression and then looked at the terrain between us and the top of the logging road. The road was ten times the distance of going straight up the mountain, but the road was smooth and flat and safe. The uphill land between the zig-zagging road was filled with brush and inclined at a 45 degree angle.

"We'll make up some serious ground and you know our horses can do it, Casey."

And with that, Casey was convinced. "Let's do it."

I steered Chance straight for the incline, leaning forward in the saddle and wrapping my fingers into Chance's mane.

"We got this, Chance," I encouraged him. His ears flicked back at my whisper and he understood his job. I kept my reins loose and trusted in Chance's choice of a path.

He dug deep into the loose dirt and pushed hard with his hind quarters, moving us up the mountain. His chest bulled through the brush. At each flat road crossing, Chance jumped into a trot shooting across the log road and then launched himself back into the steep brush. Rocks dislodged under his feet and I watched them bounce, roll, and crash down to the closest flat landing.

Rocky stayed just inches behind Chance and followed our every move. Hitting the last incline, Chance kicked into high gear and loped hard through the brush and loose ground, grunting with his strides, pushing us straight to the sky.

Bursting out onto the last stretch of flat road, Chance snorted and pranced sideways, not ready to stop. I eased him to a halt, rolling my hand down his damp neck and patting his shoulder.

"Easy, boy," I cooed.

"Nice work," Casey beamed as Rocky trotted towards us. "The next obstacle shouldn't be far ahead now."

Glancing over the edge of the road, I noted five pairs of riders still working their way up the logging road. Our short cut just put us in fourth place.

I smiled. "Now we just have to catch the rest of them."

Chance extended his stride as we trotted off the old logging road and broke into a grassy field. In the clearing, two horses, attached to ten foot logs by tight ropes, were pushing forward, dragging their logs across the ground towards the obstacle's finishing line. Their partners cheered from horseback on the other side of the second race official.

I pointed Chance's nose towards the cheering teammates. "I'll be waiting for you at the finish line," I said, nodding at Casey with a grin on my face. "I'll be the one cheering the loudest."

Casey nodded back and I kissed to Chance. He picked up a lope, gliding across the grass, but nausea engulfed my body as we approached the other side of the field and I laid my eyes on Taylor. Suddenly, I wasn't in a hurry to find my spot among the awaiting riders.

Taylor looked straight ahead as we approached. She didn't acknowledge our existence, but Star sure did. The chestnut mare flattened her ears and flicked her tail as I lined Chance up next to her. I was certain she would've grabbed Chance with her teeth if we got an inch closer. Taylor grinned at her mare's unwelcoming attitude.

Avoiding the awkward silence, I focused my attention back on Casey. He had Rocky placed in front of the pile of logs marked with red spray paint and was looping his rope in wide circles over his head. In one succinct throw, the rope snapped around the end of the smallest log and Rocky backed to take out the rope's slack. Changing directions, Rocky spun towards us and loped off, yanking the log off the pile and bouncing it along the ground.

He headed straight towards the rider in the middle of the field, Linda Green and her stocky buckskin. Linda was halfway to the finishing line, but Rocky was flying across the grass, pulling the log with ease.

I didn't even realize I was hooting and hollering until Taylor broke my focus.

"What are you yelling for?" she hissed, staring at me through squinted eyes. "You know Casey can't win this for you. Don't you?" She might as well have spat in my face.

My mind raced with all of the nasty names I was going to call her, but instead, Casey's yell jerked my attention back to the race.

"Whoa, whoa," Casey repeated, trying to calm Rocky.

Rocky was side-by-side with the buckskin gelding when he lost it. He kicked out, narrowly missing the buckskin, and hopped to the side, whipping his head back and forth. I gasped watching Casey lurch through the air, his body following Rocky's jumps as he held on through the frantic bucking.

Reins tight, Casey pulled Rocky into a small circle and the bucking began to slow. His jumps soon turned into erratic prancing and snorting.

"That's too bad," Taylor said over her shoulder as she walked Star towards the finish line to meet Linda, but I was more concerned by Rocky's episode than her comment.

Come on, Rocky. Get it together.

Casey rubbed Rocky's tense, raised neck and whispered soothing words until Rocky eased back into the steady, brave horse that he was. As Linda trotted her buckskin across the finish line, Rocky started to pull his log again. Calmed and listening to Casey's cues, he trotted across the field. His head lowered, Rocky pushed his body forward and pulled the log across the finish line.

I loped Chance to Rocky's side as Casey took the next envelope from the race official. Casey's eyes had a sharp edge to them. He looked straight forward, concentrating on something I couldn't see, and didn't mutter a word as we rode off.

"Are you okay?" I asked. "What happened out there?"

Casey broke his stare and shook his head from side to side. "Linda slapped Rocky on the butt with the end of her reins when I came up on her side."

"Are you serious?" I yelled. "You could've been thrown! You could've been hurt! What kind of person does that?"

Casey handed me the new envelope as we trotted up the dirt path. "Someone who would do anything to win."

Ripping open the envelope, all I could think about was getting back at Taylor and her shady trainer. Now I had one more motivation to cross the finish line first.

Sixteen

#3 – TEAM Obstacle
Sorting Skills.
Separate a brown steer from the herd and chase it into the corral.
Once your steer is corralled, you will receive the envelope for the final
obstacle.

"Those clouds don't look good," I noted, glancing over my shoulder. The high noon sun was beating on my back, but the eastern sky had turned navy blue and the dark color was crawling our direction.

Casey scanned the changing scenery. "Let's just hope it holds off until we cross the finish line. We've got other things to worry about right now."

Ahead of us, a herd of at least fifty black and brown steers jostled back and forth along the edge of Diamond Lake. Riders weaved through the herd in their attempts to round-up a brown steer.

All three front running teams were now in sight.

Casey nodded at the cattle ahead as we passed the empty corral. "Just like we practiced in the arena, okay?"

I nodded back, realizing this was not like the arena at all. We were over halfway to the end of the race and there was no room for a mistake. I steadied my breathing and tried to focus solely on the task at hand, but so many images thundered through my head. This was not simply a matter of winning. There was a great deal at stake here.

All six riders, including the cheaters, were immersed in the steers, breaking the herd up into several clusters along the water's edge.

"Let's hit up the far end," I said and pointed past the riders to a small group of steers broken from the herd. Rocky and Chance broke into a lope, gliding through the tall grass.

"Easy, boys," I said, slowing Chance to a walk as we approached the curious cattle.

On the edge of the group, a chocolate brown steer stopped chewing his cud. He stared at us, swishing his tail. Surrounded by black, he was the only brown steer on this side of the herd. He was our target.

Walking towards the steer, Casey and I positioned our horses on opposite sides of the animal. I knew my job was to block him from running out into the field and I had to turn him towards the corral. He couldn't get past me.

Every nerve in my body was on alert, ready to react to the slightest movement. Chance, ears pricked forward, stared with intent and we waited for Casey to dislodge the steer from his group.

With Casey closing in, the steer made a sudden decision to run. But just as quickly as the steer jumped sideways, Rocky took two huge strides forward and cut him off. And it was on.

The steer stopped in its tracks and spun in the opposite direction. Then he was running, tail in the air, directly towards me.

At my cue, Chance lurched forward. We dived towards the frantic steer, blocking him from running into the open field. I pressed my reins against Chance's neck and he turned hard, following the steer, sending chucks of ground flying through the air.

Casey and I were now racing on opposite sides of the steer as the chased animal ran at top speed. Reaching my hands up Chance's neck, I gave him the reins and leaned in. Chance surged into another gear and we caught up to the steer's shoulder, turning him in the direction of the corral.

Casey and I worked together, pushing the steer straight to the corral and through the open gate. Pulling our horses to a halt, dust billowed up through the air.

A howl rolled out of my lungs, but the heart-racing thrill was short-lived as I watched our steer trot over to a single brown steer standing next to the fence. Turning Chance around, I caught a glimpse of the winning team loping off across the field...the hind ends of a flaxen chestnut and a stocky buckskin.

I tightened my stomach muscles and balanced my body over the saddle, allowing Chance to maneuver down the rough terrain. He kept his head low, assessing each foot placement. There was no simple path to the final obstacle so, looking at the map, we decided to blaze our own trail straight down the mountain. It was the shortest distance, but not an easy ride.

We were both silent, concentrating on each step as the declining path was filled with loose footing, fallen trees and overgrown blackberry bushes. There was still no sign of Taylor or Linda. *I hope we chose the right path to catch up with them.*

"Can you read the obstacle card?" Casey asked over his shoulder as Rocky lifted his legs over a series of fallen logs. "I know the riding is rough, but it's not going to smooth out until we are close to the final obstacle. And you're going to need to know the instructions."

By default, the last obstacle would be an individual obstacle...and it was my turn. I pulled the envelope out of my pocket and ripped it open.

#4 – INDIVIDUAL Obstacle
Jump, Jump, Jump.
The second individual on your team will complete a three-jump course. Follow the marked trail that begins at the old log cabin and ends at Willow's Creek, where your partner will be waiting for you. Then it will be a race to the finish line!

"Well, what is it?" Casey asked when I didn't say a word.

"A jump course." I cringed as I remembered Taylor would be the one completing the obstacle for her team. Anxiety bubbled up my throat. "We have to beat Taylor and Linda to this obstacle. I'm going to need the extra time. Taylor is going to breeze through this one," I said without pausing between my words.

"Easy, Lu. The clearing isn't far ahead. We will get out of this brush and the jump course should be right in front of us. We're almost there."

Straight ahead, flat ground and lush green grass poked through the tree trunk gaps. And, a few hundred feet to our right, the back of a rustic wood cabin rose above the bushes.

Goosebumps covered my arms and a shiver rolled up my spine as we pushed through the last bit of brush and followed Rocky out of the trees.

"I don't see any hoof prints," Casey noted as the horses picked up a trot on the wide grassy path.

Did we beat Taylor and Linda to the last obstacle? Or were they so far ahead of us that we had no chance of catching them?

I cued Chance and he picked up a lope, bobbing his head in anticipation. Rocky followed and we made our way down the path. The horses' hooves thumped lightly on the soft ground and the rhythm gave me some comfort.

In front of the log cabin, two wooden signs hung from a knotty, tangled tree that created a fork in the path. The sign on the right had the words "Obstacle #4" engraved along with an arrow pointing towards a wide path. The second sign said "Team Partner – Follow to Willow's Creek" and pointed to a narrow, dirt path veering off to the left and down the embankment.

Casey locked eyes with me as our bodies rocked with the rhythm of the horses. "I'll see you at Willow's Creek." His eyes were intense as he tipped the brim of his hat. "You take care of Chance and Chance will take care of you. You guys can do this." And with that, Casey sat back in the saddle, tightened his reins, and slowed Rocky to make the sharp turn down the dirt path. He had so much faith in me. Now I had to have faith in myself.

I watched Casey disappear into the woods. Then I leaned forward and Chance extended his stride, whipping past the cabin. His ears flicked back and forth focusing between the path ahead and Rocky's abrupt disappearance. He let out a short, high pitched whinny, but didn't slow down.

"Don't worry, Chance. Rocky will be waiting for us at the creek. We just have to get there." I rubbed the middle of his sweaty neck with the palm of my hand. "It's just you and me right now," I whispered.

A few heavy drops of cold rain splattered onto my bare arms as the first jump came into view. A series of logs lay across the path, separated by a stride's distance. I centered my body in the saddle and tightened my reins just enough to make soft contact with Chance's bit. His body collected under mine as we closed in.

One stride. Two strides. I moved my hands up Chance's mane to give him slack in the reins. He bunched up his muscles, pushed off the ground with his hind legs, and glided over the single log. Following the landing, he took one smooth stride and then launched himself over the second jump, which was actually two trees laying side-by-side.

Realizing the third jump was three laying trees, I braced my body for the takeoff and held my breath as Chance jumped. I watched in awe as the brown tree bark blazed by underneath his belly.

Landing on the other side, Chance loped off with an extra pop to his stride. Obviously, he was proud of himself. And, I was too. I sucked in a lung full of cold air and blew it out, relaxing back into Chance's stride.

Trees spray-painted with red arrows marked the direction of the path, but it would be difficult to veer off. The path was cut into the mountain and was surrounded by a steep incline on one side and a sharp drop-off on the other. Following the arrows, I slowed Chance to trot as we approached a sharp bend. We followed the declining turn, with careful steps, that led us to a lower path going in the opposite direction. A glimpse of the second jump was now visible, further down the trail.

And then I heard the unmistakable thundering of hooves behind me. I whipped my head back to watch Taylor ride Star around the steep bend like she was circling a barrel at a rodeo. Her golden ponytail flashed in the wind as Star dove forward into a gallop, headed straight for us.

Chance jumped, startled at the sound of grass ripping below Star's hooves, and the jump allowed just enough time for Taylor to make up precious ground. Alarmed, but listening to my every cue, Chance gathered himself and burst into a fluid gallop. Taylor was only a few horse lengths behind us. We needed to run with everything we had.

As we ran, the rain began falling harder, pelting me in the face. I wiped it from my eyes, blinking to focus on the upcoming jump. Two large trees made an "X" on the path. The middle of the crossed trees looked to be two feet high, but the height increased towards the edges of the cross. We had to hit the middle.

Streams of water trickled over Chance's neck washing the salty sweat away. Chance probably welcomed the cool shower, but I knew the grass was getting slick. Our speed was too fast. I needed to bring him back to a collected canter for this jump.

Out of the corner of my eye, I could see Taylor approaching. She wasn't letting up. Star was in a full-blown run, ears pinned flat against her outstretched neck.

I wanted to gallop through the jump, but I knew I shouldn't do it. Chance could slip on the wet grass...and he trusted me to take care of him. He would do anything thing I asked him to. And, I wasn't going to let him get hurt.

"Easy, boy, easy," I said as I sat back slightly and slowed Chance's stride. It pained me to hear Star thudding up on Chance's side, but I couldn't fathom risking an injury.

Five strides from the jump, Star's shoulder was in line with Chance's. Her petite frame was lathered in foamy sweat and her nostrils flared. Taylor narrowed her eyes at me and I expected her to fly past me to the jump. Instead, she gathered her reins and slowed the lathered mare to match Chance's speed.

I gasped when I realized what Taylor was doing. She was pushing me out of the way. I couldn't make it to the middle of the jump with Star by my side. Taylor had Star positioned directly at the center of the crossed trees and I only had two choices. I could try to stop Chance and risk slamming into the solid trees...or we could jump the higher section, which had to be four or five feet tall.

My initial reaction was to stop. I closed my hands around the reins, but Chance's body told me otherwise. His alert ears, raised neck, and forward stride radiated confidence. The height didn't seem to scare him and he had no intention of stopping. His confidence sealed my decision. I leaned forward and my body surged with his.

Directly next to one another, the petite chestnut mare and the bold black gelding tucked their front legs and launched over the trees. Chance grunted with his effort. In the air, Taylor glanced over and was eye level with the sole of my boot. I fantasized about giving her a swift kick, but resisted the urge.

Star landed first and Taylor cracked her on the butt with the end of her reins. At the snap, Star jumped into a gallop, swishing her tail in annoyance.

I braced myself for a hard landing, but Chance touched ground and rolled back into a canter with grace. He extended his stride again and we closed in on Taylor. She had a good five strides on us, but relief rushed through me as I watched her ride onto dry ground. Sunbeams kissed the grass ahead. We were riding out of the rain.

The splashing of Chance's hooves turned back to pounding against the dry ground. His long body stretched out like a Thoroughbred in the last quarter mile of a race and we were gaining on Taylor. My eyes looked between Chance's pricked ears and focused on the only thing that could keep Chance and I apart . . . Taylor.

Seventeen

Positioned before a sharp curve in the path, the third jump looked like a beaver's dam, a pile of large sticks gathered into a mound. It was a few feet high, preceded by a murky puddle that covered the width of the path and stretched out a few strides before the jump.

Remembering the race map, I knew Willow's Creek was not far after that curve and I pictured Casey on the other side of the creek, anticipating my arrival. It had to be killing him to sit and wait, not knowing what was happening. I imagined his tense face morphing into a beaming smile as I rounded that corner and raced towards him. I wouldn't let Taylor's face be the first one he saw.

My body must have conveyed my desire because, at that thought, Chance stretched out his stride farther. We inched our way along Star's side, passing her rump and then her flank. Suddenly, we were nose and nose once again.

But I didn't want that to last long. I wouldn't give Taylor another opportunity to cheat, to jeopardize our win and Chance's opportunity at a new life.

I kissed and asked Chance for more. And he gave it to me. I could feel each of Chance's hooves push off the ground as though they were my own feet. We pulled ahead of Star by a nose. Then by a neck.

In a matter of seconds, we were three strides in front of Taylor and only a hundred feet from the last jump. With our lead, I eased Chance off a full gallop before we plummeted through the water.

Even with the decreased speed, Chance's hooves splashed into the dark puddle, spraying lines of water through the air like a Jet Ski skipping across a glassy lake. I didn't look back, but heard another loud crack and a few inaudible, irate words as Chance gathered his legs and pushed us over the beaver dam, landing with a few feet to spare.

Joy surged through my body as we galloped away and I peeked back to examine our lead. But instead, I was met with the image of Star, bucking and grunting behind us, her head held low, reins flying through the air...and no Taylor.

Star had cleared the jump, but Taylor was nowhere to be seen. The chestnut mare, realizing she had dumped her rider, shook her head from side to side and bounced towards us kicking up her heels.

Sitting straight up, I pushed my heels down in the stirrups and pulled Chance to a choppy stop. He pranced, confused, as I turned him around and directed him back towards the jump we had just cleared. I wanted to leave Taylor in my tracks. I wanted to keep running...but I just couldn't. Not like this.

Star whizzed by us. Her nose pointed high in the air, snorting. I couldn't blame her for her retaliation, but I hoped Taylor was okay. What would I do if Taylor had a broken arm? A broken leg? What if she was unconscious? A fall at that speed could cause some serious damage.

I held my breath as I slowed Chance to a walk. We approached the jump and my frantic eyes searched past the mound of sticks...and landed on a very unhappy face. Taylor was sitting in the middle of the shallow, murky puddle. Her knees bent above the water and her arms wrapped around her shins. Seeing me, she pushed herself up to stand.

"What do you want?" she snapped.

Taylor was soaked from head to toe. Muddy water dripped from her once-pink polo shirt and her blonde hair was plastered to the sides of her face. Mascara ran down her defined cheekbones. I couldn't tell if she had been crying or if it was just the puddle water.

Realizing my mouth was hanging open, I snapped it shut. "Are you okay?"

"What do you mean?" she shot back.

I thought my question was pretty clear, but I asked again. "Are. You. Okay?" I repeated.

But my question only warranted a stare and a lengthy pause. Something was simmering under that look.

"You turned around to see if I was okay?" Taylor asked. The doubt in her voice alarmed me. Why else would I turn around?

"Yeah, I saw Star bucking and I thought you were hurt. We were going pretty fast before we hit that jump."

Taylor blinked her eyes, her forehead wrinkled in question. "You really turned around to see if I was okay?" she asked again, tightening her crossed arms. "I wouldn't have stopped for you."

Well, that was quite honest. Even soaked in mud, the true Taylor shined through.

But, then I thought I saw Taylor's hazel eyes glass over. She looked away and cleared her throat.

"Thank you," she mumbled, staring at the puddle.

Her words nearly sounded sincere, but before I could process her bizarre reaction, the ground rumbled and we both whipped our heads in the direction of the sound. Two riders were galloping their way down the path, headed straight for us.

"I'm fine, I'm fine," Taylor shouted as she splashed through the water and onto dry ground. "Go, go! You have to win this race!"

Standing on the side of the puddle, waving her arms wildly for me to move, I saw a glimpse of Taylor that had not yet been visible to me. Maybe she wasn't such an evil person. Maybe.

But I could tackle that thought later. Right now, I had a race to win. Knowing Taylor was okay, I turned Chance in the opposite direction and the cool wind whipped against my face as we pounded down the path again, headed towards the final turn.

From the look on Casey's face, it must have been a sight to see as Chance and I blew around the corner. Red cliff rocks on one side, thick green trees on the other, and two galloping horses on our tail. At our entrance, the worry melted off his face and he positioned Rocky with his butt towards us, ready to run.

Chance soared over the narrow creek like it was a raging river, matching my enthusiasm. Casey cued Rocky and gravel spit out beneath his hooves as he matched Chance's speed. We shot past Linda who was standing on the ground, grumbling and holding the reins of both her buckskin gelding and Star.

A team of two cowboys riding two huge sorrels scrambled to catch us. They hollered in the background as we galloped out of the woods and onto the open grassy field. Side by side, Chance and Rocky's sleek bodies bunched up and lengthened further and further with each stride until I was certain we couldn't go any faster. Their front hooves reached out past their outstretched noses.

Ahead of us, the town of Three Rivers jumped and shouted, gathered around both edges of the yellow finish line. The muffled voice of the announcer rattled in the distance as I turned my eyes to Casey.

Amidst a blurry background, Casey's crisp blue eyes twinkled. His black cowboy hat had blown off his head and was hanging by the leather string around his neck, exposing his sandy brown hair whipping in the wind. And, he was wildly laughing...exactly the way he laughed that evening in the mountain when I rode Chance for the first time.

I laced my fingers through Chance's ebony mane as we galloped across the finish line and I realized Chance was going to be okay. He was going to be mine. The thought overtook my whole being and I didn't even notice the mob of people screaming at our sides. All I could think about was everything I had gained from this Chance.

Eighteen

Chance's black coat glistened in the last bit of the evening sun. He stood quiet in the wash rack, resting his top lip against the wooden hitching post. His eyes inched shut as I hosed his body down. I sprayed his legs, moved to his shoulders, and finally drenched his back. The cool liquid carried away the salt, sweat and dirt earned throughout the race.

Then, using a rubber sweat scraper, I squeegeed the excess water from his slick body and stood back, admiring my pretty boy.

"Come on, Handsome," I cooed, untying his lead and turning toward the pasture. Chance willingly followed.

Sharkie nickered at the sight of his big buddy, welcoming him back. Closing the gate behind us, I unclasped Chance's halter and rolled my fingers along his cheekbone before releasing him to his herd.

"You're home now, Chance. You're home," I repeated before planting a soft kiss on his warm, whiskered nose.

The calm in Chance's brown eyes told me he knew my words were true. He knew we had both found our place on the Red Rock Ranch.

And, the summer had only just begun.

Turn the page to start reading Showdown (Red Rock Ranch, book 2)...

143

SHOWDOWN
THE RED ROCK RANCH SERIES
- BOOK 2 -
BRITTNEY JOY

Showdown: Book 2

Taylor and Lucy mesh together like a tight cinch and a broncy horse-- an explosion waiting to happen.

Blonde and sassy, Taylor Johnson is used to guys falling at her feet. Blue ribbons always come easy and dropping a grand on new cowboy boots and a pair of chaps is the norm. Taylor's life is perfect so why does the new stablehand keep getting under her skin?

A newbie to Red Rock Ranch, Lucy Rose is comfortable in a ponytail and jeans. Her makeup routine consists of a dirt smudge and Chapstick. And, if she had her choice, she'd spend every minute with her beloved horse Chance . . . and far away from Taylor-- the rodeo princess in need of an attitude adjustment.

But, in a twist neither saw coming, Taylor and Lucy are forced to work together. Will they play nice? Or will their summer at Red Rock Ranch go out in a bang?

Turn the page to start reading...

Prologue

❤

Taylor

The screen door squeaked open and jolted me awake as it slapped shut. My heart pounded at the unwelcome sound, but I kept still, not wanting to open my eyes or move an inch off the cushioned lounge chair.

"You're going to be late for your lesson," Mom announced in her matter-of-fact tone, clicking across the deck. I peeked at her through squinted eyes, willing her heeled sandals and manicured toes to walk silently against the wood.

"Taylor, are you listening to me?" she continued, and I knew that my wish for silence wasn't going to happen.

I lifted my head, peeling my cheek from the damp beach towel, rolling onto my back. "I'm not really in the mood for a lesson," I replied, using my arm to shield my face from the hot afternoon sun. I probably soaked up more sun than I should have, but I needed the time alone, away from the world. I was still fuming after losing the Cowboy Race this past weekend and everyone around this ranch reminded me of it. Especially Lucy.

"Don't be like that. Linda's staying at the ranch an extra week to help you prepare for that show this weekend," Mom said, smoothing out the front of her crisp, white linen pants and tucking her smooth blonde hair behind her ears. She wasn't looking at me while she was talking. "And, she's going to that thing with you tomorrow too."

I stared at her, wondering why she thought it was a good idea to wear white linen pants on a ranch. "And, by 'that thing,' are you referring to the awards ceremony for the Cowboy Race...*that I lost?*" I arched my eyebrows, waiting for her response.

She finally looked at me. "Don't be a sore loser, Taylor. And, don't be late for your lesson with Linda. Your father and I are paying good money for your trainer to stay here and work with you." And with that, Mom turned and headed down the stairs. Her heeled sandals clanked obnoxiously with each step. "I'm headed to the main cabin to have coffee with Mrs. Owens."

Sighing, I stood from the chair and let the towel drop to the floor. I adjusted the strings of my red bikini and leaned against the deck railing to watch her depart. My Mom didn't get it. Actually, she didn't get me. The "horse-stuff" was like a foreign language to her. No wonder she didn't understand why I was so pissed about losing the Cowboy Race.

I started riding when I was six years old. I've had countless lessons with a world class trainer and shown against serious competition. My horse's pedigree was filled with champions. And that dang Lucy girl shows up at the ranch and beats me on some crazy black horse she found wondering through the mountains?

I closed my eyes, my jaw clenched in frustration, but the darkness didn't ease my mind. With my eyes shut, images of the race flashed through my head and I dissected each move I should have done differently. I could have won. I *should* have won. The thought made my stomach turn.

Even though my Mom didn't know the first thing about horses, her last comment stuck in my head. I shouldn't be a sore loser. I knew I'd be sore for a while, but I definitely wasn't a loser. And, I needed to remind everyone of that.

Nineteen

Lucy

Chance stretched into a long trot and I posted in the saddle. Moving along in a controlled bounce, I focused on keeping my heels down and my upper body still. I needed to stay balanced on his broad back, ready for anything - a spook, a jump. Chance and I were a new team and I was still learning his buttons.

"Sunny has to lope to keep up with Chance's trot!" Marilynn shouted with a giggle as the palomino mare reached Chance's side.

I smiled at the sight of Sunny. One of the dependable ranch horses, she was a sweet, bomb-proof mare that barely moved as she loped along. Marilynn, a fellow stablehand and new friend, looked like she was riding a golden rocking horse.

Chance seemed enchanted by Sunny as well, and cranked his head to get a better look at his riding partner. But, in doing so, he lost his balance and took an awkward stride sideways. I gathered the slack in my reins to correct his step, but wasn't quick enough. As we lurched to the side, my knee bumped into Sunny's shoulder.

"Oops, sorry," I said as I got Chance under control.

"No worries," Marilynn noted, patting the mare on her withers. "Nothing rattles this girl." She was right. I hoped Chance was learning a thing or two from Sunny.

As we approached the barn, the horses slowed to a walk and I scratched Chance's black neck. "What a good boy," I said, praising him for his efforts today. Chance lowered his head, relaxing into my touch. We still had a lot of work ahead of us, but Chance and I made leaps and bounds in a short time. We trusted each other now and that was half the battle.

"What else is on our to-do list for this afternoon?" I asked, referring to the list that Mr. Owens, the ranch owner and our boss, had written up this morning.

Marilynn brushed a loose strand of her brunette bob out of her face and pulled a piece of paper from her jean pocket, letting the reins rest on Sunny's neck. Sunny marched on like a little soldier as Marilynn read over the list.

"Let's see," she started. "What's left on the list for today? We moved the goats into the far pasture so they can eat down the blackberry bushes. We checked on the new heifers. Everyone is good there. Looks like all we have left to do is haul fresh salt blocks out to the pastures. We'll get the four-wheelers for that, though. Then we have a trail ride scheduled for this afternoon."

"Perfect," I noted, knowing how much I loved my summer job as a stablehand at the Red Rock Ranch. There wasn't a chore I didn't enjoy doing. Being around the horses all day, every day, was a dream. But, I did wonder when Mr. Owens would start giving me jobs with Casey again.

Ever since Mr. Owens stumbled upon a kiss Casey and I shared during the over-night camping trip, he had been keeping a close eye on us. Actually, Mr. Owens specifically stated that there would be nothing "inappropriate" going on under his watch and threatened to give my Dad a call if there was. I mean, it was just one kiss...*one kiss I relive over and over in my head every single night as I fall asleep*. Okay, maybe Mr. Owens did have a little something to worry about. Hopefully, he won't keep Casey and me apart all summer.

Throwing my leg over the saddle, I hopped down from Chance. "Thanks for the ride, buddy," I said, rubbing my hands up and down his neck in a mini-massage. Chance leaned into his reward.

"If you take the horses back to the barn, I'll go get the four wheelers and start loading the salt blocks." Marilynn handed me the end of Sunny's reins. "Just put them both in the cross-ties. They can relax a bit before our trail ride."

I agreed, and gathered the leather reins. With one horse on each side of me, I started towards the barn.

Stepping through the open door and onto the concrete floor, my heart skipped a beat as my eyes scanned the building. On the opposite side of the aisle, the rusty farm truck was parked, the bed full of fresh hay bales. And, I realized what Casey's chore list consisted of today.

Reaching over the open tailgate, Casey grabbed a rectangular bale from the truck bed and hauled it off by its string twine. He effortlessly carried it to the corner of the barn, swung his torso, and launched the bale to the top of the pile. Pushing it tight against the stacked bales, Casey's defined arms were hard to ignore, especially since his t-shirt sleeves were pushed up, revealing his hard-earned muscles.

I sighed involuntarily and concentrated on walking so I wouldn't trip over my own feet.

Turning back towards the truck, Casey pushed his sandy blonde hair from his eyes with a leather-gloved hand and noticed me watching him. He slowed for a second and shot me a smile - heat warmed my cheeks and I waved, the reins dangling from my hand. I tried to think of something clever or sweet to say, but words only jumbled around in my head without making a sentence.

The end of the Cowboy Race was a blur, but I specifically remember the hug Casey gave me after I dismounted. The crowd was cheering in the background and I had my head buried in Chance's black mane, both arms wrapped around his neck, tears of pure joy rolling down my face. Casey ran up behind me, spun me towards him and lifted me from the ground into a bear hug. If I hadn't been holding onto Chance's reins, I think he would have spun me in circles. It felt great...beyond amazing being wrapped in his arms and I wanted that feeling again. My heart pounded in my ears as I relived the scene, but the sharp beat of heels on cement broke my gaze.

Shiny black knee-high boots followed by clean tan breeches entered through the barn's center door and turned in my direction. Taylor. The heartbeat in my ears jumped straight to my chest.

The last time Taylor and I exchanged words was at the final jump of the Cowboy Race. She had been sitting in a puddle, drenched in mud, horseless, and defeated. But it wasn't her snarky comments that surprised me. It was the hint of gratitude in her eyes when she realized I had come back for her - to see if she was okay. I had never seen that side of Taylor before – the vulnerable side.

"Lucy," Taylor said in a minimal greeting as she strutted down the aisle and I realized I was standing directly in front of Star's stall.

"Hi Taylor," I responded, glancing side to side. Chance and Sunny were staring at me too, patiently waiting for me to lead them somewhere. Chance bumped my elbow with his nose, wondering what the holdup was. "Are you headed out on a ride? I'll get these guys out of your way."

"Lesson," she noted, pointing out my lack of specificity.

I took the hint. I clucked and the horses followed me as I got out of her way.

"Okay, do you need me to get you anything for your lesson?" I had to ask. No matter how rude Taylor was, she was still a paying guest at the ranch. And I worked here.

Taylor pushed Star's stall door open and the chestnut mare walked over to greet her. At least someone seemed happy to see her. She slipped a halter onto Star before responding, but never turned to face me.

"I don't need *your help*," she replied, and led Star out of her stall.

I forced myself to keep walking. I wanted to tell Taylor exactly what kind of help I thought she needed.

That was the Taylor I knew. I don't know what Taylor I got a glimpse of in that mud puddle.

Taylor

"I want her stretching into the bit. Long and low," Linda announced from the middle of the sand arena. She adjusted the white visor on her head and followed me with her body as I trotted Star around the arena.

"Long and low and *forward*!" Linda shouted the last word and tossed her thick blonde braid over her shoulder so it fell down her back. "*Forward*, Taylor. You need to loosen her up. Prepare Star's muscles and ligaments for the workout."

At times Linda could be harsh, but she knew what she was doing. Years of lessons under her instruction had molded me into the rider I was today. She pushed me and critiqued me and eventually praised me – which was more than I could say of my own mother who barely paid attention to my rides. At the horse shows my Mom was more concerned with her social activity than my riding ability.

I squeezed Star's belly with a light touch of my calves and felt her extend her trot underneath me. I lengthened my reins and Star lowered her neck, stretching her nose out to make contact with the bit. She was such a good girl. So smart and talented.

"Good, good. One more lap like that and then I want to see some serpentines," Linda said and then pointed to three evenly-spaced orange cones placed down the long center of the arena. "You are still warming her up so keep allowing her to reach out long and low with her neck. As you make your way through the serpentine, sit for one beat and then start posting with the opposite diagonal at each cone.”

The exercise itself was not difficult for Star, or for me, and the rhythm of Star’s smooth stride soothed me into a relaxed state.

“Good,” Linda praised in a stern tone as I passed the last cone and continued trotting along the arena rail. “Now give me some shoulder rolls. Roll your shoulders back and loosen your own muscles. I want you both loose and ready. We are going to polish your lead changes today.”

I loved lead changes. They were technical and magical. Being suspended in the air for a second between leads was a thrill. And, doing one right after the other felt like dancing.

Linda continued. “We’ll get them polished up and nobody will be able to touch the two of you in your pattern classes at the show this weekend. Now, pickup your canter and start the serpentine again. At each cone I want to see a lead change.”

A grin grew on my face – probably for the first time since the catastrophe of the Cowboy Race. So what if we got beat at some stupid race...it was practically a trail ride. It wasn’t a real competition. Star was a show horse. I was a winner. And, I had a bedroom full of blue ribbons and golden trophies to prove it.

I gathered the reins in my hands and asked Star to move into a canter on the right lead. She rocked forward into her smooth stride without hesitation. Turning towards the first cone, I began to prepare for the lead change.

“Be conscious of your balance, Taylor,” Linda reminded me. “Move with Star through the lead change. Don’t throw her off.”

In the last stride before we passed the cone, I straightened Star’s body using my reins and my seat before moving my right leg back a few inches on her belly. Star collected her whole body and switched her lead effortlessly, cantering on. The following two lead changes were as smooth as the first. The graceful movements made me feel like a ballerina.

Linda applauded with three succinct claps. "Beautiful, beautiful. Now, canter on and try three lead changes on a straight line down the long side of the arena."

Star cantered on like a champ, her long flaxen mane rolling ever so slightly with each stride. Riding on, I patted her withers and mentally prepared myself for our next lead change. But, before we hit the long side of the arena, laughter broke my concentration and my gaze shot over my shoulder.

Marilynn and Lucy were leading a line of horses & giggling kids out for a trail ride. The group trotted along the dirt path next to the arena and Lucy waved as they passed by.

Star couldn't have cared less about the ruckus, but my jaw clenched at the sight of Lucy and that black horse. I looked away without responding and tried to focus on my riding.

As Star and I circled the end of the arena and started down the long side, I asked for the first lead change. Star picked her head up, but instead of changing her lead, she pinned her ears, kicked out, and then continued on with a few crow-hops.

"What the heck?" I yelled with a squeal before pulling Star to a stop. She still had her ears pinned as Linda walked towards us.

"What happened to your relaxation? Your focus?" Linda asked with a grimace on her face.

I knew exactly what happened to it, but I wasn't going to admit that some no-name girl had thrown off my game. "I don't know. I think Star is just being crabby or something."

Linda came to an abrupt stop next to Star's shoulder. "Look at your hands. Now. Look at them," she demanded and I followed orders.

Glancing down towards the saddle, I saw my hands locked in fists around the rich mahogany leather reins. My knuckles were actually white.

I immediately released the reins, letting them fall to Star's withers. She lowered her neck and I could have slapped myself. I just caused Star's tantrum.

Linda patted Star's copper chest. "Your mare is very sensitive. Very intuitive. Even when I first started her training as a two year old she responded to the slightest of touch. You have to be aware of your body and how you affect her."

I brushed my hand over Star's silky mane. "I'm sorry. That was my fault. It won't happen again."

"All right then. As long as you know you were the cause," Linda said as she turned to walk back to the center of the arena. "Again, please."

I gathered my reins and asked Star to walk off, knowing I still hadn't gotten over my loss to Lucy. I rolled my shoulders, loosening my back, and took a deep breath. I couldn't believe I let her get in my head.

Twenty

Lucy

Mr. Owen's massive Chevy truck rocked side to side as we pulled off the gravel road and inched onto the field. After a ten minute drive, we were now on the outskirts of Three Rivers - the small town closest to the ranch. I peeked over my shoulder and through the open window at the silver stock trailer, following the truck as we turned. Both Chance and Rocky peered through the slots on the side of the trailer, assessing the situation.

Chance let loose an ear piercing whinny. I closed my eyes and gripped the nylon seatbelt constricting my chest. I hated that he was stressed.

"He'll be fine. Don't worry your pretty little head," Marilynn reassured me and smiled from the front seat. "We're going to an awards ceremony, Lucy...an awards ceremony for a race you and Casey won. It's going to be fun."

I forced a polite smile. I appreciated Marilynn's encouragement, but my nerves were wound tight. Getting an award in front of the whole town of Three Rivers was not my idea of fun. I wanted to pick up the winning check and head back to the ranch. I wasn't sure why the town had to make such a big deal out of this.

Mr. Owens stopped the rig next to a line of shiny trailers and put it in park. People were milling around, brushing and saddling their horses.

"Ladies, we have arrived," he announced, grinning from ear to ear as he covered his gray hair with a black Stetson. I should have asked Mr. Owens if he wanted to accept the award on my behalf. He was reveling in the fact that his ranch was the talk of the town, on account of Casey and me.

I jumped out of the truck and climbed on the trailer fender to peek at the boys. Chance looked like a giraffe - his head cranked high in the air, surveying the scene outside the trailer. Next to my giraffe, Casey's horse was chewing on a mouthful of hay, unconcerned.

"Thanks for being so calm, Rocky," I whispered to the gray gelding through the open slot. "This is Chance's first time in a trailer. I'm glad he was with you." Actually, I was certain that Rocky was the only reason Chance arrived in one piece. "Hang-on, boys. We'll get you out of there in a few seconds."

I climbed down from the fender and hurried to the back of the trailer to find Casey and Dusty, one of the other ranch hands, a step ahead of me.

"Hey there," Casey greeted me with a smile as he swung open the back door of the trailer. "You ready for all this again?"

I nodded my head, but the look on my face must've given me away because Casey stepped closer and put a hand on my arm. "Chance will be fine, Lu. Once he knows you're here with him, he'll settle down." His blue eyes were full of certainty.

"Thanks," I replied. Casey's words managed to make me feel a bit better.

"Coming through," Dusty interrupted and Casey and I split apart, making room for him to lead Rocky out of the trailer. Stepping backwards, I brushed my fingers over my arm, grazing the very spot Casey had just held. I could still feel the heat from his touch.

Dusty moved Rocky to the side of the trailer and Casey stepped in. "Let me lead Chance out for you this time. I'm not exactly sure how he's going to unload." Casey's words were not a question, but he still looked to me for approval. "Is that okay?"

Chance's hooves beat against the floor as he paced, shaking the trailer. I wanted to lead Chance out myself, but I nodded. I had to be reasonable - Casey had the strength to stop Chance from bursting out of the trailer. If I tried and couldn't stop him, we could both get injured. At my approval, Casey unlocked the steel divider. Chance whinnied at the top of his lungs, looking for Rocky.

"Easy boy," I said, faking a calm tone - and knowing I wasn't hiding my nerves from Chance.

Casey ran his hand up Chance's tense, sweaty neck and clipped the lead rope to his halter. Turning towards the open door, Chance began trotting in place, but Casey held tight to the lead. With his neck curled and nostrils flared, Chance looked like a live grenade - one that could go off at any second. I wanted them both out of that tiny rectangular space as soon as possible.

Reaching the edge of the trailer, Casey stepped down, but Chance bulked, snorting at the new smells ahead of him. Casey moved to the side, leaving slack in the lead rope and allowing Chance time to relax...but Chance decided he wanted out.

Picking up his front legs, Chance held himself in a half-rear like a Lippizzaner Stallion in a Levade. I sucked in my breath, imagining his head hitting the trailer ceiling and trampling Casey on his way out.

Instead, Chance launched himself out of the trailer in one smooth motion, landing squarely in front of Casey and me.

I let out my breath and Casey chuckled. Chance looked like he surprised himself as well.

"Disaster averted," Casey said. "Looks like we need to practice that maneuver back at the ranch."

"I'll put 'trailer unloading' on the to-do list," I noted with a straight face as Casey handed me the lead line. I made sure I had a good grip.

Taylor

Star's silky mane slid through my fingers as I finished one long braid which accented her slender neck. The pink ribbon laced through her flaxen hair was the perfect touch. Satisfied with my work, I patted the end of the braid and grabbed the bottle of ShowSheen from the horse trailer tack room.

"You're a show pony," I whispered to Star as I sprayed the ShowSheen on a towel and wiped the polish down her neck, chest, and finally over her crisp white blaze. "These ranch horses got nothing on you."

I reached into my pocket and Star's ears perked forward at the crinkling of a peppermint. I smiled as she lapped the treat out of my hand in one swift motion and then nuzzled my pockets, looking for more.

"Better get her bridled," Linda said as she threw the reins over Cash's withers and stepped into the saddle. Linda's heavily muscled buckskin had an appropriate name. Cash was a world champion barrel racer and I'd watched Linda rake in the titles from his back. Cash wasn't used to settling for second place either.

"Okay, let's get this over with," I muttered and offered Star one more peppermint before grabbing her bridle from the trailer.

The entire town of Three Rivers crowed the sidewalks of Main Street. Little kids lined the curbs, ogling the horses and snatching up candies. The mayor and his family led the front of the parade -

siting in an antique truck waving at the crowd as they rolled down the pavement.

Star and Cash walked side by side, their metal shoes clinking against the asphalt as we followed the trivial procession. Even though it was painful, I forced myself into rodeo-queen mode. Sitting up stick-straight and pushing my shoulders back, I cupped my hand and began a slow wave.

"I *hate* that we have to ride behind Lucy and Casey," I griped to Linda between gritted teeth while keeping a smile plastered on my face.

"Well, Ms. Taylor. They won," Linda said matter-of-factly as she scanned the spectators. "They were better than us. Take note and let's not allow that to happen again."

Linda's words hit me like a slap across the face and I lost my smile as they sank in. Not only did I let myself down, I had disappointed Linda.

My hand continued in a slow waving motion, but my eyes narrowed in on the two riders ahead of me. That crazy black horse pranced next to Rocky like a Thoroughbred being ponied to the starting gate. And, when Chance jigged sideways and bounced off of Rocky, Casey reached out for Lucy's shoulder.

I cringed as Casey slid his fingers down Lucy's arm and grabbed hold of her hand, squeezing it tight. But, something clicked as I watched Lucy relax with his touch...and then Chance slowed to a walk.

Casey was Lucy's confidence. He was the glue that kept Lucy from falling apart under pressure. She couldn't have won that race without him. She couldn't have beaten me without him.

Now, it's time I break her glue.

Twenty-one

Lucy

Draped across my chest, the pearl white sash fluttered in the wind as I hopped down from the wooden stage. My feet hit the grass and I was thankful the ceremony was coming to an end. The chaos was over and the most important thing was tucked safely in my pocket - the prize money. Running my hand over the bulge in my jean pocket, I reassured myself that Chance would *officially* be my horse after today.

I straightened my sash and turned to Casey. "I'm surprised they didn't give us crowns."

Casey chuckled. "Enjoy the spotlight for a bit, Lucy. We earned it. Besides, I think you'd look pretty good in a tiara." He winked at me and my heart palpitated as he reached out his hand. "Would my winning race partner care to join me for a dance...to celebrate?"

With my heart thumping, I froze up. I didn't dance. I was born with two left feet and they only worked together in the saddle. "Um, I'm not sure you want me stepping on your feet."

"Come on," Casey urged and grabbed my hand. His touch pulsed electricity through my fingers. "I'm not taking 'no' for an answer. I wore my steel-toe boots. You can stand on my feet for all I care."

Not waiting for a response, Casey turned to pull me away from the stage and onto the field, now filled with country music and dancing couples. He didn't have to pull hard. I followed.

Casey weaved his way into the center of the bouncing crowd and turned back to me. He raised my hand – the one he was holding - and gently placed his opposite arm against the middle of my back. My free hand fell naturally on his shoulder, against the crisp cotton of his button-down shirt.

I looked straight into his baby blue eyes and swallowed hard, hoping he couldn't feel me tremble. "I hope you're good at leading," I warned, and wondered if I'd be this nervous dancing with anyone else.

Casey grinned and his dimples appeared. "Don't you worry, Ms. Lucy. I won't throw out any of my fancy dance moves...not just yet."

Casey's dimples didn't make me any less nervous, but I couldn't keep myself from smiling. Feeling my cheeks flush, I looked away, hoping my face wasn't fire-engine red. I had to focus on my feet and looking at Casey's handsome face was too much of a distraction.

We started with little steps, rocking in a small circle. Casey kept enough tension in his arms to firmly direct my body and soon we were keeping beat with the band.

Gazing over Casey's shoulder and past the crowd, a glimpse of the open field reminded me why we were here. "Can you believe we were riding Chance and Rocky across this grass just a few days ago? Galloping them across the finish line?"

"I can believe it," Casey said with confidence as he lifted my hand to turn me in a spin. "We make quite the team."

I'm not sure if it was the directional change or Casey's statement, but my mind lost track of where my feet were going. Instead of completing a ladylike spin, I tripped myself with my own foot. The tip of my boot caught on my opposite ankle and attempts to yank it loose only pushed me further off balance. I knew I was going to fall (not so gracefully) to the dance floor and I couldn't even force out a whimper in protest of my clumsiness.

But, to my surprise, Casey managed to keep hold of my hand as I spun. Still gripping tight to my fingers, Casey's arm wrapped around my waist and his opposite arm grabbed my back – keeping me from suffering a face-plant to the grass.

Now cradled in his arms, I stared at Casey's hypnotizing eyes and perfect white smile – lingering only a few inches from my lips. "I told you." I shrugged my shoulders sheepishly. "Two left feet."

Casey laughed, his sandy blonde hair grazing his eyes. "Well, that's one way to get close to you."

The few inches between us held a clear tension. If I had known this position would come from my clumsiness, I would've been tripping all over the ranch.

Then the music stopped…or at least I think it stopped. I couldn't really tell because I was stuck in my own world – with Casey. And, the rest of the universe fell away as he held me.

"Attention race participants." The speakers crackled. "Attention race participants. In ten minutes we will be taking a group picture in the field. Please saddle your horses and bring your trophies."

The heat rushed back to my cheeks as I pulled my feet underneath myself to stand upright. I knew Casey caught me blush that time.

Letting go of me, Casey cleared his throat. "I guess I'll go get our trophies from the stage." His statement lacked his earlier confidence. "Meet you back at the trailer to saddle up the horses?"

"Yeah. Sure. Sounds good." The words fell out of my mouth faster than I could think them. I wished that had happened anywhere but here - in the middle of all these people, with Mr. Owens looming in the background.

I wanted Casey to kiss me. I wanted to kiss him. A lot. A lot more than I wanted to go get my picture taken.

"I'll see you in a few minutes then," Casey said without breaking his gaze.

"Yeah, in a few minutes," I replied and forced myself to turn away. I started walking before a full on kiss-fest was broadcast to the whole town of Three Rivers...and we both put ourselves in danger of losing our jobs.

Walk it off, Lucy. Walk it off.

My mind was cluttered with images of Casey as I approached the horse trailer - his perfect smile, his bronze skin, his broad shoulders. I had never been so fixated with someone before. What was wrong with me? I shook my head back and forth, trying to jar the images from my mind.

Luckily, Chance's familiar low nicker brought me back to reality, reminding me that the horses needed to be saddled. I looked ahead to see Chance's ebony coat and Rocky's gray dapples shining in the sunshine. The two geldings were tied to the stock trailer, happily eating from their hay nets.

"Hey there, buddy," I sighed and rolled my hand down the length of his forehead, wondering what I was going to say to Casey when he got here with the trophies. We'd already been warned. It was clear we weren't to be getting too close. Kissing was definitely out of the question. I needed to rein in these feelings before I got myself in trouble.

Chance watched me with his soft brown eyes as he grabbed another mouthful of hay. He seemed to be analyzing my thoughts as he chewed.

"Don't judge me, Chance." I grinned. "I don't know where these feelings came from...or what to do with them. Any advice for me?"

I scratched along his neck with my fingertips, thinking I should get the saddles out of the trailer just as Chance stopped chewing. He raised his head, his ears forward and alert.

I stopped scratching. "Did you spot Casey?" I whispered, wishing Chance could actually give me a piece of advice. I took another deep breath before turning around. I had to play it cool. *Play it cool, Lucy. Play it cool.*

I spun on my heels and started blabbing before I could get lost in Casey's eyes. "I guess we better get these guys tacked up for the --" But my words stopped midsentence as I locked in on the man standing before me.

"Mr. Jackson," I exhaled abruptly. Billy Jackson - Chance's former owner. Or, Chance's *soon-to-be* former owner. I still had to give Billy the prize money from the race. And, he still had to sign over Chance's registration papers to me.

"I prefer Billy," he replied and stepped forward. In the tiny space between the trailers, I immediately realized we were isolated from the crowd. And Billy's presence gave me the creeps. The last time I was alone with him I got pushed to the ground and bounced off a fence board. I wanted to get this transaction done as quickly as possible.

I grabbed the check from my back pocket and handed it to him. "Here it is. Here's the check for $5,000. I had the race committee make it out in your name."

I expected Billy to snatch it from my hand and throw Chance's registration papers at me. Instead, he cocked his head and spit a line of brown tobacco juice from the side of his mouth. A grin grew on his face, revealing his yellowed teeth.

The check dangled between us.

"Here," I said again. The small piece of paper was starting to feel heavy between my fingers.

"I don't want the $5,000 anymore," he announced without blinking.

I was certain I didn't hear him right.

"What?" The word creaked out of my mouth and my heart began thumping against my rib cage. "What do you mean?"

Billy adjusted the bill of his dusty ball cap and raised his chin. "He's a race winner, right? Seems like he should be worth more than $5,000."

Billy stood, unwavering, in front of me and I couldn't wrap my head around his statement. Did this low-life just ask me for more money?...because *Chance and I* won the Cowboy Race?

"You want more money for Chance?" The words fell from my mouth, followed by my heart, as his intentions fully hit me. I glanced back at Chance, not wanting to take my eyes off Billy for long. Chance was pacing. I wanted to console him, to tell him not to worry, but I didn't know what Billy was planning to do.

I tried to slow my breathing, not wanting this monster of a man to know I was scared – terrified that he would take Chance from me. "You said $5,000. You can't go back on your word...you just can't." I couldn't believe this was happening. He didn't even want Chance. The only thing he cared about was squeezing every dollar he could get out of "his" horse. "Five thousand dollars was the deal!" I caught myself in a scream as I turned away, reaching for Chance's lead. I pulled at the end of the rope, releasing the knot and freeing Chance from the trailer. There was no way this creep was taking my horse.

Billy was now walking towards us and I knew I had to get out of there, fast. "Give me the horse," he grumbled, reaching out his hand.

"No! Get away!" The words shot out of my throat and I threw the lead over Chance's withers. I braced myself to jump on his back and gallop far, far away when a female voice jumped in.

"What the heck is going on?" Taylor asked as she appeared from under the front gooseneck of the horse trailer. She held a bridle in one hand and a second place trophy in the other. "It sounds like a freaking Jerry Springer show over here."

Taylor was not who I wanted to see, but at least I had a witness so this lunatic wouldn't assault me again. "He's going to take Chance," I sputtered out and pointed at Billy. Tears were gravitating to my eyes.

Taylor crossed her arms and threw her blonde braid behind her shoulders with one flick of her head. "Oh for God's sake, Lucy. Are you sure?"

By this time, Linda had wondered over and was also checking out the scene. I looked from Taylor to Billy and back again. "Yes, Taylor," I shouted, baffled at her question. I didn't have time for her backhanded comments. "Yes, I'm sure. He just asked me for more money and I don't have any more to give."

Taylor's forehead wrinkled up in confusion. "I thought that horse was already yours."

"He should be," I said, swallowing my tears and wanting to spit them at Billy.

Taylor paused and the confusion left her face. She shifted her eyes away from me, to Billy. "How much do you want for him?" Her question came out in an even, cool tone.

"Ten Grand." Billy threw out the number without a moment's hesitation, focusing his sights on Taylor.

"What?!" Billy wanted $10,000, double the money I had, and now Taylor was offering to buy Chance? Every protective instinct I had was gnawing at my gut, telling me to stop the insanity. "You can't have him! Either of you!" The ground felt like it was spinning and I held tight to a chunk of Chance's thick mane, balled in my fist.

"Settle down, Lucy. Crazy doesn't look good on you," Taylor said and looked at me with one eyebrow cocked while executing a half-roll with her eyes. "I don't want him."

Was this some kind of sick game?

Taylor nodded her head towards Linda. "Can you grab my checkbook from the trailer? It's in my purse in the living quarters."

Linda froze for a second, probably just as confused as I was. "Are you buying half of that black horse? Don't you want to run that by your parents first?"

Linda's questions seemed valid, but Taylor looked annoyed by them. "I'll just buy a few less pairs of boots this month and tell my Mom I needed a new show outfit. They'll never even miss the money," she answered. "And, no, I'm not buying half of that horse."

Taylor's eyes never left mine through her explanation. She was talking directly to me. "I'll give Billy the additional $5,000 if you agree to work for me for one weekend." She paused before continuing, probably soaking in the shock on my face. "Linda's assistant broke her arm on a spill off a colt yesterday so she can't work at my show this weekend. We need someone to feed, pick stalls, groom, clean tack...someone to do all the chores no one else wants to do."

Linda stared at Taylor with her mouth gaped open but snapped it shut when she realized she was announcing her shock to everyone.

Billy spat another line of tobacco juice from his mouth. "I don't care where the money comes from. Get it to me and that horse is yours. Otherwise, I'm taking him with me right now. I'm sure I can get $10,000 out of someone else."

My pulse flicked violently against the side of my neck. I knew Taylor was basically asking me to be her slave for the weekend. I had no idea what I was in for or why she would even offer up the money, but I knew I could make it through one weekend of anything in order to keep Chance – to make him mine. I locked eyes with Taylor and shook my head up and down. I was in.

I laid flat on top of my quilt, staring at the A-frame wooden ceiling of my bunk. Today had sucked every ounce of energy from my body. I considered falling asleep in my clothes, but the thought of laying in filth all night gave me motivation to move towards the shower - a little motivation anyhow.

My fingers rubbed tiny circles on the thick paper pressed to my chest, reassuring myself that it was real. I raised the paper to eye level and examined the text I had already read a million times during the truck ride back to the ranch.

Chance's registered name was "Fool's Gold" and he was seven years old, registered to the American Quarter Horse Association. The picture in the corner of his papers showed a spindly, long legged foal standing close to the golden rump of his mother. His brown fuzzy coat and curly mohawk were a far cry from the stark black, strong gelding I knew today. But, his trusting brown eyes were the same. The picture made me smile.

But, what really made me smile was the back of the paper. The back of the paper was solely text and I scanned over my favorite part – the signature of the seller, Billy Jackson, and the signature of the new owner, Lucy Rose. Chance and I officially belonged to one another. This paper told me so.

I hugged the paper to my chest again and felt myself drifting to sleep. My eyelids slipped shut and I decided it wasn't so bad to sleep in dirty jeans.

Twenty-two

Taylor

I sat on top of my teal blue suitcase, yanking the zipper shut and examining my pile of luggage. I had one massive suitcase, a matching teal tote bag, a boot bag, a cowboy hat case, and a purse – all of which needed to be hauled across the ranch and loaded into my horse trailer. How was I supposed to do that by myself? If I was at home, one of the maids would have already taken care of it. Annoyed, I stood up and reluctantly gathered my essentials for the weekend.

The wheels on my suitcase rolled smoothly across the wooden floors of the cabin, but maneuvering around furniture with the stack of bags was quite the task. Heading through the living room, my boot bag caught on a floor lamp, knocking it to the ground in a crash. I jumped forward, startled, and managed to trip over a pair of particularly high heeled gold sandals which sent me stumbling out the screen door, my suitcase nipping at my heels.

Catching my balance outside the door, I growled to myself. Only my Mom would pack a pair of gold stilettos for our summer trip to the ranch. I cursed the gold sandals as I gathered my bags – which were now scattered across the deck.

"You okay, Taylor?" A concerned voice asked from the walking path below the deck.

Peeking over the railing, I recognized the boy in khaki cargo shorts and a Broncos baseball hat. Andy from Denver. Yesterday he wandered over, uninvited, while I was sunbathing – in my bikini. He was here with his uncle or something. Just got here a few days ago and was staying in the cabin a few doors down.

Andy was no cowboy, but I was sure those broad shoulders could carry a suitcase. Otherwise it was going to be a long walk to the horse trailer.

I gave my suitcase a push with my knee and waited for it to topple over, banging against the wooden boards. "Oh my goodness," I exclaimed and gave a loud sigh. I tossed my hair over my shoulder like a pro and walked across the deck to lean on the railing. "Hey, Andy. What you up to?" I marveled at my soap-opera dramatics.

"Do you need some help?" he asked.

"Oh, that would be great. Do you mind? I just need to get these bags to my horse trailer. They're so heavy." I cocked my head and raised my eyebrows. "I don't want to bother you if you're busy, though."

I watched Andy's well-muscled calves flex as he flew up the stairs to the deck. Mr. Athlete grabbed all of my bags before I moved an inch off the railing. "No problem. Glad to help," he said and flashed a smile.

I wrinkled my nose and gave Andy my signature grin. "Well, aren't you just a sweetheart."

Boys - they all fall for the same thing.

On the trek to the trailer, I complimented Andy on his gentleman-like behavior. "Oh, Andy. You've been such a big help." I unlocked and opened the door to the trailer's living quarters and stepped aside. It was amazing what a little ego-stroking could get you.

"No problem," he said as he tossed my bags in and handed me my purse. "Maybe we can hangout when you get back from your horse show? I'll be here all week."

"I'm sure we can." I winked at his trusting face, knowing we wouldn't hangout when I got back.

"Are you ready to load the horses?" Lucy's overly sweet voice rang through the air and I peered around Andy.

Lucy stood at the back of the horse trailer with a small duffel bag slung over her shoulder. Her mousy brown hair was slapped into a slick ponytail, like always, and there wasn't a stitch of makeup on her face. And, Casey was standing at her side. I didn't understand what he saw in her.

"Yeah, Linda will be here in a few minutes," I said, the annoyance in my voice audible. "I'll get Star and then you can load Chance." I turned my attention back to Andy. His clean-cut, city-slicker look was no match for Casey's worn Wranglers and farm-earned muscles. "Have a good weekend." I patted Andy on the shoulder and walked towards the barn without looking back. I was done flirting.

Lucy

I sat in the backseat of the truck wishing I didn't get motion sickness from reading. The horse magazines I packed were peeking out the top of my bag, taunting me, but I figured I better wait to read them. About the only thing that could increase the tension in this cab would be to puke all over the soft leather seats.

The hour long drive to the show grounds contained only essential conversation. There was no chit-chat from Linda as she drove or from Taylor in the passenger seat. In fact, in the first few minutes of the ride, Taylor turned the radio to a country station and glued her eyes to her phone's screen.

I was thankful the scenery out the window kept me entertained during our silent trip. The highway to Bend, Oregon was lined with rustic ranches and fields full of livestock. I watched two young girls canter their horses through a lazy herd of cattle...and the scene brought my thoughts back to Chance.

Yesterday, when Taylor said I could bring Chance with to the show, I was relieved. He gave me a sense of comfort and I knew I needed his presence to help me through the weekend. Plus, it would be good for him to experience new things. We could experience them together.

I'd never been to a horse show of this caliber. In the little information Taylor gave me, she explained that we were headed to the Northwest Stock Horse Championships. Since then, I'd been imagining insanely expensive horses stalled up in pristine barns and accomplished riders walking the show grounds. This was going to be a foreign world for Chance and for me.

And, to prove my imagination right, Linda slowed the rig as we approached what seemed like miles of bright white fencing. I gasped as the truck turned down the long paved driveway that ran between the manicured fields. The green pasture on our right housed a small herd of broodmares with babies at their sides. They grazed happily as their coats gleamed in the sun. And, the pasture on our left enclosed a group of spunky yearlings frolicking through the grass.

Peeling my eyes away from the prancing babies, I looked ahead to find the biggest barn I had ever seen. The sprawling building was covered in cream siding with green trim and a matching roof. The highest part of the barn was lined with classic square cupolas, topped with horse-shaped weather vanes. The gorgeous barn looked like it had been ripped from the pages of *Horse Illustrated*.

Coasting along, we followed a line of trucks and trailers as the driveway morphed into a circle - surrounding a colorful rose bed and a massive bronze horse. The metal statue seemed to watch our rig as we circled it and parked in the unloading area. Yep, I was out of my league.

Linda put the truck in park and grabbed her purse from the seat. "All right, girls. I'm headed to the show office to get us signed in. You two can unload the horses. Taylor, you know where our stalls are."

All three of us hopped out of the truck and into the chaos of the unloading area. Metal shoes clip-clopped along the pavement as horses stepped off trailers and were guided to the barn. Horses whinnied greetings to each other as their people pushed wheelbarrows full of feed and polished tack. People and horses marched in every direction, but it was controlled chaos. Everyone seemed to know where they were going. Except me.

Following Taylor to the back of the trailer, I waited for more instructions. She unlatched and opened the double doors. "Unload Chance and wait for me. You can follow me to the stalls."

"Okay," I replied as she handed me a lead rope.

I stepped into the trailer and unclipped the metal separator which kept Chance standing in one place during the ride. Swinging open the metal half-wall, I watched Chance curl his neck towards me, the whites of his eyes showing. His neck and chest were damp with sweat, but he was in one piece...unharmed. And, it didn't look like he did any damage to Taylor's trailer. Thank God.

"Don't worry, Chance," I reassured him as I clipped the lead rope to his halter and lead him towards the rear of the trailer. "We are just here for the weekend. It'll be fun. It's good to try new things."

As we edged towards the back of the trailer, I gripped the lead rope in preparation for Chance's projectile launch to the pavement. I squeezed tight, hoping I could hold on.

Chance hesitated at the floor's edge, but actually followed me to the ground with just a hop. I breathed a sigh of relief and turned to pat him on the neck. "See. We're getting better at this stuff."

Chance didn't notice my pat. His ears were pricked forward, but he was *not* paying attention to me. His eyes darted around, evaluating the busy parking lot, and his head inched higher and higher with each passing second. I felt like I was holding onto a kite in a wind storm.

"Follow me," Taylor instructed as she unloaded Star from the trailer and turned towards the barn.

I followed, hoping Chance would relax in Star's presence, but he seemed to think his friend was running away from him. Chance danced at the end of the lead rope and put his whole body into a whinny that made my ears ring. His sides quivered from the force of his shriek.

Taylor shot an annoyed look over her shoulder and my grip on Chance's lead rope couldn't get any tighter. "Easy, buddy. Star isn't leaving us. We're going with her." I hoped the stalls weren't far away. Chance needed some time to chill out in this new environment – in a safely enclosed space.

Taylor walked Star through the open barn door and into one of the aisles, which wasn't any quieter than the unloading area. Star sashayed down the center of the aisle with slack in her lead rope as Taylor nodded and waved to acquaintances. They smiled back as Taylor passed, but their facial expressions changed as soon as they laid eyes on me. And, they moved out of my way - fast.

Chance's hind end swayed side to side in protest of my slow speed and I was certain we were going to plow through anything in our way. He pulled me along like a water-skier while still prancing on his tip-toes.

I wanted to turn him in a circle, to break his focus and calm him down, but there was no room to do it. Expensive saddles, tack boxes, brooms, and wheelbarrows cluttered the aisle.

"Chance, come on," I whispered through gritted teeth and gave him a quick yank on the lead rope. He didn't acknowledge my tug and I wasn't sure how long I could hold him back. Panic sank in as I realized I was losing a battle with a thousand pound horse.

Just then, Taylor turned Star into a stall. Looking at me through the metal bars, she nodded her head towards the next stall. "You can put Chance in there."

Without stopping or saying a word, I aimed Chance towards the open door and leapt through. He nearly stomped my toes as he followed, trotting into the cedar bedding with a snort.

I slammed the door shut behind us.

We made it.

Thankful he was now enclosed, I peeled off Chance's halter and snuck out of the stall to watch him pace from a safe distance. He circled the square space and screamed into the air, nostrils flared. Star responded by pinning her ears flat to her neck and flipping her head towards Chance, apparently telling Chance to shut his mouth.

"Well, this should be interesting," Taylor said, coming up beside me and crossing her arms.

Her statement crept into my head and I suddenly wondered if it was a bad idea to bring Chance along.

Twenty-three

Taylor

I ran my fingers over the embroidery on the back of the tall director's chair. The horse image circled by gold lettering looked sharp against the black fabric, but it was the words that brought a smile to my face – "California Stock Horse Grand Champion" followed by my name, Taylor Johnson.

I took a sip of my iced latte, reading the words a few more times before I hopped into the seat. I crossed my legs and spread a glossy magazine over my lap. But before I flipped through the pages, I lingered on the cover – a picture of last year's Northwest Stock Horse Champion. The girl's face beamed with pride from atop her horse while surrounded by family, friends, and trainers. And next to the winner sat a massive gold trophy and an engraved saddle.

I wanted that. I wanted that trophy, that saddle, that picture, that moment. And, I knew Star and I could do it. We could take the championship title this weekend...and next year our picture would be featured on the cover. The thought made my stomach flutter in anticipation.

Breaking into my daydream, Star reached her neck over the fabric guard on the stall door. She nuzzled my shoulder, sniffing for a treat.

"You want it too, don't you?" I whispered before pulling a peppermint from my pocket. Star's brown eyes widened at the crinkle of the wrapper and she gobbled the candy from the palm of my hand. I gave her a kiss on her smooth muzzle. "You sure would look pretty in that championship saddle."

Star blew a few soft breaths against my cheek before she pinned her ears and bit at the stall bars, forcing Chance to step back. I chuckled at her mare-ish behavior. "I know, I know. He's annoying. But, at least he stopped screaming at the top of his lungs." Star popped her ears forward and focused her attention back on me. Sniffing around for another treat, she got a whiff of my latte and nuzzled the plastic cup while I took a drink.

"When is your first class tomorrow, Ms. Taylor?" The cheery voice caught me off guard and I looked up from my drink, mid-sip.

"Hey, Tim. I was wondering where you were. When did you get in?" Tim Green, Linda's husband, came to every show. He didn't ride, but he was there supporting Linda and her clients. He hauled horses, kept them fed, and was our biggest cheerleader.

Tim set down an armful of fabric - the stall decor - and brushed off his polo shirt before walking over to give me a hug. "Left California late last night and got here a few hours ago with the trailer and horses." He put his hands on his hips and took a breath. "So how are my favorite princesses doing?"

Tim called everyone sweetheart or darling or dear. He referred to Linda as *baby*, but Star and I were his only princesses. His nickname always made me feel special.

"We're good." I smiled. "And, our first class is western horsemanship tomorrow. Probably about 9:00 or so."

"I'll be there with bells on," Tim replied as he grabbed a footstool and carried it across the aisle.

Lucy made her way from the back of the barn and joined him, another stall drape under her arm.

"Lucy, can you grab the bucket of clasps over there? I'll need you to hand them to me as I hang these up." Lucy did as she was told and stood next to the footstool, handing Tim clasps as he hung the hunter green drapery from the top of the horse stalls. "I could get used to having you around, Lucy. I'm usually doing this all by myself while the girls ride." Tim chuckled. "It's quite the scene."

"Glad to help, Tim. That's what I'm here for."

Could she be any more of a suck-up? I closed my magazine and hopped off my chair. "Speaking of riding - I'm going to saddle up and practice my pattern for tomorrow morning. Star needs to stretch her legs."

"All right. Linda will be looking for you soon anyhow. She's outside by the practice pens," Tim noted, as he set the last clasp in place and stepped down from the footstool to admire his work. "Sure does look classy when it's all set up. Doesn't it, girls?"

"Looks great, Tim," I said. Tim always did a wonderful job of setting up our show barn. All of our stalls were now covered in hunter green drapery sporting Linda Green's name in bold, gold lettering. The aisle was lined with potted plants, sporting red and white flowers, and a cute table and chair set completed the vision.

Scanning the setup, I was reminded of the two empty stalls across the aisle. I wondered which horses Tim hauled in for the show. Whoever they were, I was ready to go find them.

Lucy

I tucked the nearly empty bucket of metal clasps back inside the tack trunk and closed the heavy lid. Completing a full turn, I couldn't believe I was standing in a horse stall. It was unrecognizable after Tim and I unloaded Taylor and Linda's trailers, filling the space with tack, show clothes, brushes and feed.

The walls were covered with a thick, hanging fabric which matched the hunter green drapery on the front of the stalls and the floor was padded with a checkerboard of rubber mats. A small radio in the corner played soft country music and I closed my eyes to inhale the scent of clean leather. The tack room was like my own little world, quiet and drama-free.

I could hear Chance in the next stall, finally munching on his hay, and I pictured myself curled up in a folding chair reading a book. That sounded like heaven.

But, I knew I had a full list of chores to complete today. No reading just yet. Instead, I pulled the draped door aside and stepped out of the tack room. In the aisle, Taylor had Star cross-tied and was fiddling with her saddle. I was glad she was heading out for a ride. She hadn't said much to me today, but she made up for the lack of communication in the form of evil stares.

I still didn't understand why she wanted me at her show – except that Linda was down an assistant. I guess the thought of doing any real work was enough to make Taylor put up with me. I knew the only reason I was putting up with her was because she wrote me a check, and helped me keep Chance.

"What's next on the list, Tim?"

He wiped his brow with the back of his hand and pondered my question. "Well, my stomach is starting to growl. I think I'm going to round up some lunch for us all. How do sub sandwiches sound, girls?"

"Sounds good," Taylor and I said in unison, catching each other's gaze and breaking it just as quickly.

"Okay, lunch will be served for the Green Team in about an hour." Tim grabbed his ring of keys from the table and chair set. "Taylor, can you let the rest of the gang know?"

"Will do," she said, while buckling the throat latch on Star's bridle.

"Actually Taylor, why don't you take Lucy with you to the practice pen? Show her around the grounds a bit while I go get lunch."

Taylor was gathering the reins in her hands, but stopped abruptly at Tim's suggestion. I was expecting a sharp comment to follow, but she gave us a stiff smile instead.

"Sure," Taylor noted and turned to me with the slight raise of an eyebrow.

"You girls have fun. I'll see you in a bit." He waved as he exited the aisle. Tim didn't realize he was sending me off with the enemy.

I followed Taylor, but kept my distance, as she led Star through the barn and into the unloading area, now occupied by just a few straggler trailers. The chaos of unpacking had dwindled and I wondered if everyone was out to lunch.

Walking along the barn, still in silence, we passed the wide entrance to the indoor arena. The metal lights blared bright from the ceiling and a single tractor spun circles in the sand footing, making it smooth. There wasn't a single soul riding around the rail.

"The main arena is closed to riders until the show starts tomorrow morning," Taylor noted. "And the warm-up arenas are located on the side of the barn. That's where we're going."

We turned around the corner of the barn and I could see where everyone was. There were three large outdoor arenas – the practice pens. They sat side-by-side and were packed with horses. Horses and riders moved in every direction – left, right, circles, straight. It was basically a three-ring circus.

"The middle arena is for pleasure horses. That's where I'm going to ride Star," Taylor said, putting a boot in the stirrup and grabbing hold of the reins.

"Do you want me to hold Star while you get on?" I offered, feeling like I wasn't doing much just standing there and watching.

"No, she's fine," Taylor responded before hopping into the saddle with the grace of a gymnast. "I see Linda. Follow me. I'm sure she has more stuff for you to do."

I followed - a little concerned that I was going to be run over on our way to the practice pens. Horse traffic was everywhere. *They should have a pedestrian crossing out here or something.*

Nearing the arenas, I spotted Linda too, standing next to the white fence and completely focused on the riders ahead of her.

"Ask him to jog. Relax. You're doing fine out there," Linda said with her arms crossed, not acknowledging our presence as we walked up beside her. "Make sure to keep your heels down and your elbows at your sides."

Taylor sat straight-backed and quiet in the saddle but she must've caught the look of confusion on my face.

"Linda's talking to one of her clients in the ring," Taylor noted and then pointed to her ear. "She has a headset on."

Oh. That made a little more sense. I was starting to wonder if Linda had lost her marbles and was muttering riding instructions to herself.

"Where's her client?" I asked, glad to have *something* to talk to Taylor about. I scanned the masses of riders making their way around the ring and noticed many of them were wearing headsets or Bluetooth devices. A line of trainers stood outside the arena, directing from the sidelines.

Taylor was scanning the crowd, too. "I'm not sure which of Linda's clients came here for the show."

"Tiera," Linda said, still not facing us, and then continued with her instructions. "That's it. Keep him jogging. That's a good pace."

"Oh. Great," Taylor grumbled and locked her eyes on someone in the crowd. I couldn't tell if her comment was meant to be sarcastic or if she was just being herself. Sarcasm seemed to be Taylor's form of communication.

She sighed and pointed to the opposite side of the pen. "See the gray horse with the baby pink saddle pad? That's Georgie and the rider is Tiera."

I stretched onto my tippy-toes and bobbed back and forth until I could get a good look through the commotion of the ring. But once I did, Tiera was hard to miss.

"Yeah, I see her."

Tiera's horse was pale gray, nearing white, and his pink gear popped against his light-colored coat. In fact, she had her horse decked out in pink – pink saddle pad, pink split boots, and pink crystals on her bridle and breast-collar. Not to mention, Ms. Tiera was sporting pink cowboy boots and a matching blouse. The color complemented her tanned skin and white blonde hair which was wrapped in a tight bun at the nape of her neck. Her horse jogged around at a perfect tempo, with a perfect headset. He didn't blink an eye at the horses bobbing and weaving around him.

I exhaled in defeat. Tiera - even her name screamed 'princess'. I was going to have to put up with two divas this weekend. Lord, help me.

"That's good, Tiera. Walk him now and cool him down. Come out here and park him next to me when you are done. We'll discuss your ride."

Linda turned in a sharp spin towards Taylor and me. I almost jumped back when she started handing out directions. "Taylor you're up next. Head into the arena and grab the headset from Tiera. I need you to run Star through a few lead changes on the rail. Get her warmed up first." Linda's sentences started and ended abruptly, but nearly ran together.

I chimed in as Star walked off. "What do you need me to do, Linda?"

Linda handed me a ten dollar bill and nodded her visor-topped head towards a white shed surrounded by picnic tables. "I really need a latte." She blurted the statement like it was a life or death situation. "Can you get me one from the food stand? Skim milk, extra shot, one pump of vanilla."

"Sure. A latte it is," I replied, stuffing the crisp bill in my pocket and repeating her order in my head. I didn't know a latte had so many ingredients.

Situated on top of a grassy mound, the snack-shack had a perfect view of all three arenas. From the latte line, I analyzed the horses and their riders – from a safe distance.

The farthest arena looked to be a warm-up pen for halter horses. The muscular animals trotted around next to their handlers and, when asked to halt, squared up their legs on command. The middle arena was packed tight with pleasure horses, loping slow and steady, but the arena closest to the snack-shack interested me the most - gamers, cowhorses, and reiners.

The horses in the third arena turned fast, ran hard, and stopped harder. The riders chatted as they loped next to each other and, for the most part, they were outfitted in jeans and baseball hats. I pictured Casey riding Rocky in that group – we'd been apart for half a day and I was already missing him like crazy.

Ten minutes later and hot latte in hand, I strolled down the hill, walking slower than usual so I could watch the horses.

Two girls walking in front of me slowed their pace too.

"He's so cute," one girl whispered enthusiastically to the other and giggled. Their ponytails bounced in unison as they scanned the arena. I didn't think they were looking at the horses.

"And, I heard he's single again." Both girls squealed.

Although I wasn't interested in their chatter, I quickly figured out who they were talking about. Along the rail came a boy, loping at a good pace on a bay horse. He looked to be about my age, dressed in dark wranglers and a black button-down. He tipped the rim of his cowboy hat and flashed his dimples at the two girls as he rode by.

Serious amounts of giggles followed and I caught myself rolling my eyes at their response. The girls continued walking and gossiping, but I stopped to watch. It wasn't the boy I was impressed with. It was his horse.

His horse's dark mahogany bay coat gleamed like freshly polished wood and emphasized his muscular build. His jet black mane floated in the wind, the ends skimming the boy's jeans as they loped along in perfect harmony. His mane had to be three feet long - like a knight's horse in a renaissance movie.

As they rounded the end of the arena, the bay horse picked up his pace across the diagonal. He stretched his frame, lengthening his neck before practically sitting in the sand and gliding into a sliding stop. Dirt sprayed out from under his feet like an ocean wave and he left 15 feet of straight hoof tracks in the ground behind him.

I sucked in a breath. Wow. He was beyond gorgeous.

I could have watched for hours, but my fingers started to burn, reminding me of the steaming hot latte I was holding. I rotated it to my opposite hand, cursing the thin paper cup separating my fingers from the boiling liquid. I needed to get back to Linda before I suffered third-degree burns.

But, as I turned to walk off, I met a sharp wave of dirt which ricocheted off my body. I froze in my tracks and caught the end of a perfect sliding stop from the corner of my eye...just a few feet in front of me.

Whipping my head around, I confirmed the identity of the horse and rider – the team I had just watched in awe. I shot my meanest glare towards the boy, knowing he saw me standing just feet from the fence, and I brushed off the front of my shirt. Little pebbles of sand fell to the ground and, as my eyes followed them, I realized the plastic top of Linda's latte was covered in arena dirt too. *Oh no. Not good, not good.*

I blew the dirt off with a quick breath and wiped the lid with the bottom of my shirt. I examined the white plastic, looking for any evidence of filth.

"Sorry about that," the boy shouted towards me, now trotting his horse in my direction. The bay horse stopped obediently at the fence and the other riders rode around him. "Didn't mean to get you dirty. Let me buy you another drink." His words came out like an apology, but his smile and dimples screamed of arrogance.

I continued with my mean glare. "You should watch where you're going." A rider with any manners would know not to execute a sliding stop just feet in front of an on-looker.

"I was," he said with a twinkle of his green eyes. "I saw you watching me ride. Thought you wanted a closer look."

I stared at him, stumped for words. This kid was obviously full of himself and expecting me to giggle and fall to pieces in front of him - just like the two girls did a few minutes ago.

"I was watching your horse...not you." *Wow. What a jerk.* But before either of us could mutter another word, I caught a glimpse of Linda approaching.

"There you are, Lucy," she said, walking towards me and holding out her hand. "I thought you ran away with my latte."

I handed over the drink. "Sorry, Linda. I was just..."

Linda continued talking, not allowing me to finish my sentence. "I see you've met Jace."

What?...Jace? I glanced at the boy. He looked as confused as I was.

Linda ignored our lack of words. "Jace, how is Hammer today? Is he stiff from the trailer ride?"

"No, he feels great. Like always."

"Good, good."

I started to connect the dots. Jace was one of Linda's clients. Hammer was the other horse that Tim hauled up from their barn in California. I wiped the mean mug from my face.

"Why don't you head to the middle of the arena and show me his spins," Linda continued and then took a big sip from her latte.

I bit my lip, hoping she wasn't getting a mouthful of sand.

Swallowing, Linda turned to me, squinting her eyes. "Did you order me a hazelnut latte?"

"No. It's skim milk. One pump of vanilla. Extra shot." I cringed inside.

Linda licked her lips and then shrugged her shoulders. "Hmmm. Tastes a little nutty."

Jace chuckled. "I think that's the snack-shack's signature drink. Right, Lucy?" He winked before trotting off.

I kind of wanted to punch him.

Twenty-four

Taylor

I lifted the reins and Star smoothly transitioned from a canter down to a walk. I bent over her withers and rubbed both sides of her neck, giving her a massage as we walked through the packed arena.

"You are a superstar," I cooed, pleased with our ride. It was practically perfect.

Exiting through the gate, I sat extra tall in the saddle and felt the crowd's eyes on me - it felt good. *That should give my competition something to grind over. We are going to kick some butt at this show.*

I scratched Star's withers with my fingernails. She bobbed her head, seeming to agree with me, but I think she just liked the scratching.

"Hey, Taylor. Wait for me." The screechy voice broke into my happy thoughts and I glanced over my shoulder to find Tiera waving frantically as her horse trotted towards me. She was leaning forward and making kissy noises with her mouth, enticing her horse to speed up, but Georgie only knew one speed - and that was slow.

I could've asked Star to trot and left Tiera in the dust, but I was feeling nice in that second. Besides, I didn't want Star exerting herself after that great ride.

"Are you headed back to the barn?" Tiera asked, as Georgie jogged up next to Star and eagerly slowed to a walk. She didn't wait for my answer. "I'll walk with you." Tiera stared at me with big blue eyes and a bright smile. She was like an overly eager puppy dog – which annoyed me.

"Just watch out for the other riders through this area. It's kind of a mess until we get closer to the barn. Don't run into anyone." Tiera's parents bought Georgie from Linda this past spring. He was a seasoned lesson horse, but Tiera was a green rider. And, I certainly wasn't going to be embarrassed by a newbie.

Tiera snapped to attention, absorbing my warning. "Thanks, Taylor. I'll be careful." She inched Georgie closer as a pack of barrel racers trotted past. Star pinned her ears in protest, but neither Tiera nor Georgie seemed to notice.

"Oh my goodness," Tiera exclaimed with an excessive amount of energy as the horses trot by. "I *love* those glittery things on their hooves! I need some of those for Georgie...in pink!"

I rolled my eyes. "First of all, those are called bell boots," I explained. "Secondly, Georgie will never move fast enough to need them."

My explanation didn't make sense to Tiera and she scrunched her petite nose. I decided to change the subject. "Has Linda taken you to any shows this summer or is this your first?"

Tiera broke her gaze from the band of trotting horses. "Oh, yes. She took me to the Pleasure Classic about a month ago. Georgie and I took first place in the walk-trot western pleasure class."

"And?" I asked, when she didn't continue.

Tiera raised her shoulders at my question. "And...I was really happy with our ride?"

"No, I meant what other classes did you ride in?"

"Just the one. That's the only one Linda signed me up for."

This conversation was becoming more work than it was worth.

"All-righty then. Was just asking." I ended our little chat with a forced smile and diverted my eyes away from Tiera while I rolled them again.

The Pleasure Classic was an annual show just down the road from Linda's stable and usually the first show she took her rookies to - for good reason. Only locals showed up and the handful of audience members consisted of proud moms with flashing cameras. It was also the first show I competed at. I rode Linda's retired show horse and cleaned house in every pleasure, horsemanship, and trail class for which I was eligible. I was six years old at the time and my legs were just long enough to fit into the stirrups.

Obviously, Tiera was a slow learner. And, I was done babysitting.

Swinging my leg over the saddle, I dismounted and walked Star into the barn. Tiera followed. Close to our stalls, I caught a whiff of warm bread, reminding me it was lunch time. My stomach gurgled as I marveled at the sight of several subway sandwiches displayed on the table in the aisle. Tim stood close, setting out paper plates, plastic silverware, and napkins. Thank God for Tim.

"You're my hero," I said, as I stopped next to the table and ogled the sandwiches.

Tim's face lit up. "Aw, thanks, Taylor. I do what I can around here. Got to keep this place running like a well-oiled machine. Help yourself when you are ready. I got a turkey-bacon-avocado sub just for you."

"Perfect. Thank you," I said as Tim entered the tack room and opened the cooler, rounding up drinks for the crew. The ice rattled as he searched. "What would you girls like to drink?"

"Coke for me, please," I said and Tiera chimed in with something about chocolate milk. I tuned her out and turned to Star. "Come on Babydoll, let's get you untacked. It's time for your lunch, too."

I took a step towards the cross-ties, but froze as I noticed a shiny bay horse and a tall cowboy walking down the aisle - headed straight for me. The boy's black hat brim covered most of his face as he chatted with Linda, but his smooth stride and lean muscular build were as unforgettable as his horse's beauty.

Jace is here?

My heart immediately bashed against my ribs, hard. I grabbed my chest with both hands trying to muffle the sound, convinced Jace would hear it thumping against my bones. I was torn between running away...or running to him. But, either way, I was certain my feet wouldn't work.

Why is he here?

My breathing was audible and, next to me, Star tensed. She arched her slender neck and snorted, loud. She was reading my body language and convinced I saw danger coming for us. She was right.

At Star's snort, Jace raised his eyes and connected his gaze with mine. *Run, Taylor. Run.*

My feet suddenly shot into motion and Star trotted with me through the open door of her stall. She danced in the bedding, but stayed close to my shoulder, her ears pricked forward, looking for the object of my panic. Every step of Hammer's metal shoes on the concrete increased my anxiety as I realized I had backed myself into a corner.

And then the black hat stepped in front of Star's stall.

"Taylor?" Jace asked, as though he didn't expect to see me here.

At his question, Star jumped and snorted like a dominant stallion. In the stall next door, Chance added to the commotion with a high pitched whinny.

Jace seemed startled by his welcome. "What's with Star?"

I took a quick breath. "Nothing. She's fine," I replied abruptly and ran an unsteady hand down her neck. "I think you scared her."

"Sorry. Didn't mean to," Jace responded and offered an easy smile. "I didn't see you in the practice pens."

I avoided his eye contact and focused on unsaddling Star. Hanging a stirrup on the saddle horn, I loosened her girth. "Didn't know you were looking for me."

Jace paused before answering my deliberate statement. "I was. Seems like it's been forever since I've seen you."

One month and two days to be exact.

"Yeah, well, I didn't know you were coming to this show." I tried to slow my breathing, but felt the hurt bubbling up my throat. "How was I supposed to know you were coming to this show, Jace? Did you forget how to use your phone? Did you forget about me until you got here?" I felt the blood pumping through my body, getting hotter with every word. I pulled the saddle from Star's back and marched through the stall door.

"Here, Taylor," Jace offered. "Let me help you with that."

"No," I responded before he could finish his sentence. "I don't want your help."

Jace stood there, holding Hammer's reins in his outstretched hands, and didn't move an inch as I walked past him. I wasn't sure if his face was plastered with pain or shock.

Pushing past the thick curtain covering the tack stall door, I flung my saddle on top of the rack and then grabbed onto it for support. *Get ahold of yourself, Taylor.* But it wound me up further knowing that I let Jace get to me - again. The heat in my cheeks boiled over into my eyes and I watched teardrops hit the leather on my saddle.

And just when it couldn't get any worse, the curtain rustled and I turned to find Lucy entering the tack room with a couple of buckets.

She stopped with only one foot in. "I'm sorry," she stammered, obviously not expecting to catch me crying. "I...I should've knocked or something. I was just going to get some grain for the horses. I can come back later."

She started to back out as I wiped my tears with my forearm. Just what I needed. This was none of her business.

"Why would you knock? This is a tack room." The words come out harsher than I meant them to and Lucy backed out of the doorway as I stomped through.

Lunch no longer smelled good. I'd lost my appetite.

Lucy

Chance nickered as I pushed open his stall door and crept in, halter in hand.

"Want to stretch your legs?" Chance had his hay spread across his stall floor, but he walked right to me and bumped my arm with his nose. "I know, I know. Sorry. You've been stuck in this little box all day while I took care of everyone else." I patted his forehead. "Now the horses are fed and tucked in for the night. And, we have a little time to play."

I felt more comfortable leading Chance through the barn now that it was quiet. Most everyone had retreated to their trailer or hotel to rest up for the night.

I walked down the aisle and Chance followed, cautiously watching me as we passed stalls filled with horses. They were all dressed in clean sheets and munching on their dinners.

"A little less scary without all of the commotion, huh?" I asked Chance and rubbed him on the shoulder.

Outside, there were a few riders still working in the practice arenas but the far pen was empty. The sky glowed with peach tones - the last bit of sunlight for the day - as I pulled the metal gate shut and unclasped Chance's lead.

He stared at me, unsure what my gesture meant.

"Go ahead," I urged and shooed him away with a few flicks of my hand. "Stretch your legs, big boy."

And with that, Chance hopped to the side and took off in a spurt of bucks which turned into a gallop. His head held high, he circled the arena - but he wasn't running in panic. He was playing.

What a difference this was from the first time I lunged Chance. Then, he ran in fear, pulling the rope out of my hands as he leapt away from me. Now he frolicked in the arena, kicking and snorting and having fun.

Relaxing, I sat in the dirt, pulling my knees to my chest and watching Chance exercise himself, getting his penned-up energy out. He really wasn't made to sit in a stall. I needed to make an effort to exercise him as much as possible while we were here - to keep him from going crazy in that little box. Maybe tomorrow night I could saddle up and ride. It was pretty peaceful this time of night.

As I contemplated the next evening, Chance trotted a few more laps and then made his way to me.

The air was cooling off and the last bit of sun had disappeared behind the trees. Chance reached his head down and I kissed his outstretched nose, wishing I could bottle this moment.

Chance's hooves clip-clopped through the barn as we explored the other aisles on the way back to his stall. Ears pricked forward, Chance was just as curious as I was.

The aisles were filled with color. Each stall was draped in fabric (just like Linda's) which displayed farm colors and logos. Severson Farms, The Jones' Stables, Rick Reedy's Ranch. Everyone seemed quite proud of their own name.

And, there were no naked horses. Every horse we passed was dressed from head to toe in a sheet and a hood. It was hard to evaluate any of the horses when all you could see were their eyes and feet. Although, I was certain they were all gorgeous and expensive.

Tomorrow they would each be unveiled, shined up and ready to perform. I couldn't wait to watch.

Finished with our outing, Chance and I headed back to Linda's area of the barn. But as we turned the last corner, I jumped, not expecting to run into anyone. But there, in the middle of the aisle, was Tiera. She stood with her back to me. Well, she was *kind of* standing.

Tiera had one foot planted flat on the concrete, but her opposite leg was pulled straight in the air, parallel to her petite body. Her hand held her ankle in place and the toe of her tennis shoe was delicately pointed to the ceiling.

I didn't know a person's body could bend like that. I knew mine sure couldn't.

I led Chance on, cautiously, both of us nearly tip-toeing along the cement. I didn't want to scare Tiera as she looked like she was lost in her own world.

As we neared, Tiera released her leg and turned her body into a blur of spins, propelling herself with her own weight, her hands posed in the air like a ballerina on a jewelry box.

Then she stopped mid-twirl, surprised to see me too. "Oh...Hi, Lucy," she said as she regained her balance and pulled the tiny white earbuds from her ears. "I didn't know you were still here."

"Sorry, I didn't mean to sneak up on you like that," I said, leading Chance into his stall and noting that Georgie's door was wide open. The big gray gelding stood obediently in his heavily bedded stall, half asleep and content with going nowhere. "I just took Chance out for a little exercise before turning in for the night. Is there anything I can do for you? Is Georgie okay?"

"Oh, he's fine," Tiera noted. "My Mom and I just stopped by because I forgot to grab my show clothes for tomorrow."

Standing in the middle of the aisle with no makeup, black yoga pants and a simple hooded sweatshirt, Tiera looked younger than I had thought she was. I really hadn't spoken to her today - other than watching her ride in the practice pen.

I tried to make small talk and break the silence. "Do you dance?" It seemed like an obvious question to ask.

Her face lit up. "Yeah, I just started this past year, but I've been learning ballet, tap, jazz, everything. I want to try out for the dance team when I start high school next year."

"Sounds fun," I noted, admiring her eagerness. "All of the balance and flexibility you get from dancing must really help with your riding."

"Yeah, that's what my Mom says, too." Tiera played with the strings hanging from her hood and then dug in her pocket, pulling out a peppermint for Georgie. Georgie perked up when she opened the plastic wrapper, but he waited for Tiera to come to him. He gently lapped the sweet out of her hand and Tiera patted him on the forehead.

Georgie could be the calmest horse I'd ever met.

"All right, Tiera. I've got a copy of your riding pattern for your horsemanship class tomorrow," a petite woman announced as she approached. I looked her up and down and there was no doubt she was Tiera's Mom. She was a brunette version of her daughter - same button nose, same ice blue eyes. They even had their hair styled in the same tight bun positioned at the nap of their neck.

"You must be Lucy," she said, holding out her hand. "I'm Amber, Tiera's Mom. Linda said she had a new helper for this show. Nice to meet you."

"Nice to meet you, too," I responded, shaking her hand.

Amber immediately peeked into Chance's stall. "Is this your horse?"

This time my face lit up. "Yes, this is my boy, Chance." I ran my hand down his neck, beaming with pride.

"He's gorgeous," she said and my heart swelled. "Did you meet our Georgie?" The slender woman practically skipped over to Georgie. She grabbed his nose with her hands and kissed him straight on the muzzle. "He's our baby. Right, Tiera?"

"Yep," Tiera responded and gave him another peppermint. Georgie's gray lip crinkled as he took the treat. He seemed used to the doting. It was pretty cute.

"He seems like a really good boy."

"Oh, he is," Amber cooed. "Well, Tiera, we better get back to the hotel and get some sleep. Big day tomorrow. Did you grab your show clothes from the tack room?"

"Got them," Tiera said and pointed to a thick garment bag laying over one of the chairs. Amber nodded and closed Georgie's door.

"Good night, Lucy," they both said in unision. Tiera waved to me with a smile.

I smiled back, realizing I had judged her too harshly. Tiera may be a bit of a princess, but at least she was a nice princess. "See you tomorrow."

It was 10:00 when I finished brushing Chance and gave him an extra flake of hay. It was time to go to sleep, but I dreaded crawling into bed as my sleeping quarters were in Taylor's trailer - the couch in her living quarters to be exact.

I had no problem sleeping on a couch. I just didn't like the idea of sleeping in the same trailer with Taylor. It was like letting my guard down in enemy territory.

The gravel parking lot was dark, but it was hard to miss Linda's massive trailer on display in the first row. The six-horse trailer with full living quarters rivaled the length of a semi-truck. Her name and barn logo were painted on both sides. The living quarters' lights were still on and I could see Linda and Tim, gathered in the kitchen, chatting and sipping red wine together. They looked like a cute couple.

Next door, Taylor's trailer looked small - only in comparison to Linda's - and I didn't see any lights on. Reaching for the door, I pulled the handle slowly until it clicked open. I tried to make as little noise as possible as I stepped inside. If Taylor was sleeping, I certainly didn't want to wake her up. She was not the nice princess type.

Inside, my eyes adjusted to the dark and about popped out of my head as I looked around. Taylor's trailer may have been smaller than Linda's, but her parents didn't skimp on any luxuries for their daughter. I don't know why I was surprised by that.

The trailer was dimly lit by the glow of a flat screen TV which hung on the wall and faced the queen-sized bed, tucked in the goose-neck of the trailer. Taylor was snuggled up amongst a mob of pillows and fuzzy blankets, zonked out. I hadn't seen her since our run-in this afternoon in the tack room. I had no idea what her tears were about, but I was glad she was sleeping and we could avoid the subject. Communication was not our strong point.

The rest of the trailer looked like a small apartment – a tiny version of a glitzy penthouse. The kitchenette was filled with stainless steel appliances and mahogany cabinets, finished off with a table for two. And, my "bed" was a smooth burgundy leather couch. A folded blanket and fluffy pillow were set on one of the cushions.

Well, that was nice of her.

I set my duffle bag on the floor and sifted through it to find my pajamas. Pulling off my jeans and sliding into my oversized cotton t-shirt, I felt the day wearing on me and sleepiness taking over. A big yawn almost swallowed my face and I about jumped out of my skin when I heard a phone ringing. My phone ringing. And, it was loud.

Oh my God. Where did I put my phone?

I frantically dug through my bag, pulling out pieces of clothing, magazines, a hair brush - trying to find the phone so I could stop the ringing. Five seconds felt like five minutes before I grabbed my phone out of my jean pocket and immediately picked it up.

"Hello?" I whispered with my hand cupped over my face.

"Lucy?" A confused voice asked. "It's Casey. Are you there?"

Casey? My heart jumped a beat.

"Hi Casey. It's me. Sorry, I'm whispering because I don't want to wake-up Taylor."

And, just like that, Taylor sat straight up in her bed, pulling the satin sleep mask from her eyes and glaring into my soul. "Do you mind? Kind of hard to get any sleep around here with you banging around and chatting it up."

She looked at me like I had been jumping on the couch and screaming at the top of my lungs.

"Um, Casey, can I call you back in the morning?"

"Sure, no problem," he responded, trying to hide the disappointment in his voice. "Sweet dreams, Lu."

"You, too." I said, forcing myself to hang-up. I really wanted to talk to Casey. I wanted to tell him all about my day...about the beautiful barn, the horses, and my time with Chance tonight. But, the look on Taylor's face made me close my phone and turn the ringer to vibrate. "Sorry," I noted as I crawled onto the couch and pulled the blanket around me, cocooning myself.

Taylor threw her body down on the bed with a dramatic sigh and I reminded myself she was the reason I got to keep Chance. I committed to working with her – actually, for her – this weekend and I needed to bite my tongue.

I opened my phone once more to send Casey a text, but there was already a text waiting for me.

SORRY TO CALL SO LATE. JUST MISS U. NOT THE SAME AT RRR WITHOUT U.

I smiled, despite the situation, and my body melted into the soft leather couch as I texted him back.

YOUR VOICE MADE MY NIGHT. MISS U TOO.

Twenty-five

Taylor

I inhaled the sweet scent, closing my eyes as I swallowed a swig of hot mocha. The whip cream coated my throat and the heat warmed my fingers, slowly waking my mind. Thank God for mochas. Thank God for caffeine. It was the only thing keeping my eyes open. If I could, I would curl up inside the warmth of this cup right now and fall asleep.

I shuffled down the barn aisle, the soles of my boots skidding along the concrete. I spent most of the night wide awake as my mind raced back to Jace. I just couldn't zone out. I couldn't get him out of my head. And every thought of Jace only increased my frustration.

A month ago Jace flat-out dumped me. He dumped me and never said one word why. He never called me again. He never returned one of my text messages. He dismissed me from his life without giving me a reason.

Who does that?

A jerk. A jerk does that…a jerk I thought I loved does that.

When I laid eyes on Jace yesterday, I was amazed I didn't punch him square in the face. I probably should have. I think that would've made me feel better.

Taking another gulp of warm, chocolaty liquid, I imagined Jace's stunned reaction as my knuckles cracked against his nose.

"Dreaming of something good, Taylor?"

I stopped my feet and opened my eyes at the sound of Linda's voice. "Kind of," I said with a shrug, watching her over the plastic top of my mocha.

"You look like crap," Linda noted without hesitation.

"Well, good morning to you, too," I replied, squinting my eyes in protest of her remark. I pulled the black sunglasses from the top of my head and placed them on my nose. "Just didn't sleep well," I added in a half-growl. "I'll be fine when the caffeine kicks in."

I'd make myself fine. Jace was not going to throw me off my game. I would not let him affect my riding.

Linda studied my face. Even with the dark sunglasses, she knew something was off. She nodded over her shoulder to the stalls. "Go spend some quiet time with Star and get your head back inline. Star is bathed and should be dry by now. She will need to get brushed out and then you can saddle her up." Linda patted me stiffly on the shoulder as she walked past. "There's fresh fruit and doughnuts set out on the table. Get something in your belly other than a mocha."

"Okay," I obliged, grabbing a banana from the table and feeling like I got a dose of mom-advice.

I walked to Star's stall and glanced at my watch as I pulled open her door. Two hours until my first class. I needed to snap out of it.

"Hey there, Babydoll." The words came out in a raspy whisper and Star turned her head to me, presenting a big mouthful of green hay. I moved closer and pressed my cheek against her withers, closing my eyes and breathing in her scent. Even through the fruity shampoo fragrance, I could still smell the wonderful aroma of horse.

It smelled like home. It was all I needed to feel better.

"Already dry, huh?" I asked, still pressing my body against her soft coat. "Linda is such a pro at bathing horses."

I picked my head up and stood back, scanning her chestnut coat from nose to tail. Not a spot of dirt. Her blaze and socks were the color of fresh snow and her coat a shiny penny.

I smiled.

But my happiness faded as obnoxious giggling rattled through the barn aisle. It was too early for giggling.

"You saved me, Lucy." Tiera laughed through her words as she appeared in front of Star's stall leading a wet Georgie. "Oh, good morning, Taylor." She continued chuckling. "You'll never guess what happened."

Her perkiness was about to send me over the edge. And, I didn't want to guess. "Was it super funny?" I emphasize the word "super," but my sarcasm was lost on Tiera.

"What?" she asked, slightly confused, but continuing with her story. "Anyhow, I was washing Georgie and I used the whitening shampoo. I got him all soaped up and then went to go find Linda because I forgot which conditioner I was supposed to use. Lucy came by and saw Georgie in the bathing stall covered in purple suds and she started rinsing him off. I forgot that whitening shampoo will turn your horse purple if you leave it on too long!" Tiera kept giggling and I wondered what planet this kid came from. "I mean, can you imagine if I turned my horse purple for the show? Thank goodness for Lucy!"

Speaking of the devil, Lucy appeared in a baseball cap and t-shirt, looking about as soaked as Georgie. "It's no problem, Tiera. That's what I'm here for."

"Yeah, that's what Lucy is here for," I noted, hoping they would both quit talking. "What are you washing your horse for anyhow, Tiera?" Tiera barely knew the difference between a forelock and a tail. I was surprised Georgie didn't turn into a purple grape.

Tiera paused to think about my question. "Well, I thought it would be fun. Plus, I've been hanging out with Lucy all morning.

She's been teaching me a bunch of stuff." Her toothy smile returned. "I even helped her wash Star."

My back straightened at her last sentence.

"Excuse me?" I thought Linda washed Star.

My eyes immediately shot back to my horse, reassessing the condition of her coat. I stepped around her to check for any imperfection.

"Tiera's a good helper," Lucy noted and my eyes shot to hers. "Is something wrong, Taylor? Did you want me to do anything else with Star before you saddle her up?" She must have caught the craze on my face – she was more observant than Tiera.

All my frustrations were now bubbling to the surface, uncontrollably. Why did *everyone* like this girl? Everyone wanted to be Lucy's friend. It was like the stars aligned for her, bowed-down for her. Tim liked her. Tiera liked her. Linda probably even liked her now. And, on top of that, she captured Casey's heart while my cowboy dumped me faster than a bag of stinky trash on a hot summer day.

I...Couldn't...Stand...Her.

I brought Lucy here to show her a thing or two - to let her know she wasn't as good as she thought she was. And now she was on my every last nerve. "This is not a play date, girls. This is a show and I am here to win. Please don't use my horse as a training device."

Tiera and Lucy looked at me like two baby deer in headlights. They didn't get it. They didn't understand how important this was to me – how seriously I took my riding. And, I wanted them out of my hair.

I continued my rant. "Tiera, you should be getting dressed anyhow. Hand Georgie over to Lucy. She'll put him in his stall."

Tiera followed my orders, turning on her heels and marching off.

"I'm sorry. I didn't mean to..." Lucy started, but I cut her off.

"The silver on my show saddle needs shining. The aisle needs to be swept. All the horses need fresh, clean bedding in their stalls, and I need you to saddle up Star while I get my show cloths on."

That should keep her busy. I only wanted to share my space with Star right now.

Lucy

I followed Linda down the aisle, carrying a bucket full of brushes, rags, and all kinds of sprays.

"You've got the fly spray, correct?" Linda asked, not looking up from her binder as she walked. She flipped through horsemanship patterns and multiple check lists as we made our way to the practice arenas. Her multi-tasking skills were impressive. I could barely carry a bucket, walk, and talk at the same time.

I scanned the bucket. "Yep, got the fly spray and lots of rags."

"Good," Linda noted. "Hammer has a fit about flies. He will need his legs and face wiped down with some spray soon. And, probably again every couple of hours."

"Got it."

Mental note - Jace's horse is a wimp.

The practice arenas were just as packed as yesterday, but now they were an array of colors. All the riders were decked out in their show clothes. There were bright pinks, flashy purples, neon greens and each color in between. A rainbow bounced along the white fence line and I glanced down at my t-shirt, full of horse snot and dust smears. I wondered how the riders kept their show clothes clean all day long.

Tim stood close to the arena, next to Tiera and Georgie. He waved us over with a smile.

Linda began walking faster. "Tiera, honey. Why aren't you in the arena warming up Georgie?" she asked. I noticed Linda took on a softer tone when she spoke to Tiera.

Tiera answered by dancing on her tippy toes, shifting her weight from one foot to the other as she handed Georgie's reins to Linda. "I really have to go to the bathroom," she whispered, her hand cupped to her mouth like it was a secret.

Linda grumbled a bit and I could see why. Tiera was dressed head to toe in pink – from her cowboy hat to her leather chaps. I wouldn't have expected anything else. But, there were zippers and buckles everywhere.

"You're not going to have time to warm-up Georgie if you run to the bathroom. And, I've got to coach Taylor, too. She is getting ready for her first class right now."

Tiera turned her blue eyes to me. "Lucy can do it. Right, Lucy? Georgie loves you."

"I...I guess I can," I stuttered. "If you really need me to."

Linda was quiet, processing her options, but Tiera never stopped dancing. In fact, her pace increased.

"Okay, okay. Hurry up, Tiera." And with Linda's approval, Tiera ran off, leaving me shaking in my mud-caked boots.

It wasn't Georgie that scared me. He was like an oversized golden retriever. It was the masses of well-trained riders in that overstuffed arena and the multitude of judging eyes in the crowd – that was what scared me.

I swallowed the spit in my mouth as Tim took the bucket from my hand. "I'll be the groom for a bit, Lucy. Go ahead."

And, in one short minute, Linda had the stirrups lowered and I was in the saddle - a very expensive, stiff saddle.

Linda tapped her hand on my knee. "Nothing fancy. I just want you to walk and trot around the ring until Tiera gets back."

Nothing fancy? I wasn't planning to do flips off Georgie's back out there. I just wanted to blend in and survive.

She continued. "Georgie is lazy. If anything, you will have to push him forward with your legs. Just get him loosened up. I'll be back after I check on Taylor. Okay?"

"Okay." Her directions were simple enough. I swallowed again but there was no spit left in my mouth.

"You look good up there, kid," Tim said. I had a feeling that Tim told everyone that.

"Thanks," I managed to squeeze out, as Georgie and I walked off towards the arena gate.

"Just follow the flow of traffic," Linda instructed.

Follow the flow of traffic? This was like rush hour in the city. Who was I supposed to follow? I almost had to close my eyes as Georgie and I merged into the mess, hoping I wouldn't collide with anyone.

Horses were nose to butt and moving at all speeds, all directions. And, I felt like Georgie and I were going to be used as a speed bump if we kept walking at his turtle pace.

I clucked my tongue and squeezed my legs, but Georgie just kept moving along at one mile per hour. I squeezed harder. "Come on, Georgie. Let's trot," I pleaded as two riders scooted around us at a lope. The last girl made an effort to sigh loudly as she passed.

I tried one more squeeze and then gave the gray gelding a quick kick with my heels. The kick broke Georgie out of his day dream and reminded him that he was supposed to be working. He hopped up into a smooth jog almost to say, "Oh, is that all you wanted?"

Horses weaved around us while animated trainers and parents yelled instructions from outside the arena. I tried to steady my breathing as we jogged along the rail and was thankful I was on an experienced horse. Nothing rattled Georgie. Georgie had been to a thousand horse shows and he was happy plodding along, doing his job. If I had been riding my horse in this mess, Chance would've fed off my anxiety and fallen to pieces.

My hips swayed side to side in a slow, hypnotic motion and, as we lapped the arena, the gelding's rhythmic trot managed to take the edge off my nerves. It was enough to take my eyes off of Georgie and assess the riders around me.

Trainers shouted directions about keeping heels down and shoulders back, but I thought every rider looked picture perfect. They were like equitation Barbie dolls balancing flawlessly on their shiny horses. My gut tightened as I realized I stuck out like a sore thumb.

As we neared the gate, I was thankful to catch a glimpse of Tiera walking towards the arena, still tucking her blouse back into her pants. She waved wildly and then gave me a big thumbs-up. At least she thought I was doing a good job.

I pulled back on the reins, asking Georgie to walk, and I quickly realized he was much more motivated to slow down than he was to trot. Instead of slowing, he stopped, right in the flow of traffic.

Before I could react, Georgie had started a domino effect.

The girl behind me grabbed her saddle horn as her horse jumped to the side, flattening its ears and narrowly avoiding a crash into Georgie's plump rump. Then there was a blur of shouts consisting of "whoa" and "what are you doing" and "watch where you are going." The yelling came from inside and outside the ring and only reinforced my thoughts of feeling like an outsider.

"Sorry," I squeaked, giving Georgie a swift kick. "Sorry." It was all I could think to say as we scooted out of the mess and through the gate. I hopped off Georgie and handed his reins back to Tiera, wanting to hide my face. I could've caused a wreck.

"I do that all the time," Tiera said as she put a foot in the stirrup, acting like it was no big deal. "Georgie is a fast stopper." The smile never left her face as she settled into the saddle. "Thanks for warming him up. You going to watch my class?"

My heart was still beating in my ears, but Tiera had a way of reminding me that this was supposed to be fun. Horses were supposed to be fun, not stressful.

I managed a smile back. "Yes, of course I'll watch you."

"Okay, follow me," she said, and clucked to Georgie.

Twenty-six

Taylor

From the second I glanced at the horsemanship pattern this morning, I knew it would weed out most of the riders in my class. There were quite a few advanced maneuvers in today's pattern, but I loved a challenge. And, Star and I were more than ready.

In the middle of the arena, where it was just me and my horse, I felt every eye watching my every move. I fed off of it. I lived for it...the attention, the pressure. Star did too. It only pushed us to perform at our best.

As one unit, Star and I sashayed down the center of the arena at a slow collected trot with a flawless transition into an extended trot. I barely moved in the saddle as I asked for a lope and then cantered through a figure-eight shape, executing two smooth lead changes and then a pin-point stop in front of the judges. Applause erupted and I nodded at the judges as Star and I walked off.

My pride only grew as I passed the other competitors, lined up on the far end of the arena where they had just witnessed my ride. Their fake, limp clapping and concerned expressions made me smile. They knew I had just won the class.

And, that I had. I patted Star's neck with enthusiasm as the announcer called out my name. "And, in first place for the amateur western horsemanship class, Taylor Johnson and her horse, Obviously A Star. Great ride, Taylor."

I leaned down to take the ribbon from the ring steward, thanking him, and clipped it to the side of Star's bridle. The cobalt blue color popped beautifully against Star's copper coat.

"You sure do look good in blue," I said, as we started our victory lap around the arena. I waved at the crowd even though the stands were only half full. I couldn't wait until Sunday's evening classes when the audience would be packed.

I breezed by the stands, but a sharp whistle caught my attention. Following the noise, my eyes shot towards a certain cowboy, clapping slow and loud. Jace rose to his feet as I loped by. He tipped the edge of his black hat without breaking his gaze and the two girls sitting on the bleachers behind him gave me a dirty look.

I patted Star on the neck and loped on, soaking up everyone's applause. Even Jace's.

I buckled the belt around my waist, running my fingers over the round crystals that covered the leather. Leaning close to the full length mirror, I double-checked my makeup and rolled bright red lipstick over my lips. Satisfied with my work, I admired the entire teal and tan outfit, watching the multitude of crystals bounce light off the glass.

Bling. Bling. Oh how I loved my new western pleasure outfit.

Ripping the tag from the sleeve cuff, I grabbed my matching tan cowboy hat, the brim lined with a teal accent, and opened the trailer door, ready to head back to the barn.

I skipped down the metal trailer steps, still high on my wins from this morning. Star and I were on a roll. If we kept up this pace, I would definitely be in line for the Northwest Stock Horse Championship Title. I nearly squealed at the thought!

"Hey, Taylor. Wait up."

I turned towards the greeting and my heart skipped a beat. Jace was jogging towards me, making his way through the parked trailers. What did he want? I wasn't ready to talk to him - especially right before my next class.

"I don't have time to talk, Jace," I said, turning my head away from him and walking faster.

"Just give me one minute," he said, grabbing hold of my arm. "Just one minute. I promise. Please just listen for one minute."

His touch was light, his words almost pleading. I couldn't imagine what he wanted.

"What?" I stopped in my tracks, crossing my arms over my chest. "What do you possibly have to say to me, Jace?"

Even with my harsh stance, he didn't let go of my arm. "I wanted to say congratulations on your rides this morning. You and Star were perfect out there. You looked gorgeous...you always look gorgeous."

Jace's emerald green eyes were soft. The tough guy confidence was gone. Truly, I just wanted him to wrap his arms around me and say he was sorry for breaking my heart, but I couldn't give in just like that.

"And?" I asked, not allowing my sudden weakness to show through.

Jace put both hands on my arms now, facing me head on. I looked up at him, trying to look right through him.

"And, I miss you," he said.

His quick words ripped apart my defenses. I looked away, but couldn't bring myself to move from his hold. "What do you mean you miss me?" I asked. "After I left Linda's barn for Red Rock Ranch, I never heard one word from you. You dropped off the face of this earth. And now you miss me?"

"I'm an idiot, Tay." Jace's use of his nickname for me nearly made my knees buckle. "I didn't know what to do. For some reason I thought it would be easier to make it through the summer if we didn't talk, if we took a break. I couldn't stand not being with you...so I thought it would be easier to just stop."

I searched his eyes and the dark features of his face for a real answer, but I couldn't find one. His words seemed sincere, but I just didn't understand his logic.

Jace continued. "And then I saw you here at the show and I knew I was idiot. I miss being with you."

It felt like the wind had been knocked from my lungs. I didn't know what to say. Jace had hurt me - deeply - and now he was in front of me, telling me he missed me?

"I've got to get to the barn, Jace. My class is in 20 minutes."

Jace took the cowboy hat from my hand and gently placed it on my head, adjusting the brim to just the right spot. I didn't uncross my arms.

"I'll be watching from the stands, Tay."

And with that, he walked off. I didn't know whether to be happy or mad. I couldn't tell if Jace had just apologized or if he had just threatened to rip my heart apart again – if given the chance.

Lucy

Chance pushed his black nose against the stall's metal bars, nickering softly and staring at Star.

"Aw...you have a soft spot for her, don't you?" I said and snuck a quick kiss on his whiskered muzzle. He kept his brown eyes pointed towards the chestnut mare as she stood obediently in the cross-ties, ignoring his nickers. I smiled. "Just keep trying to woo her, Chance. I'm sure she'll give in one of these days."

Walking towards Star, I went through a mental checklist, making sure I had everything ready for Taylor's next class.

Saddled up using the teal blue saddle pad. Check.

Tail brushed out and fluffed. Check.

Fly spray wiped on with a rag. Check.

I dug into my pocket for a carrot piece, but when I extended my hand, Star nuzzled the orange bit in my palm, analyzing it like I could be feeding her poison.

I chuckled. "You can take it, Star. It's just a vegetable, I swear."

She sniffed the mystery treat a few more times before delicately picking it up with her lips.

Chance nickered again, this time for me. "I've got one for you too, buddy. Don't worry."

I dug another piece from my pocket and handed it to Chance. He lapped it up before he even knew what it was.

"I'll be waiting outside by the arena." Her voice made me jump. "I need some fresh air before my class."

"Taylor," I said, clenching at my heart. "I didn't even hear you coming." I was half-afraid she was going to yell at me for giving her horse a treat, but she just walked by. She looked like she was in a trance. Maybe she was tired. Or maybe she was in her zone, concentrating on her next class.

"Thanks for getting Star ready."

I paused, wondering if my ears heard Taylor correctly. I didn't know her vocabulary included that word.

"You're welcome." The words came out like a question. "Do you need anything else for your class?"

Taylor responded over her shoulder. "No, I'm fine."

But something was definitely not fine. Something was off.

"All right. I'll bring Star out by the arena in a few minutes."

Tiera and her Mom took off for the afternoon, noting a mother-daughter day at the mall, and Jace's classes were done for the day. Taylor's western pleasure ride was the only class left and I wanted to watch. I tidied up our area of the barn, sweeping the aisle and organizing the tack stall before sneaking off to the arena, anxious to watch the class I had been hearing about all day.

Grabbing the first open seat I found in the bleachers, I settled in for the show.

"Please enter the arena at a jog," the announcer stated in a smooth, even tone. "After two tough cuts, this is the final cut in our open western pleasure class here at the Northwest Stock Horse Championship Show. Good luck to everyone."

Following the announcer's instructions, the horses and their riders entered the arena through the far gate, one by one, and they meant business. Their straight faces emphasized intense concentration as their horses jogged slowly, in single file, along the rail.

Taylor and Star were the last team to enter the arena before one of the show volunteers shut the gate with a clang. As always, they looked perfect, not a hair out of place. Whatever was bothering Taylor before had obviously been forgotten.

The announcer continued. "Class is complete. Please continue at a jog."

You could have heard a pin drop. I sat still, afraid I'd move and cause the bleachers to creak, breaking the tension hanging in the air.

"And, lope your horses."

At the announcer's request, 20 horses transitioned into a lope. There were four judges dressed in navy blazers and khaki pants, scribbling notes on their clipboards as the horses passed. My eyes darted from one horse to the next, trying to find a fault in any of them. I couldn't. This was the best of the best and everyone was here to win.

"Extend your lope."

The riders barely moved as they asked their horses to pick up the pace. Taylor and Star loped by, in perfect form, but as they passed, I thought I saw her shift her weight quickly in the saddle.

That was odd.

I kept my eyes glued to the pair as they rounded the next corner and Taylor seemed to lose her seamless equitation position, leaning forward and then suddenly grabbing the saddle horn with her free hand.

My hand shot to my mouth and I gasped, realizing what was happening. The girth was loose. Star's girth was coming undone and the saddle was falling to the side.

I stood up in the stands, my hand still cupped to my mouth, as the saddle slid off-center and Star's head shot straight up. Not understanding what was happening, Star scooted her butt underneath her belly and shot forward into a bucking spree. Taylor pulled on the reins, trying to stop her, but by the time Star hit the middle of the arena, the saddle and Taylor went sailing through the air, hitting the ground in a unanimous thud. The audience inhaled at once, making a giant sucking noise, as Star continued to buck, her reins now flailing at her sides.

The two judges at the far end of the arena put their hands in the air, yelling "whoa" and trying to control the escalating situation as other horses were now joining the fiasco, prancing and hopping in circles.

"Please halt your horses," the announcer demanded, the tension now audible in his voice. A few of the riders dismounted, feeling safer on the ground.

Star let out one last kick before slowing to a trot and stopping to snort. With her ears pricked forward and neck arched, she looked as stunned as the audience and her confusion gave one of the judges just enough time to grab the hanging reins.

With Star now under control, every head turned towards her dismounted rider. Taylor was sitting in the dirt with another judge kneeling by her side and she looked to be brushing him off, shaking her head. They both stood and a small group of audience members clapped, trying to show support.

A couple of the horses started to prance again. "Please hold your applause," the announcer warned and the arena became silent.

Taylor walked, a bit stiff, towards Star and took her reins from the judge. She didn't brush herself off. She didn't say a word. She walked past every stare, leaving her saddle and her bent cowboy hat in the dirt.

I watched her exit through the gate before I took off in a sprint, running past the murmuring audience. And, as soon as I hit the open air, I spotted Star. Walking next to Taylor, the chestnut mare's head was now lowered, looking ashamed at her irrational reaction.

"Taylor," I called after her and jogged to her side. "Are you okay?"

Without taking the time to stop and properly roll up the ends of her chaps, the soft tan leather scrapped across the ground, dragging through the dirt with each stride. She didn't look at me. I knew she was upset.

"Would you like me to take Star back to her stall for you?" I figured there was something I could do to help. Taylor probably needed some time to herself.

"Get away from me, Lucy," Taylor said through gritted teeth. "And, don't ever touch Star again."

"What?" I asked, baffled at her response. "I was just trying to help..."

Taylor turned on her heels, forcing me to an abrupt stop as she pointed a finger straight at my nose. "Help? *HELP ME?!* Don't you think it would have been *HELPFUL* if you had tightened the girth when you tacked up my horse?" The corners of Taylor's brown eyes were crinkled up in anger while her finger stayed pointed at my face.

My mouth dropped open as I stared at her, without words. Taylor was blaming me for her fall? She was putting the blame on me after I had followed each and every one of her bratty instructions since we got here? Not to mention, I did *NOT* forget to tighten Star's girth. I know I checked it before handing Star off. I wasn't stupid. Who did Taylor think she was?

Instead of biting my tongue, I snapped.

"Why didn't *you* check the girth on *your* horse, Taylor?" The words bubbled out of my mouth. "That's an elementary horse lesson – to check the saddle before you put a foot in the stirrup." The blood pumped faster through my veins with each word, sick of her know-it-all attitude. I wasn't taking the blame for something I didn't do.

Taylor's lips pressed together in a thin, straight line as she digested my reply. There was dirt ground into her red lipstick.

"I paid thousands of dollars for you to come here to work and you can't even tack up a horse correctly. I don't even know why I brought you here."

A crowd was gathering around us.

I balled my fists together, keeping them close to my sides so I didn't smack her. "Why did you bring me here, Taylor?" If I was going down in flames, I might as well get some answers. "Did you bring me here to rub your money in my face? Because I am not impressed."

A brief wave of shock shot through Taylor's eyes before they hardened and she spit out her response. "I brought you here because I felt bad for you, Lucy. I felt bad for you and your pathetic horse and I thought you could learn something here - make yourself a better rider. Or, maybe teach your horse some manners." Taylor paused, feeding off the situation's drama. "Obviously, I was wrong. I learned my lesson. I shouldn't associate myself with someone who is going nowhere."

Her words came out in a low hiss, hitting me at my core like a punch to the gut. I stood motionless as Taylor turned and walked away, seemingly happy with my reaction.

How could anyone be so self-centered? So wrapped up in her own world that she didn't care who she hurt? My feet started to back up as I felt my throat constrict. I needed to get out of there before I let her see me cry.

Twenty-seven

Taylor

I walked away as fast as I could - so fast that Star jogged to stay by my side. I was pissed. I thought about running, but I wasn't going to give Lucy the satisfaction.

Star's metal shoes clip-clopped against the concrete floor as we navigated the barn. I narrowed my eyes at a tall guy pushing a wheelbarrow and he quickly moved to the side, out of my way.

Back at the stalls, I came to a quick halt. I wanted to untack Star and get the heck out of there before I had to deal with anyone. I reached for Star's bridle and she jumped away, looking at me like I had hit her.

Star glared at me, eyes wide open and ears pricked forward. Her body leaned away from my outstretched arm.

She thought I was mad at her.

I dropped my arm, letting it rest against my side as I lowered my head. I concentrated on slowing my breathing. "I'm sorry, girl," I whispered, taking a deep breath. "I'm not mad at you. I promise."

I was mad at Lucy. I was mad at myself for letting the whole thing happen.

"It's okay," I said and repeated the words over and over. I reached out slowly and Star allowed me to rub her neck. She seemed to accept my apology as she let her body relax.

"Taylor." Jace's voice cut through the thick air. He was slowing to a jog as he approached. "Are you okay? I can't believe that just happened."

Neither could I. And, I didn't want to see anyone right now – especially Jace. I wanted to be alone after taking a roll on the arena floor. How embarrassing.

"I'm fine. I'm fine," I said, brushing off his question. I was fine...physically, anyhow.

"Let me help you, Tay." And Jace didn't wait for me to answer. He grabbed Star's halter from her stall door and took the reins from my hand. I didn't have the energy to fight him. And, in a few seconds, Jace had Star's bridle off and clasped her nylon halter behind her ears. He turned back to me and it felt like something snapped inside my heart.

I wasn't sure if the feeling came because I just flipped off my horse and smacked the ground, or if it was because I had been disqualified from a class I should have won, or if it was because my ex-boyfriend was standing in front of my face confusing the heck out of me...whatever it was, I'd hit my breaking point.

"I'm not really okay." I pushed the words out as a lone tear rolled down my cheek.

Jace stepped over and wrapped his arms around my shoulders. His touch sent me over the edge. Cradled in his familiar scent, I pressed my head against his chest and let my tears soak into his shirt. He rubbed my back with his hand and let me cry in silence.

But, I didn't let myself cry for long. It was embarrassing enough that Jace had to witness me like this. I didn't want to stand here and wait for Linda and Tim to find me. Straightening up, I swiped my face with my crystal encrusted sleeve, wiping away the tears and choking back the rest.

"How about I keep you company while you cool off Star. It looks like she could use a walk and a bath."

Jace's emerald eyes waited for my response.

I nodded.

And just like that, Jace handed me Star's lead and wrapped his arm around my back. The three of us walked out of the barn, together.

Lucy

I had to take a walk. What I really wanted to do was run to Chance and bury my face in his mane, close my eyes and forget the words that Taylor had just lashed across my face. But, I knew the culprit would be there, in the barn, untacking Star. And, I knew I couldn't be around her right now. One of us was bound to rip the other's eyes out.

So I power-walked, trying to leave behind the anger, the hurt. I pushed forward, quickly covering ground and making my way down the driveway, away from the barn. When I had no more pavement to follow, I stepped onto the grass and walked beside the white picket fence - towards a little band of yearlings. The youngsters were nibbling at the grass, swishing their short tails in the sunshine, and enjoying each other's company. I plopped down, taking a seat in the grass and resting my head in my hands.

Horses didn't judge. Just being near them gave me peace. Enough to calm me down anyhow.

An hour later, my mental state was somewhat in line and I headed back to the barn - which now felt like enemy territory. I walked down the aisle, looking for enemy number one and ready to retreat if necessary. I didn't know what Taylor would do if she saw me now. And, my stomach felt queasy just thinking about it. She couldn't take back the check she had written for Chance, could she?

Peeking down the aisle, I saw that Star was back in her stall, sheeted up for the evening, and the rest of the crew was gathered near. Linda and Tim were talking, examining Linda's clipboard, as Tiera and her Mom filed out of Georgie's stall, their hands full of brushes. There was no sign of Taylor.

"Hey Lucy," Tiera said, locking eyes with me and waving a curry comb in the air.

Tim and Linda both turned their heads.

"There you are," Tim said. "We were starting to get worried about you." Had Taylor told them I was responsible for her fall? Would they believe my side of the story?

"Sorry. I was watching a few of the classes and time just got away from me." It was the first thing I could think of.

"Well, we are all headed to a dinner tonight. The show committee puts it on every year. There's a big buffet. Would you like to join us?" No one was showing any signs that they knew about the fight between Taylor and me.

"Actually, I'm not that hungry." It was the truth, even though I hadn't eaten anything since breakfast. I just didn't feel like being social right now - or running into Taylor. "Do you mind if I just stay here?" A quiet barn was what I needed.

"You're going to miss out on the world-class chocolate-chip cheesecake at dinner." Tim licked his lips, tasting it in his mind. "You don't want to miss out on that. Do you?"

"Thanks for the offer, but I was kind of hoping to ride Chance. He's been sitting in his stall all day and I'm sure he's about to go crazy."

At that, Tiera piped up. "Can I join you, Lucy?" She immediately turned to Amber. "Please, Mom. I never get to ride on the trails here because no one ever wants to go. Pretty please, pretty please, pretty please." Tiera pushed her hands together in a praying motion, the curry comb hanging from her wrist by a string.

I didn't even know there were trails around here.

Amber scrunched her delicate face in apprehension, but then looked to me. "Only if it's okay with Lucy. And, you only walk and trot. And, you're back here before sunset."

She had a lot of requirements.

Tiera jumped towards me, raising her hands in the air like she had already won. "Can I, Lucy? Can Georgie and I come with you on a ride?"

A trail ride sounded like the perfect way to forget my afternoon. And, it would be nice to hang out with someone who actually wanted to hang out with me.

"Sure, Tiera."

She squealed at my approval and jumped around the aisle, doing a little happy dance.

"All right then. You girls be careful while we are gone," Linda instructed as she set down her clipboard. "Tiera, as soon as you get back from the trail ride, I want you to call your mother and let her know."

"Yes, ma'am," Tiera replied with a two-finger salute to her forehead.

Linda continued. "It's just going to be you girls here so stick together. Jace and Taylor went into town for a bit and are meeting us later tonight for dinner."

Jace and Taylor were hanging out? I hadn't seen them say two words to each other.

"Yes, Linda." I agreed with her instructions. I didn't care who Taylor was hanging out with. At least I knew she wasn't going to be here. "We'll be careful. And I'll make sure Tiera calls when we get back."

Taking a breath, I opened Chance's stall. "Okay, Tiera. Let's get saddled up."

"Thank God for you, Lucy," Tiera exclaimed dramatically as we rode side-by-side, leaving the barn in the distance. "Otherwise I'd be sitting at dinner, forced to listen to boring adult talk."

"Well, I'm glad I could get you out of that." I smiled at her honesty. Tiera seemed unaware of my crappy mood. She babbled on, keeping the conversation rolling and my mind off the knock-down-drag-out fight with Taylor. Tiera was helping me unwind, helping me forget.

I could forget for now, anyhow. There were still two more days left of the show. Eventually I would have to be in the righteous presence of Taylor again, knowing she blamed me for her fall...and basically called me an idiot who couldn't even saddle a horse.

My blood began to boil again, warming my cheeks, so I tuned out of my head and into Tiera's babbling.

"And that's why I hate those stuffy dinners," she said, ending a story I had completely missed, and then turning to see my reaction.

"I see," I said and nodded, responding to her raised eyebrows. "I don't think I'd like that either."

I didn't know what story Tiera had told me, but she seemed to appreciate that I was agreeing with her. She smirked, but was quickly distracted.

"Oh!" she gasped. "There's the start of the trail!"

I followed Tiera's pointing finger and found the green and white metal sign, hovering above a cluster of sparse bushes. As we rode closer, I could see this wasn't just some dinky trail. We were riding towards the main trailhead of the Central Oregon State Park.

"Wow," I said, slowing Chance to a stop and admiring the squiggly white lines drawn all over the metal sign. The lines connected and made up an extensive map of horse trails. "We could ride on these for days."

"I know!" Tiera squealed. "I've been dying to ride on these trails since we got here, but no one ever wants to go with me. Everyone is so wrapped up in the show."

A grin crawled across my face. "Well, I'm glad you asked me," I said truthfully. It was the first time I felt at ease since I left the ranch. "Do you want to lead?"

"You can lead," Tiera noted and ran her fingers through Georgie's short gray mane. "Chance's strides are so much bigger than Goergie's. I'll probably have to lope to keep up with his trot."

Tiera's smile widened at her comment and I was instantly reminded of her Mom's warnings.

"We better be careful. Remember, your Mom was pretty serious about only walking and trotting." I could just imagine the wrath I'd face if Tiera took a tumble in the dirt. I pictured Amber's petite frame coming completely unglued. I did not need to see that.

Tiera rolled her eyes as Georgie walked by Chance. "Blah, blah, blah. My Mom worries if I eat an apple that's not organic. Trust me. We'll be fine." And with that, Tiera gave Georgie a little kick and they loped off towards the trailhead. "Come on," she yelled, waving her hand at me without looking back.

I shook my head at Tiera, knowing I wasn't going to change her mind. But I was thankful for that.

Chance was thankful too. Anticipating a run, he bunched up like a spring and pranced in place before I loosened his reins, allowing him to follow Georgie. We quickly caught up and as soon as we were next to the gray gelding, Chance snorted into the fresh air. The horses loped along with their heads held high, taking in the open space before us.

All four of us were soaking up the freedom, leaving a trail of dust in our path.

I plopped down in one of Linda's chairs, monogramed with her name, and giggled along with Tiera as we cracked open ice-cold Cokes. Tiera pulled the elastic band from her pony tail and let her white blonde hair fall to her shoulders. She continued to laugh as she ran her fingers through, tugging at wind knots.

"I can't even believe Chance jumped straight over that creek! I can still picture the look on your face!"

"The look of horror, you mean?" I noticed my cheeks were sore, tired from our laugh-fest. "I can't believe I stayed on!"

"You sure he wasn't a jumper before you got him? You guys practically cleared Georgie & me. I don't think Chance got one drop of water on his hooves."

I shook my head and smiled, remembering the scene. "I seriously think Chance spooked at his own reflection in the water. He thought there was a big black monster staring back at him or something. He was NOT going to step foot in there."

Chance was now resting in his stall, eating his dinner and watching us as we laughed. He stared back through the metal bars with a mouthful of hay and snorted in our direction, dismissing our silly chit-chat.

"I know, I know. We'll stop making fun of you," I said, holding back a final chuckle and turning to Tiera. "I suppose I should have expected that. Chance isn't used to sitting in a stall all day long, doing nothing. He had a lot of energy to burn."

Tiera nodded her head to agree. "He needed the ride. Maybe we can try another trail tomorrow? I only have the one class in the morning."

"That'd be great," I said, but quickly remembered the real reason I was here at the show. I took a big swig of Coke followed by a long breath. "As long as I don't have stuff to do here...for Taylor." I caught the disgust in my voice as I spoke her name. I couldn't help it.

Tiera caught it too. "I don't know how you can take orders from her." She didn't know I had no choice. "I'd go crazy. She's so serious about everything. I mean, lighten up already." Tiera picked at the pink nail polish crumbling off her thumbnail. "I'm glad she didn't hang around the barn today. I can't imagine what she'd be like after her fall in the ring today." She looked at me with raised eyebrows.

"Yeah, I can't imagine," I replied, not allowing sarcasm to lace my statement. I knew exactly what she was like, but I hadn't clued Tiera in on the gossip. She didn't know that Taylor accused me of being the reason for her not-so-graceful dismount - or that Taylor and I had screamed at each other, nearly fist-fighting. I didn't want to rehash it. I wasn't going to gain anything from letting Tiera in on the craziness.

I changed the subject. "Poor Georgie must be worn out," I said, not seeing any sign of him through the stall bars. "He's already lying down."

Tiera popped up in one swift movement, abandoning her chair, and skipped across the aisle. "Oh, he's so cute when he lies down." She nearly squealed the word "cute" as she slid open the stall door.

I stood to join her. I agreed - a horse snuggled up in a thick bed of shavings was pretty dang cute. I wanted to take a peek, too, so I approached the open door with slow steps. I didn't want to scare Georgie into standing up. But then again, I didn't think there were too many things that actually scared Georgie.

In the stall, the gray gelding had all four legs tucked up underneath himself, his head and neck raised. Tiera was kneeling in the bedding by Georgie's head, a hand on his shoulder, but she pulled away as Georgie turned to nip at his own belly.

Tiera looked back at me and I caught the fear on her face. "Something's wrong," she said.

I stepped into the stall and immediately noticed the hay on the ground, still in two untouched square flakes. The bottom of

Georgie's rubber bucket was covered in grain – which he would normally have lapped up in thirty seconds. His neck was dark with sweat.

The scene in front of me was a horse owner's worst nightmare. Georgie was showing us all the signs of colic.

Twenty-eight

Taylor

Jace parked his car next to Linda's long aluminum trailer. The black leather interior of his cherry red Mustang radiated the scent of his cologne, fresh yet spicy. It filled my lungs and was hard to ignore – just like Jace. Trying not to be obvious, I silently studied his square jaw and chiseled features as he clicked the car key back, turning off the purring motor. He cocked his head towards me and I quickly looked out the windshield, afraid of what would happen if I looked straight into his eyes.

Jace Brooks was two years older than me, a senior at a rival high school in my hometown of Napa, California. But even though we lived in the same town, we'd never met until after he started training with Linda this past year. Believe me, I would remember a face like that.

At first sight, I was stunned by Jace's model-good-looks. Heck, he looked like he could stroll into an Abercrombie photo shoot and steal the show with one wink. But it wasn't his beautiful face or athletic body that did me in. It was his riding. After I watched Jace compete on Hammer, I couldn't stop myself from falling for him. I was fascinated by Jace's intensity and confidence through every perfect maneuver of his reining pattern. I had found the male version of myself – someone who would understand my love of the sport, the competition.

"It was pretty boring driving the 300 miles to this show by myself," Jace broke into my thoughts.

I rolled the seatbelt strap around my fingers, knowing exactly what he was referring to. Before I left for Red Rock Ranch, I had kept Jace's passenger seat warm on the way to a horse show in Vegas. His comment zapped my mind back to the trip - the hours we spent talking, the mounds of gas station junk food we consumed, and the songs we got lost in as they played over the radio.

"We do make a pretty good road trip team." A tentative smile curled on the edge of my lips. "Except that you always steal my Skittles."

"Well, who can resist Skittles?" Jace kidded and cracked opened the car door. "I mean, come on. You can't hold that against me. They're delicious."

Our eyes locked for a millisecond before he winked at me and stepped out onto the gravel. My heart palpated, unsure of why he was giving me so much attention. After all, Jace was the one who had pushed me away. And now he was flirting with me? And, why was I letting him flirt with me? *Be strong, Taylor. Don't let him wiggle his way back into your heart...at least not without getting some answers. And, an apology.*

I stepped out of Jace's car, leaving behind the scent of his cologne and feeling relief as the cool night air hit my skin. But still lost in my jumbled thoughts, I shut the door a little harder than I meant to. The crash echoed off of the aluminum metal of the horse trailer.

"Hey, ease up on the muscles there, Taylor. No need to get in a fight with my door."

I turned around to match his sarcasm with an equally witty comment, but the words never left my mouth as I scanned the parking lot. "Jace?" I called out for him and peeked around the back of his car. His six-foot-two frame had disappeared.

"Up here, Tay."

Following the sound of his voice, I looked to the sky and found his lean build staring back at me from the top of Linda's trailer, a dark silhouette in the dimming light.

"What are you doing?" I asked, amazed at how quickly he got up there.

"Come on." Jace waved his arm at me. "Come up here with me. It's quite the view."

I just spent all evening with Jace. He had walked with me as I cooled down Star and had kept me company as I bathed her. At dinner his attention continued, making me feel like I was the only girl in the restaurant. Looking at Jace from the ground with the sun setting at his back, I knew it was a bad idea to climb up there with him - to give in to him now.

But I did it anyway.

Jace was waiting at the top of the metal ladder as I climbed up the rungs. He held out his hand for mine and I grabbed hold, placing my cowboy boot on the metal roof. "You know Linda's going to kill us when she finds us up here, right?"

He squeezed my hand and then led me over to the square stack of hay bales nestled in the rack. "That didn't seem to stop you from coming up here," he replied with a grin. "Besides, we left dinner early and you know Tim isn't leaving without at least a few pieces of cheesecake." He hopped up on the hay bales and I followed.

"Yeah, you're right," I agreed, very aware he was still holding my hand. "They probably won't be back for another hour or so."

My palms were sweating now, unsure where this was leading, and also knowing I needed to confront Jace with my questions. If I was going to ask him for answers, this was my opportunity.

"Look," Jace said with a nod of his head, pointing the brim of his black hat towards the practice arenas. "We've got front row seats to check out our competition for tomorrow."

Wiping the palm of my free hand on my jeans, I looked ahead to the dimly lit arenas. The first two pens were filled with tall lanky horses tacked in English gear while the farthest ring held the quick-stopping reiners. I grinned, knowing Jace was just as competitive as I was.

"There are some really great riders here," I noted quietly.

Jace laced his fingers through mine and turned his gaze back to me, flashing a smile. "Nothing you need to worry about, Tay. You and Star are the team to beat at this show."

I chuckled half-heartedly. "Not after my dismount into the dirt today."

"That wasn't your fault. That stuff happens to the best of us."

I sighed, knowing I could have prevented it. "I should have checked the girth. It kind of was my fault."

"Don't worry about it. You were so far ahead on points from your wins earlier today. I'm sure you can make up the difference tomorrow. You'll be back in the running for the championship title in no time."

I stewed over Jace's words for a few silent moments. "I guess I just need to win every class I'm entered in for the rest of the weekend." I smiled. My words were meant to sound sarcastic, but the truth was hard to hide. I wanted to win the title and I was going to do everything in my power to make it so.

Jace didn't respond, but when I looked up, I found him analyzing me, his emerald eyes intense. He set his arm across my shoulders and my pulse quickened, bounding into my throat. I knew what he was doing and I wasn't sure how I should react.

I'd planned out this moment since Jace pushed me away. Since he stopped returning my calls, my texts. I'd dreamt about slapping him across the face and calling him every cuss word I could think of. I wanted to remind him what he lost and how he could never have it back. I wanted to make sure Jace hurt as much as I did. My head told me to push him off the roof of the trailer and laugh when he hit the gravel below.

But I didn't. I let Jace kiss me.

His lips followed mine, slow yet forceful. He tightened his arm around my back, pushing me into his chest, and my hand found the sharp curve of his jaw. The anger in my heart melted away with each second. This was where I wanted to be and where I shouldn't be, all at the same time.

And I nearly cried when he stopped.

"I've wanted to do that since I saw you yesterday," he whispered, just inches from my lips.

Jace's actions in the past 24 hours contradicted everything he had done in the past month. "I don't understand you, Jace Brooks," I said, searching his eyes for a hint of an explanation.

"What's there to understand, Tay," he asked with a flirty smirk.

I started to ask why he was such a jerk, but Jace pressed his lips to mine and my question disintegrated from my brain. Jace knew how to get his way.

Kissing Jace gave me a late night urge for Skittles – sugary goodness in rainbow form – but I wasn't sure where I would find candy at 10:00 on the show grounds. Determined, I pulled on my yoga pants and left my trailer on a sugar hunt. The vending machine by the show office was my only hope.

The parking lot was deserted as I walked towards the barn using both hands to finger-brush my hair into a high bun. Wrapping the elastic tie around my curls, my mind drifted back to Jace...and his kiss. His emerald eyes. His tight grip around my shoulders. His chest pressed against me.

The visions made me sigh.

There was something about him that forced my stomach to flutter, over and over again. I couldn't make it stop. And, after that kiss, I knew Jace felt the same way about me. He knew he had made a mistake and now he wanted me back. But this time our relationship was going to be different. This time I was going to be in control of the situation. I needed to set boundaries, rules. Tomorrow I would sit Jace down, looking especially cute in my breeches, and tell him we could only be together if he was exclusive - my boyfriend. I deserved that. I deserved to know exactly what he was thinking.

I sashayed into the barn, thoroughly impressed with my plan, and headed for Star's stall. She deserved a snack too - a few carrots and some love, especially after today's events.

The aisles were dark, lights off and horses sleeping, so I was surprised to see the lights blazing over Linda's section of the barn. Maybe Tim was checking the horses before bed? But as I approached the stalls, I caught the sound of Lucy's voice and I slowed my stride. Did I really want to deal with her after such a perfect evening? I wasn't in the mood for a buzz-kill.

But before I could turn around, Lucy hurdled herself out of Georgie's stall, kicking a cloud of cedar shavings into the aisle as she ran straight towards me. I froze.

What in the heck? What was she doing? Did she hear me coming and go completely insane with rage? Was she planning on beating me senseless while no one was around? I weighed my options. Lucy was tall and wiry and definitely faster than me. I couldn't outrun her so I tightened my fists into balls, ready to take a whack at crazy-train. As she got closer I braced myself for a Lucy-style football tackle. Maybe if I tripped her...

"Taylor," she shouted, like she was happy to see me.

"What?" I barked back, realizing my balled fists were now positioned in front of my chest, ready to fight. Not that I'd ever been in a fight in my life.

She skidded to a stop in front of me, nearly wiping out as her cowboy boots slid across the concrete. But instead of slapping, pushing or kicking me, she grabbed hold of my wrist and pulled, hard, taking me with her.

"Ouch!" I squeaked, stumbling a few steps before I was forced to follow. "What is your problem? I'm the one that took a flying leap into the dirt. Remember? I'm the one that should be mad and assaulting you."

Lucy didn't stop pulling, but she did turn her head to make eye contact while she ran. "Georgie is colicking. This is *not* about you."

My thoughts flipped as I absorbed Lucy's words and grasped the seriousness of the situation. Colic, a stomach pain usually caused by a blockage in the intestines, was not something to mess around with. It could take the life of a healthy horse in a matter of hours.

Realizing Georgie needed my help, I fell in step with Lucy's pace and soon we were running, side by side, towards Georgie's stall. Arriving, I grabbed the wooden edge of the open door to stop myself and Georgie flicked his ears in my direction. Lying down in the bedding, Georgie's soft gray coat was dark with sweat, mostly on his neck and chest. His eyes were droopy, and there were wet marks on his belly where he had nipped at his own pain.

Tiera was standing in the stall with her hands to her mouth. When she turned towards me, her eyes were glassy and I noticed her fingers starting to tremble. I stopped myself from gasping at the sight of Georgie. Tiera didn't need another reason to be scared.

Behind me, something crashed to the floor in the tack stall, and Lucy came out with a halter and lead.

"Tiera," I said, controlling the anxiety in my voice. She looked helpless and had probably never seen a horse colic before. "Where's your phone?"

She patted down her jean pockets and replied, "It's on the table in the aisle."

I stepped into the stall and put a hand on her arm, gripping it firmly. "Here's what I want you to do." Tiera was listening to me with every ounce of her attention. "Grab your phone and run to the show office. There's a list posted on the door with emergency numbers. Call the vet and tell him your horse is colicking. Then I want you to call Linda and tell her the same thing." Tiera nodded. "And tell Linda that Lucy and I are both here and taking care of Georgie while we wait for the vet."

Her bottom lip quivered. "Okay, Taylor," she said before sprinting out of the stall.

Lucy swooped in as Tiera ran out. She knelt by Georgie and quietly clasped a halter over his head. As she stood, Georgie laid his head down in an attempt to start rolling. His legs began thrashing through the bedding.

"We've got to get him up," Lucy yelled. "He could make it worse if he rolls."

I was thinking the same thing and jumped towards Georgie's hind end. "Come on, Georgie. Come on. Get up. Come on, boy." I clucked and waved my arms as Lucy pulled him forward with the lead rope and muttered her own words of encouragement.

Georgie managed to get his feet underneath himself and groaned as he straightened his front legs. He was trying to do what we wanted him to, but he was hurting.

There was more clucking and kissing and waving of the arms before the other horses realized something was wrong. Star whinnied and Chance pawed against his door. Hammer began pacing back and forth. Everyone was telling Georgie that he had to get up.

"Yup, yup!" I started making sounds like I'd heard Casey and the ranch hands yell during cattle round-ups. I clapped my hands and Lucy and I both held our breath as Georgie made a deep grunt and pulled himself into a standing position.

I wanted to scream for joy, but I knew we were far from being in the clear.

Lucy led Georgie out of the stall. His head hung low, but he was walking.

"We need to walk him until the vet gets here," Lucy said. "God, I hope he hurries." She walked Georgie down the aisle, but it wasn't long before the gelding tried to lie down. His front knees buckled and both Lucy and I started yelling and flailing our arms again.

Georgie walked forward a few steps at our urging. "He's really in pain," Lucy said, the worry on her face increasing. "I wonder if Linda packed any Banamine. Who knows how long it will take the vet to get here and we need to do something for him while we wait."

Banamine, an anti-inflammatory drug used to help relieve pain during colic, was a common medication for horse owners to keep on hand in case of an emergency – just like this one.

"Linda has a bottle in her trailer," I replied. I knew exactly where it was stashed. Last year I watched Linda grab it from her trailer's tack room when her horse, Cash, started showing signs of colic at a rodeo. "But, I don't know how to give an injection. We'll have to wait for the vet or for Linda…"

Lucy cut me off. "I know how to. I took an equine health class a few years ago with my 4H group. Can you go get it?"

Lucy's sudden confidence caught me off-guard, but I didn't hesitate. "Will you be okay by yourself with him for a few minutes?"

"I think so," she said. "Just hurry."

It was a good thing I was wearing yoga pants and tennis shoes because I ran like the wind, bursting out of the barn and across the gravel parking lot. I never ran, but I could have finished a marathon on the adrenaline pumping through my blood. The key pad on the trailer beeped at me as I punched in the numerical code and then swung open the door, jumped in and ripped open a cabinet drawer.

"Gotcha," I said, grabbing the white plastic tote with the Red Cross symbol and tucking it under my arm. I blazed a trail back to the barn and slowed to a jog as I approached Lucy, certain I had set some kind of record. I pulled a syringe and the glass bottle of Banamine from the emergency kit and set the rest of the tote on the ground.

Lucy took the bottle and syringe from me and handed over Georgie's lead rope. "Just keep him still," she instructed.

In a matter of seconds, Lucy filled the syringe with the clear liquid drug and tapped her finger against the plastic to remove any air bubbles. She stepped towards Georgie and placed a hand on his lower neck, finding his jugular vein.

I tightened my grip on Georgie's halter and cringed as Lucy slipped the needle into his neck, but Georgie didn't move a muscle as she injected the medication. When it was all done, Lucy popped the plastic cap back over the needle and placed her hand on Georgie's neck, keeping pressure on the injection site to stop any bleeding.

I was at a loss for words. Lucy knew exactly what she was doing. I'd watched a few injections before, but I couldn't have done that. Lucy knew every step it took to give the shot and she did it with ease.

"Okay, let's walk him again," she said and I followed her instruction, silently thankful she was here with me. "It shouldn't be long before the Banamine kicks in."

An hour later the barn was a calmer scene. The vet, an older gentleman with silver hair, pulled a business card from the front pocket of his plaid flannel shirt. He handed the card to Linda. "Georgie should be just fine now, but I would suggest watching him for a few more hours. If he starts to show signs of pain again, call my cell phone. Otherwise, I will be back to check on him first thing in the morning."

Linda held Georgie's lead rope as he stood in the aisle, his head slightly raised and his brown eyes perked-up. "Thank you for getting here so quickly, Dr. Kalen. I really appreciate your help."

"That's my job, Mrs. Green," Dr. Kalen said as he packed his stethoscope in his canvas bag of tools. "What really saved Georgie was the quick work of these three girls here." He smiled at Lucy and me and winked at Tiera. "You should be very proud of them."

Tim and Linda chimed in at the same time. "Oh, we are."

I gave a sheepish smile, not sure how to take the praise. Lucy really deserved the compliment.

Bag in hand, Dr. Kalen waved at the group circling Georgie. "I'll see you at six tomorrow morning. Have a good night folks."

As Dr. Kalen walked away, Georgie nuzzled Tiera's pockets, softly searching for hidden treats. He was starting to act like himself again. Tiera laid her head against his neck, releasing a big sigh, and kissed his gray coat.

"All right girls, it's time for you to get some well-deserved sleep," Tim piped up as he gently took Georgie's lead rope from Linda's hand. "Otherwise, you will all be zombies during the show tomorrow and zombies don't usually win their classes. I will set up camp next to Georgie's stall and watch him overnight."

Linda leaned over and planted a kiss on Tim's cheek. "Thank you, Sweetie."

Tiera and her Mom hugged Georgie before Tim walked him into his stall. I snuck into Star's stall to say goodnight to my baby as well, thankful she's never had to fight the pain of colic.

Star was standing against the wall with her back leg cocked and her bottom lip droopy, clearly wanting to fall asleep. I checked each snap on her pink plaid sheet, making sure she was comfortable and safe. Then I kissed her on the nose, holding the kiss a bit longer than normal.

"Sweet dreams, Star," I whispered. And, when I turned to leave, I noticed Lucy whispering her own affections to Chance. She was running her hand over his forelock and down his nose. My eyes locked with hers through the metal stall bars, but this time there was no hate, no hurt between us. No words were said, but I didn't think they were needed.

241

Twenty-nine

Lucy

"She did it again!" Tiera squealed over the roaring sound of applause from the audience. She hopped up and down as we stepped back, making space for the arena gate to swing open.

"She sure did," I said clapping my hands together. I was a little less enthusiastic than Tiera, but I was still clapping.

A single row of riders filed out of the arena, all in tan breeches, navy coats, and black velvet helmets. The outfits for the English classes were not nearly as thrilling as the blinged-out western outfits from the day before. These riders looked like a line of clones only differentiated by the color of their horse. And those jackets looked awfully stuffy.

Tiera kept clapping as the horses exited, blurting a positive comment to each rider. "Good job. Nice ride. Love your boots," she said, jumping back and forth on her tiptoes, squeezing her hands together.

I smiled at her honest excitement for each rider and wished there were more girls like Tiera.

As Taylor rode Star out of the arena, her smile spread from ear to ear. Star walked with her head held high, strutting and fully aware they had just won the class.

"I've got the brushes," I said, grabbing the bucket full of grooming tools and fly spray. The plastic tub had become like a purse for me. I toted it around all day, making sure the horses looked their best in the show ring. Today, I was only looking after Star and Hammer as Georgie was on stall-rest, recovering from last night's incident. I was so glad he was okay.

Tiera had to scratch her classes for the day, but it didn't seem to bother her much. Plus, she volunteered to be the assistant's assistant for the rest of the weekend. It was nice to have a helper – especially one with such a great attitude.

I handed Tiera a fresh bottle of cold water. "Can you see if Taylor needs a drink?"

"Absolutely," Tiera said with enthusiasm. "Need me to do anything else?"

"No, I think both Taylor and Jace are done with their classes for the day."

Tiera nodded and skipped towards Star. I followed, wishing I had a fraction of her energy. I was tired. It had been 1:00 or 2:00 in the morning before I finally drifted off. I'd tossed and turned trying to get situated in my bed - the leather couch in Taylor's trailer - but I was amped up from the colic scare. And, Taylor was acting really strange.

Last night Taylor was unusually quiet as we walked from the barn, following Linda to the trailers. And as we put our pajamas on and crawled into bed, she clicked on the flat screen TV and asked me if there was anything I wanted to watch. I stared at her without words from the couch before she handed me the remote. She didn't toss it. She didn't throw it at my head. She handed it over with the tiniest of smiles and then got situated in her quilted comforter.

"Watch whatever you'd like," she said. "Good night."

I was frozen on the couch waiting for some kind of sarcastic comment to follow. When it didn't, I wondered if a few drops of the Banamine drug had soaked into Taylor's skin, making her loopy. That was my best guess as Taylor had never made an effort to be friendly to me - not since we'd met. Was I being punked?

And then her friendly behavior continued today.

Taylor reached down from the saddle and took the water bottle from Tiera, unscrewing the cap. "Thank you," she said before tilting her head back and finishing off every drop. "It's so hot today. I feel like a sweaty mess. I'm glad I can get out of these clothes now."

Taylor popped down from the saddle and patted Star on the neck before handing the empty bottle back to Tiera. She didn't look like a sweaty mess at all. In fact, I was convinced her body was not capable of perspiration. She looked as clean and crisp as she did this morning - not a hair out of place or a dirt smudge found anywhere on her outfit. I, on the other hand, was a sweaty mess.

"Do you want me to take Star in the barn and untack her?" I asked.

Taylor pulled her gloves off, finger by finger, and nodded. "Yes, that would be great, Lucy. Thank you. I'll be in the barn soon. You can leave her in the cross ties and I will walk her out."

I took Star's reins and wondered who this person was. Maybe the Banamine went straight to her brain and scrambled it.

Taylor unclipped the chin strap on her helmet and pulled it off as she walked away, exposing her neat blonde bun. Her hair didn't know what helmet-head was either.

"Well, she's certainly in a good mood today," Tiera said, as she gave Star a peppermint. Star crunched it in dainty bites.

"Yeah," I replied. "Does that seem weird to you?"

Tiera shrugged. "Kind of, but wouldn't you be in a good mood if you just won three classes in a row?"

Tiera was right. I was analyzing Taylor's behavior too much. Taylor was doing what she loved – winning. Why wouldn't she be happy?

"Plus there's *that* whole situation," Tiera added and I followed her wide-eyed gaze to find Taylor lip-locked with Jace. Her hands were wrapped around his neck, the velvet helmet dangling from her fingers.

"Well...I should've seen that one coming," I said, a little stunned.

Tiera and I stood, our heads cocked inquisitively, watching the act in front of us unfold yet knowing we should look away. Jace's hand gravitated down the back of Taylor's navy blazer and I grabbed Tiera's arm, pulling her towards the barn.

"Come on," I said. "I don't want to witness Jace grabbing a handful of breeches."

Tiera spun with me and walked while still examining Jace and Taylor over her shoulder. Her gaping mouth told me I had been right about the breeches.

Tiera giggled about our piece of gossip as I clipped Star into the cross-ties. "Oh my goodness! I can't believe Jace and Taylor were making out! What if Linda or Tim saw them? I mean...are they supposed to do that?" Her eyebrows rose at her own question.

I set Star's lightweight English saddle on a metal rack in the aisle. "Well, I don't think it's illegal or anything," I said, as I shrugged my shoulders. "But, I don't think Linda or Tim would be very happy if they caught them. That was pretty ballsy of Taylor to go in for the lip-lock right next to the arena. I mean, we practically saw their tongues."

Tiera wrinkled her nose and put her hands on her hips. "Gross."

A chuckle slipped out of my mouth at Tiera's reaction to the witnessed kiss, but I muffled it as I noticed Linda, Tim & Amber making their way down the aisle.

"Do you think we should tell them?" Tiera whispered, covering her mouth with her hand.

I instantly shook my head back & forth. "No, it's none of our business." Truthfully, I just didn't want Taylor back on my case. It was nice not having to worry about her tantrums.

Tiera nodded knowingly and zipped an imaginary zipper across her lips.

Linda stopped at the table and set down her binder full of show papers. She had an unusually big smile plastered on her face. "Now that's the way to start off a show day," she noted with a head bob. "All blues for both Taylor and Jace today. If they keep this up, one of them is bound to snag the championship title."

"Green Stables is unstoppable," Tim chimed in with a jolly hurrah. "And, why wouldn't we be? We have the best riders, the best horses, and the best assistants." He winked at me and Tiera.

"And, of course, we have the best trainer," Amber added, putting her arm around Tiera's shoulders and looking at Linda.

"Well, that goes without saying," Tim said before he kissed Linda on the cheek.

I cleared my throat to break through the love-fest. "Linda, Taylor said she wanted to walk Star and cool her off herself." I brushed Star's back to wick away the sweat left by the saddle. "What would you like me to do?"

Linda looked around. The floor was spotless and everything in its place. "Why don't you take a break, Lucy? Star & Hammer are done for the day. Enjoy a few hours off before you need to feed the horses their dinner. Tim and I are going to watch some more classes in the indoor arena and Amber is taking Tiera shopping downtown for a new dance outfit."

Tiera hopped in place at the mention of a new dance outfit.

I was grateful for the suggestion of a break, but I didn't really know what to do with myself. "Okay. Are you sure there isn't anything you need me to do?"

"Not a thing," Linda said. "Why don't you ride your own horse? The reining classes are done in the big outdoor arena and it shouldn't be too crowded out there this afternoon. It would be a good place to exercise Chance."

And, as if he heard his cue, Chance pawed twice at his stall door. His brown eyes stared at me, certain I was talking about him.

"Yeah, I like that idea," I said. Chance bobbed his head up and down at my voice. It looked like Chance liked that idea, too.

I brushed Chance in his stall while I waited for Taylor to arrive and, by the time I had him saddled, she strutted into the aisle. She was humming something unrecognizable, but upbeat. Her cheeks were pinked and she spun her helmet in lazy circles around her fingers.

"I wiped down your saddle and bridle and put them back in the tack room," I told her from Chance's stall.

Taylor jumped like I shouted my statement from the rooftop and then nervously laughed at herself, putting a hand to her chest. Chance jerked his head up at her reaction, watching her like a hawk.

"Oh, wow. I didn't know anyone was still here," she said with a giggle.

I analyzed the strange sound I heard coming from Taylor – laughter – and then I continued. "I wouldn't leave Star standing in the cross-ties by herself. You never know what could happen."

Taylor took a breath and shook her head. "No, I wouldn't expect you to do that. Thanks for taking care of her."

Was that a compliment?

"That's what I'm here for," I said slowly, waiting for a back-handed comment to follow.

Taylor unclipped Star from the cross-ties. "Are you taking Chance for a ride?"

Was she really interested in what I was doing?

"Yes," I replied, unsure how to act around this new, uncharted version of Taylor.

"Great," she noted as she started leading Star away. "Have a good ride."

Chance and I peeked our heads out the stall door to watch Taylor and Star walk away. Taylor went back to humming and twirling her helmet. And, there was an extra sashay in her step. I didn't take my eyes off her as she led Star out of the barn.

"Let's just enjoy this while it lasts, Chance. She's bound to implode at some point."

I double-checked Chance's girth before I raised my knee to my chest and put a boot in the stirrup. That same precaution may not have occurred to Taylor, but I certainly didn't need another reason to end up flying through the air. I had enough of those.

As I situated myself in the saddle, Chance began to prance in place, having too much energy to be patient. I rubbed his neck with my hand and tightened my grip on the reins.

"Easy, boy," I cooed to him. "I know you are sick of standing around in that dang stall. The weekend's almost over and soon we'll be headed back to the ranch where you can run around in the pastures and hang out with your buddies. I'm sure Sharkie and Rocky are missing you." I knew I was missing the ranch...and, without a doubt, Casey.

Chance flicked his black ears back and forth listening to my story, but he didn't stop prancing. "Okay, okay," I said and gave him a gentle squeeze with my legs. My calves barely brushed his sides before Chance marched forward into an energetic walk. "Let's go find this outdoor arena Linda was talking about."

Earlier today, Jace won his reining and cutting classes in the outdoor arena, but I hadn't laid eyes on the ring yet. I stayed close to the barn and the indoor, making sure Taylor and Star were taken care of. After all, Taylor was the one who wrote me the check and the real reason I was here. Not to mention, there was something about Jace that rubbed me wrong. I made sure his horse, Hammer, was always taken care of, but I didn't go out of my way for Jace's sake. He could focus his big-headed ego elsewhere. One princess was plenty to take care of.

Walking away from the barn and past the practice arenas, I watched the riders from a distance as they moved gracefully in circles. Watching them, my mind flashed back to the panic I felt while riding Georgie in the warm-up pen and I secretly hoped the arena I was headed towards was deserted. Georgie was the sweetest, easiest-going horse I knew and I still almost caused a crash. I physically shook the memory from my head, not wanting to tense up and freak Chance out.

"Let's have a good ride. Okay, Chance?"

Chance marched with vigor as we followed a short dirt path towards a barrier of tall pine trees. In the middle of the trees there was an opening framed by two tall wooden posts, topped with a rustic sign. The sign was engraved with the words "Welcome to the Rodeo."

I liked the sound of that.

Passing through the gate, my eyes widened at what the trees had been hiding. The outdoor arena, as Linda called it, was a huge oval arena about the size of a football field. Empty wooden bleachers wrapped around the sides and the far end was made of metal bucking shoots - for the rodeo broncs and bulls. An announcer's stand rose above the metal shoots like a white cottage. A massive American flag hung from the rectangular open window on the front of the stand.

The setup looked like it came straight out of the Wild West. I couldn't wait to ride in it.

I clucked and Chance hopped into a stretchy trot aimed for the open gate. He seemed as excited as I was to try out our new-found adventure. And, we had it all to ourselves. Even better.

I posted Chance's big trot as we entered the arena and he stretched his neck to the sky, surveying our new surroundings. The dirt was freshly tilled. Only a few lines of hoof tracks left circles on the ground. Three metal barrels painted in red, white and blue stripes were strategically placed in a pyramid form.

They must be running barrels in here later this evening.

I pictured the white bleachers filled to the brim with a cheering crowd, the announcer's raspy voice blaring over the speakers, and a dark night sky brightened by the glare of the arena lights. I pictured the crowd's eyes on Chance and me as we raced around each barrel at lightning speed. It was a beautiful sight.

A grin spread across my face and Chance lengthened his trot, checking out the barrels in front of him.

"What do you think, Chance? You want to try running a pattern?" I whispered my question like it was a secret.

What the heck. No one is here to see me if I screw up. Who cares if I knock over a barrel or two.

Following my impulse, I directed Chance towards the first barrel on our right and he followed my cues. I giggled as he slowed down and jogged a tear-shape around the metal obstacle.

"Good boy," I praised him before aiming his nose at the second barrel on the left side of the arena. Getting excited by our new game, Chance broke into a canter. I didn't stop him. I just adjusted my body to the faster speed, knowing he had energy to burn.

We neared the second barrel and Chance started to turn towards it before I asked him to. He loped another perfect tear-drop shape and I leaned forward in the saddle to follow his motion. But my movement seemed to click something in Chance's head and he proceeded to kick himself into high-gear. Chance dug deep into the dirt, his front end rising like a speed boat accelerating through the water. I grabbed the saddle horn, surprised by his enthusiasm, but I was just as anxious to run as he was. I gave him the reins to go.

With ears pricked forward, Chance locked his eyes on the third barrel and I leaned into his neck. His body stretched out underneath me. And when we came to the third barrel, Chance turned with such intensity that we leaned together at a 45 degree angle, breezing around it. I grabbed the middle of his thick black mane and moved with him as he exploded towards the gate we had entered, not even 30 seconds ago. The wind nipped at my face and blew through my hair – just like a new question flew through my mind. *Where did that come from?* Chance circled that last barrel like he'd been running them all his life.

Nearing the gate, I sat back in the saddle and pulled Chance to a controlled canter just as I realized we were being watched. Immediately, my body stiffened.

"Whoa, Chance," I said, as I tightened the reins and rode him into a circle, barely missing a collision with two riders. They must have come in right after me.

Chance started to trot, showing his irritation for the slower speed by tossing his nose in the air. After another circle, he gave in and came to a stop, blowing a loud snort through his puffed nostrils. My legs involuntarily bounced against his ribs as the air left his lungs.

Halted, I was facing the two riders and their horses. Both of the girls' brows were scrunched up, looking mildly confused as they observed Chance and me. After a few seconds of uncomfortable silence, the brunette girl on a big bay horse spoke. "Did you just get here or something?"

Her question sounded irritated and I thought about my answer before responding, not knowing what she was getting at. "What do you mean?"

The second rider, a petite red-head on a lanky palomino, chimed in. "Did you just get here? We haven't seen you riding in the practice pens."

"Oh," I responded as Chance blew out another snort. "No, I've been at the show for a couple of days."

The girls pursed their lips together, still staring at me. I wasn't sure what they wanted so I continued, just trying to fill the silence. I asked them the same question. "Did you guys just get here?"

"Um, no," they said in unison, sounding offended.

"Who's your trainer?" the brunette asked bluntly and then turned to her friend. "Her trainer was probably riding her horse in the practice pens and that's why we didn't notice her." She was very sure of herself.

"Well, I don't really have one," I replied.

"What do you mean you don't have a trainer?" They both blurted, again in unison, and I wondered if they had some kind of telepathic communication.

"I don't have a trainer," I repeated. "I train my horse myself."

The girls looked at each other and started to laugh. Their bodies shook against their shiny saddles and that's when I noticed that they were both wearing black baseball hats embroidered with a trainer's name. Obviously they had a trainer, but why did they care if I had one?

"You're kidding, right?" the brunette said as she cocked her head. "Everyone has a trainer. I mean, everyone who counts has a trainer."

The girls snickered again and my patience grew short. Who did they think they were? I felt like knocking their matching hats off their big heads with a swift blow.

But before I could respond to their snickers, a voice from the fence broke into our conversation. "Not everyone has a trainer, Sandra." The statement was very matter-of-fact.

All three of us turned to look over our shoulders and found Taylor sitting casually on the top board of the arena fence. She was no longer in her show clothes, now wearing jean shorts and holding a soda. Star was only a few steps away, grazing on a patch of lush green grass. She wasn't exactly the person I wanted to see lurking in the shadows.

"Oh, hey Taylor," Sandra, the brunette, said as she sat up straighter in her saddle. I guess Sandra wasn't excited to see Taylor either. "I didn't see you there."

"No kidding," Taylor noted and continued in a cool tone. "Like I said, not everyone has a trainer. And, *some people* like to pay their trainers to do all the work with their horse...and *those people* think they can take all the credit when they win." The girls started squirming in their saddles and Taylor hardened her gaze. "How do you like your new horse, Sandra? Isn't that the gelding your trainer won the National Finals Rodeo Championship Title with last year?"

Taylor's words sounded sweet to the ear, but they were laced with disgust. She took a long, slow gulp of her soda, letting her questions sink in. "It sure is nice to have a rich daddy. Isn't it, Sandra?" Taylor finished her rant with a wink.

Sandra and the nameless red-head looked like they had been caught stealing cookies out of the cookie jar. They glanced at each other and rode off without another word. There was no snickering as they left.

I wasn't the target of Taylor's rant, but I was speechless just the same. Taylor, the girl who looked down her nose at me, who bossed me around, who blamed me for her nose-dive into the dirt...this same Taylor just had my back?

As I sat there, stunned, Taylor spun her tan legs over the top of the fence and hopped down to the ground. She walked over to Star and started braiding her flaxen tail as the chestnut mare continued grazing. I rode Chance over to the fence and watched

Taylor expertly weave the thick braid and wrap a rubber band around the end.

I wasn't sure I should be thankful for Taylor's tongue-lashing skills, but I appreciated being defended. Instead of a thank you, I said the next best thing. "Congratulations on your wins today, Taylor. You and Star make quite the team in the show pen."

A brief smile graced Taylor's face. "Thanks," she said and ran a hand over Star's muscled rump. She patted the mare a few times and then turned to face me, crossing her arms. The intensity in her hazel eyes had me wondering if I was her next victim.

"Don't let them treat you like that," she instructed. "Don't let anyone talk to you like that. You don't deserve it." My mouth must have dropped open because I felt it drying out as she continued. "Those girls could never ride a horse like Chance. They win because mommy and daddy buy them horses that are broke to death. And when they start losing because their skills can't keep up with their horse's talent, mommy and daddy just buy them a new horse."

I couldn't believe the words that had come out of Taylor's mouth. In her own way, she had given me a compliment on my riding - the thing I held closest to my heart. I watched her as she picked-up Star's lead rope from the grass and started to walk off.

"Taylor," I called after her. She stopped, looking at me over her shoulder and waiting for my response. "Thanks."

She gave me a nod and continued on. Maybe I didn't know Taylor as well as I thought I did. Maybe I didn't know the real Taylor at all.

Thirty

Taylor

My pointer finger flew down the list of names, nearly smudging the black ink as it dried on the paper. The official show rankings had been updated and posted just minutes ago as the last class of the day was now complete. Finding my name under each class I competed in, I tallied the numbers in my head. For each ribbon won, I earned a certain number of points and I was hoping I was still a contender for the all-around championship title. My stupid nose dive into the dirt could've screwed everything up.

I was halfway through the list when one of the show volunteers walked out of the office armed with a single piece of white paper. As she started positioning the new paper on the corkboard, it dawned on me what she had – the point *totals* for each competitor.

I watched her out the corner of my eye, trying to appear casual, but wanting to rip the results from her hands. I just about screamed as she took her time placing a thumbtack on each corner of the paper, making sure it hung straight.

Happy with her work, the volunteer pushed the last tack into the corkboard and walked away. As soon as she turned her back, I leaped the distance to the other side of the board, ready to devour the new information.

"Come on, come on, come on," I muttered to myself as my eyes focused on the list. My hands involuntarily clasped together at the suspense, but a squeal quickly escaped my lips as I found my name. I was in second place with one more day left of the show! I still had a shot at the championship!

My feet danced around in a little jig as I pictured Star and myself posing for our magazine shot, standing proudly next to our new saddle and golden trophy. "Yes!" I meant to whisper the word, but it came out more like I'd just completed a touchdown. I balled my fist together and jerked my arm down by my side in a celebratory thrust. However, in my celebration, I didn't notice that someone was sneaking up behind me...until my elbow connected with their flesh.

"Umph," a voice gasped into my ear and I spun around to witness Jace doubled over with a hand on his stomach. "Geez, Taylor," he said as he looked up at me. "I wasn't expecting to get pounded for trying to give my girlfriend a kiss."

"Oops." I shrugged my shoulders, but I didn't feel too bad. I was still celebrating in my head. "Don't be so sneaky next time," I instructed, half-kidding and half-serious.

At my comment, the sparkle returned to Jace's emerald eyes and he gave me a one-sided grin. "You are quite the handful, Taylor Johnson." His playful smirk was infectious and I felt my lips turning up in a grin.

"I could say the same of you," I replied, liking how he called me his girlfriend in the midst of getting elbowed in the stomach. And then I remembered why I got so wound up in the first place. "Guess who's in the top two of the point standings so far." I raised my eyebrows and cocked my head, challenging him to say anyone else's name but mine.

Jace walked towards me with slow steps and took my hips in his hands, pulling me closer. "Me and you," he said before dipping his head down and grabbing my lips with his.

Normally, a kiss from Jace would give my body tremors and send my heart into an uneven rhythm, but his three words shocked my system. They weren't what I was expecting him to say. My eyes froze open and my lips wouldn't move with his kiss. After a few seconds, Jace pulled back.

"Is something wrong?" he asked, looking a bit offended.

"What did you say?"

"Tay, I asked you if something was wrong."

"No." I shook my head. "Before that. What did you say before that?"

"I said you and I are the top two contenders for the championship title. I called the show office about ten minutes ago for an update." His smile widened again. "Isn't that great?"

The realization of Jace's statement sunk in...Jace was in the number one spot. I was behind him in second place.

"Oh," I said, making sure my face didn't fall as I gently broke out of his hold. "Yeah, that's great." I turned away, not so gently, to get a better look at the list.

Sure thing. Jace Brooks' name was at the top of the list, above mine, and beating me by five points. My body went numb as Jace put his arm around my shoulders, smiling and oblivious to my reaction.

I didn't know how to feel. On one hand, Jace was now my boyfriend, something I'd wanted for months. I should probably be happy for him, show him support. That's what girlfriends were supposed to do. On the other hand, he was the only thing keeping me from taking home the Northwest Stock Horse Championship title, an award I'd worked so hard for, wanted with every fiber of my body. And on top of that, I surely would have been in the number one spot if I hadn't botched up my western pleasure class with a stupid loose girth.

Jace turned his head towards me and gave my shoulders a quick squeeze. "Pretty exciting. Right, Tay?"

In that moment, I was thankful for my years of rodeo-queen experience. I flashed my best plastic smile and nodded my head while my insides screamed.

Jace kissed me again. "I'll see you tonight at the bonfire, right?"

"Yeah, for sure," I said with all the enthusiasm I could muster. Every muscle in my face tightened to force another grin.

Jace pulled me into a half-hug and winked as he turned away. My eyes followed him as he walked, but my mind was clouded with calculations. I had two more classes tomorrow, both of which Jace was also competing in – mountain trail and the freestyle horsemanship class. He'd be tough competition. But, if I could win both classes, I would earn enough points to take home the championship award.

I folded my arms across my chest, wondering what Jace's reaction would be if I beat him. What would my reaction be if he snagged the title from my hands? Neither of us liked to lose, but there could only be one champion.

I was beginning to wonder if there was any way I could win – whether I took home that champ saddle or not.

Star's head popped up as I approached her stall and she blew out two soft nickers at my arrival - nickers meant only for me.

"Hey there, Babydoll," I said, reaching through the metal stall bars and picking a single strand of hay from her flaxen forelock. Star batted her long, black eyelashes as I ran my fingers down her forehead to the soft fuzz of her nose. "Make sure to get your beauty-sleep tonight. We've got some serious butt-kicking to do tomorrow."

And, as though she understood the seriousness of my whispers, Star reached for her hay net with vigor. She chomped her teeth around an excessively large chunk of hay and ripped it from the nylon net. She tossed bits through the air with a few flicks of her nose, showing the hay who was boss.

Her aggressive approach to eating made me chuckle. "Now that's the kind of sass I like to see."

Just as Star settled from her hay-beating, my ears caught the sound of oats rattling against plastic. Star heard it too, and a few seconds later, Lucy emerged from the tack room, four feed pans stacked on top of one another. Her arms were wrapped around the balanced heap.

All four horses whinnied in eager anticipation.

"Hey, Taylor," Lucy greeted me with a timid smile. Her chestnut ponytail was peppered with hay bits. I felt the need to pick them out.

"Hey," I responded as she walked towards me. "Which pan is Star's? I can give it to her."

"That'd be great. Her grain is in the second pan." Lucy stood still as I took the top two feed pans off her stack, taking Star's and rearranging the other pan back on the pile.

Pushing open Star's stall door, I set the plastic feed pan on the ground and Star dug in. As she ate, I watched Lucy distribute the rest of the grain. Across the aisle, she fed Hammer and Georgie, patting them each on their foreheads before closing their doors. As she walked towards Chance, he nickered in the same soft tone that Star had just greeted me. Lucy rolled open his stall door, whispered a few words and then held his grain pan against her chest. Chance lapped up the oats and watched Lucy as he chewed. He gazed at her like she deserved his full attention.

I cleared my throat. "So, how long have you been practicing barrels on Chance?"

Lucy turned her head, looking surprised by my question. I thought it was obvious small-talk after witnessing her run barrels in the outdoor arena. She raised her shoulders slightly. "I've never practiced barrels on Chance."

"What?" I asked. The word shot out of my mouth. "You've *never* practiced a barrel pattern with him? No way."

"No, I haven't. I promise." Lucy raised her shoulders higher like she was shocked herself. She whispered her next sentence like she was afraid she'd done something wrong. "That ride in the outdoor arena was the first time I've tried him on a barrel pattern."

I chuckled, but it wasn't meant to be condescending. It was a stunned chuckle. "No way," I restated. "He ran that pattern like he knew what he was doing." I would have accused Lucy of lying, but I knew she wasn't capable of it.

She glanced back at Chance as he licked up the last pieces of grain. "I honestly don't know where that came from. It was like something clicked in his head when we turned around the second barrel...like he knew what he was doing."

"Something clicked?" I asked. "Like a memory? I didn't think he was broke when you and Casey found him. I mean, I saw him explode and toss you through the air like a wet noodle." Lucy gave me a small smile and I knew she didn't take offence to my comment. I wasn't being rude. It was the truth. Chance went rodeo-bronc-crazy the first time Lucy got on him. And, I was pretty sure he did it a few times after that.

"I really don't know much about Chance's past other than he came from Billy Jackson's place." Her eyebrows wrinkled sharply at Billy's name. "And I don't think Billy was running barrels on Chance. He couldn't even get close enough to put a halter on him. I'm certain he didn't even like horses. The cops told us he inherited a bunch of them from his Dad."

"Maybe his dad rode Chance?"

She shrugged again. "From the picture the cops painted of Billy's dad, I think he was more of a horse trader than a rider. I'm thinking he picked Chance up at an auction somewhere hoping to resell him and make some money."

"Maybe Chance had some training before he ended up at the Jackson's?" There had to be an answer to this puzzle. Chance didn't learn those moves on his own.

"It's possible, but I'm not sure I'll ever know his full story. It's not like I'm going to call up Billy and ask him for the details."

"Yeah, he seemed pretty shady," I responded, remembering Lucy's confrontation with Billy at the Cowboy Race's awards ceremony. In particular, I remembered the way Lucy screamed at him, and the fear covering her face.

"'Shady' might be an understatement," Lucy noted as she closed Chance's stall. From her tone I could tell there was more to the story, but Lucy didn't offer it up and I didn't press the issue. "Is Star all done with her grain?"

Star was already mowing down on her hay and I grabbed the grain pan from the stall floor, handing it back to Lucy. She did a good job of looking after the horses. She obviously cared about all of them – not just her own horse.

"You've got Chance's registration papers, right?" I asked, thinking I could probably help with a piece of Chance's puzzle.

Lucy gathered Hammer's and Georgie's feed pans and responded over her shoulder. "Yeah, I've actually got his papers in my duffel bag in your trailer. I've been meaning to Google his sire and dam..."

I didn't let her finish. "I can do better than that."

Thirty-one

Lucy

I followed Taylor into her trailer and watched as she grabbed an iPad from the kitchen table. She plopped down cross-legged on the leather couch, as the tablet screen came to life. She started tapping before looking up. "You just going to stand there?" she asked, raising her eyebrows and then giving a pat to the leather with her hand.

I was still standing in the doorway. "Oh," I noted. "Guess I could take a seat." It was hard to forget that this was Taylor's space. I felt like I needed to respect that. But...she was technically sitting on my bed.

I walked over and took a seat opposite Taylor. "So you think you can find out where Chance came from? His past?" My stomach fluttered at the thought. I was excited and anxious at the same time. What if we stumbled on something I didn't want to know? What if the Jacksons were thieves? Maybe they stole Chance from some little girl who's been crying every night since he disappeared. Maybe they grabbed him from a stall at a rodeo.

I pictured Billy pecking away at a keyboard, creating fake registration papers to ensure he'd get his money from me. Although, I had to admit, Billy being savvy with a computer was a far-fetched idea. That gave me some comfort.

"I'm a member of the Quarter Horse Association," Taylor said, making a few more swipes at the Ipad with her finger before she continued. "That gives me access to online records. It allows me to look up information on any registered quarter horse."

"Really?" I asked, zoning in on the kind of information we were about to find on Chance...on my Chance. "What kind of stuff? What kind of information do you have access to?"

"Bloodlines, show records, past owners. Stuff like that." Taylor seemed to find what she was looking for on her Ipad. "Where are Chance's papers?" I stood up and unzipped a pocket on the side of my duffel bag, pulling out a thick sheet of tan paper, folded once. Taylor continued her instructions. "There should be a registration number in the upper right hand corner of the paper. Read it to me."

I read off the numbers, one by one, waiting as Taylor typed them into the online records system. I held my breath when she pressed enter and almost told her to stop. Chance was mine, as far as I knew, and I didn't want anything to change that. Would Taylor keep my secret if we found out he didn't actually belong to me?

I swallowed hard and tried to ignore the questions growing in my head, but they only multiplied as I watched Taylor's reaction to the new information. She turned her body towards me, slowly, her lips parted, ready to spew out Chance's story.

I shook my head. "I take it back. I don't want to know. Don't tell me whatever you just read." Taylor was being nice to me now, but she wasn't *that* nice. If Chance wasn't mine, she wouldn't keep that to herself. "I really don't want to know."

"Oh, I think you're going to want to know this," she said, her eyes wide as she ignored my babbling. "Chance's registered name is Fool's Gold, right?"

I nodded hesitantly.

"Do you know what Cash's registered name is?"

"Linda's horse?"

This time Taylor nodded.

I didn't know what Cash's registered name was. The only time I had spent around Cash was during the Cowboy Race and at the awards ceremony. The only thing I knew about him was that he was a gorgeous buckskin and Linda had won about a thousand championships on him. Well, maybe a thousand was exaggerating a bit.

"No," I responded. "Why does that matter?"

"Because Cash's registered name is Gold Rush." Taylor sat still, her mouth gaped open, obviously waiting for me to put the pieces together.

"Does that mean their related?"

"Yes," she exclaimed and snorted out a breath - like she didn't believe it herself. "They have the same sire, Blazing Gold. And, they came from the same barn in Texas. It looks like Chance was born at South-Star Stables and sold about four years later." Taylor set the Ipad on her crossed legs and looked at me like I'd just won the lottery. "The trainer at South-Star Stables is a five-time world champion barrel racer. And, Blazing Gold is her prized stallion. He's sired more champions than I can count."

The pieces of Chance's past were falling together and starting to make sense. "If Chance was sold at four, that means he probably had at least a year of training at that barn." I was amazed at this revelation, but at the same time, those things didn't really matter to me. I loved Chance before I knew his bloodlines, his training, which barn he came from. "So...does your Ipad say Chance is mine?"

Taylor cocked her head and I thought she was going to tell me I was a few bricks short of a load. "Yes, crazy." She handed me her Ipad. "After South-Star Stables and about five other names, you are listed as Chance's current owner." Taylor pointed to the middle of the screen. "See. It says Lucy Rose right there."

I let out a sigh of pure relief and let myself relax into the couch.

Taylor sat back too, thumping her slender body against the cushion and taking a minute to think. "Do you know how much Linda paid for Cash?" She started laughing before answering her own question. "She wrote a check for $20,000 when he was a yearling. Twenty thousand dollars!"

I couldn't help but to gasp.

"She paid thousands of dollars for Cash and you found a horse roaming around in the mountains with the same bloodlines and *more* training." Taylor's body shook with laughter. "Now that's funny stuff. I can't wait to tell Linda that one."

"I'm thinking she's not going to find it quite as funny." Actually, I was certain she wasn't going to find it quite as funny.

But, it kind of was.

A giggle grew and bubbled up from my chest and soon Taylor and I were laughing together...that surprised me more than Chance's bloodlines. But, it felt good. The two of us laughed until we both melted into the soft leather of the cushions and were out of breath.

Taylor sighed, holding her stomach as she glanced at the digital clock on the microwave. "Oh, crap. It's already 6:00?"

I watched her jump from the couch. "Do you have somewhere to be?" I was being sarcastic, but Taylor opened a closet door and started scanning through the tank tops and jeans she had hanging in a neat row. I guess she did have somewhere to be.

She pulled out a turquoise tank top and looked at me over her shoulder. "You want to go to a bonfire, Lucy?"

The bonfire Taylor invited me to wasn't noted on the show schedule, but she informed me it was only a short walk away. After a quick change of clothes, Taylor and I left the trailer, walked along the white fence of the rodeo arena, and hiked through a field towards a thick patch of trees. Once in the brush, Taylor located a weathered fence and hopped over a broken board. She turned back as I hesitated, skeptical of where she was leading me.

"Come on," she said, waving her hand at me. "I promise I'm not leading you blindly into the wilderness."

I gave her a doubtful stare. "I'm not sure I trust you this much yet." Which was true.

She shrugged her shoulders, but grinned at the same time. "I wouldn't trust me either. But if you don't come, you're going to miss out on some killer barbeque. Tanner Wilkenson's Mom is like the Martha Stewart of the grill. Plus, there'll be s'mores."

I stood still for another second and then gave in. Who could resist s'mores? "I'll trust you this one time," I noted before grabbing hold of the fence and jumping over. But, as my feet touched the ground, a whiff of spiced brown sugar goodness hit my nose. Taylor and I inhaled together, closing our eyes to relish in the sweet, smoky aroma. "Okay, I believe you," I said, as my eyes opened.

"Told you so."

Taylor didn't waste any time and stepped towards a beat-down dirt path. It looked like this area of the woods had seen some traffic. "So this Tanner is a friend of yours?" I asked, following along as my stomach growled.

"Yeah, Tanner's whole family shows horses. They're at all the big events. Everyone knows the Wilkensons," Taylor said, making a sharp turn at the end of the dirt path. She pushed aside a few leafy branches and we stepped out onto a well-manicured lawn. "And, since they basically live next door to the show grounds, they have a barbeque every year on the last night of the show."

"Well, that's awfully nice of them."

Taylor shrugged. "I think they just like to party. But, whatever. They always have amazing food."

Taylor and I strolled across a sprawling lawn towards a classic red barn with white trim and an iron weather vane. We passed three square pastures, each with a few grazing horses. The fourth pasture, closest to the barn, had a wide open gate and smoke rising from a well-built bonfire. A group of laughing teens hung within range of the flames, sticks in hands.

Taylor nodded her head towards the bonfire as we passed. "The s'mores area is over there and the barbecue's next to the barn."

My mouth started watering in anticipation.

Outside the barn, there was a smoldering charcoal grill and a table full of typical summer dishes. Taylor handed me a paper plate which I filled full of potato salad, corn on the cob, baked beans, and sauced ribs. By the time we made it to one of the picnic tables, I had already finished a rib, balancing my plate in one hand.

"Hey, Taylor." Friendly faces at the table greeted us as we sat.

Taylor smiled and flipped her blonde braid over her shoulder. "This is Lucy," she said before making herself comfy on the wooden bench.

The group greeted me in unison, as well. I recognized most of them from the show, even without their fancy outfits. And, with Taylor's introduction, they accepted me instantly. No questions asked. The group chatted away as we filled our bellies, telling stories of their horses and the show year. I listened, chiming in with one word agreements between mouthfuls. It was nice to relax and be part of the group, instead of the worker-bee for a change.

Taylor and I scraped our plates clean at the same time and I glanced at the bonfire.

"You got room for a s'more?" I asked.

Taylor licked her lips and rose from the bench. "I always have room for dessert."

"It was nice to meet everyone," I said with a wave as we left the group.

After more introductions at the bonfire, Taylor and I roasted marshmallows and created four of the best looking s'mores I had ever seen - golden goo oozing over melted chocolate and graham crackers. I sighed at the sight of them. They were almost too pretty to eat.

Taylor grabbed one in each hand. "Come on," she said. "I've got to show you one of the Wilkenson's colts. He was born late in the season so he's only a few days old. He's adorable."

Without question, I grabbed my two s'mores and scurried off with Taylor to the barn. We headed down the aisle and straight to an extra large stall in the middle of the barn. I held one of Taylor's s'mores as she pulled open the door to reveal a dark bay mare munching on a mouthful of hay. Next to her side was a miniature version of mom with wobbly legs and a fuzzy, black mohawk for a mane. I couldn't help it – I squealed.

Taylor looked at me knowingly. "Isn't he just the cutest thing ever?"

I wanted to reach out and touch his baby soft coat, his tiny muzzle, the fuzzy puff of his forelock. But I held back, not knowing how the mare would react. "Do you think she will mind if we get closer?"

"Tanner said she's starting to get used to people around her baby, but she's a first-time mom. She's a little nervous." Taylor took a few quiet steps into the stall. "We probably shouldn't get too close, but we can watch them from a distance."

Taylor lowered herself into a cross-legged position in the cedar bedding. I tiptoed in her steps and sat down beside her. We were just a few feet from the cracked door, giving the mom and baby plenty of room, but the mare turned her head to blow soft breaths against her colt's neck - checking to make sure he was okay with the new visitors. The bay colt responded by nuzzling his mother's cheek. With his nose pressed against her, the colt's lips wrinkled up, exposing his pink toothless gums.

Taylor's eyes lit up and she smiled at me without words, but I knew we were thinking the same thing. What a special moment we were witnessing. And, in that moment I recognized that Taylor and I shared the same love for horses, even though we lived in different worlds. Sitting there on the stall floor, just a few inches from each other, I wondered if we could actually be friends.

"Thanks for bringing me here," I whispered.

Taylor opened her mouth to respond, but a slew of footsteps and laughter cut her off. The mare's head jerked up at the noise.

"We should probably leave them alone before we stress them out," Taylor noted, pulling her feet underneath herself to stand, but stopping as she heard her name leave the mouth of a boy in the barn aisle.

"So you and Taylor Johnson are back together, huh?" The boy teased. "Or were you guys just sucking-face for the heck of it today?" He was obviously teasing Jace. I glanced at Taylor, wondering if she was offended by the boy's rude comment, but she only rolled her eyes and awaited Jace's answer.

"Yes, Scott. We're back together. Why? You keeping notes on who I'm dating?" Another boy snickered at Jace's remark. "Or you just jealous?"

I could tell egos were flaring up and I didn't like where this conversation was going - especially since the boys didn't know we were within earshot. I squirmed, eager to make our presence known, but Taylor placed her finger in front of her smiling mouth, shushing me. For some reason, she wanted to hear what they had to say about her.

"Well, obviously I'm jealous," Scott replied and then chuckled. "Except you guys aren't going to be together long once she finds out what you did."

Now I had a view of the group through the cracked stall door. The guys stopped, facing each other, and I watched as Jace shot a dirty look at Scott.

"It's not like I meant for that to happen," Jace replied.

"What? What happened?" The third kid chimed in.

Scott continued, loving whatever he had hanging over Jace's head. "Jace didn't tell you?" He laughed at the secret he was holding.

Jace laced his thumbs in his jean pockets and shook his head. "You're such a loud-mouth, Scott."

Scott playfully punched Jace in the shoulder. "Oh, come on. It's funny!"

The third kid was dying to get clued in. "What are you guys talking about?" he pleaded.

Scott raised his eyebrows and tipped his cowboy hat towards the third boy. "You remember yesterday when Taylor was ahead of Jace in the point totals? When she was on her way to winning the all-around championship title?" The other kid nodded his head. "You remember when she cartwheeled off her horse and took a nose-dive into the dirt?" Scott waited for the kid to nod again before continuing. "That wasn't a coincidence."

Both boys looked at Jace, slowly.

"What?" he said, shrugging his shoulders at the accusation. "I didn't mean for her to fall off. I just loosened the cinch so she'd have to stop in the middle of the class and forfeit. I didn't expect her to keep riding with a loose saddle."

The s'more I was holding rolled off my fingers and dropped to the ground as my hand popped up to cover my mouth. I whipped my head around to face Taylor. She was in the same crouched position, but the color had completely drained from her face, along with her smile. I didn't know what to do. I didn't know what to say. I could barely comprehend what I just heard. Jace, who was apparently Taylor's boyfriend, had sabotaged her ride. Worse than that, he intentionally put Taylor in danger. There were a thousand things that could have happened to her...things much worse than just hitting the dirt.

I pulled my hand away from my mouth as I remembered the minutes before Taylor's class. "Jace held Star for me while I got her bridle out of the tack room," I whispered in disbelief. "He must have loosed the girth when I wasn't watching."

Taylor looked sick to her stomach, her breaths increasing. I didn't know if she was going to cry or throw-up. Trying to comfort her, I reached over and placed a hand on her knee, but my touch only jolted her body into action.

Taylor snapped her mouth shut and leap-frogged over me, bursting through the stall door. The overly-cocky group of boys suddenly looked like they were witnessing a ghost march across the aisle. I barely had time to get to my feet before Taylor got to Jace.

She didn't let him speak. In one swift movement, Taylor circled her arm around and smacked Jace in the face - with a handful of s'more. He flinched at the attack, his hands flying up in surrender and his back hitting the wall behind him, but Taylor didn't back down. She stepped closer, glaring up at his six-foot frame with vengeance as she slowly ground the graham cracker-marshmallow-chocolate mess into his face.

"I can't believe I wasted a second of my time on you," she snarled, leaning closer and wiping the gooey leftovers across the front of his starched, clean shirt. "Don't ever talk to me again. I mean it. Don't *ever* talk to me again."

The other boys stepped back. Jace didn't utter a word.

And finishing her attack, Taylor picked her foot up and stomped her wooden boot heel down on Jace's toe, hard. *Really hard.*

I stood in the doorway of the stall, stunned, as Taylor turned on her heels and marched off. She stomped across the floor in a heated exit, leaving Jace cussing and hopping on one foot, but I caught her bottom lip quivering as she passed me.

I took off after her.

Taylor

Sweat rolled down my back, dampening the gauzy fabric of my shirt, and my calves burned, protesting my run through the woods. I never looked back, but I knew Lucy was following me. She called out my name at first. When I didn't reply, I only heard her footsteps.

The heat rose from my chest and into my face as I thought of Jace. *Why would he do that to me? How could he do that to me?* That good-for-nothing, lying, scum-of-the-freaking-earth...a growl rolled up my throat and turned into a screech as it left my mouth. Two girls exiting the barn jumped and scattered out of my path as I blew by. I didn't care what they thought. They hadn't just had had their hearts ripped out of their chest. They hadn't been slapped in the face by someone they thought they loved.

I wanted to get to my trailer, to be hidden away from the world while I crumbled, but the pressure in my eyes wouldn't stop. I couldn't keep the tears from coming. Instead, I made a hard left into the tack stall, whipping aside the fabric curtain as hot tears ran over my cheeks.

I dropped myself down on a stack of dirty sheets just as Lucy walked in. She took a few steps towards me.

"Leave me alone," I said, followed by a sob I was trying to hold in. "I need to be by myself." I couldn't handle being with anyone right now. I couldn't trust anyone.

With my head in my hands, I could see Lucy's boots through my fingers. They didn't move.

"I'm not leaving you alone, Taylor," she said, barely above a whisper. "You shouldn't be alone right now." Another sob escaped my throat, but Lucy didn't go away.

Jace's betrayal cut me like a knife. I thought he cared about me. I thought he loved me. Everything I thought was wrong. He sabotaged me because he wanted to win. I hit the dirt because of my boyfriend...my ex-boyfriend. The tears flew down my cheeks and I buried my face into my knees, wrapping my arms around my legs. "I feel so stupid," I mumbled into my jeans.

Lucy's footsteps fell across the ground and the sheets crinkled as she took a seat next to me. "That guy's a jerk. A complete jerk." Her words were steady, but I caught the disgust in her voice. "Nobody with any sense in their head would put another person in danger, for any reason." Lucy put her hand on my arm and gave it a soft squeeze. "He doesn't deserve you."

I tried hard to control my breathing as my jeans soaked up the tears. I stayed in that position, cradled and afraid to move until the crying slowed. My heart physically hurt, my eyes burned, and through it all Lucy never moved an inch, her hand still on my arm. She didn't tell me I was stupid for falling for Jace. She didn't remind me that I had blamed *her* for my accident. She just sat there and listened to me cry.

I raised my head slowly, setting my cheek against my knees and swallowing the lump in my throat. I bit my lip to stifle a sob.

Lucy looked straight into my blurry eyes, her lips pressed together in a straight line. "That guy deserves a lot more than a s'more to the face."

Thirty-two

Lucy

Half an hour later, I helped Taylor to her feet, leaving the crumpled pile of horse sheets on the floor. I grabbed three bridles from the metal rack, handing one to Taylor, and we exited the tack room. We had a plan. Well, sort of.

"First, we need to find Tiera," I noted. Taylor gave me a sideways glance with her red eyes, but she didn't protest. "Just trust me."

Taylor nodded.

I pulled my phone from my jeans and dialed Tiera, giving her a shortened version of the recent fiasco with Jace. Just seconds after ending the call, a blur of pink came running down the barn aisle headed straight for Taylor. Taylor winced as Tiera wrapped her arms around her and squeezed, pressing her head against Taylor's chest. Tiera held tight, her cell phone still in her hand.

Taylor raised an eyebrow at me, stuck in the awkward embrace. I cracked a grin.

"I can't believe he did that to you," Tiera exclaimed as she pulled back, still holding Taylor's arms. "What a...what a..."

I chimed in, stopping Tiera from trying to find a word suitable for Jace. "I can't believe it either. And, he certainly doesn't deserve to win the championship title."

Taylor wiggled out of Tiera's embrace, taking a step back and a deep breath.

"Of course he doesn't," Tiera said, her mouth open in disgust. "We need to report him to the show office, to the judges. They'll disqualify him for cheating."

Taylor's voice cracked as she finally spoke. "And what am I supposed to tell the judges?" She crossed her arms over her chest, cradling herself. "That I was hiding in a horse stall at a barbeque and I overheard Jace bragging to his friends that he loosened Star's girth before my ride?"

Tiera looked back and forth between Taylor and me and shrugged her shoulders. "I think they'll believe you. I mean, why would you lie about something like that?"

"We have no real proof," I said. "It would be his word against ours and I don't think he's going to fess up. Owning up to cheating, to putting Taylor in danger, would be suicide for Jace. They'd strip him of his winnings. Heck, the association probably wouldn't let him show again. Ever."

Taylor dug her nails into the flesh of her arms as she processed my words. "Lucy's right," she said, and shook her head. "Jace will never fess up to that. He'd never jeopardize winning the title or being banished from the show ring. We're going to have to beat him at his own game."

Tiera leaned in closer, waiting to hear our plan. I filled in the details we had so far. "Taylor and Jace both have two classes to compete in tomorrow – mountain trail and the freestyle horsemanship class. Taylor feels confident she can beat Jace in the trail class, but she needs our help to beat him in the freestyle class."

Taylor jumped in. "Jace always wins the freestyle class. Hammer's spins and sliding stops are killer. And, on top of that, he just had a new ride choreographed and the music was put together by some top-notch DJ his Dad knows in LA."

Tiera's face scrunched up in confusion and I felt an explanation was in order. "I didn't know what a freestyle horsemanship class was, either, until ten minutes ago. Basically, a rider has four minutes to put on a show, set to music, and certain movements are required during that time."

Taylor continued the explanation. "The riders have to complete a lead change, stop, pivot, and present all three gaits during those four minutes. And, you can show off any other trick or talent you want to. The judges score the riders on each maneuver, but a third of your score actually comes from the audience. The louder they scream, the more points you get." Tiera's eyes widened as Taylor described the class. "But Jace knows my music. He knows my whole plan for the freestyle class because I bounced ideas off him when we were dating...the first time we were dating. For all I know, he could have stolen all my ideas to use himself."

"I wouldn't put it past him," I said. "Cheating obviously doesn't bother him one bit."

"What can I do to help?" Tiera asked, genuinely concerned.

I stepped towards Tiera and handed her a bridle. "We need to put our heads together and come up with a brand new presentation with brand new music. And, we have one day to do it."

"I'm in!" Tiera squealed making both Taylor and me jump. "It's like we're the Saddle Club or something!" She clasped her hands together and jumped on her tippy toes.

After the shock of her squeal wore off, I couldn't help but laugh. Taylor, on the other hand, was looking at Tiera like we just teamed up with a crazy person.

"What?" Tiera stopped jumping, still holding her hands to her chest. "Was that a little too much?"

The sun cast a peach shadow over the open field and, in the last rays of light, we gathered our horses in a powwow, their noses nearly touching. From our saddles, Taylor, Tiera and I absorbed the music flowing out of Tiera's phone one last time.

The last few beats of the melody pumped through the air before Tiera lowered her phone to her thigh. "Who knew the remix music from dance class would come in handy after the recital? I'm glad I saved it on my phone."

Taylor was biting her lip, her eyes closed as she went through the routine in her head.

I rested my hand on the saddle horn. "I think we've got it down."

Taylor opened her eyes. "Maybe we should do it one more time? Just to be sure."

"Taylor, it's going to be dark soon and we don't want to wear the horses out. They've all got to be ready for tomorrow – especially Star."

Taylor paused and then nodded. "Yeah, you're right. Let's head back to the barn." She rolled her fingers through Star's flaxen mane, smoothing it against her neck. "I just want the performance to be perfect, you know? I don't want to give Jace any advantage."

Her usually confident brown eyes revealed a hint of uncertainty and I realized Taylor was looking for my reassurance. "Taylor, you just do what you do best – ride. Tiera and I will take care of the rest."

I hoped my words sounded stronger than they felt.

After a not-so-restful night of sleep, Tiera and I sat in the bleachers, literally on the edge of our seats, watching the mountain trail class. The course, spread out across the indoor arena, was made of an array of obstacles and completely different from the classes Taylor had been competing in up to this point.

"These obstacles look freaking scary," Tiera whispered to me out the corner of her mouth.

I agreed. There were multiple log obstacles and jumps, a bridge that teeter-tottered when stepped on, and even a man-made pond surrounded by stuffed animals (not the soft, fuzzy ones). I knew Chance would take one look at that fake elk's pointy rack and he'd run in the opposite direction. Every obstacle was a test of the rider's relationship with their horse.

"Here comes Taylor," I said and we straightened up in our seats. Taylor rode into the arena at a lope and approached the first obstacle - the double log jump. "This one is right up her alley." And she proved me right as Star easily popped over both logs, looking relaxed.

So far, none of the riders - including Jace – had completed a perfect round. There were even a few riders that had to get off their horses and lead them out of the arena, without completing the course. But most had finished, making it through the obstacles in one form or another. And there were a handful of riders who rode it well, making few mistakes. Currently, Jace was in the lead with the most points and quickest time, but even Hammer had baulked at a few of the obstacles.

Loping away from the log jump, Taylor slowed Star to a walk, getting ready to tackle the miniature mountain. This obstacle was a dirt hill covered in thick branches and rocks. Taylor took her time, allowing Star to lower her nose and check out her footing. Being cautious, Star took slow steps over the closely placed objects and climbed to the top of the mound where there was a flat spot, just big enough to turn around. A 180-degree pivot was required and Star made it look easy, turning in a tight half-circle and carefully retreating down the same path.

Tiera grabbed my forearm. "She's doing awesome." There was a squeaky tone to her voice.

"Don't jinx her," I replied. "She's got half the course left."

Tiera squeezed my arm tighter. "You're right. You're right."

Next was the pond, surrounded by stuffed elk, deer, and turkeys. They approached the water at a trot until Star was just a few feet away from the edge...and she suddenly spooked. Star dug her hooves into the ground and back peddled, snorting at the herd of unknown animals. I clenched my jaw and sucked air through my teeth, but Taylor looked unfazed, allowing Star to stand still and sniff the air.

"It's taxidermy," I explained to Tiera. "Those are real hides from dead animals."

"That's gross." Tiera wrinkled her nose.

"I'm sure Star is freaked out by the smells. Her instincts are telling her to get out of there."

Taylor patted Star and seemed to be talking to her, coaxing her. Slowly, Star's neck lowered and she stepped towards the pond, all her senses on high alert. She put one hoof in the water and then burst through the shallow pond with a high-stepping trot, spraying droplets through the air and leaving the dead animals behind.

Next, the pair cantered back and forth in an S-shape through a line of closely placed trees. She swooshed through the obstacle like a gamer running poles. I looked at the clock blinking on the wall above the arena. Taylor was making up lost time, but it was going to be close. All of the top riders completed the course in around three and a half minutes. And, the clock just passed the three minute mark.

"Come on, Taylor. Come on. You got this," I mumbled under my breath, squeezing my knees with both hands. I heard Tiera muttering the same words.

Star stopped just short of the next obstacle, the bridge, and Taylor asked her to step on. This time Star didn't hesitate, getting her front feet on the wood...but she didn't expect the bridge to move under her hooves. Tiera and I gasped as Star launched her body away from the perceived danger.

"Poor Star wasn't expecting a teeter-totter!" Tiera exclaimed as Taylor rode Star into a circle, trying to calm her down. Star made her displeasure known, wringing her neck from side to side.

By this point, my fingers were digging into the metal of my seat, wrapped tightly around the edge. "I don't know if she's going to step foot on that bridge again. And, they have to make it across or they're disqualified."

The crowd was now in a murmur, watching Taylor and the clock.

Approaching the bridge again, Star hesitated, but trusted Taylor enough to follow her cues. She moved forward, placing one hoof on the bridge to test it. The wood creaked, falling under her weight. Star waited for it to settle before following with her other front hoof. With tentative steps, Star inched her way across the bridge and then launched off the opposite end as it teetered down. It wasn't pretty, but they made it across.

"They have one more obstacle!" Tiera squealed, as we both jumped to our feet, watching Taylor and Star blaze around the end of the arena and turn back towards the gate. Taylor's blonde hair hung in the wind behind her as they soared over the last jump, a thick fallen tree, and broke into a gallop towards the finish line.

Tiera and I screamed, pumping our fists in the air as the clock ticked away. As Star blew past the electric timer, the blinking numbers stopped at three minutes, thirty-four seconds. I gasped, and Tiera looked to me for an explanation.

"It's not the fastest time, but Taylor could still win, depending on what the judges awarded her for points on each obstacle." And there was one more ride to go before the final scores were announced. That was too long to sit still. "Let's go find Taylor."

Tiera and I burst out of the arena and found Taylor dismounted and standing next to Star. She shook her head as we got closer.

"I should have given Star more time to look at the obstacles," she said, still shaking her head. "Dang it."

She was beating herself up for honest mistakes. "You had one of the top times, Taylor. You could still easily win."

Taylor chewed her lip. "I'm going to walk Star around while the last rider goes. This wait is going to kill me." And with that, Taylor turned away and Star followed. Tiera and I were left standing by the arena.

"I'm going to walk with her," Tiera said, but I put a hand on her arm as she stepped forward.

"I think Star is the only thing that can calm her nerves right now. Let's let her be."

Tiera nodded, understanding, and we waited to hear the results.

Most of the riders, including Jace, were on their horses, gathered around the arena gate as they watched the last competitor. I scanned Jace up and down, wondering when he got the idea to loosen Star's girth or why that thought would even cross his mind.

Jace caught my stare and I whispered to Tiera. "Hammer doesn't deserve a cheating, big-headed jerk for an owner." Jace couldn't hear my words, but my face must have conveyed their meaning. He quickly broke eye contact and looked away.

Tiera snapped her fingers. "True dat, sister."

Finally, the announcer's voice cracked over the speakers, breaking my gaze. "All right, folks. We have the official results for the mountain trail class. The top three rides were separated by only a few points. As your name is called, please enter the arena for your ribbon." All chit-chat stopped. "In third place...we have Taylor Johnson."

I cupped my hand to my mouth. "Oh, crap." I scanned the crowd and found Taylor, back in the saddle and riding towards the arena. Before she could get there, the second and first place winners were announced.

Jace's name was last.

"Oh no," Tiera whined. "What does that mean? Does Taylor still have a chance at the championship?"

Taylor jogged Star through the center of the group gathered at the gate. Her shoulders were back, her equitation in perfect form, but when she passed Jace, the look on her face could have peeled paint from barn wood. Jace flinched. A wave of fear flashed across his face. Did he think Taylor was going to rat him out? She probably should've.

But Taylor didn't slow down. She didn't speak one word. She rode into the arena and picked up her yellow ribbon, even flashing a smile for the clapping audience.

And I scraped together the words to answer Tiera's question. "That yellow ribbon means Taylor needs to get a blue one tonight. No other color will win her the championship."

Thirty-three

Lucy

Taylor weaved the last of the silky ribbon into Star's braided mane as I walked out of the tack room, fastening the buckle of my borrowed black chaps.

"I told you they'd fit you. You look good in chaps." Taylor shot me a smile as she tied off the last braid. "At least I'm not making you wear a leotard." She winked and I chuckled at the thought.

"You would've gotten a fight out of me if you tried to stuff me into one of those things. Spandex? Ugh." I grinned back, looking over Taylor's getup. She sported the same leather chaps, but instead of a black t-shirt, her outfit was topped with one of Tiera's dance leotards. Metallic purple and blue fringe hung from the back of her sleeves and draped her shoulders. Her long blonde ponytail fell down her back in curls. "But, the leotard suits you."

She cocked an eyebrow. "Thanks...I think."

"Okay, you guys. I'm ready," Tiera announced as she jogged down the hall in a matching black leotard with fringe, black tights and a metallic purple tutu. She hopped along in her cowboy boots, carrying her ballet shoes in her hand. She was all smiles. "Horses and dance. The perfect combo!"

Chance wasn't as sure about her statement, snorting at her bouncing tutu as she jogged past.

"Looks like the horses are ready, too," Tiera said, patting Georgie as he tried to get a mouthful of fringe.

Star, Chance & Georgie stood patiently, tacked up and full of braids and ribbons. Their gleaming coats were sprinkled in glitter. I took a deep breath, wiping my sweaty palms on my shirt. "Okay, girls. Let's do this."

Dusk settled over the outdoor arena as we rode up, side-by-side as a team. The wooden bleachers were packed, the overhead lights blaring, and the announcer's voice boomed through the evening air. It was just as I pictured it when Chance and I ran barrels the other day. Only this time it was for real. I swallowed a growing lump in my throat and glanced at the other girls. All three of us were quiet, lost in our own thoughts.

Taylor was serious but relaxed, swaying with Star's stride. And her straight face warmed when she caught me looking her way. I knew how much this meant to her. I now knew how hard she worked for each one of her wins, how much she cared about her relationship with Star. I wanted Taylor to win this championship, not in spite of Jace, but because she had earned it.

We slowed to a halt, joining the group of riders waiting by the closed gate and I jumped as an electric guitar squealed out of the speakers, followed by crashing drums. It sounded like a rock band was exploding somewhere in the arena.

"Jace is riding," Taylor said, peering through the crowd.

Both Tiera and I craned our necks, trying to get a glimpse, but I only caught a flash of bay as Hammer whizzed by and the rock song played on. Whatever Jace was doing, he was doing it at high speed. The audience hooted and whistled, rising to their feet at the end.

"That was Jace Brooks, folks. Current leader for this year's Northwest Stock Show All-Around Championship title. He is certainly giving his fellow competitors a run for their money, isn't he?" The announcer's words shattered through the cheers as Jace trotted out of the arena on Hammer, pumping his fist in the air.

"And next we have another top contender for the title, Taylor Johnson. Her performance tonight is called *The Dance-off*." At his introduction, the riders in front of us parted and I felt my lungs constrict. This was it.

Taylor, Tiera and I rode in a line, together, stopping in the brief safety of the chute - only a few feet from stepping into the arena. All three horses pricked their ears towards the bright lights. Star stood in the middle of the pack, Georgie and Chance edging her in.

In the few seconds of quiet, Taylor dropped her reins, resting them on Star's neck and reached her hands out for ours. I grabbed hold, giving her a hand a squeeze, and I watched Tiera do the same from the other side.

"Thank you," Taylor mouthed, first to me, and then to Tiera. Her two simple words brought peace back to my mind as the lights went dark.

Taylor

My hands were still warm as I picked up the reins and watched Lucy and Tiera leave my side. They directed their horses towards the single spotlight on the black arena floor. Light glistened off the metallic ribbons floating from Chance and Georgie's hair and butterflies moved through my belly as I watched them trot, knowing I would join them soon.

The audience was hushed now, but I planned on making them roar. Nothing about performing made me nervous - only excited.

This is what I live for. And it was time to show everyone what I could do.

A second spotlight moved in my direction and I brushed Star with my legs. She obliged and we stepped out onto the dirt, inching towards the horses as Tiera dismounted.

Lucy took Georgie's reins from Tiera, guiding both geldings out of sight and leaving Tiera in the middle of the arena. In the circle of light, Tiera stood perfectly still, her legs together and toes pointed out. Her arms were suspended in front of her, bent at the elbows and her fingers nearly touched. Her slick blonde bun glowed in the light. She was the silent image of a ballerina.

Star and I approached and stopped to face her. In the quiet of the arena, Tiera completed a curtsy, crossing her legs while bending forward, holding the outer edges of her tutu.

I cued Star to respond and she began lowering her chest, shifting her rear into the air. She folded one front leg underneath herself, taking her knee to the ground while the opposite leg stayed straight, extended in front of her. Star's nose nearly grazed the ground as she held the bowing position and the crowd whispered.

I winked at Tiera as the soft classical music started and both Star and the ballerina rose to stand. I shifted in the saddle, realigning myself before the real riding began.

As the violins played over the speakers, Tiera arched her arms in the air and began spinning, one leg floating through the air in a circle around her. Her body rotated in the ray of light over and over until she stopped abruptly, facing me with two legs on the ground again.

Star's ears pricked when she knew it was our turn. I lightly guided the reins to the right, pressing my left calf to her side, and Star began crisscrossing her front legs. I centered my body in the saddle, balancing myself as she picked up speed. She moved her front around her rear in an increasingly intense spin...faster and faster. Her flaxen mane, laced with ribbons, blew parallel to the ground and the audience became a black, soundless blur until Star stopped on a dime, facing Tiera again.

There was a deafening pause before the whistles, hoots, and hollers brought a grin to my face. I was warming up the crowd.

Tiera didn't wait for the audience to quiet before she began floating across the arena, arms in the air and her legs following as she leaped in an elegant zigzag. Her tutu bounced and her toes touched with each jump - like a graceful gazelle. At the end, she turned back towards me with a beckoning curtsy.

I put my fingers to the brim of my black cowboy hat and tipped my head, accepting her challenge as Star pushed forward into a canter. We looped around Tiera a few times, stretching into a quick pace before turning across the diagonal of the arena.

Taking a breath, I eased Star into a slower speed and prepared us for our first lead change. With a subtle move of my leg and a hint of a weight change in the saddle, Star bounced from her left lead to her right lead with ease and we received a gracious clap from the crowd. We executed a second lead change just as we passed Tiera and she dramatically set her hands on her hips, getting a giggle from the audience.

As we rounded the end of the arena, I gathered my reins in my fingers and began cantering straight down the long middle of the arena.

"Here we go, girl," I said, sucking in a breath. "This is what we have been practicing for." Star gathered herself and we began a line of single lead changes. With every stride, Star changed her lead, practically floating through the air. She bent her body from left to right to left to right, each stride zigzagging with the change of direction. We danced together, merely skipping down the center of the arena - moving as one unit with the rhythm of the music.

As we finished our last lead change, my focus zoned back to reality and I immediately noticed the screams from the stands. Reacting to the noise, Star rung her tail, knowing she did a great job, before coming to an abrupt stop in front of a pouting ballerina. I tipped my hat once more, this time with a wink.

At the wink, Tiera flew off into a stream of jumps. Launching herself through the air, her legs rose until they were parallel to the dirt, over and over again. Finishing her last jump, she landed just a few feet from Georgie and hopped up into the saddle. Feet in the stirrups, Tiera joined Lucy as they trotted their horses to the middle of the arena.

The crowd hushed again, waiting for my response, as Lucy pulled a long, purple ribbon from her saddle bag. With one swift throw, she tossed an end to Tiera. Tiera grabbed the ribbon and they both backed their horses until Georgie and Chance were a few horse lengths apart, still facing each other and pulling the ribbon tight.

The music morphed into a fast tempo, increasing the crowd's anticipation. But, I wasn't done yet. I wasn't going to leave anyone sitting in their seats.

Reaching forward, nearly laying on Star's neck, I threaded my fingers under her leather bridle, gently pulling it over her ears. I waited for Star to release the bit from her mouth before letting the whole thing drop. The bridle piled into a heap at Star's hooves and the arena gasped as one.

Still stretched across Star's neck, I took a second to close my eyes and inhale her sweet scent. Kissing Star on her glossy coat, I whispered, "Let's finish this, baby girl. Let's show them what we can do."

Sitting up in the saddle, I took in the vision of the mob surrounding me - all leaning on the edge of their seats - and my heart pumped faster, following the speed of the music. Without a bridle, I was completely reliant on my relationship with Star. But, I didn't have a doubt in my mind. Star and I were a team. We worked as one unit and I could always count on her.

With a slight movement of my leg, we pushed off into a canter, circling the arena and increasing our speed with every lap. Raising my arms up, the fringe whipped from the back of my sleeves and I pumped my arms in the air, asking the crowd for more. They responded with whistles and hollers which swelled as we moved into a gallop.

As we turned towards the middle of the arena, I asked Star to decrease her speed, just enough that we were balanced for our final act. Slowing, I locked my eyes on Lucy and Tiera - sitting in their saddles and holding a single ribbon which closed the gap between their horses.

Star moved underneath me like an extension of my own body. I felt every movement - each leg as it hit the ground, each breath as it blew from her lungs.

And, a stride before the ribbon, Star gathered her whole body and catapulted us into the air. Her ears slapped back against her neck as she put all she had into that jump.

Leaning forward, her mane whipped me in the face as we soared upwards. And, as Star's body evened out over the top of the ribbon, I sat up and launched my own arms into the air. My sight was blinded by the blaring spotlight, but I knew the vision we were creating. We were flying through the sky – bridleless and seemingly weightless. The light was bouncing off Star's chestnut coat as the ribbons and fringe lashed in the wind.

We rolled through the air in slow motion, but when gravity connected us with the ground, the crowd's roars filled every crevice of the arena and my heart burst with pride. I immediately latched onto Star's neck as we cantered off. Happy tears fell from my eyes. I couldn't put into words how much I loved Star. But I knew she understood.

The crowd's cheers continued, but my performance didn't feel complete. I looked back at the two girls that built me up when I was down and I wanted to be next to them. I wanted to share this moment with Lucy and Tiera.

Star and I glided across the arena and stopped between Chance and Georgie. Grabbing the girls' hands again, we raised our palms to the dark sky, smiles plastered on our faces and a silent bond passing between our eyes.

Who knew I'd come out of this show with two new friends?

Thirty-four

Taylor

The bright morning sun warmed my arms as I reached up to hand Star a carrot. Popping her head out of the open trailer window, she snatched it up, breaking the veggie in two with one crunch. As she chewed, Star pinned her ears and snaked her head at Chance - who was watching patiently from the next trailer window. He batted his dark lashes at me.

"Be nice, Star," I said, patting her on the nose. "Would you like a treat too, Chance?" His chocolate eyes enlarged as I stepped towards him and, when I offered the second half of the carrot, Chance wrapped his lips around the gift and gently removed it from my hand. "Did you see that, Star? You might want to take a tip or two on manners from this guy." I chuckled and Star replied with a hasty snort before two swift honks grabbed my attention. I turned to find Tim driving the big rig alongside my trailer. The diesel truck rumbled as it approached and both Tim and Linda were waving their hands out the open windows.

"Call me when you get back to the ranch so that I know you made it safely," Linda instructed.

"Will do," I said with a smile and a wave.

"Great job this weekend, Ms. Northwest Champion! Keep up the good work with Star and we'll be headed to the World Show next year." Linda flashed one of her rare beaming smiles and I knew she was proud of me. Her words warmed my heart. "Tim and I will see you in a few months. Enjoy the rest of your summer at Red Rock, Taylor."

"Take care, Princess," Tim chimed in with a wink before rolling the rig towards the driveway. I smiled as they departed, knowing I would miss them, but having a renewed excitement to enjoy the rest of my summer at the ranch.

Ready to head out, I turned my attention back to the horses, but caught a glimpse of red as I spun. As the six-horse trailer passed, a cherry red mustang emerged, following in its path. The car crawled unusually close to the bumper, trying to hide in the trailer's dust, but I stood watch, holding my gaze as the mustang approached.

Beneath the dark windshield I saw Jace's outline, his cowboy hat pulled low over his eyes. I was certain he couldn't wait to get out of here. He raised two fingers off the steering wheel in some kind of greeting – or maybe his version of an apology - and I simply gave him a nod. I didn't rat Jace out to the authorities, but I think like he learned his lesson – cheaters don't win...in the show ring or in life. *And,* if you cross Taylor Johnson, she will smash a s'more in your face and beat your pants off in the arena.

"Good riddance," I muttered under my breath at the back of the mustang. "I don't know what I saw in you in the first place." And I wasn't going to waste another second of my time or energy on Jace. I had better things to focus on.

Turning back to the trailer, I closed each window, prepping for the drive back to the ranch. Just as I snapped Chance's window shut, I heard a car door slam. Feet pounded across the pavement and I was tackled in a bear hug before I could even turn around.

"I caught Lucy in the barn and gave her a big hug, too. I'm going to miss you guys so much," Tiera squealed, hugging me tighter.

"We'll miss you too, Tiera," I said, turning to hug her back. My words even surprised me. "Let's plan on a trail ride in early September when I get back to Linda's barn, okay?"

"Okay. You and Lucy better call me with updates from the ranch," Tiera instructed as she gave me one more squeeze. "I might just have to join you guys there next summer."

Tiera released her embrace and jogged back to the waiting Mercedes. I called after her. "Maybe we could both learn how to rope a steer?"

"That would be awesome!" Tiera shouted as she hopped in the car and waved goodbye.

I completed one more safety check on the hitch and then climbed into the driver's seat just as Lucy opened the passenger door. She jumped in holding a disposable plastic cup in each hand and balancing her cell phone between her shoulder and her ear.

"This one's for you," she said, stretching her arm out to me. "Mocha with extra whip cream."

I took the drink from her hand, excited to get it to my lips. "Yum...thank you," I replied before taking a sip.

"I was talking to Taylor," Lucy commented into the phone as she snapped her seatbelt into place. "Yes, it's just Taylor and me driving her trailer back to the ranch. And, no, I promise we won't kill each other on the way back." She caught my eye and stifled a giggle. I grinned, realizing how much our relationship had changed in just a few short days.

"Is that Casey?" I mouthed to her and she nodded, wrapping up her conversation.

"Yeah, I'll fill you in when we get to the ranch. I've got a lot to tell you. Talk to you soon." And, with a smile, Lucy set her phone on the truck's leather seat, next to the gigantic trophy – which was strapped in with its own seatbelt. Her fingers left the phone and touched the etching on the trophy's plaque, reading the words aloud. "*Taylor Johnson, Lucy Rose & Tiera Alexander ~ Northwest Stock Horse Champions*. I still can't believe you had the show staff put our names on the trophy too."

I took another sip of my mocha before turning the key to start the truck. The engine roared to life. "It's our trophy, Lucy. It was a team effort."

Turn the page to start reading the next Rodeo Daze (Red Rock Ranch, book 3)...

RODEO DAZE
THE RED ROCK RANCH SERIES
- BOOK 3 -
BRITTNEY JOY

Rodeo Daze: Book 3

Lucy always dreamed of competing in a horse show— but she'd never thought it'd become reality. When a big competition comes to Three Rivers, the whole town's talking about who will win the title. Lucy is happy to stay on the sidelines to watch— until a tragedy causes her to step up and participate with her horse, Chance.

With frenemy Taylor as her coach and a bitter new rival to challenge, Lucy isn't sure she can handle the pressure. Plus her relationship with Casey is growing, and she needs to know where she stands. Lucy doesn't want to be "just friends" with the cute cowboy.

Can Lucy get over her stage fright and make all her dreams come true— in the arena and with Casey?

Turn the page to start reading...

Thirty-five

LEATHER GLOVES, POCKET KNIFE, WATER BOTTLE. I went over the list in my head as I stuffed the gloves in my pockets and grabbed the half-empty water bottle from the barn floor. Wiping the sweat from my brow, I filled the bottle to the top using the hose hung on the barn wall. I'd need every drop of water out in the field this afternoon. Heck, it was only 10 a.m. and my jeans were already sticking to my legs.

"Ew, Lucy," a voiced squeaked, and I looked up from the hose to see Taylor walking down the barn aisle. She was leading her mare, Star, and must've just got done giving her a bath. Star's copper coat was unusually dark and a track of wet hoofprints followed her on the concrete floor. "You know that hose is used to fill the horses' water buckets, right?" She wrinkled her nose in disgust before stopping Star and clipping the crossties onto her halter.

I raised a sweaty eyebrow at Taylor. Of course I knew the hose was used to fill the horses' water buckets. I was the one to fill them— twice a day.

"It's the same water that's piped into the tack room sink," I replied with a shrug of my shoulders. Not to mention it was ten steps closer than the tack room. If the hose had been outside, I would've pressed my mouth to the spray and gulped, but I didn't want to make a mess in the barn. "I mean, I kiss my horse on his mouth anyway. What's the difference?" My horse, Chance, loved kisses and I loved giving them to him— especially on his wrinkly, whiskered nose skin.

Taylor grinned at me before disappearing into the tack room. "You do have a point."

I knew I did. Because Taylor loved to give Star kisses as well. She was just a little more discreet about it than I was.

"Where is everyone, anyhow?" Taylor asked from inside the tack room. "It's like a ghost town around here."

"Casey and Marilynn went to hook up the truck to the flatbed trailer," I said, securing the lid on my water bottle and winding the hose back on its hanger. "Mr. Owens has been baling hay all morning and said it's ready to get picked up in the field."

Mr. Owens was my boss and the owner of Red Rock Ranch. The ranch had been in his family for nearly a hundred years and he was very involved in the everyday activities— running machinery, hauling cattle, and often joining trail rides. But more than that, he and his wife were the faces of the guest ranch. They greeted every guest when they arrived and were present at every meal. However, Mr. Owens mostly left the barn and the horses up to the stable hands— me, Casey, and Marilynn.

Taylor sauntered back into the aisle, picked up a brush, and started to comb through Star's long, flaxen mane. "Can I help?"

Her question confused me. "With what?" I asked, certain Taylor was *not* referring to stacking hay.

"With the hay, silly," she added. "With the picking-up part." Taylor tossed her long blonde braid over her shoulder and I almost laughed.

I cleared my throat instead. "We'll be picking up bales from the field and stacking them on the trailer. Then we'll unload them into the barn. You sure you want to help with that? It's not very glamourous. And it's like a thousand degrees today." I was *not* overexaggerating.

"Yeah," Taylor agreed, like I'd just asked her to go get ice cream in town. "I mean, I already rode Star and gave her a bath. What else am I going to do all day? Hang out with my mom in the cabin?"

I wiped my hand on my pant leg. "Okay. As long as Mr. Owens is fine with it. I don't think too many of the ranch guests help with loading hay." Actually, I was sure of that. Stacking hay was the only thing I didn't like about horses. It was hard, sweaty, dirty work, and if I was a paying guest at this ranch, like Taylor, I'd probably choose to spend my afternoon watching the horses graze, cleaning tack, or reading a book. Anything other than stacking hay.

Taylor led Star into her stall and took off her halter. "Well, I'm not just *any* guest," she said, and gave Star a peppermint before closing the stall door. "I'm sure Mr. Owens will let me help." Taylor gave me her signature movie star smile. I knew it usually got her what she wanted.

I assessed Taylor, knowing she was not prepared for what she *thought* she wanted to do. Her jean pockets were outlined with rhinestones. Her makeup was freshly applied. And I had no earthly idea how she kept her white tank top clean while she rode and then gave Star a bath.

"Well, okay," I said, pressing my lips together. "Let's find you some leather gloves, then."

"Great," Taylor replied with more enthusiasm than I was feeling.

As Taylor followed me into the tack room, I couldn't picture her picking up hay bales in a field under the blazing hot sun, but she'd surprised me a few times since I arrived at the ranch. At the start of the summer, Taylor intimidated me. No, she *frightened* me with her icy glares and sassy comments. But, after being forced to spend time with her, I learned that Taylor came across as tough, but she was really a softy. She'd do anything for her mare, Star. Taylor and I were different in many ways, but we shared one thing— a deep love of horses. And if she wanted to throw some haybales around today, then so be it. Maybe she'd surprise me again with some mad hay-throwing skills?

"I saw a pair of gloves in here the other day," I muttered, opening cabinets, one by one, searching. "Somewhere in here." I pushed aside rolls of vet wrap and bottles of leather conditioner.

"Maybe they're in the saddle bags," Taylor offered, and started unzipping the pack bags hung on the wall.

"Maybe." I opened another cabinet and peeked around fly spray and tubes of de-wormer. Just as I thought I'd have to run to my cabin and grab my extra pair of gloves, I saw yellow fingers poking out from behind a tub of horse treats. "There they are," I announced, and I heard Taylor walk up behind me.

But when I moved the tub of treats and grabbed the leather fingers, I felt more than just the gloves. Before I realized what was happening, a small gray creature scurried over my hand and up my arm. Its beady eyes glared at me as it ran toward my face, and I was sure the scream that came out of my mouth could've been heard from the pastures.

"What the—" Taylor asked, but her question quickly turned into a scream that matched mine and we danced around the tack room like our feet were on fire.

"Mouse!" I managed to yell as the nasty little thing flew from my arm and onto the floor. Taylor jumped and grabbed onto me as we watched it zigzag around before finally scurrying out the tack room door.

"Gross!" Taylor squealed, her eyes wide, both hands clamped on my arm.

I shook my body and stuck out my tongue, disgusted that the creature had run across my bare arm. I was sure I'd have nightmares about little feet shimmying across my skin for years.

Amid the mouse attack, I hadn't noticed footsteps in the aisle until a tall body appeared in the doorway. It was Casey— peering into the tack room like he might have to save us.

"Are you two okay?" he asked with a smirk on his face. He hooked his thumb in his jean pocket and waited for an answer. It was then that I realized Taylor and I were basically hugging each other. I let go of Taylor and stood up straight, trying to wipe the fear from my face.

"Yeah, we're fine," I replied, feeling my cheeks heat up. "I mean. We saw a mouse."

"I figured that much," Casey said, pulling the brim of his baseball hat a little further down on his head, like he was trying to cover up his smile. "I thought maybe you guys were fighting off a monster. Or you saw a ghost or something."

"It was a *mouse*," Taylor said and raised her eyebrows at Casey. "And it ran across Lucy's arm! Nasty!"

Casey shook his head. "You two ride thousand-pound animals and you're scared of a little mouse?" He couldn't hide his smile any longer, and I suddenly felt very silly for screaming as loud as I did.

"It caught us by surprise." I shrugged. Even though I was embarrassed, I found myself smiling back at him. I couldn't help it. Casey had a way of making me blush, even when my blood wasn't pumping from getting scared senseless.

"Oh, it surprised us alright," Taylor added and executed a shimmy with her shoulders. "Yuck."

I was silently glad Taylor witnessed the mouse with me and I wasn't the only one that screamed at the top of my lungs.

Casey stepped back from the door. "The mouse is fully contained now. You're safe to come out of the tack room. Jaycee caught the little escapee."

Taylor and I shuffled out of the tack room, not sure who Jaycee was. In the barn aisle we met two sets of eyes— a girl and a boy. They looked to be our age, probably sixteen or seventeen, and the girl wore a t-shirt that said *This Ain't My First Rodeo*. Her well-worn cowboy boot was balanced on top of an over-turned bucket, and I assumed she was the mouse catcher. A black and white border collie stood next to her and stared at the bucket like there was a treat that would pop out of it at any given second. The tall boy stood a few strides behind them both.

"Taylor, Lucy," Casey said with a nod of his head. "This is Jaycee. That's Levi." Levi grinned and waved, giving us a much less judgmental look than Jaycee. "They both help with odds and ends around the ranch. They'll be helping with hay today."

"Hi." I waved, biting my lip as I realized everyone in the barn heard me screech and jump around. All because of a tiny mouse.

"I'll get rid of it," Jaycee said, casually. She had one hand on her hip. The other pointed at the bucket.

When she reached for the overturned bucket, I couldn't help myself. "What do you mean you'll get rid of it?" There was a finality to Jaycee's words.

Jaycee looked at me from under her ballcap. Her thick, dark ponytail spilled over her shoulder when she did. "The mouse," she clarified. "I'll get rid of it."

"Like kill it?" I asked, swallowing.

Jaycee looked confused. I couldn't blame her. A few seconds ago, I'd been screaming bloody-murder because the mouse touched me. But I didn't want it to die.

"You can't do that," Taylor jumped in, sounding offended. "Can't we just let it go?"

"Sure," Jaycee said, and I felt my shoulders relax. I wasn't going to be responsible for a mouse murder. Even if it had scared me silly. "We can let the mouse go, if you want him to run right back to the tack room and surprise you again tomorrow."

Jaycee was definitely being sarcastic.

"We'll shut the tack room door to keep him out," Taylor said, trying to help. This made Jaycee look at the both of us like we were crazy instead of silly.

I turned to Casey, not sure what to say. I didn't want the little mouse to find its way back into the tack room and make a mess. I also didn't want Jaycee's dog to grab it the second Jaycee took her boot off the bucket.

"Mice are pretty sneaky. They can get into about anywhere they—" Casey started, but stopped when he looked at me. Taking a breath, he motioned to Jaycee. "Just leave him. I'll take the mouse out to the field and let him go." He caught my eye and gave me a defeated grin. "That way he'll have a fighting chance."

Before anyone could protest, Marilynn shouted from the other end of the barn. "Let's go!" Her voice carried like she was standing next to me.

Marilynn wasn't much older than the rest of us— seventeen, and only beating out Casey's birthday by a few months. She was also the smallest of the ranch crew, but Marilynn had a way about her that demanded respect. She spoke. You listened. That was how it worked.

"Mr. Owens is waiting in the field," Marilynn shouted. The diesel truck rumbled just outside the barn. "No time for lolly-gagging or whatever you guys are doing."

At that, Jaycee took her boot off the bucket. "Come on, Patsy. Leave it," Jaycee said, and the border collie followed her as she walked away. Levi did too.

I turned to Casey and gave him a thankful smile. I knew he offered to save the mouse's life on my behalf.

Casey kept his blue eyes on me. There was something about his stare that made my stomach flip-flop.

"I'll rescue the mouse," he said. "You better get in the truck. Marilynn doesn't like to wait."

"I've got shotgun," Taylor said with a little hop as she jogged off.

Casey suddenly looked confused, and I shrugged. "She wants to help. Told her she could if it was okay with Mr. Owens."

The truck horn beeped and I remembered what I was originally searching for.

"Gloves," I blurted, and turned on my heels. "I was going to grab some for Taylor."

Hurrying into the tack room, I found the gloves in the open cabinet, but hesitated before snatching them, hoping the mouse hadn't left any friends behind. When I grabbed leather instead of a rodent, I sighed and jogged back into the aisle. By that time, Casey was on the other end of the barn. He was carrying the bucket and yelled something to Marilynn as he passed the truck. Bucket in hand, he was heading toward the pasture. I thought he'd never looked cuter.

Thirty-six

THE TRUCK RUMBLED as it crept across the freshly cut field. Marilynn's elbow hung out the driver's side window. She had one hand on the wheel as she navigated between two rows of bound hay bales. The rest of us were on foot, in charge of picking the bales out of the field and stacking them on the flatbed trailer.

Casey, Levi, and Jaycee walked alongside the trailer, plucking rectangular bales from the ground. They swung them up onto the trailer by their twine, and Taylor and I stacked them. I hopped across the top layer of bales like a circus acrobat, working hard to keep up with the onslaught of tossed hay.

"Incoming," Casey yelled as he launched another bale through the air, making sure it landed in front of me. He threw the bale exactly where it needed to go— like he'd been throwing hay all his life. Maybe he had. I simply had to bump the bale with my knee to press it tightly against the growing stack. Thankful for his expertise, I turned and watched Casey pick up the next bale. His t-shirt sleeves were rolled up to his shoulders and I unknowingly let myself get so distracted by his arms that I lost sense of where I was walking and nearly tripped over the bale Jaycee threw at my heels.

"Easy, Cowgirl," Jaycee warned and caught my attention, stopping me just shy of the rolling bale.

"Oops!" I caught my balance, but only because I bumped into Taylor and grabbed her shoulder.

"Whoa, Lucy," Taylor squeaked, and let go of the bale she was carrying. It dropped to her feet and she stumbled, but Levi was at the edge of the trailer and caught her arm. He looked happy to steady her.

I gave her an apologetic look. "Sorry. Wasn't watching where I was walking." To be exact, I was watching Casey's sweaty muscles.

Taylor straightened up, brushing off my clumsiness with a quick shake of her head, and Levi gave her a smile.

"Eyes on the bales, ladies," Jaycee said, mostly to me. Then she added a wink and I knew she'd caught me staring at Casey. Heat rushed to my cheeks and I grabbed the offending bale behind me.

Focus, Lucy, I told myself as I heaved the bale up onto my thigh. *So far today, everyone witnessed you scream at the top of your lungs because a tiny critter touched you. Let's not take a nose dive off the trailer, too. No more getting lost in Casey's arms.*

Casey tossed another bale onto the trailer, oblivious to my ogling and stumbling.

"Only about five hundred more bales to go," he said, joking about the fact that we'd just barely started. Then he wiped the sweat from his forehead with a handkerchief.

"Five hundred?" I asked, like my biceps weren't already burning. "That's easy. I could do this in my sleep." *What was I talking about? Why do I babble when I'm nervous?*

Casey laughed at my joke and grabbed another bale just as Marilynn stopped the truck and turned off the engine.

"Water break," Marilynn yelled before she opened the truck door. "Everyone needs to stay hydrated." She jumped out of the truck with an armful of water bottles. Her brunette bob bounced as she passed the plastic bottles out like candy.

Parched and sweaty, I followed Taylor off the back of the trailer. We hopped down the bales like stairs and joined the group on the shaded side of the haystack. It was nice to get out of the beating sun. Everything was sticking to me— my jeans, my hair, my sports bra, even my gloves. I felt like a cat that had accidently fallen in a water trough.

"Take a five-minute break," Marilynn announced. "I've got to ask Mr. Owens a few questions." Then she turned and marched off across the field, headed for the tractor pulling the baler.

Everyone was quiet for a minute, guzzling water. I closed my eyes, thinking cold water had never tasted so good. In the heat, it was sweeter.

"It's like a big puzzle," Taylor said, plopping down on the ground and setting her water bottle against her leg. She was sweaty too, but somehow, the sweat on her skin looked more like glitter. "You've got to get the bales stacked just right or it messes everything else up."

"Haven't you loaded hay before?" Jaycee asked, like Taylor's observation was pretty obvious. However, she looked more curious than judgemental as she brushed hay bits from her bare arms with gloved hands. Jaycee definitely had experience in the hay department. She had no problem keeping up with the boys.

Taylor shook her head. "I board Star at home. No hay loading involved." She said it matter-of-factly and pulled off her gloves. If her explanation hadn't convinced Jaycee, her manicured nails sure did the trick.

"Really?" Jaycee lifted an eyebrow, like she didn't know another human being that had never stacked hay.

Taylor shrugged. "Really."

Casey cut in. "Jaycee, Levi, and I've been bucking hay together every summer since we were twelve." He took another swig of water, his sandy hair dark with sweat at the base of his neck.

"It's not glamourous, but it sure beats hitting the gym," Levi added, and then gave a mock "gun" show, curling his arms into the air like a body builder. Levi was tall and lanky with black hair and olive-toned skin. If he'd been a horse, he would have been a Thoroughbred. A bay Thoroughbred. "These are home grown farm muscles, ladies. Try to contain yourself."

Casey chuckled, nearly choking on his gulp of water. Coughing, he wiped his mouth with his arm and said, "Good thing, because Three Rivers doesn't have a gym. Your game with the ladies would *really* suffer if you didn't buck hay."

Levi gave a few more over exaggerated faces and fancy arm curls before he laughed at himself. His chuckle was contagious and the group joined. Jaycee play-punched Levi in the shoulder, stopping his gun show.

"Put those away," Jaycee said, teasing Levi like a little brother. Her raven ponytail swayed with her punch. In the chuckles that followed, I realized that Casey, Levi, and Jaycee knew each other well.

"Come on, Jaycee," Levi whined, rubbing his shoulder where she had punched him. "Just because your muscles are bigger than mine doesn't mean you have to beat me up." He gave her a sly grin like he was teasing her, but the way he kept rubbing his arm told me otherwise. "I have to haul barrels around tonight at the Round-Up. You don't want me doing that one-armed, do you?"

"Actually, I'd love to see you do that one-armed," Jaycee replied, with a smile that wrinkled her nose.

"What's the Round-Up?" I asked. Jaycee and Levi looked at me like I was an alien that just landed from somewhere far, far away.

"Lucy's not from here," Casey said, putting his baseball cap back on his head. His hair curled out from under the edges of his hat.

Jaycee squinted at Casey. "Well, duh," she said. "We have exactly thirty-six people in our class. If Lucy lived in Three Rivers I *probably* would have seen her around. Geez." She looked at me like, *Can you believe this guy?*

"Where you from?" Levi interjected and leaned against the hay.

"Willow," I replied, fiddling with my bottle cap. "It's about an hour from here."

"She's here for the summer," Casey added. "Working on the ranch."

Taylor jumped in, bringing the conversation back to its original subject. "So, what's the Round-Up?"

"She's not from her either," Casey said, pointing a thumb at Taylor and giving Jaycee a sarcastic grin.

Jaycee rolled her eyes at him but answered Taylor's question. "It's like a combination of a rodeo and a horse show. It's a big deal around here. Try-outs start tonight."

Taylor's eyes got big. I thought she might jump up from her seat on the ground. "A competition?"

"Yeah," Jaycee replied, surprised by Taylor's sudden interest.

"Are you trying out?" I asked Jaycee, but Levi laughed. Jaycee immediately swung at him but Levi jumped away before she connected with his shoulder.

Jaycee steadied herself after the missed punch and shook her head at Levi. "Not my thing. Plus, my horse is kind of a hot mess. He likes to run fast in a straight line, but not much else. Except buck. He does like to buck." She shrugged like this was no big deal. Something about her honesty made me smile. "Part of the competition includes barrel racing. The other is a horsemanship pattern. I'd rather wrestle a steer."

"Can anyone try out?" Taylor asked, getting to her feet. "Or do you have to be from Three Rivers?"

"You got a horse?" Jaycee asked. Taylor nodded. "Then you can tryout."

"What time are tryouts?" Taylor replied, quickly.

"Seven o'clock tomorrow night," Casey replied, leaning against the trailer load of hay next to Levi. "You should do it." Then he turned to me and added, "You too, Lucy."

I laughed, thinking he was joking. When I saw that he wasn't, I started stuttering. "What? No. I can't." Everyone looked at me, forcing me to expand on my immediate denial. "Not my thing, either."

Taylor furrowed her brow at me, but it was Casey that pressed the issue.

"What do you mean it's not your thing?" he asked. "You just won the Cowboy Race. I seem to remember you're pretty good at that *riding thing*. You should tryout."

"Oh, *you're* the girl that won the race with Casey." Jaycee said it like she'd just figured out all my secrets. "Yeah, you should totally tryout. Why not?"

"Not my thing, guys," I repeated, and just as I thought all four of them were going to gang up on me and drag me to tryouts against my will, Marilynn broke their hungry stares.

"Break time's over," Marilynn yelled and started up the truck. The rumble diffused the interrogation.

I cleared my throat, welcoming the distraction from my lame excuse. "Back to work, I guess." I jumped onto the trailer and positioned myself for more hay-catching.

Marilynn put the truck in gear and turned the radio up. A catchy country song trilled out the open windows and the chorus boasted something about "little white lies." Casey was singing along, a bit louder than necessary. He gave me a wink as he picked up a bale and I wondered if he knew me better than I thought.

Thirty-seven

MY STOMACH GROWLING, I left my bunk and walked down the gravel path toward the main lodge. I wanted to run, but didn't think my limbs or my sweat-soaked jeans would allow me to do so. Instead, I settled for a fast, limpy walk.

Oh my goodness. I scrunched my face up and willed my body to move normally. After loading and unloading six loads of hay, muscles hurt that I didn't even know I had.

"Hey, Lucy! Wait up!" Taylor yelled. I slowed and looked over my shoulder. Taylor was running down the path, waving at me, looking rested and fresh. She helped with the first load of hay but opted to go back to her cabin after that. I didn't blame her. I wouldn't have thrown hay around if I wasn't getting paid to do it.

Taylor made a weird face at me when she got close. "Aren't you going to shower before dinner?"

I narrowed my eyes at her, glad the muscles in my face still worked. "I'm really hungry. And Marilynn said it was okay to head straight to dinner since we worked so late. Most of the ranch guests should be done eating by now anyhow."

It was nearly eight o'clock and the sun was setting, silhouetting the main lodge, making its long, curvy log walls look black. The kitchen would be closing soon and all I could think about was cheeseburgers. I didn't care that I looked like I just ran through a dust storm.

"Oh, okay," Taylor replied, with a shrug like my sweaty, dirty body was now acceptable.

"I washed my arms. And my face," I offered, remembering how the cream-colored washcloth turned black as I scrubbed.

"Whatever, Lucy. Nobody cares. It's a ranch. Everyone's dirty. I was just asking." Taylor smiled and started walking. I followed, knowing she didn't mean any harm. That was just Taylor. She said what she thought, no matter what.

As we walked, Taylor was quiet. I thought quiet-Taylor was stranger than say-whatever-Taylor.

"Is everything okay?" I asked. She seemed like she was pondering something.

Taylor bit her lower lip. "Why don't you want to try out for the Round-Up?" She looked at me, mascaraed lashes and all.

"I mean," I started, surprised she cared one way or the other. "It's just not my thing."

"But you were great in the Cowboy Race."

I looked away, unsure I wanted to put my fear into words. "It's not the competition that freaks me out."

"What is it, then?" Taylor pressed. When I didn't answer, she continued to stare. I had a feeling she wasn't going to let it go.

"It's the crowds," I said with a breath, feeling silly for admitting it. It wasn't the riding that scared me. It was the eyeballs— the people that would watch my every move and judge me if I screwed up. "I hate riding in front of tons of people. Makes me really nervous. Like I'm going to throw-up." Taylor wrinkled her nose. "The Cowboy Race only had an audience at the starting line and the finishing line. There weren't crowds of people watching me every minute."

"But you rode in front of hundreds of people this past weekend when you helped me at the show for my Freestyle Event." Taylor raised her eyebrows at me, thinking she was making a point.

"That was different."

"How?"

"I did it for you." I wasn't thinking about myself. I rode at the show to help Taylor.

Taylor's face softened. She looked away, ahead at the lodge.

"Oh," she replied. I thought I saw her smile.

"I wasn't in the spotlight. You were," I added. "And I was still nervous. I just knew you needed me and Tiera to help you." That was all truth. I felt nauseous right before Taylor, Tiera, and I rode into the arena, but I would've been paralyzed if I was the one competing. That was more pressure than I wanted to deal with.

Taylor twirled toward me, her blonde waves following her spin. She grabbed my shoulder, stopping me mid-stride.

"Will you help me again? I want to enter the Round-Up and I need an assistant," Taylor said, a wide smile on her face.

I paused, but only because Taylor nearly knocked me over. However, in the state my body was in, a stiff wind could have done the same.

Taylor's smile faltered and she added, "I'll pay you."

"No," I replied, and Taylor's face melted as though I'd told her a puppy died. "I mean, no, you don't have to pay me."

Taylor paid me for my time and assistance at her show this past weekend, but that was different. At the time, I needed money to buy my horse, Chance, and Taylor needed a worker for the weekend— to clean stalls, feed horses, bathe Star. Basically, she needed someone to do all the manual labor so she could focus on competing. But now, I felt like Taylor was my . . . friend?

"I'll help you, Taylor. You don't have to pay me. It'll be fun." I smiled at her.

"Great," Taylor said and put her hands in her jean pockets. "Thanks." She gave me a crooked, uneasy grin.

"Grub's on!" Marilynn yelled from the lodge's front porch and my stomach gurgled, breaking into our conversation.

Taylor chuckled, her unease fading. "Let's go eat."

"I'm going to need three cheeseburgers," I noted as we started walking. "And a basket of fries. And four of whatever dessert is."

Taylor laughed. I did too, but my laugh sounded desperate as I limped along like an old man. I wasn't kidding in the least.

After tacking Chance up, I walked him out of the barn and into the sunshine, excited to ride. We finished loading and stacking the hay a few days ago and I was thankful to be back to regular work tasks. My body was still sore, but nowhere near as bad as it was the first day.

I stopped Chance next to the paddocks. "You're the most handsome horse I've ever seen," I cooed as I smoothed his thick, black forelock. He closed his eyes and I stroked his tresses a few more times. I straightened the leather browband that ran across his forehead and pulled my cell phone from my pocket. "Let's get a picture of your cute face before I get in the saddle. Okay?"

Chance looked at me curiously, trying to figure out my question, and I turned to pose for a selfie. I didn't usually take selfies. Most of the time, I thought it was obnoxious to take a picture of yourself, but having Chance's handsome head next to mine made it seem okay.

"Say cheese," I said, extending my arm out as far as possible. I wanted to make us both look cute and get the barn in the background so I snapped about ten pictures, smiling and trying not to giggle as Chance sniffed and nuzzled my cheek. Picking the best one, I sent the picture to my dad and gave Chance a kiss on his nose.

Before my lips left his velvet-soft skin, my phone rang. Actually, it cantered. The ringtone made multiple horse-hoof sounds before I picked up the call.

"Hey, Dad," I said, grinning at how fast he'd called after I sent the picture.

"Hey, sweetie," he replied, a sing-song to his voice. "We just saw your picture and thought we'd call to check in on you."

"We?"

"You're on speaker phone," a squeaky voice called from the background. I recognized my little sister Molly's voice immediately. "And *we* didn't get to see your picture yet. Dad just told us how adorable you looked with Chance, nearly burned himself on the pizza as he took it out of the oven, and then called you." She laughed at her own description of what was going on in the house, and I chuckled, too. I loved Molly. She was nine years old, seven years younger than me, but we were thick as thieves. Hearing her laugh squeezed at my heart and made me miss home.

"Hi Molly," I said, and Chance nuzzled my shoulder, probably wondering what I was doing and who I was talking to.

"I'll show your sisters the picture when I get off the phone," Dad said, and I could hear the pan rattling as he sliced dinner up. Pizza was my dad's specialty. The frozen kind.

Another voice joined the conversation. "Yeah, I want to see this new horse of yours. I can't believe you got another one. Especially when you could've used that money to buy a car."

My older sister Jackie's voice was the opposite of Molly's. Jackie was a glass-is-half-empty kind of girl while Molly and I always saw the glass half-full. So did Dad. But I loved Jackie despite her ornery attitude.

"Hi Jackie," I replied, shaking my head. Jackie was eighteen and leaving for college this fall. She was going to Oregon State and couldn't wait to peel out of the tiny town of Willow. She'd bought a car when she was fourteen and had been itching to leave ever since. "You'll like Chance. He's black and shiny. Just like your car."

"Except my car has a motor and can hit seventy in six seconds and—"

Jackie was promptly cut off by my dad, "You sure as heck better not be hitting seventy in six seconds." Then there was quiet, and I could feel Dad's serious stare through the phone.

"Well," Jackie started, and then thought better of it. "No. I don't do that."

"You better not," Dad added, and brought the conversation back to Chance. "Grandma said you can keep Chance at her place. She said Stella needs a friend, anyhow."

"Awesome," I replied, knowing Stella was fine on her own. She'd always been a solo horse, ever since Grandma bought the little paint mare for me, Molly, and Jackie. Well, mostly for me and Molly, because Jackie only liked to feed Stella carrots. She didn't live and breathe horses like Molly and I did. She didn't jump out of bed every morning thinking about feeding and riding and brushing. She didn't dream about cute horse noses and—

Dad cut off my mind-babbling. "But you have one-hundred percent responsibility for him. That means you clean his pen. You feed him. You pay for his hay and grain. Okay?"

"Absolutely," I said. "I wouldn't have it any other way."

"And I'll help you!" Molly yelled. I heard her scoot around on her chair like she couldn't contain her excitement.

"Thanks, Molly." I petted Chance's neck, knowing he'd love living with us in Willow when the summer was over. "I'd love that. How's Stella doing?"

"She's great. Since you left, I feed her every morning and every night," Molly said, proudly.

Our grandma lived just three doors down on five acres with a little red barn, so it was easy for Molly to run over and take care of Stella herself.

Molly continued, "And we've been going for a ride just about every day. Mostly around Grandma's house or over to Prestly's to ride with her."

"Good. I'm glad you're taking such great care of her while I'm gone." I could practically hear Molly beam through the phone. "And when I get home at the end of August, I can ride Chance, you can ride Stella, and we'll go on trail rides together."

Molly squealed, and Dad laughed.

"What are you up to tonight?" Dad asked as Jackie said something about her ears hurting from Molly's squeals.

"I'm riding into town with Casey and Taylor. I'm going to help Taylor audition for this thing called the Round-Up."

Molly squealed again, "That sounds so fun!"

"Be careful," Dad said. "Are you going to be riding on the roads?"

"It's only a mile into town, and Mr. Owens wouldn't let us go if it wasn't safe," I reassured him. "I promise I'll be safe and I won't ride on the roads if I don't have to."

"All right," Dad said, sounding leery. Just then Casey walked out of the barn leading his horse, Rocky, and I figured I better get off the phone before Dad decided that riding a mile into town was too dangerous. I didn't want him nixing my evening plans.

"I'll text you when I get back to my bunk. How about that?" I offered. "I've got to get going though. Don't want to be late."

"Okay, be safe. We love you," Dad said and two more "love you's" echoed in the background.

"Love you guys, too," I said before ending the call and sticking my phone back in my pocket. I missed my family, but I was finding my stride here at the ranch. I loved my summer job and I was making friends. Chance blinked his big brown eyes at me. I knew he was a big part of why I felt at home here. "I'm sure glad you found me," I whispered to Chance, and put the reins over his neck.

The clip clop of Rocky's hooves closed in and Chance nickered at his dapple-gray friend as he joined us near the paddocks.

"You ready, Lu?" Casey asked from the saddle. Taylor wasn't far behind him, riding Star. "We need to get there a little early. Levi said his arm still hurts where Jaycee punched him and asked if I'd help him set barrels." Casey laughed and then went serious. "Don't tell Jaycee that, though."

I put my boot in the stirrup and hopped up into the saddle. "It's our little secret," I said, hiding my grin. Then I joined Casey and Taylor and we rode off toward town together. I was ready to see what this Round-Up thing was all about.

Thirty-eight

RIDING TO THREE RIVERS was about the least dangerous thing I'd done since I got to the ranch. Casey, Taylor, and I followed a quiet gravel road that passed fields full of crops and cows. We rode side-by-side on a wide, grassy shoulder and chatted as birds chirped from treetops. Only one truck passed and the driver slowed down to say hi. Casey knew him by name and introduced the older man as his math teacher's dad.

The man waved as he drove away, and Taylor asked, "Does everyone know everyone in this town?" She looked around like people were watching us.

Casey adjusted his reins in his fingers. "Pretty much."

"That's creepy," she added.

He chuckled, but also looked confused. "Why?"

"Everyone knows your business. Like, if you go get a latte at the café, pretty soon Sally Mae's next-door neighbor's half-cousin knows what time you were there and what flavor you got. Right?"

I huffed a laugh at Taylor's fake scenario.

"Well, probably not," Casey replied, and Taylor gave him a squinty-eyed challenge. I was riding between them and leaned back so Taylor could give Casey the full effect of her face. "They'd probably never know what kind of latte you got because the café doesn't serve lattes. Coffee, only."

Taylor gasped and put her hand to her chest. "Oh my God. How do people survive around here?" She did *not* sound sarcastic. I wondered if Taylor started every morning off with a shot of caffeine.

"I think it's nice," I chimed in, and Taylor gave me a squinty face too. "Not that the café doesn't have lattes. That's a travesty." Taylor relaxed her stare when she realized I wasn't defending the town's lack of flavored caffeine. "I mean, I think it's nice that everyone is so friendly."

Casey nodded and smiled at me. "It is nice, isn't it?"

I caught Casey's glance and got a little lost in his blue eyes. "Reminds me of home." *Warm. Friendly. Wonderful.* My body tightened as I suddenly wondered if I was describing my hometown . . . or Casey. I changed the subject. "How much farther?" I asked, looking at Taylor even though she didn't know where we were going either.

"I think we're here," Taylor replied, forgetting about the latte conversation.

Casey gave a nod and I looked ahead. Past the next bunch of fir trees, there was a herd of horse butts, a big outdoor arena, and a ton of pickup trucks.

"Come on," Taylor chirped, and started trotting Star. Casey and I followed.

"Wow," I said to myself, posting in the saddle to keep up with Chance's big strides. "It looks like the whole town is here."

"Most of it," Casey replied over the clip-clop of hooves as we trotted across the road. "This is where all the action is on Friday nights. There's always something going on at the Ring."

The enormous arena was set on the edge of town and wrapped in weathered fencing. A row of houses bordered one side. Fir trees and farm land bordered the other. Above the bleachers on the opposite end of the arena, there was a wooden sign boasting big, bold painted letters which spelled out *The Ring*.

"This is awesome," I uttered. Horses filled my vision in every direction. Riders of all ages were camped out on their horse's backs, talking with friends, relaxing in the saddle. Kids climbed on the fence and sat on the top rail. Trucks were backed up to the arena— acting as big lawn chairs for tonight's event. It was like the horsie-version of a high school football game.

I looked at Taylor. Her face was lit-up, too.

"Where do I sign-up?" she asked, her eyes eager.

"I'll show you," Casey said. He waved his hand, and Taylor and I followed as he weaved Rocky through the crowd, saying hello to everyone as he passed— like he was the town mayor. When we finally got to a small white trailer, a middle-aged woman with really big hair stepped out the open door. Casey tipped his hat at her. "Hey, Marcy."

"Hey, Casey," Marcy replied, giving Casey a mega-watt smile that matched the intensity of her teased brunette curls. She had a clipboard in one hand and a stack of orange cones in the other.

"This is Lucy and Taylor," Casey said, and I gave her a little wave. "Taylor is going to try out and needs a number."

"Alright, Sweets," Marcy said, as though she was talking to one of her kids. "Will you take these cones to Levi? I'll get Taylor all set up." She handed the stack of cones to Casey. He placed them on top of his saddle horn, balancing the stack on the pommel. Rocky could have cared less, but Chance gave a little snort. I patted him, letting him know it was okay that Rocky had a pile of orange plastic on his back.

"Do you need any help getting ready?" I asked Taylor as Marcy flipped through her clipboard and pulled out a cardboard number. Earlier today, I'd helped Taylor run through a few practice patterns at the ranch, but I wasn't sure what I could do during the auditions except cheer her on.

"No, I'm fine. Just need to get Star warmed-up in the arena," Taylor said, while Marcy pinned a number to Taylor's saddle pad.

"Go help Casey. If I need help, I'll find you, but I think I'm good." Taylor looked relaxed and excited at the same time. I could tell she was ready to get in the arena and start riding.

"Okay, good luck. Knock 'em dead out there." Then I added over my shoulder, "And make sure your cinch is tight."

Taylor gave me a shake of her head and a chuckle. "I already checked it. I won't make that mistake again."

Casey prodded me as we rode off. "What was that about?" he asked, holding the cones with one hand and directing Rocky with the other.

"Inside joke." I shrugged. "I'll explain later." I smiled to myself, thinking how crazy it was that I had an inside joke with Taylor. Just a week ago we were at each other's throats. I guess it took a horse show, a hard fall, and a jerk of an ex-boyfriend to figure each other out.

"Okay . . ." Casey drawled out his response, looking at me like I better not forget to tell him later. Then he got distracted and yelled, "Hey, Jaycee!"

His voice carried over music which blared out of a nearby truck. I followed his look and saw Jaycee riding toward us. She was on a tall leopard Appaloosa and was wearing a dark brown t-shirt that said, *Boss Mare.* The color of her shirt matched her horse's spots. The saying on her shirt matched her sass.

"Where did you get that shirt?" I asked when she got close, wishing I had the gumption to wear a shirt like that. "I love it."

"Thanks." Jaycee looked down at her shirt like she forgot what she was wearing, but then she beamed. "It's one of my favorites. Got it from the tack shop in Bend." She brushed a smear of dust off her chest.

"I've got to take these cones to Levi," Casey interrupted. "Can you stay with Lucy? Show her around?"

"Can do," Jaycee said, and Casey gave me a wink as he rode off. When Rocky's dapple-gray butt disappeared into the masses, Jaycee looked back at me. "Is that your horse, Chance?"

"Yeah," I said, and Chance whinnied. I petted his neck. "It's okay." Up until then, he was being so good in the new, chaotic environment. But now he wouldn't stand still, wondering why his buddy was leaving him.

"Let's go closer to the arena," Jaycee offered as Chance started to prance in place. "Chance will be able to see Rocky from there." She turned her horse and led me past a couple of bays and a group of paints, finagling us through the crowd.

When we got to the fence, I scooted Chance close to Jaycee and her Appaloosa. "Thanks. He's still getting used to stuff like this." I sighed as Chance spotted Rocky in the arena and relaxed.

"It takes time. And you've only been riding him like a month, right?" Jaycee asked, and I nodded. Casey must have told her about Chance. "I've been riding my horse, Nauti, for about ten years now." She reached back and patted her horse on his butt.

"Your horse's name is *Naughty*?" Jaycee's horse reminded me of the dotted Dalmatian dogs that rode on fire trucks in parades. He was spotty, but he didn't look particularly mischievous. "He doesn't look like his name fits him."

Jaycee reached in her pocket and pulled out a carrot chunk. She held it down by her knee and her horse turned his head to nibble it out of her hand. "See the patch around his eye?"

I did. The Appaloosa's left eye had a bunch of chocolate-colored spots around it that blended together, making it look like he was wearing an eye-patch.

"When we first got Nauti, my brother saw the patch around his eye and wanted to name him *Pirate*." Jaycee rolled her eyes. "My sisters and I didn't like the name, but Mom said we had to agree on one name, so we compromised. We all agreed on *Nautical*. My brother was happy, because it was pirate-like. I was happy because

I liked the nickname. I call him 'Nauti' for short. And, believe me, it fits him."

I laughed. "I like it. It's original."

Jaycee grinned and grabbed another carrot piece from her pocket. "For Chance?"

"Sure." I took the carrot from Jaycee, thinking that was awfully nice of her to offer. "Thanks." Chance quickly lapped the carrot from my hand, having already watched Nauti get a treat. Then he stood still, deciding the spot on the railing was safe. I was sure the carrot helped sway his decision.

"I was out of town the other week so I didn't get to see you and Casey ride in the Cowboy Race. But Casey told me about you and Chance— how you guys found him and how you've trained him. Pretty cool." Jaycee looked at me out the corner of her eye and seemed impressed.

Pretty cool. I let Jaycee's words replay in my mind, wondering if those were her words or Casey's. "Well, Casey helped me with him," I said, feeling my cheeks heat knowing Casey had talked about me to his friend.

What else had Casey told Jaycee about me? Casey and I had shared a kiss— a kiss that made my stomach flutter every time it crossed my mind. But ever since I got back from the horse show with Taylor, there'd been no more kissing. I was beginning to wonder if Casey changed his mind about me. Was I a one-kiss-wonder? Did he think we'd be better off as friends? Was it too weird to date someone he worked with?

"What did Casey tell you—" I started, thinking I could squeeze a clue out of Jaycee.

Just then Star loped by and Taylor waved at me and Jaycee. I stopped talking and gave Taylor a thumbs-up, thinking she looked like the poster-child for equitation. She'd have no problem securing a space in the Round-Up. Then I realized I wasn't the only one watching Taylor glide down the railing on her show pony. A group of cowboys sitting on the fence waved at her, too. In fact, one guy nearly fell off backwards, only catching himself because his buddy grabbed him.

My stomach clenched as they swooned. Casey had liked Taylor at one time, too. If he wasn't interested in her, did I even have a chance at keeping his attention?

"That boy needs to toughen up," Jaycee chuckled, and her laugh broke my gaze from Taylor. "I barely hit him."

Pushing my wandering thoughts from my head, I followed Jaycee's stare. She was looking at Levi. He was in the middle of the arena, pushing a barrel across the ground— with one arm— and gave Jaycee an overexaggerated scrunched face. When he shook a fisted hand at her she laughed, obviously entertained by his antics.

But her laugh was cut short when Nauti pinned his ears and popped his hind end in the air with a kick.

There was a shuffling noise behind us and when I looked back, a girl on a Palomino was giving Jaycee a nasty look.

"Jaycee, where's his ribbon?" the girl snapped, and I assumed Nauti had kicked out at the Palomino. Sometimes, riders tied red ribbons in the tails of horses that were prone to kicking. It served as a warning to others.

Jaycee looked rattled by the fact that her horse had kicked out. "Oops, sorry," she started, but when she turned and saw who was speaking, her shoulders relaxed. "*Amanda*, you know Nauti kicks. Give him some space. Duh."

The girl gave a dramatic sigh, but rode off instead of arguing Jaycee's logic.

Jaycee leaned toward me. "I hate ribbons, but I usually have one braided in Nauti's tail when I ride. My sister must've taken it out. But don't worry. Nauti never makes contact. Just likes to give out warning shots." Jaycee shrugged, and I wasn't sure if I was shocked or amused.

I guess Nauti did live up to his name. He also managed to make me forget about Casey's lack of kissing me. For now.

Thirty-nine

IT WASN'T LONG until the tryouts started and instead of the bleachers, Jaycee and I watched from our saddles. I thought I had the best seat in the house. After a few riders blazed around the barrels, Casey and Levi joined us. Casey parked Rocky next to Chance, and Levi snagged a seat on the fence. We all had our eye-balls glued to the action in the arena.

The tryouts consisted of running barrels and then riding a horsemanship pattern, which was a tough combination. Barrel racing was a speed event in which each rider had to complete a cloverleaf pattern around trash-can sized barrels (which Levi set in place with one arm). Then, if the rider was fast enough during the barrel racing portion, they moved on to the next round—the horsemanship piece, which included a pattern judged on precision, not speed.

When it was Taylor's turn to enter the arena for the barrel portion, she blew in like a Thoroughbred at the Derby. Star flew around the barrels in a rush of tight turns, lead changes, and thunderous galloping. Casey, Levi, Jaycee, and I screamed at the top of our lungs, pumping our fists in the air as Taylor and Star finished their run and clocked-in with a time that ultimately earned her the fifth fastest speed overall and got her to the next round.

"This would be so hard," I said as the horsemanship portion started. I knew the horses would be amped up from running barrels, but for the horsemanship pattern, they would have to chillout, slow down, and complete a pattern on a loose rein. That was a tough combo.

This first girl rode into the arena on a little Paint that was barely holding it together. He was supposed to be trotting toward a line of orange cones, but the Paint's mind was apparently still on running barrels. He jigged and zigzagged, wanting to run as the rider grasped tight to her reins. When they got to the first cone, the girl asked her horse to lope and the Paint lost it. He gave her three big bucks instead.

Jaycee inhaled sharply and we all sighed with relief when the girl managed to stay on.

"That would totally be Nauti," Jaycee whispered as the girl in the arena waved at the judges and then trotted out the gate, forfeiting her turn. "Only he'd put me in the dirt."

Casey laughed, and Jaycee told him to shut his mouth.

I held my breath as I watched the next rider, but there was no bucking this time. The next rider completed the pattern, but her horse was still anxious, shying away from the cones like they might bite her.

When it was time for Taylor's ride, I sat up tall in the saddle, watching intently, knowing Taylor was a pro at horsemanship. But even Star looked a little rattled when she entered the arena. Star gave a swift shake of her head, looking irritated, but Taylor rubbed Star's neck and spoke a few words. With Taylor's reassurance, Star regained her composure as though she immediately realized it was time to compete.

"She's amazing," I said, admiring how Star was completely in tune with Taylor. Taylor rode, looking like she wasn't doing anything, but I knew she was giving Star subtle cues with her legs and her seat. They glided effortlessly through the pattern, completing trot to canter gait changes, a perfectly round circle, and a spot-on halt at the last cone.

"You talking about Star or Taylor?" Levi asked, honestly, not taking his eyes off the arena.

"Both," I replied, and we all clapped when Taylor nodded at the judge, noting she was finished with her pattern. As she trotted out of the arena, Taylor gave us a huge smile from under her black cowboy hat and I knew she was happy with her rides. I also knew she was a shoe-in for the Round-Up.

When all the rides were complete, we hung out near Levi's truck, chatting and waiting for Taylor. She had secured the top spot overall after her beautiful horsemanship pattern. Casey and I sat on the open tailgate, hanging onto our horses by their reins. Jaycee sat on Nauti and Levi was behind us, perched on a big metal tool box in the front of his truck bed.

"How many go on to the competition?" I asked, amazed at the amount of talent in this little town. It seemed like everyone in Three Rivers had been riding since they could walk. Or maybe before.

Jaycee swung one leg over the front of her saddle, getting comfy, and I hoped Nauti didn't decide to kick out again.

"The top fifteen," Jaycee replied, playing with the toe of her boot. "The winner gets a college scholarship, a tiara, and a lot of pats on the back." She said it like it was no big deal, but after watching the tryouts I knew the top-ranking girls were unbelievable riders.

"You forgot to mention the cool jacket, Jaycee." A voice entered our conversation and I looked over my shoulder to see a girl on a chestnut Paint. She rode up to Levi's truck, and I recognized her horse immediately. He was a flashy horse, almost red in color with white patches on his neck and rump that slid down his body. It looked like someone had dumped a can of paint on him and let it drip over his coat. He was gorgeous and I remembered his rides today— they rivaled Taylor's.

"How could I forget the *cool* jacket?" Jaycee responded. "I mean, you do wear it every single day. Even when it's summer and most people are in tank tops."

The girl on the Paint was wearing a burgundy jacket that reminded me of the letterman jackets the football players wore at my school. It had gold lettering across the chest and last year's date. I figured she had to be last year's winner.

The girl looked offended. "I get cold easy." Then she gave Jaycee a little glare.

"Hey Breklynn," Casey said, diffusing the banter between the two girls. "Nice rides today."

Breklynn beamed. "Thanks, Casey. Whiz was really on his game." She tucked her short, red hair behind her ear. A few strands fell back in her eyes. "We do have a title to defend this year. Speaking of that, who's your friend? The one on the chestnut."

I noticed she didn't refer to Taylor as the top rider today.

"Taylor?" Casey asked.

"Yeah, the one you rode here with," Breklynn replied, and I remembered Taylor's comments about everyone in Three Rivers knowing your business. I grinned, thinking she might be right. "Where's she from?"

"The ranch," Casey replied, and his simple response looked like it confused Breklynn.

"Like she lives there?"

"California," I added, and Breklynn looked at me.

"Hey, aren't you the girl that won the Cowboy Race with Casey?" Breklynn tipped her head like she had a new focus. "You aren't from around here either, are you?"

I squirmed, feeling like all eyes had turned to me, even those that weren't part of our conversation. I wanted to flip the subject back to Taylor, but Casey replied on my behalf.

"Her name is Lucy. And, yes, she won the race." Casey looked back at me with a smile. My cheeks warmed.

"*We* won the race," I said, mostly to him. "Together."

"Well, look at you, Casey Parker. Making friends with girls from all across the country." Breklynn sounded sweet enough, but there was grit in her comment. "So, how come you didn't try out for the Round-Up, Lucy?"

I was getting ready to give my canned response about how this "wasn't my thing," but Taylor rode up behind me on Star and answered before I could get the words out of my mouth.

"She's going to try out next year," Taylor said, matching Breklynn's tone in a way that told her to back off. "Right, Lucy?"

My mouth popped open, but I closed it when Breklynn replied with, "Well, isn't that wonderful. We *love* out of towners here." She gave a tight smile that was anything but welcoming and rode off before I had a chance to gather my thoughts. The gold letters on the back of her jacket sparkled in the last of the sunlight.

What just happened?

"I don't think she liked what you had to say," I said to Taylor, but it was nice that Taylor had my back— even if she wasn't telling the truth.

"Ugh," Jaycee moaned when Breklynn joined another group of riders next to the bleachers. "I don't like her."

"You don't like anyone," Casey replied.

"Truth," Levi added with a laugh.

Jaycee smirked at their jesting. "You guys are lucky I like you."

"*So* lucky," Casey added, and Jaycee waggled her head at him. "Besides, Breklynn is harmless."

"Harmless like a fly in pudding," Jaycee said.

Casey shook his head and smiled.

"What does that even mean?" I asked.

"She buzzes around and then ends up where you don't want her," Jaycee explained.

I couldn't help but to chuckle. "I see." Jaycee certainly had a way of summing things up.

Taylor cleared her throat. "Well, regardless of flies or pudding, you *are* going to try-out for the Round-Up next year. Right, Lucy?" Taylor spoke with certainty, but I thought she was just on an adrenaline-high from her rides. "You'll come back and work at the ranch next summer, right?"

I hadn't thought ahead to next summer, but I nodded. Working and living at the ranch was like a dream come true. Of course I'd come back next summer. "Yeah. I mean, I want to."

"Good. I'm sure I'll be back too and I'll help you practice on Chance," Taylor said. "You can totally do this. I don't know why you didn't try out this year."

"Well," I started, thinking that I'd only run one barrel pattern with Chance and we'd never attempted anything that looked close to a horsemanship pattern. "I've never done anything like that." I waved my hand at the arena, trying to get my point across.

"It just takes practice," Taylor said, nonchalantly from her seat on top of her show pony.

"Exactly," I replied. "I'd probably need to practice a few of those things before I got in front of a huge crowd and did something embarrassing."

"Come on now," Casey said, and he brushed his shoulder against mine, nudging me. "Who do you think you're kidding? You could do this. No problem."

"Lucy, you can do it. You rode through a flipping mountain, chased cows, jumped jumps. Why do you think you can't run some barrels and complete a pattern?" Taylor stared at me. Her question caught me off guard. I knew I did those things. But the Cowboy

Race was different. I was fighting for Chance. I had to compete. I had to win.

"Taylor's right," Casey added. "You should do this. Next year. When you come back for the summer." There was a glint of excitement in Casey's eyes when he mentioned next summer, and I hoped it was for me.

"I don't know," I replied, but even as I said it, I was considering how fun it would be to ride in the arena, to circle barrels at blazing fast speeds, to be so connected to Chance that we could blow everyone's minds with our beautiful, perfect horsemanship pattern. "I guess I'd have enough time to practice before next year."

"Yeah! It's settled then," Taylor said quickly, throwing a hand in the air. "I'll help you practice and next year *you* will enter the Round-up and kick butt."

"Yes," Jaycee added with a fist pump. "Then I can watch you *both* beat Breklynn."

I smiled at Taylor and Jaycee's enthusiasm for next year's auditions and Casey nudged me with his elbow, a little harder than he had with his shoulder.

"Okay, okay," I said. "I'll do it next year." My circle of new friends cheered and my heart swelled with their excitement. "As long as you guys help me practice."

Everyone agreed, and I figured the practicing might be more fun than the competition. Besides, I had a whole year to get ready.

Or, I *thought* I had a whole year.

Forty

I AIMED THE wheelbarrow at the wooden ramp and gave a grunt as I pushed it up the incline. At the top of the ramp I dumped the load of dirty bedding into the manure spreader and gave the wheelbarrow an extra shake to make sure it was empty. Then I set it down and took a breather. Casey had a few guests out on a morning trail ride, and Marilynn was helping Mrs. Owens with a children's activity at the main lodge. From the top of the ramp, I could see Marilynn and Mrs. Owens out on the lawn in front of the lodge with a group of kids, doing something that resembled a stick horse race. I smiled, but was glad I was in the barn, cleaning stalls instead of wrangling kiddos.

Three done and two more to go, I told myself, wanting to get the stalls cleaned before Casey got back with the guests. This week there was a group of women that were staying at the ranch. They were from northern Washington and hauled their horses with them. Said they were on a well-deserved vacation from cooking, cleaning, and work and I wanted their horses' stalls to be perfect when they got done with their ride. Plus, Casey and I still needed to move the young heifers to a fresh pasture. Mr. Owens said they needed to be pushed over to the next field where there was more grass, and I couldn't wait to work the cattle with Chance. And Casey.

Moving through my morning checklist in my head, I grabbed the wheelbarrow again and shuffled down the ramp, intending to head back to the barn. But Taylor's voice stopped me. In fact, it made my head snap up and, surprised at her tone, I dropped the empty wheelbarrow off the side of the ramp.

"Lucy!" Taylor yelled.

There was a distinct desperation in her call. I looked for her, expecting her to be running. She wasn't. Taylor was slowly walking up the path from the arena, headed toward the barn. Star was at her side, saddled, but she was . . . limping?

"Is Star hurt?" I asked, and abandoned the tipped-over wheelbarrow. I made it halfway to the barn before I saw the red and my heart stopped. One of Star's front legs was cut— right below the knee. Blood darkened her copper coat and dripped onto her white sock. "Oh my God."

"She spooked when we were riding. Jumped and cut her leg on the gate," Taylor stuttered. Her face was pale, her eyes wide. "I don't have my phone. I . . . I need to call the vet."

I immediately grabbed my phone out of my pocket. As it rang I asked, "Are you okay?"

"I'm fine," Taylor replied, not looking fine at all. She looked frightened.

I pressed the phone to my ear and Taylor knelt next to Star, getting a closer look at the injured leg. There was a good-sized flap of skin that hung down and I hoped that was all it was— skin that could be stitched back together. Not something worse. Star had her leg cocked, trying to take the weight off the injury and her head hung low. She knew she needed help.

Dr. Sam answered after two rings and I explained what I saw before me. She said she'd be right over and told me to keep Star still until she got there. "We are right next to the barn," I told the doctor before hanging up. Then I called Marilynn.

"What?" Marilynn asked, yelling over screaming kids in the background. I only had to repeat myself once and she was on her way. Marilynn ran from the lodge to the barn in about ten seconds and took over all the necessities. She called Mr. Owens and hurried to the barn to grab clean rags. I stayed with Taylor, trying to think of something to say to make her feel better while we waited for the vet.

"She'll be okay," I said softly and put an arm around Taylor's shoulders. "Star will be okay. Dr. Sam will know what to do." My words seemed to make the situation worse. Taylor's lip trembled and I knew she was on the verge of crying. I squeezed Taylor's shoulders tight and she dipped her head as tears escaped her eyes. "I'm so sorry, Taylor."

Dr. Sam was practically a neighbor and made it to the ranch in about five minutes. I'd only met Sam once before when she stopped by to do a few vaccinations, but I thought she was the nicest vet I'd ever met. She was a tiny woman with a short, dark pixie cut, and she had a magical way with horses. She was quick and kind. The horses barely noticed when she had to poke or prod them. She cooed sweet words and petted them as she worked which seemed to lull all the animals into a dreamy state.

After she arrived, Sam determined that Star was able to walk and she helped us lead Star to her stall. Then she gave Star a shot to sedate her, cleaned the wound, and stitched her up. Taylor stayed near Star's head through it all, holding her, giving her kisses, and whispering encouragement as Sam worked her magic. Marilynn, Mr. Owens, and I pitched in where needed— handing Sam supplies from her vet bag and fetching her buckets of clean water.

"I know it looked bad," Sam said when she finally rose from her kneeling position next to Star's newly bandaged leg. "But it was a clean cut. A flesh wound. There shouldn't be any permanent damage."

"That's good news," Mr. Owens said with a heavy sigh. He looked at Taylor, expecting her to comment, but she only nodded. Taylor hadn't said much since the doctor arrived. "What should we do with Star now?"

Sam placed a hand on Star's shoulder and ran it over her coat a few times, like she wanted to do more to soothe her. "She'll be sleepy for another hour or so until the sedative wears off. Keep her in her stall until tomorrow and I'll be back in the morning. I want to check the stitches and change the bandage." Sam gave Taylor a sympathetic smile. "And I'll show you how to change her bandage as well. We'll want to keep her leg clean, so the wound doesn't get infected."

"Okay, thank you." Taylor's voice was small, like she was trying to keep from crying again.

Dr. Sam tucked a partial roll of vet wrap in her front overall pocket and stepped out into the barn aisle. "Once Star perks up you can give her some hay. But wait at least an hour. I want the sedative to fully wear off before she eats anything."

"Absolutely," Mr. Owens replied. Marilynn and I both nodded, acknowledging Sam's instructions.

Sam turned back to Taylor. "Call me if you have any questions. You have my cell number and I'll be back tomorrow morning, about eight. Try not to worry too much. Star will be just fine. And I'm sure you girls will take great care of her tonight. She'll need an extra carrot or two and lots of loves."

"Thanks, Dr. Sam," Taylor said, choking back tears. "I'll see you in the morning."

I reached down and picked up Sam's vet bag and handed it to her. "We'll all keep watch on Star."

Sam gave me a smile and took her bag. She walked off with Mr. Owens and I peeked back into Star's stall. Star's head hung low, her forehead pressed to Taylor's stomach like she might topple over if Taylor stepped away. But it didn't look like Taylor was going anywhere.

"I'll switch spots with you if you need a break," I offered.

Taylor rolled her hand over Star's flaxen mane before replying. "It's okay. I got this. I'm going to stay here until she wakes up."

"Okay. I'm going to finish cleaning stalls. Just yell at me if you need anything." As I walked away, my heart ached for Taylor. I was sure she felt worse than Star.

Forty-one

I KNOCKED THREE times and barely got my knuckles off the cabin door before Taylor appeared. She jerked the door open and stared into the night, at me. It was after eight o'clock and I probably should've texted instead of just showing up unannounced.

"Is everything okay?" Taylor looked terrified. She must've thought something was wrong with Star.

"Star's fine," I replied quickly. Taylor had stayed within a ten-foot radius of Star's stall all day and only retreated to her cabin when Mr. Owens urged her to get some rest. "I checked on her just before I walked over here."

Taylor's face relaxed. "I was going to check on her again about midnight, but I'm not sure I'll be able to sleep. I might just grab a cot and sleep next to her stall." Taylor's hand was on the door, and she had a tight grip on the knob.

"Casey is doing night-check on the horses in another hour or so. And I'll be at the barn feeding by six in the morning. Star will be okay. Just keep your phone by you while you sleep. We'll let you know if something is wrong, but she's been doing great since Dr. Sam left." I raised the two mugs in my hand, showing them to Taylor. "I just thought you could use a friend. And some hot cocoa." I smiled tentatively, hoping I wasn't bothering Taylor. She probably did need some rest.

Taylor's shoulders lowered and she looked embarrassed. "Oh," she said with a sigh. "Yeah, that'd be great." She opened the door to her cabin, inviting me in.

It was the first time I'd been in a guest cabin. My bunk was a one room A-frame, closer to the barn. The guest houses were on the opposite side of the ranch, nestled behind the main lodge. They were cozy cabins set among the fir trees. People rented them out, usually for a week at a time, but Taylor and her mom rented this one for the entire summer.

I stepped into the living room and saw Taylor's mom in the kitchen. She was wearing a fluffy pink robe and had her long blonde hair in a messy bun on the top of her head— just like Taylor. They looked so much alike.

"Hi, Mrs. Johnson. I'm Lucy," I said as she turned to me, feeling like I needed to explain why I was knocking on their door so late. "I just wanted to see how Taylor was doing. I hope I didn't wake you."

"Hi, Lucy. Nice to officially meet you. Taylor's told me all about you."

"Mom," Taylor moaned as she walked over to the brown leather couch. "You make me sound like a stalker." Then she plopped down on the couch.

"You can call me Christine," Taylor's mom said, ignoring Taylor's comment and leaning against the edge of the counter.

"I brought Taylor some hot cocoa from the lodge." I raised the mugs again. "Well, kind of. I mean, I brought the mugs, cocoa powder, and marshmallows." I gave a shrug, knowing I'd need some hot water.

"Here," Christine said, and walked over. "I've got a teapot going on the stove. Let me make those up for you girls." She took the mugs from me and smiled. "Why don't you make yourself comfortable? That was very nice of you to stop by and check on Taylor."

I replied with my own smile, thinking Taylor's mom seemed pretty nice. I'd only heard Taylor complain about her, so I'd imagined her much different.

Taylor snuggled into the couch pillows and pulled a blanket onto her lap. Then she motioned for me to join her. "There's another blanket if you'd like."

"Sure," I said, kicking off my boots near the door and joining Taylor on the couch. Taylor tossed me a fuzzy blanket. It was black with little white running horses all over it. I tucked it around myself, covering my sweatpants and most of my well-worn sweatshirt. I'd had the shirt since I was thirteen. It was my favorite— red with hoofprints down the sleeves. "Star's doing good. She's quiet in her stall and not bothering her bandage." I didn't have to tell Taylor this. She knew. I just wanted to remind her. Maybe it would help her relax.

Taylor pulled the woven blanket closer to her chest. "I've just . . . I've never seen her hurt. Not like that. It really scared me."

I nodded, understanding. The cut looked really bad before Dr. Sam got there and Taylor didn't have to explain her fear to me. I got it. "It was an accident. She's going to heal up just fine."

There was clinking in the kitchen and Christine came over with two steaming mugs. "I'm going to bed, but stay as long as you'd like, Lucy."

"Thank you." I took the mug topped with marshmallows. When Christine gave Taylor her mug, she gave her daughter a little squeeze on the shoulder.

"Thanks, Mom," Taylor said and took a sip, staying quiet as her mom padded through the kitchen and closed the door to her bedroom. "Star doesn't usually spook like that. She'll jump every now and then, but those cows really scared her."

"Can you blame her? I'd be scared, too."

When we were feeding Star her dinner, Taylor told me the details of what happened. She'd just finished practicing patterns in the arena and was riding Star out the gate when a huge branch broke free from a tree in the closest pasture. There were about ten cows standing under the tree and they panicked when the branch came falling to the ground. The combination of a crashing branch and a running herd of cattle made Star flee. Before Taylor knew what was happening, Star had blown out of the arena and managed to slice her leg on the open gate during her scramble.

Taylor shook her head and took another sip of her hot cocoa. She licked the chocolate from her lips. "Thanks for this, Lucy. I think it is making me feel a little better."

"Chocolate and marshmallows. Always works for me."

Taylor gave me a grin, but it quickly slipped away when she added, "It's too bad I can't ride in the Round-Up now. I was really looking forward to it. Would've been really fun. But I'm just glad Star is going to be okay."

"We can still go watch it together," I offered, but knew that's not what Taylor wanted to hear. I saw the gleam in her eyes when she was riding at the Ring. She loved to compete. "Or, maybe you can ride another horse? I'm sure stuff like this happens. Maybe with a vet note the committee will make an exception?"

Taylor's eyes shifted. "I don't think so."

"It wouldn't hurt to ask. And I'm sure Mr. Owens would let you ride one of the ranch horses. Sunny or Tank? Or, you could even ride Chance if you wanted to."

Taylor lifted her brows at my offer, knowing it was a big deal for me to offer up my horse for her to use. But I knew I could trust her. I always knew she was a good rider, but watching her with Star today had shown me how big her heart truly was.

"That's really nice of you," Taylor started. "But if I can't ride Star, there's no sense in me competing. Winning only means something to me if I do it on my own horse . . . on Star. Does that make sense?"

"It makes total sense," I replied, knowing what she meant. "I get it." I plucked a gooey marshmallow out of my mug and put it in my mouth, still feeling bad that Taylor had such a crappy day.

"Hey, Lucy," she asked, and I swallowed the sugary goodness. "Do you want to stay and watch a movie? There's this new one on Netflix about this girl that saves this horse and ends up winning the Derby with him."

"Oh, I've been wanting to watch that one. Yeah, that sounds great."

Taylor grabbed the remote from the end table and turned on the TV. "I'm not sure if it's any good, but I've never watched a bad horse movie."

"Me either," I replied, and we both snuggled deep into the couch pillows and fuzzy blankets. As the movie started, Taylor finally gave me a smile that met her eyes.

Forty-two

THE NEXT DAY flew by quickly. Dr. Sam was at the barn bright and early to check Star's leg. She showed Taylor how to change a bandage and clean the wound, and said she'd swing by at the end of the week again. In the meantime, Star was stall-bound and not very happy about it. Especially when Casey and I took the Washington ladies out on a trail ride and Star was left by herself in the barn. Marilynn said Star whinnied for ten minutes straight until Marilynn brought Freckles, the kind Appaloosa mare, in from the pasture and stalled her across the aisle from Star— which made both mares happy. Freckles enjoyed eating an extra flake of hay and Star was content to be near another horse.

"Thanks for the beautiful ride," Barbara, one of the ladies from Washington, said with a wave. Casey and I had taken them to Diamond lake where they'd had a picnic on horseback. We'd been gone most of the day. "We can't wait to do it again tomorrow, but I think the lodge deck is calling us now." Barbara gave a wave as she walked out of the barn with her three friends at her side.

"And a glass of wine," Sylvia, the tall redhead, added.

"Or two!" Barbara said, and all four of them laughed.

I waved back as I unhooked Chance from the cross-ties. "See you in the morning. We'll take you guys up to the red rocks tomorrow."

My comment started more lively chatter. I gave Chance a good scratch around his ears until their voices disappeared. Then I led him down the aisle and around the back of the barn, where Casey was waiting for us. He was standing next to Rocky, a curry in his hand.

"Shampoo, bathing mitts, and sweat scrapers are lined up and ready to go." Casey pointed at the row of goodies on the ground near Rocky's hooves.

We had some extra time and decided to give the boys a good bath. The Washington ladies were our only guests for the next few days. They all brought their own horses and enjoyed brushing and tacking them up themselves. That meant Casey and I had some extra time to spend on Chance and Rocky.

I joined Casey on the cement slab, which acted as a wash rack, and tied Chance to the hitching post. Chance gave Rocky one soft nicker.

"Conditioner, too?" I asked.

Casey paused before answering, unraveling the hose from the hook on the barn wall. "Yes, but you better not tell anyone I use conditioner on Rocky. It might hurt his tough reputation." He gave me a quick wink. "And mine."

I laughed. "Oh, come on. Being tough doesn't mean you can't have a silky mane and tail, right?" Casey gave me a pointed glare and I ran my fingers over my mouth like I was zipping it shut. "Your secret is safe with me." Kind of. I knew I'd give Casey grief about it later on. He was just too fun to tease.

"Ladies first," Casey said, walking over to hand me the green hose.

I took it with a playful smile and turned toward Chance. "Easy, buddy." I sprayed the ground for a few seconds before turning the hose on his front legs. I wanted to make sure Chance knew what I was doing and that he wouldn't spook at the sudden rush of water. "Good boy," I continued as I moved to spray his chest and then his back, soaking his coat, mane and tail before handing the hose off to Casey.

"Must be nice to have a black horse," Casey noted as he drenched Rocky, darkening his dapple-gray coat.

I poured a dollop of shampoo on a bathing mitt and scrubbed Chance's coat into foamy, white bubbles. Chance lowered his head and licked his lips, enjoying the scrub.

"He is pretty easy to keep clean." Just then I knelt down to scrub his left front sock. Other than the tiny star on his forehead, Chance's sock was the only white on his body.

Casey hung the hose over the hitching post and started scrubbing Rocky, making sure to hit the grass stains on his hip and a dark, unknown stain on his hock. "Rocky likes to roll in anything and everything he can find. If there's a mud puddle or a random manure pile, he'll find it. And he'll roll around in it. Right, big boy?"

Rocky looked at Casey like he understood his question and was not impressed with his comments, but Casey continued. "It's like he doesn't know he's gray. I think he secretly wants to be a paint and just keeps adding spots when he can."

I stopped lathering Chance's mane and laughed. "You're going to hurt his feelings." I turned and pointed a foam-filled hand at Rocky. The gelding confirmed my jest. He'd turned his head away from Casey like he was disgusted. "See. Look what you did. You better apologize to him." I chuckled again, knowing Rocky was probably just disgusted with the fact that he had to stand still for a bath.

"Aw, Rocky," Casey said, walking toward Rocky's head with his hands held out. "You know I love you and I wouldn't change a thing about you. Stains and all."

Rocky perked his ears, but instead of fully acknowledging Casey's approach, Rocky grunted and shook his whole body like a dog after a bath. A shower of water and foam flew through the air. Casey flinched as the wetness hit him.

"Oh, come on," he said. "Not cool, Rocky. Not cool."

Casey turned to me, his hands still in the air and I folded over in laughter. Casey's white shirt was splattered with dirty water, making it look tye-dyed, and dollops of frothy foam had settled on his arms, face, and hair.

"You *definitely* hurt Rocky's feelings," I said, putting my own foamy hands on my knees, steadying myself as I laughed.

Casey pursed his lips like he was considering this. "Now I'm just as dirty as him. Figures. Guess I deserved that."

"You did deserve that."

Casey cocked his head at me like he was challenged by my comment and I froze, knowing what he was going to do just before he did it.

"You—" He took one quick stride and closed the gap between us catching my arm as I squealed and grabbed the hose that was hanging over the hitching post. Casey moved like he was going to give me a big bear hug. I was not about to let him share all his horse-sweat-water-and-foam-shower with me. I managed to put the hose nozzle between us. Casey froze, his mouth agape in mock astonishment.

"One move and you're toast," I challenged him with a grin, holding the spray nozzle with both hands, my thumb positioned over the trigger.

"You wouldn't." Casey's pale blue eyes slatted. He had both hands on my arms. They were sudsy and slippery, but stayed fixed on my wrists.

"Try me," I said, suddenly realizing how close we were. When Casey replied with a crooked grin, his dimple showed up and my hand got a mind of its own. I squeezed the nozzle, hard, and a solid stream of water shot out and hit Casey right in the chest. But my move backfired because the spray ricocheted off Casey and blasted me as well— in the face. Instinctively, I closed my eyes and dropped the nozzle. We both yelped and when I opened my eyes again, Casey had his mouth open and his shirt was soaked.

"I can't believe you did that," he said, not able to keep a straight face. We both broke into laughter. The horses were looking at us like they weren't sure if they should ignore our craziness or be scared.

I tried to wipe the cool, dripping water from my face with my arm since my hands were still full of foam. "Well, maybe you don't know me as well as you think you do."

I was kidding, but Casey closed his mouth and stepped closer. He still had a grin on his face, but there was something about him that had turned serious.

"Truce?" he said, holding up his hands. "Will you abandon your weapon?"

"Truce." I grabbed the hose from the ground. I went to hang it back on the hitching post but thought twice before doing so. Casey would probably grab it and douse me, head to toe, getting his revenge.

Just as I started to pull the hose away from his grasp, Casey reached out and grab my hand. My other hand. The one that didn't contain a weapon.

I froze and let out an audible gasp.

His hand slide around mine, slick and warm, and held tight to my fingers.

"Hey, Lucy," he started, sounding like he was going to ask me a question. Shampoo bubbles were splotched on his cheeks. The adorableness of it made me wish he would kiss me.

"Yeah?" I replied, like I'd just run out of breath.

"Do you think that maybe you'd . . ." Casey paused, and I couldn't handle the anticipation.

Was he finally going to ask me on a date? Was he going to ask if he could kiss me? Was he going to ask me some random, weird question just to make me laugh? The way he was looking at me made my stomach flip.

"Yeah," I said, again, like I suddenly knew no other words.

"I thought that maybe we could—" This time, Casey stopped, but only because he was interrupted by yelling.

Casey and I both jerked our heads toward the sound. Taylor.

"There you are!" Taylor yelled as she ran toward us. She was holding a piece of paper high in the air, and my chest caved when Casey let go of my hand. "You're never going to guess what I found out!" Taylor stopped in front of us, waving the paper around, obviously excited about something. Then she looked back and forth between me and Casey and her eyebrows scrunched together. "Umm . . . what are you guys doing?"

Suddenly, I was aware that I still had the hose nozzle aimed at Casey's chest. Casey looked like he'd just run through a car wash, and my hair was soaked and sticking to the side of my face.

"Giving the horses bathes," I replied, casually.

"Oh, okay." Taylor raised an eyebrow. "Seems like you might want to turn the hose on your horse instead of Casey. Just a thought."

Casey grinned, and I lowered the hose, thinking about turning it on Taylor instead. But I gave her a pass since she'd been through a lot in the past twenty-four hours. Plus, it looked like she had news that just couldn't wait.

Taylor disregarded the awkwardness. "So, I went to go talk to Marcy. You know, the coordinator at the Ring. The one with the big hair."

"Taylor," Casey said. "That's not very nice."

"What? I didn't say big hair was bad. I love big hair." Taylor cocked her head at him like she couldn't believe he thought *big hair* was a criticism.

"Well, in that case, continue." Casey wiped his still foamy hands on his beyond-dirty shirt and I cracked a grin.

"As I was saying, I went to go talk to Marcy. I let her know about Star's injury and that I needed to scratch from the Round-Up, and she told me about this loophole in the rule book that not too many people know about."

I set the hose on the ground and pushed my hair out of my face with the back of my hand. "What's that?" I figured Marcy had convinced Taylor to ride another horse in the competition or told her she would be automatically qualified for next year's Round-Up.

"She said you could take my place!" Taylor spit out her secret so fast that I thought I heard her wrong.

"Excuse me?" My voice made a weird screechy noise.

"Marcy said that the winner of the Cowboy Race gets an automatic entry in all competitions at the Ring for an entire year." Taylor stared at me with pure glee on her face, but looked confused when I didn't respond. "That's you. You won the race, Lucy."

"I . . . " I was at a loss for words. I didn't feel the same excitement about this revelation as Taylor did. "I mean . . . I know what you're saying, but—"

"But, nothing. You don't even have to tryout. All you need to do is fill-out this sign-up sheet and you can ride Chance in the Round-Up next weekend." Taylor waved the paper in the air again and I blinked at her.

"That's awesome," Casey chimed in. I looked at them both like they'd lost their minds.

"Are you sure you didn't fall off and bump your head and you didn't tell me about it?" I asked Taylor, not sure why she was so excited about the idea of me riding in the competition. "I can't ride in the Round-Up."

"Why not?" Taylor asked.

"Yeah, why not?" Casey jumped in.

"Did you *see* the riders at the try-outs?" I asked, not sure why I had to explain this. "They were amazing."

Taylor put a hand on her hip. "And you're not?"

"You're just as a good of a rider as any of those girls," Casey added. Maybe he'd bumped his head too.

"Those girls have years of practice and competitions under their belts. I've never even taken a real lesson. I'd make a total fool out of myself." I pictured riding into the arena, letting my nerves get the best of me, and trying to stay in the saddle as Chance freaked out.

"Lucy, we watch you ride every day." Casey crossed his arms across his chest like he wasn't going to let me get away with what I was saying. "We both know you're a great rider. Right, Taylor?"

"Duh," Taylor said, putting her other hand on her hip, making it very clear that they were teaming up on me. "I mean, come on. You beat *me* at the Cowboy Race. Do you think I'd let someone else win for the fun of it? No. You beat me because you had a better ride." I could tell Taylor had a hard time saying that last bit.

"You guys," I said, looking at them both like I didn't think this was a good idea . . . AT ALL. I loved riding. I loved horses. But competing in front of a huge crowd, by myself, sounded terrifying. "I just don't think I can do it."

"Just because you haven't had lessons?" Taylor asked. I shrugged, knowing that was one of the reasons. "I'll help you. I'll give you lessons, and you know Chance already knows how to run barrels. We figured that out at the horse show this past weekend. Now you just need to practice and I'll give you tips. How's that sound? You said you wanted to do it. I heard you with my own ears."

"Yeah, I said I wanted to do it *next year*." I pressed my lips together, looking at the confidence in Casey and Taylor's faces and wondering if they ever got stage-fright.

"Look, let's just get you signed-up today," Taylor offered. "Then we'll see how you feel about it over the next week. You can scratch any time between now and the competition, okay? It'll be fun, I promise."

I swallowed, hard. Back home, I'd basically grown up on my mare's back, but that consisted of riding Stella around my grandma's farm and going on trail rides with the neighbors. We didn't have an arena or a horse trailer, so I'd never taken Stella to a show or a rodeo. Not that I hadn't dreamt about it.

"I . . ." I started, not believing I was even considering Taylor's hair-brained idea.

"Come on," Taylor urged, leaning in like she knew I was thinking about it.

When I reluctantly nodded my head, Taylor jumped up and down and clapped her hands together. Then she grabbed my hand and pulled me toward the barn. "Let's get a pen and fill this out.- Then I'll help you finish bathing Chance because it looks like you might need a lesson in bathing more than you need a lesson in riding."

Taylor pulled me along. I heard Casey's hearty chuckle behind me, reminding me of our water fight, hand holding, and almost-something. And as Taylor dragged me into the barn, I wasn't sure I had enough room in my head for all the feelings that had rushed through it in the past five minutes.

Forty-three

BACK IN MY cabin, I cleaned up for dinner. I pulled on a fresh shirt and jeans, washed my face, and brushed my hair. It was barbeque night at the main lodge. A sweet tang hung in the air, mixed with smoke, and the scent snuck in through my open window, calling to me. I quickly smoothed my hair into a ponytail, hurrying so I could meet Taylor for dinner. This afternoon, Taylor helped me fill out the sign-up sheet and put it in her pocket, saying she'd turn it into Marcy tomorrow. She didn't trust that I would hand it in and said her mom had to go into town anyhow. She was probably right. If I let myself think too much about what I'd agreed to, I would tuck that piece of paper away where no one would find it.

Checking my chestnut ponytail in the mirror one more time, I got a glimpse of the stack of books on the dresser and turned to stare at their colorful spines. I brought my favorite books to reread this summer—*The Racing Hearts* series, about a teenage girl that trains race horses. The horses always started off as underdogs, but the main character would find a way to make them winners. Then there were the *Horse Haven* books about another teenager that rescued troubled horses, figured out their problems, and saved them. I'd burned through both series, daydreaming that I was the main character in each book— saving horses, bonding with them, and magically making them winners.

I sighed. Who was I kidding? I *did* really want to ride in the Round-Up. I just didn't think I was ready. But Taylor seemed to think I was. Casey too. And I really hoped they weren't lying to me or just trying to be nice.

Maybe it's like a Band-Aid? I thought, running my fingers along my books' spines and thinking of how my dad always says to yank a Band-Aid off quickly. It somehow made the pain less. I knew that because one time I tried to pull an extra sticky one off slowly and I could feel every hair plucked from my arm, one by one.

Maybe the competition wouldn't be as scary as I imagined? Maybe Chance and I would enter the arena and work together like a flawless team, one that had been practicing for years?

I don't need to win. I just want to be proud of our rides.

I picked up my favorite *Horse Haven* book and smiled at the cover. Andrea, the main character, was staring intensely at a rearing, wild horse, but I knew how the story ended. I knew she ultimately got through to that horse. She tamed him. She won him over. And that was worth more than any ribbon.

I cracked open the book, wanting to read a few pages, but a knock at my door stopped me. Taylor had probably gotten sick of waiting for me and came to hurry me along.

"I'm coming," I yelled, setting the book on my nightstand, wanting to get lost in its pages tonight before drifting off to sleep. "I was just—"

I opened the door, but stopped talking when I saw Casey standing on my steps. There was a screen door between us, but it didn't hide Casey's grin.

"Hey," he said. He was dressed like he'd just done something very cowboy-like. Instead of his signature baseball cap, Casey wore a black cowboy hat, the brim speckled with dust. Leather chinks covered his jeans and Rocky was standing quietly behind him, a rope tied to his saddle.

"Hey," I replied, thinking Casey could be a cover model on one of the *Horse Haven* books. "I was just going to go get dinner. Did you need my help with something?"

"No, I—" Casey replied, and pulled a hand from behind his back. He was holding a small bouquet of wildflowers. "I mean, Rocky and I picked some flowers for you. We saw them when we were out checking cows in the upper pastures. Thought you'd like them."

"For me?" I asked the question as though there might be some other girl hiding in my cabin that he meant to give the flowers to.

"For you." Casey grinned wider.

I opened the screen door and joined Casey on the steps. Reaching out, I took the flowers. My heart melted. The bouquet was made of lavender, pink and yellow petals. The stems were wrapped with a piece of baling twine. "They're beautiful," I replied. "Rocky helped you?"

"Well, he mostly ate the grass around the flowers while I picked them. But he likes to think he helped."

I chuckled and my next comment snuck out before I thought too much about it. "Are these like thank-you-for-being-a-great-coworker flowers?" After the wash rack incident where Casey took my hand, I wanted Casey to give me more than just a hint that he liked me. But as soon as I asked the question, I held my breath, hoping he didn't say yes, call me buddy and give me a playful punch to the shoulder.

"They're more like I-want-to-get-to-know-you and will-you-go-to-the-dance-with-me flowers?" Casey smiled.

My heart did a double-beat and my mouth only allowed me one word. "Dance?"

"I know you don't really like to dance, but there's this dance after the Round-Up. It's always really fun. There'll be a band and food and everyone goes to it. And I was wondering if you wanted to be my date."

Date? I stopped myself from uttering another one-word question. Instead, I cleared my throat. "I like dancing. With you."

Casey looked mesmerized by my answer. I wanted to bottle up his look so I could peek at it over and over.

"It's a date then," he said.

"It's a date," I repeated as Casey backed down the stairs and gathered Rocky's reins. He kept his eyes on me as he patted Rocky's neck. When he finally walked off and looked away, I did a little tap dance on the top step and pressed the flowers to my nose, taking a deep breath.

They smelled sweet. Like happiness.

I found myself half-skipping to the lodge and really wanted to tell Taylor what had put a permanent smile on my face, but there were way too many ears at dinner. At the long dinner table, Taylor sat across from me and Marilynn sat next to me. Marilynn had half a pulled pork sandwich in one hand and a pen in the other as she checked things off a list in a small notebook. I was certain Marilynn didn't want to hear me gush about a boy, especially Casey. Jaycee joined us and I made *sure* my lips were sealed. She'd been helping Mr. Owens string up fencing all afternoon. I certainly was not spilling the beans about Casey in front of one of his good friends.

Instead, I enjoyed the barbeque, potato salad, and cornbread, and kept my excitement to myself. For now.

After dinner, Jaycee walked with Taylor and I back to the barn. Her dog, Patsy trotted alongside us and chased birds, butterflies, and squirrels— basically anything that moved.

"I better get to pedaling," Jaycee said, grabbing the bike that was propped up against the barn. "When I ride Nauti to the ranch, I can cut through Dr. Sam's property, cross the creek, and get here in like five minutes. But with my bike, I've got to take the roads all the way back into town. Takes me like fifteen minutes, and I've still got to clean Nauti's stall because Lord knows my sister didn't do it." Jaycee rolled her eyes as she swung a leg over her bike.

"How come you couldn't ride Nauti?" I asked, thinking that seemed like the better choice for multiple reasons.

"My brother was using him for roping practice. He's a multi-talented horse." Jaycee's eyes twinkled. "But his spotted-handsomeness is all mine tomorrow. I'll be back to help sort cattle. Night, Lucy."

"Night, Jaycee. Be careful on the roads."

Jaycee waved as she pedaled off. Patsy loped behind the bike.

Taylor was already in the barn and had Star in the cross-ties. She'd removed the bandage on Star's leg and was looking closely at the stitches. I walked over, wanting so badly to tell someone that Casey had asked me to a dance, but as I neared, I saw the seriousness on Taylor's face and I thought twice about telling her. I didn't want to sound like I was bragging. After all, Taylor had liked Casey at some point. Would I be rubbing salt in her wound? She was already upset about Star.

Instead of sharing my news, I sat on an overturned bucket close to Taylor. "Her leg is looking good."

"Dr. Sam said I could stop wrapping it," Taylor replied, throwing the bandage and wrap in the trash. "She said fresh air will help with the healing."

"Good." I grabbed a comb from the ground and started spinning it in my fingers. Star looked at me like she wondered why I was sitting on a bucket. Her flaxen forelock spilled over her eyes and I stood-up. "You want me to braid her forelock?"

Taylor paused and stared at me. "Okay, what gives?" She sounded like she was accusing me of something.

I stopped spinning the comb in my hand. "What do you mean?"

"I mean, you've been acting weird all night. At dinner you had this glowy, giddy thing going on, like you just won the horsie-lottery or something. And now you're being all quiet. What gives? What happened? What aren't you telling me?"

Taylor stared at me, a bottle of iodine in her hand. She looked ready to interrogate me.

"Nothing," I replied, not really knowing why I didn't want to tell her. Casey liked me. I should be able to tell my friend that. I shouldn't need to keep that a secret.

Star's ears flicked side to side as she looked back and forth from Taylor to me, following our conversation.

"Did something happen with Casey?" Taylor prodded, softer this time.

I bit my lip. I needed to tell her. She was going to find out anyway, and it would be better if it came from me. "He asked me to a dance." Instead of feeling happy about my secret, I felt like I was confessing something I did wrong.

Taylor almost dropped the iodine. "A dance?"

I started babbling. "I didn't want to tell you because I didn't want to hurt your feelings. You're already dealing with Star's injury, and I just didn't think—"

"Lucy, you should be excited. Why would you think that would hurt my feelings?"

I stared at her, feeling like a deer caught in headlights. "I thought—"

"Oh," Taylor said, looking like she suddenly understood. "You think I still like him, don't you?"

I shrugged, not knowing, but really hoping she didn't. Taylor and I hadn't talked about Casey at all. When I first came to the ranch, there was obviously something between them. In fact, Taylor had literally screamed at the top of her lungs when she saw Casey and I kiss that night near the pond.

"I just . . ." I started. "I really like him."

"I know," Taylor replied, and gave me a soft smile. "It's obvious you guys like each other. It's about time he actually did something about it."

"Really?" Was Taylor truly excited for me?

"And I want you to know I don't like Casey. Not like that. I came to the ranch pretty heartbroken. You saw what happened with Jace at the horse show this last week. He broke up with me not long before Mom and I came here for the summer."

I nodded, remembering Jace and his cocky attitude. I wasn't sure how Taylor could fall for that guy, but she obviously had. That was clear when Jace betrayed her and Taylor lost her marbles. He'd fixed one of Taylor's classes, loosening Star's girth so Taylor would have to stop riding and forfeit the class— just so he could beat her in overall points and win the championship. Instead, Taylor's ride ended up in a slipping saddle, a frantic bucking Star, and Taylor on the ground. I ended up sitting next to Taylor in the tack stall, comforting her as she cried, for more reasons than just hitting the dirt.

"I remember."

"I think I was just trying to get over Jace when I was flirting with Casey. Casey was so nice to me. And I just wanted my heart to stop hurting. There never was anything between us other than flirting. And that stopped on his end after he got to know you." Taylor looked down for a second. "Lucy, I'm sorry for being such a jerk before."

"You don't have to apologize."

"Yes, I do." Taylor started rubbing Star's shoulder like she was trying to soothe herself. "I was really mad before. I was mad at Jace for dumping me. I was mad at my mom for taking me away from home for the summer, again. And I took it all out on you . . . just because I could see that Casey liked you. That was really crappy of me."

I bit my lip, not sure what to say. Taylor had really hurt me when I was new to the ranch, but now, her apology felt sincere. And I only wanted to get to know the real Taylor from now on. The one that let me in. The one that told me her secrets and truly wanted to be my friend.

"I promise I won't keep any more secrets from you if you promise to do the same." Then I raised my hand, holding out my pinky finger. "Pinky swear?" It was a gesture I'd done a million times with my sisters, mostly when we had to keep something from my dad, but now it felt like the first step to a true friendship with Taylor.

Taylor reached out and wrapped her pinky finger around mine. "I pinky swear to never keep secrets from you."

"Besides, if I never told you about the dance, I don't know who I'd ask to help me pick out an outfit."

Taylor's brown eyes sparkled at my suggestion. "I've got like a million different shirts or dresses you can borrow. And I'll do your hair."

"Perfect. Because otherwise, I'm wearing my work jeans, a tank top, and my hair will be in a ponytail."

Taylor made a face, appalled by my comment. "No, you certainly will *not* be wearing that to your first dance with Casey." She tapped her finger against her chin, thinking. "I'm picturing something with crystals, and I think I'll curl your hair."

"Nothing too crazy. I still want to look like myself." I didn't need to look like some half-baked version of Dolly Parton.

"Who said you can't look like yourself while still rocking some crystals and curls?"

I chuckled and spun the comb in my hand again. "Okay. I'll trust you on that." Then I reached up and started combing Star's forelock, glad I'd spilled my secret to Taylor.

Forty-four

THE NEXT DAY Jaycee, Casey and I were in the upper pastures, sorting the open heifers from the cows with calves at their side. I was riding Tank, the big bay gelding. He was great with cattle, but I would've preferred to ride Chance. However, Taylor convinced me to ride one of the ranch horses so I could save Chance's energy for tonight. Tonight we were to have our first practice session, and Taylor kept sending me text messages, urging me to let Jaycee in on my secret— to tell her I'd signed up for the Round-Up.

When we were done sorting cattle and riding back to the barn, I finally mentioned something to Jaycee and was surprised by how good it felt. Jaycee danced around in her saddle, then moved Nauti close to Tank to give me three or four high-fives. She gave Casey a mean glare when she realized he was in on the secret and hadn't told her. Casey shrugged and trotted Rocky away from Nauti, probably thinking Jaycee would chase him down and give him a good shoulder punch.

Back at the barn, Taylor was waiting for us. She'd been hand walking Star and had Chance tacked up for me. She also convinced Casey and Jaycee to stick around and help me practice riding patterns with Chance. I argued, not sure I was ready for an audience, but Taylor said it would help me get over my nerves. I agreed, not sure how she got so good at convincing everyone of everything.

After I unsaddled and brushed down Tank, I put him in the pasture and hopped on Chance. Then all four of us made our way to the ranch's outdoor arena. Taylor was on foot, leading Star. The rest of us were in the saddle. Jaycee's border collie, Patsy, trotted eagerly behind Nauti, wondering if we were going to chase more cows.

"Jaycee, go stand in the middle. Casey, line-up with Jaycee, but more toward the far end of the arena." Taylor's hand pointed as she gave out instructions, and Casey and Jaycee rode their horses to their designated spots. Star stood at Taylor's side and nuzzled her arm, looking happy to be out of the barn and doing something with the other horses.

"Let's pretend that each horse is a cone," Taylor said, waving a hand at Jaycee and Casey. "Star will be a cone, too, and I'm going to tell you to do certain things at each cone."

"Okay," I replied, feeling a little uneasy about everyone watching me try to complete my first horsemanship pattern.

"At the competition, you'll get a printed version of the pattern well before you ride it, but until that time, we won't know what you'll have to do in the ring. The good thing is that I've done like five bagillion horsemanship patterns and I can basically make them up in my head and give you lots of different scenarios."

"Five bagillion?" Taylor's humor distracted my nerves.

"Well, maybe not that many, but I've definitely done a lot of them. *We've* ridden a lot of them. Isn't that right, Star?" Star lipped Taylor's arm at the sound of her name. She knew she was a topic of discussion.

"I'll try my best to do whatever you tell me to."

"And I'll watch you and yell out tips as you go along. We'll try out a couple of different patterns. I'll go line Star up with the other horses and you go stand by the gate. When you're ready, I want you to jog Chance to Star and stop. Then you'll lope to Nauti and make a big circle to the right. When you get back to Nauti, transition down to a jog and jog to Rocky. When you get to Rocky, stop and back-up five steps. Got it?"

"I'm not sure." Taylor rambled off the pattern so quickly that I was sure I was going to forget it by the time I rode to Star. "Can you repeat it for me?"

"Don't worry. I'll yell it off as you ride it. You got this." She led Star away and lined her up with Nauti and Rocky. All three of the horses stood in a straight line, but were separated by about twenty feet.

"Okay, Chance, let's give this a shot," I whispered, and gave him a little nudge with my legs. He walked to the gate and I turned him toward the other horses and stopped. Chance looked curiously at his friends, wondering what kind of game we were playing. I scratched his withers and added one more whisper. "I promise I have a peanut butter granola bar waiting for you in the barn when we are done here." They were his favorite.

"When you're ready, jog to me and halt. Okay?" Taylor said from her stance next to Star.

I nodded and gave Chance a cluck, asking him to jog. He obliged and happily jogged toward Star. I kept him in a straight line by making sure my reins were even and my body was straight in the saddle.

"Start thinking about halting Chance a few strides before you get to Star." Taylor watched me ride and when I got closer to Star, she added, "Start relaxing your body and sit deeper in the saddle. Then ask Chance to halt."

I followed Taylor's instructions just as she said them, letting my body relax and melt down into the saddle seat before I gently pulled back on Chance's reins and said, "Whoa."

Chance stopped right away, exactly when I asked him to, and cocked his head toward Star to say hello. They touched noses and Taylor laughed.

"When you actually ride a pattern, you won't have a real life horse distraction at each cone," Taylor noted. Then Star's nose nuzzling turned into a nip and she squealed at Chance. "Seriously, Star. Don't be such a mare."

Chance looked shocked for a second and then looked away, put in his place by the sassy chestnut mare. "Don't worry, Chance. Star likes you. She's just extra sassy because she's been on stall rest," I consoled him.

Taylor ignored her mare's spunk. "Anyhow, that was awesome. Great job! Now, ask Chance to lope off on his right lead and ride to Nauti. When you get to him, start making a circle to the right. Ride all the way out to the fence and back to Nauti. Got it?"

"Got it." I thought about all the pieces of my body that needed to work together to make those things happen. I prepped Chance for a lope departure. I kept my right leg at his girth, but moved my left leg back a few inches and pressed my calf against his belly. Then I tipped my upper body forward, just slightly, and kissed to Chance. He was a little unsure and hopped into a trot for a few strides, but then he moved into a lope. He took the right lead. I silently squealed to myself and Jaycee gave me a thumbs-up as Chance and I loped past her and started a circle.

"Look up," Taylor yelled, and I realized I was looking at my reins as I tried to direct Chance into a round circle. Our circle was looking more like a square, but after Taylor reminded me to look up, Chance understood where I needed him to go and the second half of our circle was more geometrically correct.

"Good. Now think about transitioning into a jog a few strides before you get back to Nauti." Taylor's words were loud but calm, almost soothing, and her reminders came at just the right time.

I asked Chance to jog as we finished our circle and approached Nauti. The first few jog strides were fast and choppy, but he was paying attention to my cues and quickly slowed down into a nice, smooth jog as I aimed him toward Casey.

"Halt when you get to Rocky and make sure to let Chance rest for a second before you ask him to backup."

Again, I prepared for the stop and Chance listened.

When we halted in front of Rocky, Casey said, "Great job," and gave me an encouraging smile. I almost forgot to ask Chance to backup because I was so lost in my delight at my very first complete horsemanship pattern with Chance. Also, Casey's cuteness was distracting.

"Remember to backup five steps," Taylor reminded me from afar.

"Oops." I pulled back on Chance's reins and counted each step as he took it. *One, two, three, four, five.* "Whoa."

I heard clapping from behind me and gave Chance an excited neck rub with both of my hands.

"See that wasn't that hard, was it?" Taylor asked as she walked over, Star in tow.

I couldn't believe it, but I agreed with her. "Actually, no. That wasn't so bad."

"See!" Taylor was obviously excited by my response. "Now I'll give you some tips on how to polish up those maneuvers, and you can try it again."

I nodded, and Taylor proceeded to explain a few tips for riding the pattern. She told me to aim for completing a transition when Chance's nose was at a cone. That would get me a better score. She also explained how to look ahead when I'm riding a circle, telling me that my body position would follow where I was looking and that would help give Chance cues as to where he needed to be.

I rode the same pattern again and it went even better.

"Good boy!" I exclaimed, and gave Chance a pat on his rump after we backed up.

"Awesome," Taylor said. "You made a much rounder circle and your transitions were quicker. I think that's probably good for today. We can try out a few different patterns tomorrow. Besides, we'll want to get over to the Ring so you can ride in the arena before sunset."

"What?" I asked. Taylor's comment sucked the excitement right out of me.

"Monday nights are open riding at the Ring, but apparently the arena lights only come on for events, so we'll want to get over there as soon as possible. It's six-thirty now and the sun sets by nine. That's why I said you should ride Tank today, so Chance has enough energy to practice."

I wasn't expecting to ride at the Ring just yet. "Are the other girls going to be riding too?"

"Probably," Taylor said, tossing her hair over her shoulder. "But they don't need to know your practicing for the Round-Up. It's open riding so anyone can use the arena. And it'd be good to get Chance in there. Being in the arena is totally different from riding around the outside of it. There's banners and tons of weird stuff that you will want Chance to see before the day of the competition so he doesn't spook at that stuff."

"I don't know, Taylor," I started, not sure I was ready to ride with all the girls I'd seen at the auditions, but a honking truck interrupted my dispute.

"I texted Levi and he's going to give me a ride to the Ring since Star is still out of commission. I'll see you guys over there." Then Taylor walked off, leading Star back in the barn.

Levi waved at us from the open window of his truck's driver side door.

"Do you think she'd be mad if I didn't show up?" I asked Casey and Jaycee, but I knew the answer to my own question. If I skipped out, Taylor would have Levi drive her back to the ranch and she'd pester me until I gave in.

"Yes," Jaycee and Casey replied at the same time.

"Come on, we'll ride with you," Casey laughed. I shook my head, not quite sure what I was in for at the Ring.

Forty-five

I RODE ACROSS the gravel road toward the arena, Casey and Jaycee riding alongside me. Taylor got to the Ring well before we did and was sitting on the arena fence. She waved at us and Levi was standing next to her, his arm resting on the top board.

"There you are!" Taylor announced, and hopped down from the fence. "Perfect timing. There's half an hour left of open riding and then there's individual time slots for practice runs on the barrels. I signed you up."

"Taylor," I said, my voice tight. "I'm really not ready for that."

For a second, Taylor looked surprised. Then she added, "You don't have to run the barrels. I thought it'd be good to get Chance in the arena by himself and you can just trot around the barrels. We'll work on speed back at the ranch. It'll be fine. Everyone is just practicing and having fun. They won't even be watching you."

I looked around. It wasn't as crowded as the last time I was at the Ring. There were probably ten riders in the arena, trotting and loping, focused on schooling and exercising their own horses. Furthermore, there wasn't a lingering audience like at the tryouts. There were just a few kids, sitting on their horses and talking to each other on the outside of the arena.

I pressed my lips together, stuck somewhere between nerves and excitement.

Taylor grabbed the end of my boot and squeezed down on my toes, bringing my attention back to her. "Hey, take a few deep breaths." She spoke quietly so that only I could hear. "That's what I do to calm my nerves." Then she took a deep breath through her nose and let it escape out her mouth.

I followed her example. Breathing in and out until I felt some of my jitters fade.

"Go in there and warm Chance up. You can just walk if you want to. Okay?"

"Okay," I replied and gave Taylor a small smile, glad she was helping me through this. *You can do this, Lucy. Don't chicken out.*

Urging Chance forward, I rode into the arena through the open gate. I took up the slack in my reins, wanting to make sure I had control of Chance if he spooked, but he was acting more curious than scared. We walked a few loops around the ring and Chance only snorted once at the plastic banner on the far end. It hung on the fence and was advertising the Friday night burger special at the local diner.

"It's okay," I reassured Chance. "The banner won't jump out and bite you." I let him sniff it a few times. As he did, I took a few more deep breaths, wondering if I was making a bigger deal out of this than necessary. If Chance could handle it, so could it. Deciding to push myself a little further, I asked Chance to trot and he bounced forward. I held tight to the reins and pulled back, slowing him down. "Easy, buddy. Let's just jog."

Chance reluctantly slowed his stride, but just as I got him into a smooth jog, a thundering of hooves approached quickly from behind and Chance jumped, unsure what was approaching.

"Whoa, easy," I managed just as a lanky bay blew by us. The horse was moving fast and his rider's leg was only a few feet from mine. Wanting to get away from what he thought was a threat, Chance scrambled sideways and I grabbed the saddle horn. But I couldn't stop us from banging into the fence. My knee whacked a post and I winced.

When Chance saw it was just another horse running by, he thankfully stopped. We watched the inconsiderate rider as she cantered away. It was then that I noticed a group of riders just on the other side of the fence from me.

Breklynn, the girl that had ranked up with Taylor at the try-outs, was in the middle of the group, staring at me from atop her paint horse. She raised her eyebrows at me. I knew she'd watched Chance jump and smack me into the fence.

"You okay?" she asked, but her question sounded sarcastic rather than concerned, and my earlier bravery washed away.

"I'm fine," I replied quickly, and stopped myself from rubbing my throbbing knee. Instead, I started walking Chance again. I made a loop around the arena and when I got to the gate, I exited. I couldn't get out of the arena fast enough. I would have galloped out, but that would've caused a bigger scene.

Taylor was waiting for me just outside the fence. Casey, Jaycee, and Levi were behind her, talking and laughing. They'd obviously not seen Chance spook.

"You okay?" Taylor repeated the exact same question Breklynn had asked me, but Taylor's concern was sincere. I felt my cheeks flush, embarrassment getting the best of me. "That girl shouldn't have run past you like that."

"It's fine." This time I let myself rub my knee in small circles, knowing I was going to get a good bruise.

"Don't worry about it. It's almost about time for the individual time slots and you're seventh on the list. You'll have the arena to yourself for ten minutes with no rude riders bugging you. That'll be better."

I nodded, knowing I'd have the arena to myself, but also knowing that meant all eyes would be on me and Chance.

Everyone here would be watching me ride. *Judging. Examining. Picking me apart.*

Taylor stood next to Chance and ran a hand down his neck as the arena cleared and the barrels were set up. Casey and Levi ran out to help. We watched as individual riders went in and out. Watching each ride only amped up my anxiety. These girls weren't playing around. They blazed through practice runs, zipping through cloverleaf patterns at breakneck speeds. Some riders schooled their horses, using training techniques I had no idea how to implement. They stopped their horses at particular spots near the barrel, or they'd canter past the barrel toward the fence, seeming to make their horses turn tighter and run faster in the few minutes they had in the arena.

Not everyone had a perfect ride, but all the girls seemed to know exactly what to do to help their horses get better.

"Taylor, I don't think this is a good idea. Let's come back another day when there's not so much going on." My chest had tightened like there was a cinch around my middle.

Taylor looked up at me. "I looked at the schedule. There's something going on every evening at the Ring. Monday's open riding is the only time to get in and practice. You'll be fine once you get in there. I know it." She brightened up as if she'd just remembered something. "I almost forgot, I brought my helmet for you." Taylor walked to the fence and bent down to grab a backpack. She unzipped the bag and pulled out a black helmet with teal and magenta roses printed on the sides. "I always wear one when I run barrels. And I thought it would make you more comfortable."

She offered me the helmet and I took it, thinking that was thoughtful of Taylor.

"Thanks." I put the helmet on my head and clasped the strap under my chin.

"It looks good on you," Taylor said. Her kind gesture had distracted me from my nerves for a minute.

A loud *clang* came from the arena, and I looked up to see that a rider had hit one of the barrels as her horse turned around it. The barrel tipped over and rolled, scaring her horse into a few rears and a head toss.

I bit my lip and watched in anticipation until the horse stopped his fit. Levi ran out and set the barrel up again. I was just about to ask Taylor if she'd ever knocked over a barrel when a cackle distracted me. Near the gate, Breklynn and her group of friends were sitting on their horses, watching, but instead of looking worried for the rider that had just hit the barrel, they were pointing and laughing.

I looked at them in horror, and when the girl rode out of the arena, Breklynn and her friends giggled. They didn't say anything to the girl, but they didn't have to. I could tell the rider felt horrible and she quickly trotted away.

I was too stunned for words, but I was even more horrified when Breklynn rode toward me and looked like she needed to tell me a secret.

"She should probably wear knee pads when she rides if she's going to keep hitting barrels with her legs. Actually, you might need some, too." Breklynn rode past me, letting her words hit me like little daggers. Then she added, "I'm just kidding. Lighten up."

"What did she just say?" Taylor asked, dipping her head around Chance to look at Breklynn as she rode away. "Did she seriously just say what I think she said?"

I didn't respond. I felt sick, like all my nerves had just exploded in my stomach. Breklynn was not *just kidding* and I didn't want to enter that arena again. I'd surely be made fun of.

I gathered Chance's reins in my hands. "I don't want to ride, Taylor. Not tonight."

"But you're next," Taylor said, her voice sounding irritated as she watched Breklynn ride. She turned back to me and the anger slid from her face. "Are you okay?"

I shook my head, knowing I wasn't. "I just want to go back to the ranch. I don't feel good." That much was true.

Taylor stood frozen for a moment. They she said, "Okay. I'll go with you."

"No, stay here. I'm fine. You don't need to go with me." Taylor didn't even have a horse to ride. Did she think she was going to walk alongside Chance all the way back to the ranch? "Ride back with Levi."

I turned Chance and rode off as Casey, Jaycee, and Levi all looked at me in silent confusion. I could hear Taylor explaining to them that I didn't feel well. I could also hear Breklynn galloping her horse through the dirt— pounding across the ground just like she'd stomped all over my dreams. Then I only heard Chance's hooves clack along the gravel road as we headed back to the ranch.

Forty-six

WHEN I GOT to the barn, I untacked Chance and spent an extra-long time brushing him. I smoothed his black coat with a soft body brush and spread detangler through his tresses. I ran a comb through his mane and tail and scratched him in all the places he liked to be scratched after a ride— near the base of his ears and along his cheekbones.

As I was scratching, Levi's truck pulled up to the barn. Its tires crunched on the gravel as he rolled to a stop. Taylor hopped out. She said something to Levi before shutting the door. Levi gave me a wave and I waved back before he drove off.

I went to gather my brushes from the floor as Taylor walked down the barn aisle slowly, her boot heels clacking. I was sure she was going to lecture me on all the reasons I shouldn't have run off. Heck, I'd been lecturing myself since I got back to the ranch.

"I shouldn't have pushed you to do something you said you weren't ready for." Taylor stopped in the aisle and fiddled with her nails. "I'm sorry."

I stood up, my arms full of brushes and combs. "It's not your fault." Taylor hadn't really pushed me to do anything I didn't want to do. "Honestly, I want to ride in the Round-Up. I want to be able to run barrels and be proud of my rides. I want to show everyone how amazing Chance is. I just . . . I just got scared. I freaked out." I swallowed, unsure what Taylor would think of my confession.

Taylor bit her lip, thinking. Then she walked over to Star's stall and grabbed the halter from the hook. "Want to go hand-graze Star and Chance? Star could use some time out of her stall." Star banged her leg against the stall door when she saw Taylor grab her halter. Taylor scolded her. "You better not be pawing with your injured leg, Missy."

"Sure," I replied, wondering if Taylor was going to ignore my confession or if she just didn't know what to say. I guessed it was the latter.

We walked out of the barn in silence, leading the horses to a big patch of grass that never got mowed. It was on the far side of the pastures. The grass was knee high, wispy, and smelled like summer. Chance and Star immediately dug in, grabbing mouthfuls and chomping away. Behind them the sun set, turning the sky pink, peach, and then dark blue before I said anything else.

"I want to ride in the Round-Up," I started, trying to explain myself again. "But I'm not like you."

Taylor gave me a look like she couldn't decide whether she should take offense to that. "Just because you haven't had lessons?"

"Kind of." There were other reasons too. "I mean, I've never had a *real* lesson. Like with a trainer. My grandma taught me how to ride. She would give me instructions from her porch as I rode around her backyard. I've never competed at a show, either. Riding in the ring with you at your show was as close as I've ever gotten to a horse show. I'm not like you, and I'm not like all those other girls at the Ring who have practiced for years and years." I twisted the lead rope in my hand, feeling doubt rising from my belly. "I felt like an impostor tonight, like I wasn't supposed to be there."

Taylor glanced at me and then shifted her gaze to her boots. Her blonde hair fell over her shoulders. "We're all scared of something." She said it quietly. I knew she was trying to make me feel better.

"Like what?" I asked, wanting to know what Taylor Johnson worried about. "You never seem like you're scared of anything. You didn't seem nervous before you went in any of your classes at the show. Even when you did your freestyle class in front of an entire coliseum of people." Taylor looked up at me, studying my face. "You had a spotlight on you while you performed. And you killed it. None of that scared you. I would've been so nervous I probably would have fainted, or puked or fallen off."

Taylor stepped toward Star and took a piece of her long flaxen mane in her hand. She twirled it in her fingers as Star nibbled the grass around Taylor's boots.

"I don't get nervous," Taylor confessed. "Not when I'm riding Star."

I took a deep breath, not sure if Taylor was the right person to confess my stage-fright to. I figured she'd tell me she gets butterflies, even if she didn't. Instead, she confirmed that competing didn't scare her, not in the least. Now I officially felt like a head case. Chance deserved a stronger rider.

"But you know what does scare me?" Taylor stared at me expectantly, and I hoped she wasn't going to say spiders or snakes or the boogie-man.

"What?"

"Riding any other horse besides Star."

I cocked my head, confused. "I don't. . ." I trailed off, losing my words.

Taylor gazed out, past our horses and the wood fencing. She seemed to be looking at the horizon, where the ranch horses were grazing. "Have you ever seen me ride any other horse besides Star?"

Baffled, I thought about Taylor's question. No, I hadn't ever seen her ride another horse. But I didn't think that was strange. Star was Taylor's horse, and she adored her. She didn't need to ride any other horse. At least, not until Star got injured.

"No. I guess not," I replied, and my brain flashed images of Taylor with Star. Since the first day I'd arrived at the ranch, Taylor had ridden every single day. She'd taken Star on trail rides, practiced in the arena, chased cows with her. But since Star got injured, Taylor hadn't been in the saddle. She never asked to use one of the ranch horses. Not once. As a paying guest at the ranch, Taylor could ride a different horse every day if she wanted to.

"I had a bad accident before I got Star."

"What happened?" I asked, as gently as I could.

"My parents bought me Star for my tenth birthday, but before then, I leased this gelding from Linda. His name was Cody. I learned to ride on him. He was one of Linda's old show horses. He was kind and sweet. He never spooked or got upset. Nothing rattled him. But after I'd been riding and showing him for two years, Linda decided it was time for Cody to be retired. He was in his mid-twenties by that time and was getting arthritis. Linda wanted him to live out the rest of his years eating hay and being pampered. And even though I was sad, I agreed that Cody had earned it."

Taylor paused, and I urged her on. "It sounds like Cody was a great horse to learn on."

"He was," Taylor nodded, and brushed her hair over her shoulder. "He never gave me any grief. He always did what I asked him to. In the show ring he would practically change gaits when he heard the announcer say 'trot' or 'lope.'" Taylor smiled at this, but it melted away quickly. "But because Cody was so good to me, I had this inflated ego. I thought I could ride anything, no problem. So after Cody was retired, I told Linda I wanted to start riding Dancer. She was this fancy mare that Linda only let her advanced students ride. Linda told me no, that I wasn't ready for that. I pulled a complete brat-move and saddled her up when Linda wasn't in the barn."

My eyes widened, knowing Taylor's story wasn't going to end well.

"I was riding Dancer by myself in the indoor arena, and it went well at first. Then she got a little frisky and I thought she was going to buck. I didn't know what to do, so I pulled back on the reins and held tight, thinking that would make her stop. It did the opposite. It sent her into a panic and she started to run. I couldn't stop her. She was too strong and too scared. And when she did actually start to buck, I flew through the air and smacked into the arena wall. I still remember the sound of my body thudding into the wood."

I released a breath, feeling Taylor's pain, knowing what it felt like to take a hard fall. I'd taken many a fall, though nothing that serious.

"Were you okay?" Obviously, Taylor was standing in front of me so she'd survived, but the fall sounded like a bad one.

"Linda always made me wear a helmet when I was learning to ride. And luckily, I had my helmet on when Dancer tossed me because I hit my head hard, against the wall. I broke my arm. But worse than that, something inside me broke, too. All of a sudden, I was scared. If I couldn't ride Cody, I didn't want to ride at all. I didn't think I could. Not to mention my arm was in a cast for months."

"Really?" I asked, not able to picture Taylor scared to get in the saddle.

"I still went to Linda's every day. I just didn't ride. I watched her work her show horses and give lessons. Linda had just bought Star, and I was fascinated by her. She took my breath away the first time I saw her, and Linda noticed. She asked if I wanted to help her with Star while my arm healed, so every day I'd come to the barn and brush Star, tack her up for Linda, spend time hanging out with Star in her stall or in the pasture. While my arm healed, I took the time to get to know Star— all her quirks, likes, dislikes. I grew to trust her long before I ever had the gumption to get back in the saddle."

"But you've ridden other horses since, right?"

Taylor shook her head. "I got back in the saddle with Star and I haven't been on another horse since."

I stared at Taylor, shocked. She was a flawless rider. She had won trophies and ribbons and been to countless horse shows and rodeos. She didn't bat an eye when she entered an arena full of stellar riders and well-bred show ponies. Yet she was saying she was scared to ride any other horse except Star?

"Star gave me back my confidence," Taylor continued and patted her mare again. "But I still don't trust myself to just jump on any horse. Not like you, Lucy."

"Like me?"

"You worked with Chance and gentled him. I saw him buck you off. I saw him pull you across the arena on the end of a lunge line. But you didn't give up. You kept at it. At first, I thought you were crazy. But then I saw all the improvements you were making with him."

"I mean," I started, dumbfounded. "Just because I kept working with Chance doesn't mean I wasn't scared sometimes."

Taylor nodded. "Well, I hope that someday I can be like that, too."

"Like what?"

"Like you, Lucy. Not scared. I hope someday I can get up enough courage to ride all kinds of different horses."

My lips parted and my mouth fell open. All this time I'd been admiring Taylor's confidence, not knowing that she . . . that she admired mine as well?

"Wow, I had no idea," I whispered. "But you're an amazing rider, Taylor. You aren't giving yourself enough credit."

Taylor put a hand on her hip. "Ditto." She gave me a one-sided grin. "You're just as capable of riding in the Round-Up as any of those other girls, and I don't want you to give-up. I know you can do it. If you want to ride in the Round-Up, then you should, and don't let some sassy-mouthed Breklynn-girl mess with your head. Okay?"

I squeezed Chance's lead rope and listened to him chew. Then I nodded. "Okay." I couldn't believe it, but Taylor had just talked me off the ledge.

"Good," Taylor said, and I wondered if there was really only one person I needed to prove myself to— and her name was Lucy.

Forty-seven

"THANKS FOR TAKING such good care of my baby boy this week," Barbara said as I pulled the wheelbarrow out of the stall. I set it down in the aisle and hung the manure pick back on the wall with the brooms and shovels.

"You are very welcome." I smiled, liking the way Barbara referred to her horse as her "baby boy," even though he was a seventeen-hand draft cross that made Chance look small. "Gus's stall is all ready for him. Fresh bedding and all."

"Did you hear that, Gus?" Barbara asked the big bay gelding standing next to her. He cocked his head like he was waiting for Barbara to answer her own question. She did. "Ms. Lucy got your stall all cleaned and put fresh fluffy bedding in there for you to sleep in tonight. Isn't that wonderful?" Barbara dug into the small fanny pack that hung from the belt around her breeches and offered Gus a carrot piece. He lapped it up.

Earlier in the week, Barbara had explained that she cut up three carrots every day and kept them in her fanny pack so she could reward Gus for good behavior. She even gave him treats when she was riding. Gus would stretch his neck around and gobble them up from her hand. Best I could tell, Barbara gave Gus a treat about every fifteen minutes or so for no other reason than he was being cute.

"All of your stalls are cleaned and your horses' hay racks are full," I announced to the four ladies as they milled about the barn. Barbara led Gus into his stall and was giving him another carrot piece. Sylvia was pulling the saddle from her horse's back as he stood in the cross ties, and the other two ladies were brushing their horses as the radio played softly in the background.

"Perfect. Thanks, Lucy," Sylvia said as she carried her dressage saddle into the tack room.

All four of the ladies rode dressage and had an array of different horses. In addition to Gus, there was an Arabian, a Fjord, and an Appaloosa. Throughout the week, Casey and I had learned that these women had been friends since middle school and originally met at a boarding stable. Now, they lived in different areas of the state, but always got together for one horse-themed vacation a year. Last year it was riding on the beach. This year it was a "real cowboy vacation" at the Red Rock Ranch. But mostly, they just wanted to go on trail rides, laugh, and eat good food. I thought they were the most adorable group of ladies. I hoped I had a group of girlfriends like that when I was their age.

"I'm going to go get some dinner, but I'll check on your horses before I go to bed. Come find me at the lodge if you need anything, okay?"

Barbara poked her head out of Gus's stall. She had his halter and lead hung over her shoulder. Gus was nibbling at his hay behind her. "Don't you worry about us, Lucy. We're just going to spend some time loving on our babies before we go to dinner."

"Do all the loving you want," I replied, and grabbed the wheelbarrow. I pushed it down the aisle and outside. As I was dumping the dirty bedding, I noticed Levi's truck rolling down the driveway toward the barn. His truck was hard to miss. It was lifted, making it look like one of those monster trucks. It was also a very obnoxious lime green color, which reminded me of the glow-in-the-dark plastic stars I had glued to my bedroom ceiling at home.

I waved as Levi pulled his truck to a stop in front of me. Casey hopped out the passenger door. I saw that Taylor was sitting between the boys.

"Want to go get dinner at *The Tack Room*?" Casey asked, looking excited as he mentioned the local diner. "They've got great pizza, and Marcy makes an amazing marionberry pie."

"Marcy? Like the same Marcy that organizes the events at the Ring?" I set the wheelbarrow down.

"Yeah, Marcy does all the baking for *The Tack Room*. She makes a killer marionberry pie and her apple crisp is to die for too. Actually, everything she makes is to die for. How 'bout it?"

"Jump in," Levi added, his arm resting on top of his steering wheel. "I've got room for one more."

Taylor scooted closer to Levi, making room on the bench seat. Levi's eyes got wide at her proximity.

"Come on," Taylor said, seeming oblivious to Levi's reaction. "You can sit next to me."

Casey looked at me, waiting on my decision.

"Sure. I love marionberry pie," I replied, and Casey grinned. Then he held out his hand.

"I'll help you into the truck," he offered.

Grabbing hold of Casey's hand, I balanced myself and took a big step up, pulling myself into the truck using the door and the metal running board for further support.

"Geez, Levi," I breathed as I settled in next to Taylor. "You might need to get a ladder for this truck."

"It's not that high," he said, shifting into drive as Casey plopped down beside me and shut the door. "Actually, I was thinking of putting in a bigger lift kit. I want to add about six inches."

Casey chuckled, and Taylor looked at Levi like he'd lost his marbles.

"What?" Levi asked and turned the radio up as we headed to town.

Casey was right. The pizza at *The Tack Room* was great. It was thick and cheesy and piled with sausage chunks the size of meatballs. But the marionberry pie . . . it was the best marionberry pie I'd ever had. I ran the edge of my fork against the little white plate, picking up the last bit of flaky crust and homemade whipping cream. Then I closed my eyes and let the sweetness melt in my mouth.

"You weren't kidding," I said to Casey, wondering how I could get here every night this summer for a piece of Marcy's pie.

"I told you so," Casey replied from his seat next to me. We were on one side of the booth while Levi, Taylor, and Jaycee were on the other. "To die for." Casey popped a few more fries into his mouth. He'd finished his slice of pie well before I did and was working on polishing off the basket of crispy fries with Levi.

"Marcy's pies are the best," Levi agreed, looking happy to be squished between Taylor and Jaycee on the other side of the booth. "But her chocolate chip muffins are my favorite. She only makes them on the weekend and you have to get here before eight o'clock. Otherwise, they're all gone." He waved at Marcy who was behind the kitchen counter, apron on. She looked like she was baking desserts for tomorrow. She waved back, her hands dusted with flour.

All five of us seemed to sigh at the same time. It was just past seven o'clock. The sun was still out, peeking in through the frilly curtained windows, but I felt a food coma kicking in and knew it was going to be an early-to-bed night for me. The week had been busy— full of work, and then practicing with Chance. My body was tired and the pie had just put me over the edge. I set down my fork and scooted back, the bench seat squeaking as I leaned my shoulders against it.

Casey sat back too and leaned toward me, letting his shoulder press into mine and his hand graze my pinky finger. The light touch quickened my pulse. When I looked over, Casey was watching me. I was suddenly awake again.

Jaycee cleared her throat, but she was smiling. "So, how long do I have to keep this secret?"

I looked across the table and realized my closeness with Casey was obvious to more than just me. Taylor and Levi both had sly smirks on their faces, and Jaycee looked like she'd just seen her brother make googly eyes at a girl.

I avoided glancing back at Casey, but kept my shoulder and hand pressed against his. "What do you mean?" Was she talking about my crush on Casey? The fact that he'd ask me to the dance?

Jaycee leaned over the table and whispered, "The Round-Up." She over-pronounced the words with her lips to make sure I understood. "I'm horrible at keeping secrets, and this one is killing me. When can your secret be announced to anyone outside of this table?" She looked eager for me to give her the go-ahead— as if she wanted to jump on top of the table and shout my secret to the whole restaurant.

I sat up. "I don't want to make a big deal about it, but I guess you can tell people if you want." My stomach fluttered at the idea of my secret being announced to the whole town. That would mean it was real, that I was committed, that I couldn't back out at any given second.

"Let Lucy tell people when she's ready to," Taylor added. Jaycee scrunched up her face like she couldn't hold her tongue any longer.

"What's the big deal? You're going to do it, right?" Jaycee asked.

As far as Jaycee, Casey, and Levi were concerned, they still thought I left the Ring the other night because I didn't feel good. Taylor was the only one that knew I left because I was freaking out, that I was terrified to make a fool of myself. And Taylor had kept that information to herself. I didn't even have to ask her to keep my secret. She just did.

"She's going to do it," Casey jumped in and wrapped his pinky finger around mine, locking our fingers against the leather seat and making my heart beat fast— for more reasons than the scary competition.

A bell jingled as the door opened, and Jaycee was distracted from her questions as Breklynn and her crew piled into the restaurant, all giggles and chatting.

Jaycee rolled her eyes. "She's going to wear that coat out," Jaycee said. Breklynn was wearing her award jacket again. As soon as I looked her way, Breklynn caught my eye and walked over to our table. I cringed.

"Hey guys," Breklynn addressed the table like we were all buddies. Her girlfriends followed, but were having their own conversation behind Breklynn.

Casey and Levi replied with a friendly-enough "Hey." Jaycee raised an eyebrow. She really did not care for Breklynn.

"We just got done running barrels at my place, and we're famished." Breklynn gave an overexaggerated sigh, like she'd just run a marathon and was exhausted. "Whiz just keeps getting faster and faster. No one is going to be able to beat us during the speed portion of the Round-Up. Especially now that you had to scratch." Breklynn was looking at Taylor. Her stare had a tangible superiority to it.

Taylor shrugged, unimpressed with Breklynn's conversation, but that only seemed to urge Breklynn on.

"I don't think we should be letting out-of-state riders compete in the Round-Up, anyhow," Breklynn added, pushing her hands in her jacket pockets, reminding us all that she was wearing it.

Taylor licked marionberry off her bottom lip. "Is that because I beat your time on barrels and had a better ride than you in horsemanship?" she asked Breklynn, her tone flat.

Breklynn huffed, offended. "Whiz was having an off day. I don't think I warmed him up enough before the auditions."

"Anyhow," Taylor replied, brushing off Breklynn's excuse. She was trying to change the subject, but Breklynn didn't want to let Taylor's comment go— especially since her friends were now paying attention to the conversation.

"I won last year, you know," Breklynn said, loud enough for everyone around us to hear.

"Taylor didn't compete last year," Jaycee added under her breath, but Breklynn caught her comment and her jaw tightened.

"Well, part of being a winner is keeping your horse in top condition, and obviously Taylor isn't capable of doing that." Breklynn's words came out fast, like a lunge whip cracking, and Taylor's mouth gaped. "If you'd taken better care of your horse, she wouldn't have gotten injured, and then you could have competed this year." Breklynn cocked her head. The sparkly bobby pin in her red hair caught the light from above. Then she turned her back on the table and walked away.

I looked at Taylor, stunned, and saw the pain in her eyes. She looked like she'd just been slapped across the face and didn't know what to do to retaliate.

"That's not true," I said, immediately. "She doesn't know what she's talking about."

"I can't believe she just said that," Jaycee said, and scrambled around in her seat. If she hadn't been caught between Levi and the wall, I was sure Jaycee would have chased after Breklynn and given her a piece of her mind.

I reached for Taylor's hand across the table. When I touched it, her eyes went glossy. She looked away and said, "I have to go to the bathroom."

Taylor stood up and walked off. I was appalled that Breklynn had the nerve to accuse Taylor of not taking good care of Star.

What was she talking about? Why would she say that to anyone? Especially Taylor.

Before I knew it, I stood up from the booth and was walking toward Breklynn and her friends. They were already on the other side of the restaurant, making themselves comfortable in a round corner booth. Breklynn looked dismissive when I approached.

"Can I help you?" She was sitting in the middle of the horseshoe booth, her elbows on the table. Her friends sat at her sides, looking at me curiously.

I wanted to flat-out call her a jerk and tell her to take her stupid, backhanded comments back, but I knew poking a mean girl only made them meaner. I learned that in middle school and I wouldn't play into Breklynn's game. So I kept my name-calling to myself. *Jerk*.

"You don't know what you're talking about," I said, sharply.

"Oh, I don't?" Breklynn put her hand on her chest, like she was offended. "Because I sure do have a lot of trophies that tell me otherwise."

I ignored her absurd comment about trophies and crossed my arms over my chest.

"Taylor is an amazing rider, and I watch her take care of her horse every day. She knows what she's doing, and you have no right to accuse her of anything. In fact, you should think about what you say before you say it. A real winner is actually nice to other competitors. Instead of making Taylor feel bad, you should have asked her how Star is doing. That would have been what a real winner would have done."

Everything fell out of my mouth in one breath. Breklynn looked like she'd just eaten something sour. One of her friends made a low whistle, but before Breklynn could muster up some sarcastic rebuttal, I added, "And it's too bad you have a thing against out-of-towners competing in the Round-Up, because I'm taking Taylor's spot."

"What'd you say?" the girl closest to Breklynn asked.

I leaned in. "I said, I'm taking Taylor's spot. The rulebook says the winner of the Three Rivers Cowboy Race gets an automatic entry into the Round-Up. And that's me." I pointed to my own face. "I'm the winner. And I didn't need any knee pads to take home that trophy." I gave Breklynn a stiff smile, and her smug face paled. "See you at the Round-Up, Breklynn. I hope you have a better attitude then."

"Oh, snap," some kid said from another booth. I turned and walked away, leaving Breklynn behind me.

It felt good to stand up for Taylor, but as I walked across the restaurant, I saw all the faces staring at me. I wondered why I had to throw in the last bit about me riding in the Round-Up. My secret was out. I couldn't take it back out now.

Forty-eight

MARILYNN WAS THE first one to say it. "Heard you've signed up for the Round-Up," she announced the second she stepped into the barn.

I was pouring Star's morning grain into her feeder and my arm hung in the air, stuck. Star nudged the feed scoop aside and buried her nose in her grain, not tolerating my hesitation.

"Where'd you hear that?" I withdrew my arm from Star's stall, certain she was going to nip me if I kept getting in the way of her breakfast.

Marilynn moved one of the wheelbarrows close to the stack of hay bales. "My cousin called me." She rolled a bale into the wheelbarrow and cut the twine with a pocket knife. "Said he was at *The Tack Room* last night and heard you tell Breklynn off."

I paused, and then spit out, "I didn't tell her off." Gus nickered gruffly and I moved to the next stall, knowing the horses were anxious for their breakfast. "I just told her she should be nice to Taylor."

I scooped grain out of the bucket hanging on my arm and poured it into Gus's feeder through the open stall window. I suddenly wondered how the Three Rivers gossip-train would interpret last night's public conversation with Breklynn. Maybe Taylor was right when she said it was creepy that everyone knew everyone else's business in this town.

Marilynn followed behind me, breaking hay free from the bale and tossing flakes into each horse's stall. "He said you stomped across the restaurant, told Breklynn to get off your friend's back, and you said you were going to beat her butt at the Round-Up and she better watch out."

I set the grain bucket on the ground, feeling faint. "That is *not* what happened *at* all." The other three horses hung their heads over their stall doors and nickered, afraid I would forget to feed them.

"I'm just telling you what I heard." Marilynn shrugged.

"Well, it's not the truth." I picked the bucket back up and went to feed the rest of the horses. "Breklynn was really mean to Taylor. Made a comment about how Taylor would still be in the competition if only she knew how to take care of her horse. Like it was Taylor's fault that Star got hurt."

Marilynn made a *tsk-tsk* noise with her tongue, knowing that kind of comment wouldn't go over well with Taylor.

"Exactly," I added. "She was being a big bully and really hurt Taylor's feelings."

"So you told her off?"

"I didn't tell her off." I gave Marilynn a serious look as I strode by and put the grain bucket back in the feed room. "I told her she should be nice. And then somehow, I thought it would be a good idea to tell Breklynn that I was taking Taylor's spot, that I would be riding in the Round-Up. I guess a few people overheard."

Marilynn laughed as she threw the last few hay flakes to Franz, the Fjord. "Yeah, I think a few people heard. Not to mention, Breklynn is the queen of gossip. She's like a real-life version of Google. Want to know who's dating who? What brand of cowboy boots so-and-so wore to the rodeo? Who just bought a new horse? Ask Breklynn. She'll tell you." Marilynn wheeled the empty wheelbarrow back to the haystack, filling it with another bale to take to the horses in the pasture. "You're the hottest topic of conversation at the watering hole. And it's not a very big watering hole."

Marilynn wheeled the hay out of the barn and I swallowed, wondering what my big mouth had done and if I could take it back.

By the afternoon, it was confirmed. Everyone in the entire town of Three Rivers knew that I was going to ride in the Round-Up. And, somehow, they all thought I was challenging last year's winner. I might as well have asked Breklynn to a dual— with swords. I would've been better off with a competition that involved weapons.

Jaycee sent me a text that said her little sister wanted to be me for Halloween because she thought I was the coolest, most courageous cowgirl she'd ever heard of. Mrs. Owens said she'd bake a cake the day of the Round-Up and host a party in my honor. Even Taylor's mom heard about my late entry when she went into town to get coffee. And every time the rumor mill spun and someone else asked me about the Round-Up, my stomach twisted tighter, like a towel being wrung out.

I should've kept the secret between me and my friends. I could've surprised everyone else the day of the competition. Now everyone thought I was making a big deal about it— that the winner of the Cowboy Race was challenging the winner of the Round-Up to a ride-off or something. I had unknowingly put a big, fat spotlight on my head, and now everyone would be analyzing my every move in that arena. It was *exactly* what I didn't want to happen.

"You're really quiet," Casey said, riding up next to me. We'd been riding for an hour or so, leading the Washington ladies on a trail ride to the Red Rocks. We were nearly there and I'd spent most of the time in my own head, thinking about how I could back out of the Round-Up.

"Sorry. Just thinking about stuff, I guess."

Barbara and her friends laughed behind us and then moved into awed silence as we rounded the last switchback and the Red Rocks came into view. Sandy red walls of rock climbed the mountain, and huge, flat slate pieces littered the ground. It looked like an abandoned rock quarry.

"Are you guys ready for lunch?" Casey turned back and asked the ladies.

They all chimed in with agreements before dismounting their horses and getting comfy on one of the big slate rocks. The four women used the rock like a couch and let their horses graze at their feet.

Casey pulled a paper bag from his saddle bags and handed it to Barbara.

"Lucy and I are going to go check on the herd just down the hill while you guys relax and enjoy the view, okay?" Casey pointed to a small herd of cattle that could be seen from where the ladies were sitting.

"Take your time," Barbara said as she took the bag from Casey and peeked inside. "This is what we came to the ranch for. Relaxation and good company. And how can you beat this view?" She raised her hand and sighed as she looked past us. From the Red Rocks, you could see the entire ranch and all the farm land that surrounded it.

"And the snacks," Sylvia added. "We came here for the snacks, too." She winked as she dug into the bag Barbara had opened.

Casey chuckled. "Okay, call me if you have any issues. Otherwise, we'll be back in about an hour."

As we rode off I heard Sylvia ask if Mrs. Owens' oatmeal raisin cookies were hiding in the bag. They all cheered when Barbara discovered them. I cracked a grin at their enthusiasm.

"That's better," Casey urged. "I'm not used to seeing you without a smile." Rocky walked close to Chance and Casey leaned over in the saddle, closing the gap between us. "What's wrong?"

I guess I hadn't been hiding how I was feeling even though I'd kept my thoughts to myself. I rubbed the leather reins between my thumb and pointer finger. "Do you ever get nervous about something even before it happens?"

"Like what?"

"Like riding in front of an audience." I glanced at Casey. I didn't specifically mention the Round-Up, but I saw the recognition on Casey's face.

"What are you worried about, Lucy?"

Every worse-case scenario flashed through my head. "What if I fall off?"

"Then you brush yourself off and get back on."

"What if Chance freaks out and runs around the arena like a race horse?"

"Then you do everything you can to calm him."

"What if he's scared of the lights or the announcer, or a random kid running around with cotton candy?"

Casey shrugged and Rocky nipped at a fly on his chest. "All those things could happen."

I gave Casey a sideways glance. "I know. That's why I'm worrying about them."

Casey wrinkled his forehead. "What if everything goes the way you want it to?" he countered, and stopped my onslaught of worse-case-scenarios. "You know that could happen too, right?"

We neared a metal gate and I digested what Casey said as he rode up to it.

Honestly, I hadn't really thought about what it would look like if everything went the way I wanted it to. I was so focused on what scared me that I hadn't thought much of what it would feel like to have a good ride at the competition.

"Why think about everything that could go wrong?" Casey asked as he reached down and unlocked the gate before guiding Rocky through. "Seems like a lot of wasted energy."

It was a lot of energy— to think about what scared me. But how else was I supposed to prepare myself?

"Because things do go wrong and I want to make sure I'm ready for what could happen," I confessed, finding my thoughts drifting to my mom. One day she was baking cookies in our kitchen, laughing at Jackie's silly dance moves, letting me eat dough straight from the bowl, and holding Molly on her hip.

The next day she was gone, taken from our lives in a split second because a man was distracted behind the wheel. He sideswiped her car, and one bad decision changed my life forever.

I rode Chance through the open gate, not sure how my thoughts had jumped from a riding competition to the day I lost my mom. They weren't at all comparable.

"If I run through all the scenarios in my mind, I feel like they won't be as scary if they happen." That time I *knew* I was talking about my mom, not about riding. I never once pictured life without her. Not until the day she died. And then I didn't know what to do with myself. I was lost without her.

Casey furrowed his brow at me, looking like he was trying to understand, but I couldn't bring myself to tell him what I was really thinking about.

"Can I give you a piece of advice?" he asked gingerly, like he was aware I was upset, but not sure why.

I nodded as he pushed the gate shut and rode Rocky over to Chance again.

"My grandpa always said, worry is like a rocking chair. It gives you something to do but never gets you anywhere." Casey watched me as he swayed in the saddle. "And my grandpa always gave good advice."

I looked down at Chance, remembering that Casey lost someone close to him as well. He'd told me how his grandpa had taught him to ride, how they'd spent every day together. When he passed, Casey's parents couldn't afford to keep the family ranch, and he'd been devastated when they had to move to Three Rivers.

"Sounds like your grandpa was a very smart man. I'll try my best to follow his advice," I replied quietly, knowing that if anyone understood what I was feeling, Casey would. "What was his name?"

"My grandpa?" he asked, and I nodded. "His name was Gene. Good, strong cowboy name, isn't it?" Then Casey looked off into the distance for what felt like a long time.

"It is," I agreed, and his silence tugged at my heart. I wanted to tell Casey about my mom, too. "My mom's name was Laurel."

Casey's eyes shifted to mine.

"She passed away when I was little."

"I'm sorry," Casey replied.

Usually, when someone said that to me, it made me angry— like those two words weren't enough, that words could never make it okay. But when Casey said it, somehow, I felt closer to him, like there was a new, unspoken connection between us.

"Thank you," I replied, and set my hand on my saddle horn. Chance twitched an ear at me, trying to figure out if I was giving him a cue. "And I really like what your grandpa said about worry and rocking chairs. I never thought about it like that. Makes sense." I really shouldn't waste my time thinking about all the bad stuff that could happen. How was that really helping me?

Casey gave me a small grin. "Well, he also used to say that chickens are the only ones that get anything accomplished by sitting on their butts. So, not all of his advice was as good."

A laugh bubbled up in my throat and escaped my mouth. It felt good. "That is true though."

Casey chuckled too. Then we didn't say another word as we rode through the cattle, eying up the cows and calves, making sure the animals looked healthy and happy. They were munching on green grass and dozing in the summer sun. They didn't look like they had a care in the world. And for the first time that day, I let myself relax, too.

Forty-nine

I SUCKED IN a breath and sat straight up in bed, knocking the open book from my chest. It hit the floor with a *thud,* and I jerked again before realizing I'd fallen asleep while reading.

I'd woken in the middle of a dream. I was in an arena, one much bigger than the Ring. The bleachers soared high above my head and every single seat was full. I was riding Chance, and the entire audience was laughing at me. Then their laughs turned to booing. I yelled at them to stop, but they started throwing things at me— hot dogs and shoes. I was scared for me, scared for Chance. I tried to get out of the arena, but there was no gate. I was stuck, riding frantically in circles.

"It was just a dream," I reassured myself, pushing damp hair out of my face. I fumbled through the dark, feeling for the lamp on the nightstand, but before my fingers found the switch I heard a tapping noise.

I froze and my heart gave a few quick pounds.

"Lucy? Wake up." A strained whisper streamed in from my cracked window.

"Taylor?" This time my fingers connected with the lamp switch and clicked on the light. It filled my cabin. I saw Taylor's face pressed against the window screen. "Oh my God. What are you doing? What time is it?" I grabbed my phone on my nightstand, but it was dead. My eyes traveled to the cord. It was laying on the rug. I hadn't plugged it in before I fell asleep.

"It's midnight. I tried to text you and call you, but your phone is off or something." Taylor had her hands over her eyes like a visor as she peeked in the window. "Want to go for a ride?"

"What?" I shuffled out of bed, half wondering if I was dreaming, and fully opened the window. "Have you lost your mind?"

"I asked her the same thing," a voice said from somewhere behind Taylor, and I jumped when I realized it was Casey. I looked down at myself, thankful I wore a big, oversized t-shirt to bed.

Taylor jerked her thumb at Casey. "Except I didn't have to scare Casey out of bed. He actually had his phone on like a normal person."

"Like a normal person that was sleeping at midnight?" I asked, not knowing what was going on.

Taylor shook her head as though I was being silly. "I was thinking we could take the horses over to the Ring and you could ride Chance in there tonight. By yourself."

"What?" I wiped the sleep from my eyes. "In the middle of the night?" That was crazy.

"That way you can ride in the arena and you won't have to worry about anyone else. You can just focus on yourself and Chance, and you'll be more comfortable when it comes time for the competition."

I looked at Casey and he shrugged. "It's not a bad idea."

"In the dark?" I blinked at them both. "How am I going to see where I'm riding?"

Casey pointed up at the sky. "It's a full moon. It's pretty bright outside. And there isn't going to be another time when you'll be able to ride in that arena by yourself. If you want to ride Chance without a bunch of people watching you, we should go now."

Casey shifted his eyes to Taylor. She caught his glare and they both looked a little guilty, like they'd dished my secrets to each other and decided to team up on me.

I stared at them, thinking they'd both lost their minds.

"We already tacked up Rocky and Chance," Taylor said. "They're tied in the barn and Jaycee let me borrow her bike. Just put on some jeans and a sweatshirt and get out here. I know you'll feel better about everything if you have a good ride on Chance in that arena. Linda always tells me that you can't end a ride on a bad note, and your last ride ended when you freaked out."

"I remember," I noted, wondering if Taylor would go back to bed if I closed the window on her.

"Come on," she continued. "Chance needs to know that arena isn't scary, that it's a fun place to ride. Same for you."

I sighed and gave in, knowing she was right.

"I'll be out in a few minutes," I said, and Taylor smiled. Then I dug through my dresser, grabbing a sweatshirt and wondering if this was the smartest or dumbest idea I'd ever committed to.

Taylor was just ahead of Casey and I, pedaling on Jaycee's bike, leading the way down the gravel road. The bike had a headlight, but Taylor left it off, not wanting to bring attention to our midnight excursion. But we did have a plan if someone caught us meandering about. We'd explain that Casey's dog got out and we were looking for him. Luckily for us, we didn't encounter a single car or person on our way to the Ring. Apparently, the whole town was sleeping— except us.

When we got to the arena, Taylor hopped off the bike and leaned it against the fence. "See. That wasn't so bad, was it?"

I patted Chance's neck. He was alert, wondering what in the heck we were doing. There's no way I would have rode Chance through the countryside at midnight by myself, but Rocky's steady presence gave him confidence, made him brave.

"I hope we don't get arrested for trespassing or something," I replied with a lighthearted tone, but I was actually serious.

"Oh, come on." Taylor walked through the open gate, her blonde hair spilling over her pink hoodie. "There's like a million other things we could be doing right now. It's not like we're out partying or drinking. We're just riding at midnight. Well, you guys are riding. I was pedaling and sweating." She winked at me.

"Not sure the cops would be okay with that," I called after her, but nudged Chance with my calves anyhow, urging him forward. He followed Taylor into the arena.

"Cop." Casey corrected me. "Singular. There's only one cop in Three Rivers. His name is Chuck and he only gets out of bed for real emergencies. I don't think this counts as one." He tipped his baseball cap at me. I was glad to hear there was only a small chance we'd get arrested tonight.

The full moon cast a blue light over the arena, illuminating the smooth dirt and empty bleachers, like the neon sign that hung above the diner. It was an eerie and beautiful sight.

"Go for it," Taylor said as she skipped over to one of the metal barrels. It was still setup from the other night, part of the three-barrel cloverleaf pattern, and she crawled up on it. Once on top, Taylor sat and swung her legs. Her heels tapped the barrel in a steady rhythm. "It's all yours. You're the captain of this arena." I knew she was smiling even though I couldn't see her face.

"If you say so," I replied into the night. *Here goes nothing.*

Wanting to get a ride in before we were discovered, I gathered the reins in my hands and wondered what I should do first. Maybe trot some circles? But when my reins tightened, Chance bumped his mouth against the contact and did a tiny hop, dancing on his tip toes. "Chance," I scolded, and directed him in a small circle to grab his attention.

"He's excited," Taylor said from her barrel-seat. "He's probably remembering all his training on the barrels and he can't wait to show you what he knows."

"Or he's just frisky," I added, knowing that horses got an extra pep in their step when temperatures dropped. Even though it was summer, it was a brisk night. "And I'd rather not end up face first in the dirt, forcing one of you to go wake up the one cop in town because there happened to be a *real* emergency." I clucked to Chance and he hopped again, this time trotting and shaking his head. Trying to redirect his energy, I moved him into a few sweeping figure eights, staying close to Taylor and Casey.

"Can I join you?" Casey started trotting Rocky. "Maybe he just needs a buddy to take the edge off."

Chance's attention jumped to Rocky as soon as the gelding moved, thinking his friend was going to run off without him. I let him trot over to Rocky.

"Long trot with me around the arena until he settles down?" I held tight to my reins and Chance's neck curled high in the air.

"Yep, you just tell me what to do, and I'll do it," Casey replied. I closed my legs around Chance. I barely brushed my calves against his ribs and Chance jolted forward, lurching into a canter for two strides, but I kept my grip on the reins and sat as still as I could in the saddle until he broke back into a trot.

"Good boy," I said, low and smooth. I gave him a little slack in the reins, trying to give him the means to relax into the bit and lower his neck, but he took that slack and managed another heave into a canter. This time he threw in a few crow-hops and went back into a canter.

Casey was posting as Rocky trotted steadily at Chance's side and we rounded the arena, passing shiny vinyl banners and the towering announcer stand. As we circled, I repeated what I did before. I tightened my reins and sat still in the saddle until Chance calmed and realized I wasn't about to let him gallop free-willy to his heart's desire. He came back to a trot and I let the reins inch through my fingers. This time, Chance followed the release of pressure with his nose and stayed at a trot. I uttered another praise and scratched his withers with my fingers.

Casey stayed quiet, watching me as Rocky kept pace with Chance's unsteady trot. I kept my butt in the saddle even though Chance was moving like a toddler that'd had too much sugar—bouncing and going more sideways than forward. But I kept going, repeating my cues and giving Chance praise when he listened to them. After a few minutes and a couple of exciting laps around the rail, Chance decided he was done with his nonsense and he could do what I was asking him to.

"There we go," I said to Chance as he stretched into a long trot and settled into a steady pace. A smile took over my face as I posted in the saddle, finding an easy rhythm to match Chance's stride.

I looked at Casey, wanting to share in my accomplishment, and I saw that he was smiling too. The moon highlighted the blond in his hair and when he turned his head to me, the pale light also glinted off his blue eyes. He didn't say anything, but the way he looked at me made me proud.

Pretty soon I was riding Chance around by myself, doing laps at a canter, the moon illuminating my path around the arena. It felt good. No— it felt great. Chance was full of spunk but listening to my cues. Then, when I started trotting around the barrels, he stayed at the speed I asked of him, even though I could tell he wanted to run. Taylor threw out a few tips, but generally acted as my personal cheerleader, pep-talking me from atop the barrel as I guided Chance around her and onto the rest of the cloverleaf pattern.

As I rode, I forgot my fears. I forgot what could go wrong. Instead, I enjoyed what was going right.

And I realized that Taylor was a genius. Going for a midnight ride was exactly the medicine I needed to clear my head.

When we got back to the ranch, Taylor watched Casey and I untack the horses. She stood in the barn aisle, balancing the bike on her hip, her hands on the handlebars. She shined the headlight like a spotlight so we could see what we were doing. We didn't dare turn on the barn lights for fear of Mr. Owens waking in the middle of the night only to see barns lights on from his bedroom window across the ranch. Or worse, chancing Marilynn's attention. Her bunk was only a few bunks down from mine and I could just imagine what she'd say if she caught us unsaddling in the night. Her wrath was not one I wanted to endure. *Especially* because she oversaw my daily duties. If Marilynn caught us, I was certain I'd be scrubbing buckets and cleaning the barn bathroom— probably with a toothbrush.

"Okay, I'm headed out," Taylor said as she walked the bike out of the barn. She turned off the headlight before she stepped outside, and I followed her, leading Chance. Casey was right behind us with Rocky. "I'll see you guys tomorrow." Taylor leaned the bike against the barn and waved as she headed toward the path to her cabin. "That's enough pedaling for me to last me a lifetime. The next time we ride at midnight, I plan to be back on Star."

"It's a deal," I whisper-called after her, thinking I kind of liked this riding-at-midnight stuff. "Good night, Taylor."

Leading the horses in the opposite direction, Casey and I put Rocky and Chance in their pasture and let the boys free to join the herd. Rocky immediately put his nose to the ground and grabbed mouthfuls of grass, looking like he needed to make up for lost time. Chance, on the other hand, opted for a good roll.

I shook my head as my horse wiggled around in the dirt and kicked his legs in the air.

"He'll need a good brushing tomorrow," I chuckled, and stepped out the gate as Casey closed it. "Once again, I'm sure glad he's black."

Casey leaned against the fence, resting his arms on the wooden plank and looking out at the horses. "It's so peaceful here at night. I think I'd rather camp out here than sneak back to my bedroom."

"You won't get in trouble, will you? For sneaking out?"

Casey shook his head. "My room is on the first floor so it's easy to hop out my window. And I always park my truck next door behind my dad's shop. As long as my truck is back by the time my dad goes to work, nobody will know the difference."

I stepped forward and joined Casey at the fence. "Thank you," I said, setting an elbow next to Casey's. "For getting out of bed and riding with me tonight. I really appreciate it. Having Rocky there was what kept Chance together. If you hadn't been with, I—"

"You kept Chance together," he interrupted me.

I found my lips wanting to protest, but my tongue fell still as I discovered there was a part of me that agreed with him. I *had* kept Chance from escalating. I kept myself calm and Chance followed my lead.

Instead of agreeing, I turned and gazed out into the pasture with Casey. A few of the horses were grazing, others were sleeping. Casey and I stood next to each other, enjoying the serenity, our elbows touching as we leaned against the top rail.

"What do you want to do after high school?" I asked, still looking at the horses. Chance had joined Rocky in the tall grass.

"Be a cattle rancher."

I guessed Casey's answer before he said it. He looked at home in a saddle, especially among the cattle.

"Like your grandpa?"

"Yeah." Casey nodded. "I've known since the first time my grandpa put me on a horse. Maybe one day I can buy back his ranch and raise cattle of my own in the same place that he did."

Casey's ballcap brim shaded his eyes, but I knew how much he wanted that. I could hear the need and dreams in his voice. And I wanted it for him, too.

"It will happen. I'm sure of it," I said, and a cool breeze brushed my neck. It smelled of juniper.

"And you," Casey started. "What do you want to do?"

His question tied into what I felt tonight in the arena— accomplishment and pride in riding through a problem. I took another breath and said, "I want to be a horse trainer." I'd known this since I was little as well, but was never sure if I was good enough to make it happen, to make a career out of my riding. I told my parents, sisters, and grandma. They said I'd be great at it, but they were family and had to say things like that. Tonight was the first time I'd spilled my dreams to someone I wasn't related to.

"You're already a horse trainer, Lucy." Casey squeezed my arm. He seemed to be as certain of my dreams as I was of his. "The only difference between now and then is that one day you'll get paid to do what you love. To train horses."

I smiled and rested my chin on my arm. For a second, I wondered if we could make our dreams happen together— Casey raising cattle, me working with horses, us living happily ever after someplace where pastures rolled on for infinity. I knew it was a silly thought, as I'd only known Casey for a fraction of a summer, but I couldn't help it. The thought flew through my mind.

"Thanks." It was the only word I could utter to explain how I felt— about the night, about Casey, about my time at the ranch, about the blessing of Chance.

Casey and I stood there in silence under the twinkling stars, and when Casey turned toward me, I wondered if he was going to kiss me. I wanted him to kiss me.

Instead, he put a hand on my shoulder. "I better get going, before we're discovered and have to explain what we're doing. I don't think anyone will believe we're staring into the horse pasture looking for my lost dog. Good night, Lucy," he said, ending in a whisper. He started to walk away, but let his fingers gently fall down my arm. When they got close to my hand, I grabbed them, and my heart thudded when Casey stopped and looked back at me.

His eyes fell on our intertwined fingers. Then they traveled upward and his gaze locked on mine, creating this strange rush of panic and excitement that shot through my body. Casey swiveled toward me and leaned in. I closed my eyes. It felt like forever before his lips touched mine, but when they did, my legs went weak. Despite that, I managed to stand on my tippy-toes and kiss him back.

He never let go of my hand. When I put my heels back on the ground, he squeezed my fingers and kissed my cheek.

"Maybe I could stay a little longer," he whispered, his lips nearly brushing my ear. "To watch the stars."

"Watch the stars?" I let our intertwined fingers fall against my thigh. I only wanted him to watch me.

Casey's blue eyes grabbed my gaze. "And talk. To you. If that's okay?"

A smile swept across my face and I nodded. Casey pulled me close, kissing me again. Softer this time.

"It's a little chilly out here though," I said, and Casey's face fell slightly before I squeezed his hand. "Wait right here." I ran back to my bunk and snatched the quilt off my bed.

Casey's grin widened when I returned with a blanket bundled in my arms.

"Good idea," he said, and took the quilt from me, throwing it around our backs before we settled onto a spot in the grass. I laid down and nestled next to him, sliding my head on his shoulder and my arm across his chest before peering up at the stars. They shimmered like the flecks in Casey's eyes and the excitement in my belly.

"This is so much better than going back home," Casey whispered as he tightened his arm around my shoulders. I nodded my head against his shirt.

Then, for the rest of the night, Casey and I snuggled under the stars, wrapped in a quilt, not sleeping a wink. We shared sweet kisses, quiet laughter, stories of our pasts, and dreams for our future. I wanted to bottle up every moment so I could live it again and again— especially when the first hint of dawn crept over the mountain. I wished the sun would go back to sleep, but also knew it was time to part ways. Casey kissed me one more time before he drove off and I reluctantly tiptoed back to my bunk knowing I wouldn't get one second of shuteye before work. Nothing could've made me happier.

Fifty

THE REST OF the week went by in a blur and, for the most part, I felt good about the Round-Up. The competition was quickly approaching, but I kept practicing. Every night after work, Taylor and I met at the barn. I'd tack up Chance while she brushed Star and tended to her healing leg. Then we'd spend an hour or so in the ranch's outdoor arena, running through patterns and techniques. After every session, my confidence boosted. I started to see I was just as capable of competing as any of those other girls.

Saturday— the day of the competition— started off good. Mr. and Mrs. Owens hosted a pancake breakfast in my honor and filled the main lodge with tons of friendly faces, floating balloons, and a big banner that read *"Good Luck, Lucy!"* It hung over the fireplace and everyone at the party signed it like a big card. Mrs. Owens happily chatted with guests and flipped pancakes onto plates. Mr. Owens wore his best cowboy hat and gloated about how his employee was going to win the first-place trophy, just like she had for the Cowboy Race. Kids raced between tables, chasing each other with little lassos. But the most important people sat with me at the long table in the middle of the room. Casey, Levi, Jaycee, Taylor, and Marilynn surrounded me. We drenched our plates with syrup and forked fluffy cakes into our mouths, chewing between smiles and laughter.

I rode away from the ranch feeling full of good vibes, but as I left the security of the ranch, nerves slowly crept back into my mind.

Levi drove his truck at an idle down the gravel road, leading me into town. Taylor, Marilynn, and Jaycee sat on the toolbox in his truck bed. Casey and I rode behind on our horses. It was like my own personal parade. People waved at us from front porches and lawns.

And it was fun— until Levi honked his horn, trying to get the attention of a man on a riding lawnmower.

Levi's horn was nearly as loud as a semi truck's and it jerked Chance out of a calm walk. Chance jumped sideways, alarmed by the blaring horn. I stayed on through his spook, but managed to catch my shirt on the saddle horn and pop off two buttons right above my jeans.

When Chance jumped, Jaycee reached around the truck and slapped Levi through the open window. "What are you doing?" she asked, and Levi stopped waving to the man on the lawn mower. "You scared the crap out of Chance."

Levi looked in his side mirror. "Oops! Sorry Lucy. You okay?"

"I'm fine." I reassured everyone and smoothed the fabric along my stomach as I steered Chance back to Rocky's side. I was wearing one of Taylor's highly-starched show shirts. It was pale purple with crystals on the collar and sleeves. "Good thing I wore a tank top underneath," I added, feeling bad for ripping apart the beautiful shirt.

"I've got safety pins," Taylor said, and held up her purse. She didn't look like she was worried about the missing buttons. "And double-stick tape. And bobby pins. And lip gloss. Don't worry. I'm prepared for anything."

I smiled tightly at her and tried to ignore the nerves that prickled under my skin. I was sure lip gloss wasn't going to ease them.

As we approached the Ring, I saw the amount of people waiting to watch the show and my nerves became impossible to ignore. The nagging prickles quickly turned to stings.

The arena bleachers were full. Not a single seat was empty. The audience spilled over onto the grass and parking lot.

"I'll go get your number," Taylor said when Levi parked his truck. Jaycee opened the tailgate and Taylor promptly hopped down from the bed. Jaycee followed her, but Marilynn made herself comfortable on the tailgate. She opened a small red cooler and dug through ice.

"You want anything, Lucy? A water?" Marilynn asked as she dug.

"Not right now. Thanks, though." My stomach was turning. I didn't want to get in a situation where I had to dismount and find the porta-potties. Instead, I watched the other riders. They were warming up their horses, riding circles in the flat grass next to the parking area. The arena was being prepared for the day's events. As I watched the riders, Casey tried to distract me with some comment about puppies or unicorns or cows. Actually, I had no idea what he was saying as I turned my focus to the amount of people that filled the stands. Did they bus people in from neighboring towns? Was half of Oregon visiting the town today?

"Hey, Lucy." I heard my name, but jerked when a hand touched my knee.

I looked down and Taylor was standing next to Chance. She was holding my number and kept her hand on my knee. I watched her face fall.

"Are you okay?" she asked.

I shook my head, trying to pull myself together.

"Yeah. I mean. I think I'll be—" My own stuttering startled me.

Taylor took a big breath and blew it out, moving her hands through the air in a twirl like a yoga instructor. "You have to remember to breathe. Come on now. Do it with me." She took another breath and I followed her suggestion.

"That's better," Taylor said after we'd both taken a few deep breaths together. "Right?"

I nodded, mostly for Taylor's sake.

"Good. I've got your number and I need to pin it to your back. Actually, maybe Casey can do it, so you don't have to get off Chance?"

"Sure." Casey offered, and moved Rocky close to Chance. He took the number and metal pins from Taylor. When he did, a black number fifteen stared at me from the white cardboard.

"I'm fifteen?"

"Yep," Taylor replied, cheerfully. "You're last in the line-up, which gives you the advantage of watching everyone run before you ride."

Taylor and I were obviously looking at this piece of news from two totally different angles. To me, going last meant I'd have to endure my nerves, try not to throw up, and watch all these amazing riders kill it in the ring *before* I entered it. I found myself wishing I could ride first so I could get this over with.

Casey pressed the cardboard against my back and pinned it in two places.

"I think I'm going to walk Chance around," I said, feeling like a zombie and wanting to redirect my focus to Chance. He was watching the other horses as they rode across the grass in front of us, not nearly as concerned about the full bleachers as I was.

"Good idea." Taylor stepped out of my way. "They're going to start barrels after the arena is dragged. This would be a good time to warm him up and work out his kinks."

Kinks. That was one way to describe it. Except I felt like all the kinks had gathered in my body, not Chance's. He was more amped up when we rode the other night in the dark.

I motioned for Chance to walk and we joined the other riders. Most of the girls were trotting their horses, warming them up. Everyone was silent, concentrating. I looked from face to face and the intensity I saw rattled me further.

A big, heavy rock grew in my belly.

I was in over my head and shouldn't have agreed to this. I should've signed up for a schooling show— something where the whole state wouldn't witness my ride. My goal for the day went from having good rides to just wanting to get through this.

Focus on one thing at a time, I told myself, and gathered my reins. *Get it together.*

Chance cocked an ear at me, paying attention, and I asked him to trot. He picked up his pace and trotted in a big circle with the other horses. I scratched his withers with two fingers, thankful one half of my team had his wits about him. As we trotted, Chance's rhythm and willingness started to soothe me and I found myself focusing on him more than my fears.

At least until a woman stepped out of the crowd. She appeared in front of me like a ghost. I stopped Chance just before running into her. She didn't look the least bit scared by my big black horse's fast approach. In fact, her smile widened.

"Lucy Rose, right?" Her eyes brightened, matching the sparkles that covered a wide belt slung across her hips. She had flame-red hair and a shirt that matched.

Chance tossed his head, unsure of the abrupt stop, and I ran a hand over his neck to let him know it was okay. I cleared my throat. "Yes, that's me."

"I'm Adrianna, from Channel Eight News in Bend." I suddenly noticed a man with a camera behind her. "I'm covering the Round-Up and was wondering if I could ask you a few questions. You have perfect timing because I was just talking with Breklynn Cole. It'd be great to get you both on camera at the same time. Is that okay?"

"Sure," a voice responded for me, and I turned my head to see Breklynn. She was on her horse, standing close to the arena fence and surrounded by a few other girls, also on their horses. Before I could reply, Breklynn rode her chestnut paint over and stopped him next to Chance.

"Great," Adrianna responded and gave a few cues to her cameraman. Before I knew it, the camera was rolling, and Adrianna was asking questions.

"As we learned in the last segment," Adrianna started, "Breklynn was last year's winner of the Three Rivers Round-Up and she's planning on securing the title again this year. She's been riding since she could walk and her horse, Whiz, has been her partner for the past five years. They had one of the top scores at the auditions and are the team to beat this year. *That was* until a late entry surprised everyone."

Out the corner of my eye I saw Breklynn's face transform from beaming to tight lipped. "Lucy Rose won The Cowboy Race earlier this summer and is now trying for a second title." Adrianna extended her arm and there was a microphone in her hand. "Lucy, what's your game plan when you enter the arena today?"

My mind went blank. Was this really happening? The bleachers were full of people waiting to judge me, and now there was a microphone stuffed in my face? I didn't have a game plan. I barely had a sane thought in my head.

"Stay in the saddle," I blurted.

Adrianna's face froze, but then it warmed. "A little humor to break the tension, I see." She laughed like I'd made a joke. "Folks, the winner of the Cowboy Race's game plan is to keep from hitting the dirt. Seems like a pretty good plan to me. Isn't that what we all hope for when we put a foot in the stirrup on a day like today?"

She pointed her microphone at Breklynn and asked the same question. I faintly heard something about relying on years of experience and hard work. Then Adrianna was facing the camera and signing off.

When the man lowered his camera, I felt my stomach turn. I knew I had to get out of there.

"Excuse me," I said, and Adrianna thanked me for my time.

I turned Chance quickly and trotted away from the camera, away from the riders and the humming crowd. I guided Chance into and through a patch of fir trees and stopped him on the other side, just before the field of berry bushes.

I didn't know why, but I felt like crying, and I could hear my heartbeat in my ears. Everything was just so . . . so overwhelming. Over the field of berries, I could see the ranch. If I left now, nobody would find me until the competition was over. Especially if I rode into the mountain and up to the red rocks.

Fifty-one

NOT SURE WHAT to do, I got off Chance. I swung out of the saddle and put my boots on the ground. Maybe it was to keep myself from fleeing? Maybe it was because I felt sick and didn't want to puke from horseback? Either way, I moved close to Chance. Reins in one hand, I smoothed his forelock with my other. I took deep breaths, just like Taylor had shown me, and I set my eyes on his.

Chance blinked at me curiously like he wasn't sure what kind of game we were playing. He checked my pockets for treats, nuzzling gently with his nose, and he looked longingly toward the arena as though he wondered when we would go back and play with the other horses.

I took another breath and blew it out my mouth. "You're fine, aren't you?"

Chance swiveled his ears, listening, and I knew the answer to my own question. Chance was completely fine. The audience, the newscaster, the other riders— none of it bothered *him*. It was me that was rattled.

Still staring into his brown eyes, I thought back to all the times my grandma had cheered me on from her back deck as I rode circles around her house on Stella. I remembered how my dad blindly told me I was good at everything I tried, even when I wasn't. And tears welled in my eyes, knowing how my mom loved horses with her whole being, just like me. She would want me to do this simply because I loved riding.

"We can do this, can't we?" I swallowed, knowing I wanted to, knowing I couldn't let my fears and doubts get the best of me. I couldn't just run away and pretend this never happened. I wanted to ride. I'd been practicing and working hard. I wanted to compete.

"Lucy?"

I glanced over and saw Taylor walking toward me through the fir trees, looking worried. I waved at her like it was normal for us to meet by the berry bushes, not wanting to make a big deal out of my mental breakdown.

"Are you okay?" She'd asked me that once before already. I started to reassure her.

"Yeah," I started, but my words jumbled and morphed into the truth. "Actually, not really. I'm really nervous."

Taylor bit her lip like she was churning over my answer. I thought she was going to tell me that everything would be all right, that I'd have a great ride, or that I didn't need to worry so much.

Instead, she asked, "Why are you doing this?"

I stared at her, stunned.

"Why are you riding in the Round-Up?" she clarified.

The short answer was that the person standing in front of me had to forfeit and then she forced me to take her place. But the long answer was that I'd pictured myself doing this since I was little. I'd dreamt of it. In every book I read where the girl won the race or gentled the wild mustang, I'd imagined myself doing the same. I'd spent countless hours with my sister in my grandma's backyard, taking turns on Stella, putting on pretend "horse shows" with obstacle courses made of flower pots and lawn chairs. The long answer was that I was doing this because I wanted to, not because anyone was making me.

"Because I've always wanted to," I replied and hearing my own words somehow made me feel strong.

Taylor nodded. "That's what I thought. Then you just need to go out there and do what you've been practicing."

She made it sound so simple. "When I was practicing it was just you and me. Or maybe Casey or Jaycee. Now I'm going to be riding in front of hundreds . . . or thousands of people." I thought of the camera and Channel Eight News.

"So what?"

"What if I royally mess up?"

"I mess up all the time, Lucy. Remember when I took a nose dive off Star in my western pleasure class and she went bucking around the arena until the saddle came flying off her back?"

I nodded, picturing Taylor's cowboy hat and blonde hair flailing about. I about fell out of the bleachers when I watched it happen.

"That didn't stop me from riding in my next class, did it?" she asked.

I shook my head, marveling at how Taylor gathered the confidence to move on after hitting the dirt.

She pursed her lips. "And you didn't hear me worrying about what everyone thought of my fall, did you?"

I hadn't paid attention to that part at the show, but now that Taylor said it, I realized I never heard her utter a word about being embarrassed or worried that it would happen again.

"But you—" I started.

"You should only be worried about competing with yourself. Linda told me that a long time ago, and it stuck with me. Every time you enter an arena, you only need to worry about having a better ride than *you* did the last time." Taylor pointed at my chest. "It doesn't matter what anyone else does or says. When you're in the arena, you should only be thinking about yourself and your horse."

I stared at Taylor like she'd just read from some handbook that was written just for me. My nerves didn't magically disappear, but I realized I had to do this for myself, not for anyone else. I would ride today because I wanted to prove to myself that I could do it, that I was good enough. I shouldn't be trying to prove that to anyone else— not the crowd and not the other competitors.

I was the only one that could make my dreams come true.

"You're right, Taylor. I should do this for myself, not for anyone else."

Taylor smiled, and I put Chance's reins back over his neck. Then I put a foot in the stirrup.

"Wait," Taylor said, and I froze with one leg in the air. She dug around in her pocket and pulled out two shiny metal pins. "I also came to fix your shirt. You think I'm going to let you ride around with your shirt half open?"

I looked down. I'd completely forgotten that I hooked my shirt on the saddle horn and popped a few buttons off. Looking at the gap forced out a chuckle.

"What would I do without you?" I stood still as she pinned my shirt together.

"That's what friends are for, right?" Taylor looked up at me from her crouched position as she examined her work. "I know you'd do the same for me."

I nodded at her, knowing that I would. Then I put my foot in the stirrup and got back in the saddle.

Fifty-two

THE SUN HUNG high in the sky. I was parked next to Levi's truck, watching the Round-Up from Chance's back. Taylor, Jaycee, and Marilynn sat on the open tailgate while the boys stood in the bed, leaning against the cab. All our eyes were glued to the excitement in the arena as each competitor took their chance at the barrel portion of the competition.

Each horse and rider burst out of the gate, skimmed around three barrels, and flew down the homestretch, racing back to the gate as the crowd went wild. I cheered along with the crowd and was surprised to find that yelling made me feel better. It was like my body was happy to release my nervous energy into a cheer.

I rooted for each and every rider as they tackled their pattern. When a barrel was hit or someone made a wide turn, I cringed like I'd done it myself. I wanted every rider to have a great run—even Breklynn. I cheered for her just as loud as I did for the other girls and she had a beautiful ride, looking like a pro at the National Finals Rodeo as she zipped through her pattern and secured the top time.

When there were just a few rides left before mine, I started warming Chance up, trotting him in the grass. My hands shook and my heart thumped like a bass drum. My nerves were still there, maybe worse, but I wasn't going to let my nerves talk me out of this. I took deep breaths and talked to Chance in a low, quiet tone as we trotted around. I tried my best to keep my worries from affecting him, but Chance was getting riled up as well, raising his head and trotting with a quick stride. I kept my cues consistent, just like I had during our midnight ride.

When my name was called over the loud speaker, my stomach shot into my throat, but the cheers from Levi's truck took me out of my panic. All five of my friends were standing in the bed of the truck, yelling my name. In addition to the yells, they were jumping and fist pumping and when I looked at them, my throat made a weird laugh-cry noise that I was glad no one heard. They were so excited for me and I hadn't even set a hoof in the arena.

A huge smile took over my face. One of those smiles that makes your cheeks hurt.

I knew I'd won something much bigger than any trophy or jacket.

With my friends cheering in the background, I pointed Chance toward the gate and focused solely on him.

We can do this. We can do this, I repeated to myself ten times before we got to the gate.

Chance started to dance when we entered the alley way, anticipating what we were about to do, but he wasn't rearing or shaking his head like I'd seen a few of the other horses do. He was excited and moving on his tip-toes, but he was mentally with me. He was listening to me.

The alley way was a dirt path enclosed on two sides by fence panels. It reminded me of a tunnel. Before I let Chance canter into the arena, there were a few seconds were the world muted and it was just me and Chance. In that tunnel, I gathered up my courage and visualized our run going just like we practiced. I leaned forward and let Chance go.

He shot into a canter and burst out of the alley way. Once in the deep dirt of the arena, I turned him toward the first barrel on the right, which was the start of our cloverleaf pattern. Chance was moving fast so the first barrel came up quick, and I tried to remember everything that I'd worked on with Taylor.

Stay centered. Don't brace your arms. Sit down through the turn. Don't look at the next barrel until you've finished your turn on the first.

Chance spun around the first barrel like a boomerang and charged at the second. I repeated the same mantra in my head as we approached the next turn and Chance dug in deep, cutting the barrel even tighter this time. His power, speed, and control took my breath away and as we ran to the third barrel, I forgot about the audience beyond the fence. I vaguely heard a roar of clapping and yells, but it was background noise. I was lost in the connection I had with Chance. I was consumed by how proud I was of him.

As we neared the third barrel, I prepared for our last turn, knowing a gallop back to the gate would follow. But as soon as I asked Chance to turn, I knew I had asked him too early. I was excited. He was excited. And when I asked him to turn, he moved off my leg and reins like I had snapped him with a rubber band. Chance dove into his turn and even though we were moving at breakneck speed, I watched his shoulder graze the barrel in slow motion.

He bumped it and the barrel wobbled, but I forced myself to look away. I had to focus on what was ahead. We had to finish our run and I didn't want to slow Chance down by turning my body to look at a barrel that could or could not have fallen.

Instead, I pressed my body forward and flung my hands far up Chance's neck, nearly touching his ears. I tried to make myself invisible on his back, staying balanced so all Chance had to do was gallop. We sliced through the arena and I only dared to move when we entered the alley way. I might as well have been riding black lightning.

When we came out the other side of the alley way, I had Chance slowed to a trot. He was prancing like a carousel horse, bouncing up and down rather than forward. A crazy, wonderful energy had taken over my body and I felt like I was floating. I guessed Chance was feeling the same and I frantically rubbed his neck, telling him what a good boy he was. I rode toward Levi's truck where my friends were all still jumping and cheering in the bed, rocking the frame.

They were shouting all kinds of praises, but when I halted Chance at the open tailgate, I glanced back at the arena and saw that I *had* knocked over that last barrel. It was laying in the dirt waiting for someone to pick it up.

I didn't care.

Knocking over a barrel would add a five second penalty to my time and would probably put me at the bottom of the rankings, but I was so stinking proud of what I'd just done. I was so proud of Chance and all the effort he had given me. I was so proud that I had practiced and worked hard and fought for something I wanted. I was proud of me.

My friends were too. That was all that mattered.

After I cooled Chance down, I got off and replaced his bridle with a halter. I tied him to the arena fence next to Rocky and gave him two big carrots. As he crunched his treats, I kissed him on his forehead and hugged his whole face. I hoped he knew how proud I was of him, of how much I loved him.

"Lucy!" a chorus of voices cried, and I pulled my cheek from Chance's forelock, immediately recognizing the shouts.

My sisters, Molly and Jackie, were running toward me. My dad was two steps behind them.

Molly got to me first, wrapping her spindly arms around my waist and crashing her nine-year-old body into mine. I grabbed her in a hug, thankful she was half my size. Jackie came in next and my dad finished off the group hug by wrapping all three of us in his arms.

"That was awesome!" Molly squeaked into my shirt, muffled by bodies. Dad and Jackie chirped praises as well.

"What are you guys doing here?" I cried, knowing I had barely mentioned the Round-Up. I didn't want to make a big deal out of it, especially because I wasn't sure I'd even go through with it. I told my dad I entered a local event with Chance but hadn't elaborated on the details.

Dad gave one more big squeeze, pushing us all together. "Mr. Owens called me, wanted to let me know about the pancake breakfast he and Mrs. Owens were putting on for you before the Round-Up. When I told him I didn't know anything about this round-up thing, he brought me up to speed." Dad loosened his grip and my circle of family stared at me. "Why didn't you tell us? You know we wouldn't have missed it for the world. The girls helped me deliver two loads of feed this morning, so we could close up the farm store early and make it here in time to see you ride."

I stared at my dad's scruffy beard and my sisters' expectant faces, and I thought about telling them that I didn't know how important today would be until right before I went into the arena. Instead, I smiled and pulled them all into another hug.

"It'll never happen again. I'm so glad you guys are here."

They all agreed and hugged me back.

While we waited for the next portion of the competition to start, Molly got to know Chance. She fed him carrot pieces and groomed him even though he was clean as a whistle. When she'd circled him multiple times, brushed every piece of him she could reach and lulled Chance into a nap, Molly exclaimed that she loved him. Then she asked Casey if she could groom Rocky.

"You sure can," Casey replied, and Molly did a little dance as she gathered the brushes and combs from the ground. Casey gave her a big smile and handed her a curry she dropped. I wanted to kiss him for being so sweet to my little sister.

"His hair is so silky," Molly said as she combed Rocky's gray tail.

"Good thing you used conditioner," I whispered at Casey with a playful wink.

He gave me a shushing noise but grinned at my comment.

Behind us, there was chatter and laughter. My dad was talking to Mr. Owens, lost in some conversation about tractors and horsepower. Mrs. Owens was giggling with Dr. Sam as two small children ran circles around their feet. My sister, Jackie, was sitting on Levi's tailgate. Jaycee handed her a pop from the cooler. Taylor and Marilynn were giving Levi a hard time about why his truck had to be so tall, and Levi was doing some weird bicep curling maneuver. Even the ranch guests, Barbara and her friends, had come to hangout and watch "all the real cowgirls" ride.

There was so much distracting me that I barely thought about the horsemanship pattern until it was time to get on. I didn't have time to get myself riled up and freaked out. And now that I'd run barrels, I wasn't as worried as earlier in the day. I'd knocked over a barrel and no one was upset, not even me. My friends and family were here to support me. They didn't care if I won a trophy or took last place. They would root for me no matter what.

I put Chance's bridle back on, gave him a kiss on his nose, and mounted up.

"You're going to do awesome, *again*!" Molly jumped up and down, a brush in one hand, a curry in the other. Next to her, Casey beamed a mega-watt smile.

"Your sister's an awfully smart kid," he said. "And I *know* we're looking at a winner."

I blushed. Molly nodded and pointed a thumb at Casey. "I like this guy," she said.

I laughed and my name was called over the speakers. "Looks like I'm up. Wish me luck."

"We would, but you don't need it," Taylor called from the truck bed. "You got this! No problem."

Everyone in our group chimed in with agreements. I felt like I was glowing as I rode Chance to the gate.

Unlike with barrels, I thought going last in horsemanship was an advantage because I watched fourteen riders complete the same pattern before it was my turn. The pattern was now burned into my brain. Furthermore, the contestants were given the pattern yesterday and Taylor went through it with me last night, piece by piece. She had me walk the pattern with her on foot before I rode it. It seemed silly at the time, but I found it easier to visualize the pattern when I got back in the saddle.

Now, riding toward the arena for the second time today, my nerves were still present, but they were more like a flutter— not an earthquake.

"Let's do this," I whispered to my handsome boy as we walked into the alley way and the line of orange cones came into view. I knew I'd be judged as soon as I rode out of the alley and onto the arena sand so I gathered my reins, making soft contact with Chance's mouth, preparing him for a jog. But as soon as I touched him with my legs, Chance broke into a lope and braced against the bit.

"Whoa, easy," I said, sitting back and pulling hard on the reins. Chance's quick jolt forward sent my heart into my throat and I barely stopped him before he bolted out of the alley into the arena. "Easy, boy," I said again, my voice tight as I pulled him into a sharp circle. The crowd hissed and groaned in reaction. The sound bit through me like an icy wind, bringing my nerves to the surface.

I held tight to the reins and Chance pranced in a circle, making me extra aware of the eyeballs staring at me. People were watching from atop the fence, near the gate, and in the stands. A loud whisper traveled through the crowd like a secret and I thought the whisper was worse than the initial groans and hisses.

They were talking about me. About Chance. They were whispering about our ride and waiting to see what I would do.

My whole body tensed, from my toes to my fingers, and I did the only thing I could think of. I turned Chance in circles until he finally listened and slowed to a walk. Then I closed my eyes, just for a second, and took a breath. I let it out slow.

"This isn't barrels," I told Chance as I opened my eyes, but I understood why he was getting excited. "We aren't going to run." I repeated this to him a few times.

I halted Chance and his body was just as tight as mine. If I didn't do something to soothe him, we were going to blow into the arena like a firecracker. I ran a hand down his curled neck and knew I had to contain my own emotions. Chance was excited, and I was winding him up further.

Think of something happy, I told myself, trying to force my thoughts into something positive— which was difficult as I stared down a line of orange cones and hundreds of waiting stares.

The first thing that popped into my head was an image of my friends. I thought of Taylor, Jaycee, and Casey as they pretended to be cones. I pictured them in the ranch arena— Jaycee and Casey camped out on their horses and Taylor calling out instructions from beside Star. I remembered their smiles and encouraging words, and a grin grew on my face. Happiness seemed to travel down my body— from my lips to my shoulders and all the way down to my toes. Chance must've felt it too because he lowered his head as though he realized he was being over-dramatic with his prancing and impatience.

"Come on, boy," I said with a sigh. "We got this."

Before my nerves could wiggle their way back into my head, I gave Chance a light squeeze with my legs and he walked forward. He didn't hop. He didn't protest. And when we got to the end of the alley way, I asked him for a jog. He did as he was told, and we sashayed our way to the first cone. Then we loped to the next.

I made sure to breathe and I pictured myself riding in the arena with my friends. Anytime my nerves bubbled up, I imagined my friends' friendly faces instead of the intimidating orange cones or the humming crowd. I kept my thoughts positive and succeeded in completing all the maneuvers in the pattern. I made a round circle at an extended trot, a snappy halt, and a full turn on the haunches. By the time I asked Chance to reverse, a wide smile had made its way to my face. I nodded at the judge, completing my pattern.

Chance and I didn't do every maneuver perfectly. We also didn't knock over any cones. I considered that a major success.

Fifty-three

BACK AT THE ranch, Taylor met me in my cabin so we could get ready for the dance together. She brought a suitcase full of clothes, jewelry, and makeup and acted as my personal stylist, voting for the third outfit I tried on for her. Then, as she swept blush on my cheeks, I glanced at my seventh-place ribbon— the one I won today. It hung on the full-length mirror, was a pretty shade of purple, and would serve as a daily reminder that I could accomplish whatever I set my mind to.

In addition to the ribbon, I'd also been presented with a gold pin— a tiny pair of metal cowgirl boots engraved with "Three Rivers Round-Up Finalist." Taylor insisted that I wear the pin to the dance.

"There. That's perfect," Taylor announced as she pinned the tiny boots to the thin silk scarf she'd expertly tied around my neck. Happy with her work, she handed me a rose-colored lip gloss. "Finish it off with this."

I swiped on the lip gloss and turned to the mirror.

"Wow," I muttered, and put my hands on my hips. "You're good."

Taylor had curled my hair and pulled it into a high pony. I tilted my head and stared into the mirror, not understanding how she'd created so much volume with just hairspray and a comb. She'd also dusted my eyelids with a golden shimmer that highlighted my brown eyes. The flowy cream-colored tank and expensive-feeling square-toed boots she lent me went perfect with my favorite dark denim jeans. "I feel so fancy."

Taylor looked me up and down in the mirror. "You look fancy, and Casey is going to fall over backwards when he sees you. Mission accomplished." Taylor threw the remainder of the clothes strewn across my bed into her suitcase and zipped it up. "I'll see you at the dance. Levi and Jaycee are picking me up in a few minutes."

I grabbed Taylor and hugged her before she stopped talking, making the fringe on her yellow sundress swish.

"Thank you, Taylor. For everything." I hoped she knew I was talking about more than just the outfit.

"Ditto, Lucy." Taylor hugged me back but pulled away when there was a knock at the door. We both knew who it was. "I better get out of here." She smiled. "I'll see you guys over there."

I nodded. Taylor scooted out the door, her suitcase in tow. I heard her say hello to Casey, and I took a deep breath before approaching the door. When I saw Casey standing on my steps, my heart did a double-beat.

He wore pressed jeans and a sharp blue shirt that perfectly matched his eyes. His hair was combed and styled, not hidden under a baseball hat. When his eyes landed on me, his mouth parted and my cheeks warmed.

"You look gorgeous, Lu." Casey reached up to open the screen door, and I noticed the bouquet of flowers he was holding close to his chest. He also held a bundle of carrots. "These are for you." He held out the white daisies and I took them, brushing his fingers as I did.

I pressed my nose to the petals. "Thank you. They smell amazing."

"And I thought we could give Chance and Rocky some carrots before we head to the dance."

My heart swelled. I couldn't have imagined a more thoughtful gift.

"You sure know how to impress a girl, don't you?"

"You're the only one I want to impress," he replied, and held out a hand to guide me down the steps. "Shall we?"

I took his hand and the screen door squeaked closed behind me.

We walked over to the pasture and Chance trotted to meet us at the fence when I whistled and called his name. Rocky was right behind him. As soon as they craned their necks over the railing, I offered up the treats. They gobbled each carrot out of my hand and pulled them into their mouths like they were slurping spaghetti noodles. As Chance chewed, I kissed him on his black, whiskered nose and giggled when I saw the glossy pink lip print left behind. I wiped it away and told Chance, once again, what a good boy he was. He bumped my shoulder with his nose, wanting more treats and kisses. I handed him another carrot.

"He sure likes you," Casey said, glancing from Chance to me. I scratched Chance on his forehead, and Casey added, "I've got a feeling he isn't the only one."

I rubbed my hands together, brushing away the carrot remnants. "Are you saying that you like me, Casey Parker?"

"That's exactly what I'm saying." Casey's gaze was steady. "And maybe you'll let me take you on a real date next week. Just you and me?"

"Like to dinner?" I imagined us sharing a sausage pizza and a slice of marionberry pie at the diner.

"I was thinking more like a trail ride up to Diamond Lake and a picnic." Casey watched me tentatively, and my stomach fluttered. "How does that sound?"

"I think that sounds perfect." I couldn't imagine anything better. That would even top the marionberry pie.

Casey's face lit up. Then he stepped toward me and offered up his arm. "We better get going. Everyone is waiting for us at the dance. Levi already texted me like six times."

I gave Chance one more peck on his nose and took Casey's arm. The horses meandered back into the pasture and Casey escorted me to his truck.

"Don't worry. I cleaned it," he said, opening the door for me. His truck was a red Chevy built well before my dad was born. I'd seen Casey drive it many times before, but had never been in it myself.

"I appreciate that." I knew how dirty a truck could get when you were around horses all the time, but sliding onto the bench seat and scooting to the middle, I thought Casey's truck smelled just like him— a mix of pine and cinnamon. It was the perfect combination of manly and sweet.

When Casey got in the driver's side, he sat down and brushed his leg against mine. Feeling bold, I leaned into him and slipped my arm under his. We didn't say much during the quick drive into town, but the permanent grins on our faces did enough talking for the both of us. Snuggled up next to him, I wanted Casey to keep driving forever, but when he parked next to the town square, I couldn't help but to gasp.

The grassy park normally reserved for dog walks and bench-sitting had been transformed for tonight's dance. White lights were strung around every tree and twinkled nearly as bright as the stars in the sky. A band played in the gazebo and a big group danced to a catchy beat. At the edge of the dance floor, there were smoking grills and tables full of food.

"I see Taylor and Jaycee." I squeezed Casey's arm and he opened his door, sliding his fingers into mine and helping me out of the truck. I followed him, excited to hangout and celebrate with our friends.

Taylor, Jaycee, and Levi were by the food. Taylor waved excitedly when she saw us walking toward them, hand in hand.

"Didn't take you long to find the food," Casey said to Levi just as Levi took a huge bite of a hot dog. With his mouth full, Levi just smiled and shrugged.

Taylor grabbed a few paper plates from the table. "We're starving." She handed me and Casey plates. "You guys want to eat first?"

"Thanks," I said, taking the plate, but I paused when I glanced over Taylor's shoulder and caught Breklynn staring at me. She was standing with a group of girls on the edge of the dance floor. I handed the plate to Casey. "Actually, can you make me up a plate? I need to take care of something. I'll be right back."

Casey saw who I was looking at. "Do you want me to go with you?"

"No, I'll be right back. I'll make it quick. I promise." Before Casey could stop me, I left his side and strode over to Breklynn and her friends.

"Hey, Breklynn." Every head in her circle turned to me. "Can I talk to you? Alone?"

I hadn't talked to Breklynn since the interview with the news crew, but I had watched her horsemanship pattern. Breklynn had a beautiful ride, but when she got to the end of her pattern, she completely forgot to back her horse— which meant she didn't get a score for that portion of the pattern. Breklynn exited the arena looking like she knew she'd won the competition, but when she realized her mistake, her face fell.

Breklynn looked at me. She raised her dark eyebrows and pursed her lips. "Okay," she muttered after a few uncomfortable seconds of silence.

We walked over to the sidewalk, away from prying ears, and faced each other under the white, twinkling lights. Breklynn was wearing last year's trophy jacket over a sparkly black tank top and jeans. She had the third-place ribbon from today's event pinned to her jacket.

I took a breath and gathered my thoughts. "First of all, I wanted to say congratulations. You did an amazing job today. You had two beautiful rides." That was true. I wasn't here to rub anything in her face or remind her that everyone makes mistakes— even the all-knowing Breklynn. I wasn't going to treat Breklynn the same way she'd treated Taylor.

Breklynn cocked her head at me like she was waiting for me to take a dig at her.

"I also wanted to tell you I didn't like the way you talked to Taylor the other night," I started, keeping my tone even. I wanted to get my point across. I didn't want to start another tiff. "Taylor's my friend, and she's a talented rider. More than that, she's an amazing person, and she loves her horse. She didn't deserve the way you talked to her in the diner. I think you know that."

Breklynn stared at me, grinding over my comments, but she didn't interrupt, so I continued. "And I wasn't challenging you or telling you off that night. I didn't mean it like that. I was mad because you hurt my friend. I just wanted you to know that wasn't right. You shouldn't talk to anyone like that."

Breklynn bit her painted lip and I was sure she was going to tell me to go pound sand. Instead, she swallowed, like she was preparing to say something she didn't really want to. "I shouldn't have said those things to your friend." She spoke quietly. Her posture was stiff.

I could have pushed it further. I could have reminded Breklynn of my other comment at the diner—that a real winner should always be gracious— but I didn't. Instead I took my own advice and opted for the high road. Besides, I was done with this unnecessary drama.

I offered up my hand. "Truce?"

Breklynn paused. Then she pulled her hand out of her jacket pocket, slowly. "Truce." She took my hand and added, "You had some great rides today too. If you hadn't hit that barrel, you would've been in the top five."

"Thanks," I replied, but it didn't matter to me what Breklynn thought of my rides. I was proud of them.

"You going to compete again next summer?" Breklynn asked. I couldn't tell if she was making conversation or sizing up her competition for next year, but I nodded.

"Yeah. I think I will." I gave her a smile and ended the conversation with, "Have a good night, Breklynn." I turned and walked back toward my friends, feeling like I'd accomplished what I set out to do. Maybe Breklynn would think twice before throwing out another snarky, thoughtless comment. Regardless, I wanted to forget about Breklynn and enjoy the night.

"Everything okay?" Casey asked as I approached the picnic table and joined my friends. Casey, Taylor, Jaycee, Marilynn, and Levi were staring at me expectantly. They'd obviously been watching me talk to Breklynn.

"Everything is great." I scooted onto the bench next to Casey. He had a plate of food made up for me— barbeque, potato salad, corn on the cob, and chocolate chip cookies. I took a big bite of a chocolate chip cookie and Casey smiled at me.

Behind me, the band started a new song. Before the first line was over Taylor slapped her hands on the table and squealed.

"Oh my gosh! I love this song!" She sprung from the bench and ran around the table to grab my arm. "Come on. Let's dance!"

I still had a mouthful of cookie, but knew Taylor wouldn't take no for an answer, so I hopped up and jogged with her to the dance floor. When Taylor pulled me into the crowd and started dancing, I finished chewing and waved dramatically until the rest of the table joined us.

Then we all danced into the night— in our shiny boots under the twinkling stars. And I didn't just stand in a circle and bounce my shoulders. I pulled out all kinds of moves, because I knew my friends loved me just the way I was. Silly dance moves and all.

THE END

Review Request

Thank you for joining me at the Red Rock Ranch. I hope Lucy, Casey, Taylor, and all their furry friends touched your heart the way they touched mine. If you have a few minutes, I'd love it if you would post your honest review on the site you purchased your book from. Reviews help me understand what stories readers enjoy. They also help me decide what to write next. Your review is greatly appreciated.

BONUS: Interview Questions

Brittney Joy

When did you start writing?

I've always been a reader. In middle school, I devoured *The Thoroughbred Series* by Joanna Campbell— especially before I had a horse of my own. I loved the riding scenes. In fact, I didn't like the scenes where the characters were in school or doing anything non-horsie. I was like, "get back to the horses, already!" Ever since I got hooked on The Thoroughbred Series, I knew I wanted to write a young adult book with an equestrian theme . . . someday. When I was sixteen, my parents gave me a journal for my birthday and I starting writing down all my thoughts, secrets, and feelings. The journaling is really what allowed me to discover the fun of writing as well as the emotional release and reward it gave me (and I journaled frequently through high school & college). However, I didn't dabble in writing fiction until my late twenties. I knew I wanted to write a book, but I didn't know where to start or if I was any good at this "writing-thing." So, I took an online course called "Writing for Children & Teenagers." As I received feedback from my instructor on my short stories, I slowly gained confidence in my writing and it was after I finished that course that I started the first draft of *Lucy's Chance*.

How long does it take you to write a book?

That depends on the book. Here's my writing process… I usually take about a month to free-write about the characters. During this time I ask myself lots of questions. *What would Lucy's perfect day look like? What would break Taylor's heart? What is Lucy's greatest accomplishment?* I ask myself questions about the characters and when I write a response to those questions, I often come up with scene ideas and plot ideas. During this first month of free-writing I also create a plot outline so I have a loose idea of the beginning, middle, and end of my story. After that first month, I start writing my first draft. First drafts take me anywhere from a few months to a year to write. In fact, *Rodeo Daze* was my fastest first draft to date. It took me just 45 days to write! Because *Rodeo Daze* is the third book in the Red Rock Ranch series, I already had a deep sense of my characters and when I finally sat down to start writing, the words flowed out. However, my young adult fantasy books (The OverRuled Series) each took me about a year to write (the first drafts). Then, after I'm done writing a first draft it takes me six months to a year to edit, edit, edit to a final manuscript.

What character are you most like?

I wouldn't say I'm exactly like just one of my characters, but my personality and inner thoughts are closest to Lucy's. In middle school and early high school, I was extremely shy and not super confident in my riding skills. I always felt like the underdog in the showring and I connected with my horse more than most people. However, even though I connect most with Lucy, there's a piece of me in every single one of my characters. For instance, I'm competitive like Taylor. And, even though I wouldn't say (out loud) many of the things Taylor says, I certainly think them in my head. I'm internally sassy like her and Taylor won my heart as I continued to write her. In book one, she started off as the villain, but the more I got to know her, the more I understood her actions. Taylor may just have her own book someday.

Where do you get your inspiration?

The short answer is: everywhere. I think to be a good writer you must be extra aware of your surroundings. Inspiration can come from real life experiences, news stories, or a story your girlfriend tells you over coffee and cookies. I keep notebooks all over (my office, my nightstand, the living room, my car) and any time I think something is interesting, I write it down as a possible future plot, scene, or character. For instance, The Cowboy Race in the first Red Rock Ranch book was inspired by a real competition I rode in. I participated in a competitive trail ride with my horse, Cheli, in which I rode through a beautiful outdoor trail course that totaled about seven miles and included an obstacle every mile or so. I had so much fun (rode with girlfriends) and afterwards I thought the same type of competition would be super fun to write about in a book . . . hence, The Cowboy Race. Also, the opening scene in *Rodeo Daze* where a mouse surprises Lucy in the tack room? That happened to me last summer. And I screamed like my feet were on fire. I always have my eyes and ears open. I'm continuously looking for inspiration.

Do you really ride?

I sure do! I started riding when I was about ten years old and was lucky enough to get my first horse (Austie) when I was thirteen. As a teenager, I worked at a local barn to help pay board and my passion for horses has only grown with every passing year. I love all kinds of riding disciplines. I grew up trail riding and showing western pleasure. In college, I dabbled in reining and also competed on the Intercollegiate Horse Show Team. Now, my husband and I own some land and I'm able to keep my two horses, Cheli and Stella, in my backyard. I thoroughly enjoy taking care of them every day. I compete in Cowboy Dressage with Cheli and I love to trail ride. When I trail ride I always take both of my babies (I ride Cheli and pony Stella). Horses will always be a huge part of my life and that's one of the reasons I enjoy writing about them. I want to share the joy of horses with anyone that will listen.

BONUS: Short Story

Sugar Cookies & Peppermints

Georgie's breath puffed against my cheeks as I kissed him, over and over. The whiskers on his nose were softer, shorter than the pokey hair on his lower lip and I couldn't help but giggle when he nuzzled me back. He was everything I'd ever dreamed of, better than I imagined, and my heart swelled to the point of bursting as I remembered that Georgie was my horse.

A squeak escaped my lips as I kissed his gray muzzle again. "I can't believe you're mine." Georgie's fuzzy ears flicked forward at my confession. He batted his brown eyes. "I get to brush you and feed you and ride you and spoil you whenever I want." I stepped back and patted the red ribbon tied around his braided forelock. My cheeks were sore from the smile I couldn't wipe off my face.

"Tiera? You in here?" Mom called as she opened the barn door. A gust of wind blew her chocolate brown hair across her face. She squinted against the chill, but smiled when she stepped inside and laid eyes on me. "I don't know why I asked that question. Of course you're in the barn." She wrapped her cardigan tight around her chest and pushed the hair from her eyes. "It's the coldest California

Christmas I can remember and you're outside playing with your horse."

I playfully rolled my eyes at her. "Come on, Mom. It's like forty degrees. I'll be okay." She was overprotective, but had to know the weather wasn't going to keep me from the best Christmas present I'd ever received. "I'm wearing my hat and gloves like you said." I raised my hands and pointed to my head to show her that I was following her rules. "And it's not that cold when you're out of the wind." I gestured for her to move away from the door and she did, keeping her thick sweater wrapped tight around her middle.

Mom walked over and patted Georgie on the forehead. His ears bounced with each tap. "Your grandpa did good."

"Better than good," I added, putting my hand next to hers to scratch Georgie until his eyes closed.

"Your grandpa always did have an eye for a good horse." Mom brushed her fingers down his nose and admired my snow-white Christmas horse. Then she turned to me and said, "Speaking of Grandpa, I need your help making his favorite cookies."

"Sugar cookies with marshmallow frosting and sprinkles?" I asked, knowing the answer.

"Yep." Mom brushed the short white hairs from her hands. "I'll make the batter while you pick out the cookie cutters. Deal?"

"Deal," I said as I placed another flake of hay in Georgie's stall. "Although I'm thinking Grandpa deserves a lot more than cookies for getting me my very own horse."

Grandpa sat in the overstuffed chair with a handful of warm cookies and a mug of milk. He bit into a heart-shaped cookie and listened to me recap my first day with Georgie: our ride through the pasture, how Georgie loves peppermints but spits out baby carrots, how he nickered at me from his stall. And just as I started gushing about how cute Georgie looks with his forelock braided, I saw my older brother, Jake, roll to the floor from the couch and dramatically flop onto the ground. With the way Jake acted, it was hard to believe he was sixteen. I acted way more mature at fourteen. Most of the time anyhow.

With his hands above his head and his body sprawled across the carpet, Jake sighed. "Tiera, I've heard these stories like a thousand times already."

I squinted at him and cocked my head, making sure he knew I didn't care if he was bored by my stories. "Well, Grandpa hasn't."

"Ugh," Jake sighed again, resting an arm over his eyes.

"Come on Jake," Grandpa urged as he set his mug on the coffee table. "I've heard about every bolt and headlight you've put in that truck of yours, right? Now, let Tiera tell me all about Georgie."

Jake peeked out from under his arm, the fireplace casting a flickering glow on his cheek. "I guess," he said, unwillingly. "But my truck is a lot more exciting than Tiera's horse."

Grandpa gave a gruff chuckle. "I love both kinds of horse power. Go on, honey. Tell me more about Georgie." His eyes twinkled like the white lights strung around the tree and I was thankful he enjoyed my stories. I stuck my tongue out at my brother and continued on until the scent of honey ham wafted in from the kitchen and it was time to set the table for Christmas dinner. I could have gone on all night. And I'd only had Georgie for one day.

The next morning, Grandpa and I walked to the barn together, pink remnants of the sunrise still hanging in the sky. I'd been awake for exactly ten minutes, had thrown a coat over my flannel pajamas and didn't bother to put socks on before my cowboy boots. A piece of hay poked the bottom of my foot, but I didn't care. I couldn't wait to get to the barn and feed my horse. I would've run down the gravel road, but Grandpa couldn't move as fast as I could. And I didn't want him to slip on the early morning frost.

Taking hold of his arm, I gave him a gentle squeeze. "Do you like living with us, Grandpa?" I asked my question with a warm smile, knowing the past month had brought a lot of changes. Grandpa sold his farm, my parents sold our house in town, and we moved into a house in the country, together. I was loving the change, but I wasn't so sure about Grandpa.

Grandpa used his cane to steady his short stride. "I do, princess." He smiled back. "That farmhouse of mine seemed to get bigger and bigger every year. Unfortunately, it was too much to take care of on my own." He sighed, his breath hissing. "But I am glad I get to see you and your brother every day now."

"Me too. And I can bake cookies for you whenever you want." I was being serious, but Grandpa seemed to think that was funny.

"Oh, I don't think I can just sit around and eat cookies all day. Though I appreciate the thought. Maybe I can help you with your horse here and there?"

"Anytime you want, Gramps. You can even ride him if you want." I let go of his arm and gave a huff as I pulled open the heavy barn door. Georgie nickered at the sound of the door rolling over its metal track.

"I think my days in the saddle have passed," Grandpa replied with a grin. "But I'd love to watch you ride."

We walked into the barn together, passing a stack of hay bales, pitch forks, and shovels. "Well, you're in luck. Cherry is coming over in a couple of hours and we're going to spend all day with Georgie. We'll ride in the front pasture so you can watch us from the house."

Grandpa nodded. "That sounds like a plan. Then I can watch a little football too."

I wrinkled my nose. "I guess somebody's got to," I said as our boots clunked across the wooden floor. Ahead, Georgie poked his head out his stall window, looking much sleepier than I felt. His eyes blinked against the barn lights which cast a glow from the pitched ceiling. "Not an early riser?" I teased, thinking his slack lower lip was adorable.

"I'm sure he'll perk up when he hears his breakfast."

As though on cue, Georgie let out a low trill of nickers when I dug a scoop into the grain bin. His nicker was like music to my ears and I shook the scoop of pellets just to hear him sing to me again.

"Here you go, Georgie." I reached into his stall and dumped the grain into his feeder. Grandpa followed behind me with a few flakes of green hay. Then we watched Georgie munch contently on his breakfast, licking the feeder clean before starting on his hay.

"Pearl loved her gray horses," Grandpa said, resting a shoulder against the stall door. "They were always her favorite."

I nodded. I never met Grandma Pearl, but enjoyed listening to stories about her. "They're my favorite too."

"I figured. That's one of the reasons I picked Georgie for you. But besides being handsome, he's got a good head on his shoulders. You take care of him and he'll take care of you. He's the type of horse that'll teach you to be the best rider you can be."

Georgie popped his head up from the ground as though he knew he was being referenced. A few squiggly stands of hay lay on his forelock and I reached through the window to pluck them off.

"I've wanted a horse my whole life," I breathed. And that was true. At least for as long as I could remember.

"You inherited your love of horses from your Grandma, sweetie." He brushed my blonde bed-head back from my face. "If she were here, she'd be just as excited to have Georgie as you are."

Grandpa swallowed and I put my hand back on his arm. "Grandpa?"

He looked at me and quickly cleared his throat. "Yes, sweetie?"

"Thank you for giving me Georgie. He's the best present I could've hoped for."

We both smiled.

Cherry jumped out of the car before it fully stopped and her mom scolded her as I tackled Cherry with a hug, squishing her auburn curls against her neck. I'd sprinted up from the barn and still had a pink curry comb in my hand.

"He's so handsome," I yelled, pulling back from our embrace.

Cherry's brown eyes were wide with anticipation. "I can't believe you got a horse for Christmas!"

"I can't believe it either, but I did!" I took her hand and we ran off to the barn as my mom chit-chatted with Cherry's mom in the driveway.

Cherry had been my best friend since elementary school and we'd been taking riding lessons together for the past year. We shared secrets, shoes, and lip gloss and now I couldn't wait to share my horse with her. "His registered name is Georgie Porgie. He's fifteen hands and eleven years old," I puffed as we slowed down to enter the barn, not wanting to scare Georgie. He greeted us with perked ears, standing obediently in the cross-ties.

Cherry stopped dead in her tracks. "He is gorgeous!" she said before her mouth dropped open. "You are the luckiest girl alive!"

"We are the luckiest girls alive," I reminded her and tugged her forward. "Come on. You can comb his mane while I finish currying."

Georgie contently watched us zip around him in circles as his hair was brushed, combed and polished. Then we saddled him, together. Cherry threw the pad on his back and I placed the saddle on top. Cherry tightened the cinch and I bridled him. And, as a team, we led him out of the barn, each holding a rein, walking on opposite sides of Georgie. Then Georgie further proved his perfection: he never baulked or shied as we crawled onto his back and rode double around the yard, waving at Grandpa every time we passed the living room window. Georgie had been in my backyard for two days, and he acted like it had been his home forever.

"I love him." I draped my arms around his neck.

"Me too," Cherry chimed in. Then I sat up and our helmets clunked together, causing us to giggle uncontrollably.

"Hey, you two silly girls," Mom said, poking her head out the back door. "You ready for some hot cocoa?"

The tips of my fingers were numb, even inside my gloves, and hot cocoa was tempting, but that would mean we'd have to get off Georgie.

"Can we take Georgie down the road first, Mom?" The first hints of dusk were settling in the air. "I want to show Cherry our neighbors' Christmas lights."

Mom gave me a look like she was afraid we were going to starve to death if she didn't get us out of the saddle. "You guys can ride down to the stop sign and back. That's it. Okay? Then it's time to come inside for a bit."

"Okay," Cherry and I agreed together.

The dead-end road was the length of three or four city blocks and dotted with farm houses and old trucks. We saw more chickens than cars—which was the only reason Mom let us ride on the road.

"This house has the prettiest lights," I said, pointing at a white house trimmed in red and green lights. A wreath hung on the front door. Candles glowed in every window.

"So pretty," Cherry cooed as Georgie trotted slow and smooth down the dirt road. Then she pointed across the road to a bright star beaming from the top of a red barn. "But I think that's my favorite."

"Oh, wow," I agreed. "I didn't see that yesterday. Next year, we'll have to put a star on our barn too."

"I'll help you."

"Okay, but first we'll have to convince my mom to let us climb on the barn roof." We chuckled, knowing that would be a feat in itself.

At the stop sign, we turned around and headed back, picking out a few more favorite decorations on the way home. Cherry decided the neighbor's inflatable snowman outranked the barn star and I was telling her she was crazy when we passed a small house I hadn't paid attention to before. It was across the street from Georgie's pasture, but nearly hidden by overgrown bushes. In what little I could see of the house, I noticed the curtains were open, but it didn't look like anyone was home. There weren't any lights on and not one Christmas decoration to be seen.

"Who lives there?" Cherry asked.

In the few weeks since we'd moved into the new house, I'd only met the Johnson family that lived directly across the road. "I don't know. It kind of looks empty."

We both stared at the little rectangular house.

"It kind of looks creepy," Cherry added. Just as she did, there was movement in the front window. "Did you see that?" she squeaked.

I decided we shouldn't stick around to find out who or what was watching us. "Let's go," I squeezed Georgie with my legs. He popped into a trot and it was the first time I wished he moved faster.

I didn't tell Mom about the creepy house. I figured it would only give her reason to keep me from riding down the road. And I didn't want that to happen.

"I'm glad you girls had fun yesterday," Mom said as she stirred dinner on the stove. "What did Cherry think of Georgie?"

"She loved him." I climbed onto a stool at the kitchen counter. "I mean, how could she not?"

Mom smiled and then nodded over her shoulder. "Sweetie, can you grab two eggs for me?" She stirred the pan again and it sizzled.

"What're you making?" It smelled sweet and spicy at the same time.

"Lasagna."

"Yum," I replied. My stomach gave a growl, but when I opened the fridge, it looked to be eggless. "I don't see any in here." I searched behind the gallon of milk and a head of lettuce.

"I just bought a dozen a few days ago. We should have some left."

"Are you sure?" I was still searching as Jack roamed into the kitchen and grabbed an apple off the counter. He bit into it and I peered at him around the fridge door. "Did you make one of your monster omelets this afternoon?" He was the only kid I knew that thought an omelet was a snack. He never stopped eating.

"Yeah." He crunched into the apple. "What's it to ya?"

"Jack," Mom addressed him and he stopped chewing. "You could've at least told me you used the last of the eggs. Now I don't have any for the lasagna."

"I didn't know lasagna had eggs in it." He lifted his shoulders, now chewing with his mouth open. "I can go get some, I guess."

"It's twenty minutes to the store, Jack. Why don't you and your sister go see if we can borrow a few eggs from one of the neighbors."

Jack groaned as I blamed him for our egglessness, but Mom shooed us both with a flick of her hand. "Now."

I grabbed my coat on the way out of the house and followed Jack down the driveway, but when we got to the end of the pavement, Jack went right and I went left.

"Where are you going?" I pulled my hood up to fend off the wind. "The Johnsons aren't home. Mom said they were going on vacation over New Year's."

"No she didn't."

"Um, why would I lie about that?" I asked, thinking Jack was the most stubborn person I'd ever known. I also knew he only wanted to knock on the Johnson's door so he could flirt with their oldest daughter, Becca. "Becca's not home and she doesn't have any eggs for you."

"Whatever, Tiera. You go that way and I'll go this way and the first one home with eggs doesn't have to do dishes tonight."

I squinted at him as he walked away. Then I whispered to myself, "Well, it looks like I'm not washing any dishes." Turning on my heels, I headed for the house with the inflatable snowman—where Cherry and I spotted two clucking chickens yesterday.

I jogged along the pasture fence and whistled at Georgie as I went by. He picked his head up from the grass and I waved at him. He looked so handsome in his royal blue blanket. "After I find eggs for Mom, I'll clean your stall and get you some dinner," I yelled. He cocked an ear before putting his nose back to the grass and I started skipping, wanting to get done with my chore as fast as possible.

I looked ahead for the inflatable snowman, but my heart jumped as I discovered a person instead. A cloaked figure watched me from across the road—standing in the dirt driveway that led to the creepy house. I halted and considered climbing over the fence and running away until the creeper pushed the hood from her head and smiled. And she didn't look like a creeper at all.

"You must be Tiera," the elderly woman said, waving a gloved hand before grabbing a stack of envelopes out of an open mailbox. She had tightly curled, white hair. Red lipstick framed her smile. Gold rimmed glasses hung from a dainty chain around her neck. "Mrs. Johnson told me she met the new neighbors. Welcome to the neighborhood. I'm Bettie."

I stood there with my mouth open, my hands still up in the air, in skipping mode.

Bettie started again. "Beautiful Quarter Horse you have. What's his name?"

I realized I was being totally rude and ridiculous. "Georgie. And, yes, I'm Tiera." I clasped my hands in front of my waist. "Nice to meet you."

Bettie tucked the stack of mail under her arm. "Did you say you needed some eggs?"

I nodded, feeling a silly for yelling to my horse about my need for eggs. "Mom is making dinner and my brother used all the eggs."

"Well, I happen to have extra. If you can wait a few minutes, I'll grab you some. How many do you need?" Bettie turned toward her house but took an uneven step on the gravel. She teetered and caught her balance, but I ran across the road anyhow and clasped hold of her elbow. For a second, Bettie stared at me. Then she placed her hand on my shoulder. "Thank you, dearie. It pains me to say it, but I'm not as nimble as I used to be." A flash of embarrassment moved across her face.

I offered a smile and a shrug, trying to show her I understood. Then I changed the subject. "Two eggs would be great." Bettie nodded and I kept hold of her arm as we walked to her front door, passing blackberry bushes that climbed the siding and brushed the roof.

"Sorry for the mess." Bettie waved her fingers at the bushes. "I have a hard time keeping up with the landscaping by myself."

I couldn't imagine Bettie trying to trim the prickly bushes herself and made a mental note to get Jack over here with a pair of pruners. He was good for something, at least.

But as Bettie pulled open her front door, the inside of her home looked nothing like the outside. It was warm and tidy and smelled of cookies, though I didn't see anything baking in the oven.

Every pillow was perfectly positioned on her sofa. Christmas music hummed from a radio on the kitchen counter.

Bettie peeled off her cloak, revealing a red cardigan with embroidered Christmas trees and I wondered if she got dressed up to get her mail. "Two eggs, you said?" Bettie asked as she shuffled to the fridge, looking happy to be able to help.

"Yes, please." I scanned the pictures hanging on her wall and gasped when I realized many of the photos had horses in them.- Some were in black and white. Others in color. But I noticed a certain blonde woman in many of the pictures. The woman donned the same red lipstick that Bettie now wore. "Is this you?" I asked, pointing to an image of a young woman with long blonde curls and a white cowboy hat. She was kissing the muzzle of a big bay horse. A glittering crown sat on the brim of her hat.

Bettie turned. A warm smile covered her face when she realized what I was pointing at. "As a matter of fact, that was me. That's the year I won the Miss Rodeo USA pageant. And that was my horse, Gussy."

My mouth popped open and hung. "You were Miss Rodeo USA?" I'd always admired the rodeo queens in our town's parade. They looked beautiful as they waved from their floating thrones, but they weren't just gorgeous. They had to be skilled riders to earn a crown.

"Miss Rodeo USA 1967." Bettie walked over and handed me a plastic bag with two eggs inside. Then she pointed to another picture with a dapple gray horse. In that picture, Bettie held the horse's lead in one hand and a golden trophy in the other. A handsome man stood at her side. His smile was just as big as hers. "That's my late husband, Johnny, and our prized stallion, Silver Jet." She kissed her fingertips and placed them on the photograph. "I miss them both."

My heart hurt for her, but Bettie wore a smile and seemed happy to relive her memories with me, so I asked her about another photo. As Bettie talked, I discovered she and her husband bred, raised, and trained Quarter Horses. They'd never had children. Their horses were their babies. They'd traveled the country together, showing horses, winning buckles, and making memories.

Bettie told me the registered name, pedigree, and story behind each horse pictured on her wall and I was in awe of her accomplishments and experience.

"Oh, look at the time," Bettie said, after finishing her last story. "I don't want to keep you from dinner."

Glancing at the clock, I jumped, realizing a half hour had passed. "Oh boy, I'd better get going. Mom is probably wondering where I am." Actually, she was probably freaking out. "Thanks so much for the eggs, Bettie." I raised the little baggie. "It was really nice to meet you."

"You as well." She smiled, but the sparkle left her face as I walked to the door.

"Bettie?" I asked as I put my hand on the doorknob. "Will you be around tomorrow afternoon? After lunch?"

She looked surprised by my question. "Yes. I'll be here."

"Can I stop over again? I don't think I'll need any more eggs, but I'd like to hear some more horse stories. Would that be okay?"

Bettie nodded and swallowed. "Any time, sweetie. Any time."

The next day I braided Georgie's mane and fastened each plait with a red ribbon and a little silver bell. My fingers hurt when I was done, but it was worth it. Georgie looked like a special delivery straight from the North Pole. He jingled with each step as I led him out of the barn and across the road—to Bettie's house. She opened her front door to greet us before we were halfway down her drive.

"Hi, sweetie," Bettie called. She was dressed in another sweater. This one had embroidered horses cantering across the front. Her hair was curled. Her lipstick was freshly applied. Bettie clasped her hands together in front of her chest as we approached. Georgie walked on one side of me. My Grandpa was on the other.

The three of us stopped at Bettie's doorstep.

"Bettie, I'd like you to meet my Grandpa Harry and my horse, Georgie," I said. "One loves sugar cookies. The other loves peppermints. And they both wanted to meet you."

There was a glossy sheen to Bettie's eyes and Grandpa gingerly shook her hand.

"So lovely to meet you." Grandpa smiled at Bettie and proceeded to tell her how he'd surprised me with Georgie on Christmas morning. As Grandpa told the story, Bettie beamed. Then she ran her knobby fingers down Georgie's velvet nose. In that instant, I knew Georgie wasn't just my Christmas present. He was a gift to my Grandpa and to Bettie. And I intended to share him with them both.

Also By Brittney Joy

Maple Bay Series:
Sweet Small-Town Cowboy Romance
Starting Over in Maple Bay (book 1)
Second Chance in Maple Bay (book 2)
Country Stars in Maple Bay (book 3)

OverRuled Series:
Young Adult Fantasy
OverRuled (book 1)
OverRun (book 2)
OverThrown (book 3)

Sweet Small-Town Romance Novella:
Christmas in Silver Leaf Falls

Never miss a new release ~ Sign-up for Brittney Joy's newsletter:

http://www.brittneyjoybooks.com/newsletter

Checkout Brittney Joy's Maple Bay Series

Starting Over in Maple Bay, book 1:

An inheritance from a mother she never knew. But can this fixer-upper mend her heart?

Hazel didn't think there was anything a homemade apple pie couldn't fix—until her husband divorced her and left her broke. Trying her best to raise her ten-year old daughter and make ends meet, Hazel is desperate for a fresh start. When she inherits a fixer-upper in the small town of Maple Bay, Hazel and her daughter head to the country for the reading of her biological mother's will. But a clause in the will says Hazel and her sister—the sister she didn't know existed—must live together on the rural property for one summer, or forfeit their inheritance.

If Hazel can tough it out in the country for a few months, she stands to gain a historic carriage house. It needs renovation, but Hazel thinks she can fix it up, sell it as a bed-and-breakfast, and use the profits to begin her life anew, back in the city. She isn't planning to stay in Maple Bay, or to fall in love with her sister's best friend, Jesse—a single dad and handsome cowboy who is recovering from heartbreak of his own.

Hazel and Jesse are from two different worlds, but this horse-whisperer just might know how to speak to Hazel's broken heart . . . until Hazel discovers a box of letters and a secret from her past that changes everything.

More information here:
www.brittneyjoybooks.com